MW01716256

DEAD GONE

A gripping crime thriller full of twists

T.J. BREARTON

JOFFE BOOKS

Published 2016 by Joffe Books, London.

www.joffebooks.com

This book is a work of fiction. Names, characters, businesses, organizations, places and events are either the product of the author's imagination or are used fictitiously. Any resemblance to actual persons, living or dead, events or locales is entirely coincidental. The spelling is American English.

ISBN-13: 978-1-912106-70-7

For Joy.

CHAPTER ONE

MONDAY

Tom was awake when the alarm clock buzzed. He switched it off, stared up at the twirling ceiling fan a moment and then went downstairs.

The sign hanging on the living room wall read: *Congratulations, Tom!*

He collected a couple of empty beer bottles and stuck them in the recycling bin. The coffee was already brewing, the timer set for six.

He stood in his sweatpants, watching the coffee drip into the pot, considering a half-remembered dream.

Tommy . . . Tommy help me.

His cell phone rang in the bedroom, snapping him out of it. He bounded back up the stairs and grabbed the phone.

"Lange," he answered.

"Special Agent Lange. Good morning." It was Director Turnbull.

"What can I do for you, sir?"

"Well, Lange, looks like day one for you is going to be a big one."

"Okay, sir. I'm ready."

"Are you familiar with Paddle Creek Tours?"

"No . . ." Tom found his notebook next to his badge on the dresser and plucked a pen from the coin dish. He scribbled down *Paddle Creek*.

"They do kayaking. Like canoeing, but one person per boat. You know where Rookery Bay is?"

"Yes, sir." Rookery Bay was a nature preserve, a large mangrove estuary fed by the Gulf of Mexico.

"Okay, good," Turnbull said. "Shell Island Road. You drive past the Research Reserve headquarters. Down a half mile on the right is where you want to be. Special Agent Blythe will meet you there."

"Blythe, sir?" He wrote that name down, too.

"Yes. She's who you're sharing the field office with, you'll be taking your cues from her." Turnbull paused. Tom heard police radio chatter in the background. Whatever was going on, it sounded big. "A body was found in the bay. Everglades County Sheriff's Office is already there. Check in with Blythe, I'll speak to you later. Good luck."

Turnbull hung up before Tom could ask any more questions. *A body in the bay*. He shed his sweatpants and took a fast shower. He dressed in a gray suit, stood at the dresser and clipped his badge to his belt. He looked at the framed photograph while he straightened his collar. Him and Nick in the picture, just kids, many years before.

Tom went to his nightstand and took out his service weapon, a Glock 37 Gen4. He ran through the safety procedure, then loaded a fresh mag and closed the action. He put on the belt holster, slipped the gun in and made sure the retention kept it in place.

The condo was already getting warm as the Florida sun rose outside. He grabbed his keys off the kitchen counter and went into the adjoining garage where the old white Jeep Cherokee was sitting in the gloom. It would be his ride until he was issued a vehicle by the department.

He jumped in and fired up the engine. When he hit the button clipped to his visor the garage door rolled open.

He realized his hands were shaking as he gripped the steering wheel.

Tom sat for a moment, eyes closed. He took a few deep breaths, inhaling through his nose, clearing his thoughts. Once he felt more settled and in control, he drove out into the sun-drenched morning.

* * *

The dirt road bisected tangles of brittle underbrush. The Jeep axles squealed and the frame rattled as Tom jounced over the potholes. He passed a speed limit sign — 10 mph — and realized he was going way too fast. He slowed, leaning over the steering wheel, peering out. The next sign was for the *Rookery Bay National Estuarine Research Reserve* and there was a small building tucked into the vegetation. The last sign along the road read *Paddle Creek Tours*. Tom could already see the flashing lights before he turned into the dirt parking area.

Law enforcement was everywhere. Three Everglades County cruisers, several unmarked vehicles, and a truck embossed with the Reserve logo — a wading bird on stick legs. Tom found a place to park.

As soon as his feet hit the mushy ground he realized he'd worn the wrong footwear. Dress shoes had no business in this place. The mosquitos whined past as he walked over to a tall, slender woman in her early fifties, with grayish blonde hair and angular cheekbones. At least she was wearing a suit, too. There was a badge clipped to her belt. Tom thought this must be Blythe.

She turned to face him, holding a phone to her ear. He waited, noticing a uniformed deputy talking with a woman dressed in cargo shorts, an athletic top and wide sunhat. Tom bet the woman was a guide for Paddle Creek Tours. Beyond her, a middle-aged couple sat on a log beside the underbrush. They were wrapped in silvery emergency blankets and wore blank, shocked expressions.

Blythe put away her phone. They stood facing the shallow water surrounded by twisty mangrove. Three kayaks were on the shore, the vessels brightly colored, top of the line. And there was a boat in the water, a flat-bottomed skiff with a small trolling motor on the back. People waded in, loading supplies in the boat. Getting ready to head out.

"So you're Lange."

"Yes, ma'am."

She looked at him out of the corner of her eye. "Turnbull says you got a perfect score on your SOCE."

Tom blushed. He didn't like anyone talking about his certification test or his training. Turnbull also liked to call him a Boy Scout. *You're a real Boy Scout, huh, Lange?* They all seemed eager to impart to Tom that the world out there was a lot different than it was in training. A lot darker. But Tom just kept silent, didn't tell them he already knew that.

"Nice to meet you, Special Agent Blythe."

She glanced down at his hand for a moment before she took it. Her grip was cool and dry, strong. She let go and pointed to another woman, short and stocky, dark hair pulled back. "That's Detective Machado with County CID." Machado was standing by the kayaks with a man in frumpy shorts and a dress shirt. He held a large duffel bag. "And that's Dr. Ward, with the Medical Examiner's Office."

Blythe pointed to the woman in the wide-brimmed hat. "That's Susan Libby. She owns Paddle Creek Tours. She was taking those two . . ." And now Blythe nodded to the man and the woman seated on the log. ". . . out for a sunrise paddle. They're the VanCotts. Libby only does the sunrise tour twice a week, Monday and Tuesday, they book well in advance."

"So what's Florida Department of Law Enforcement doing here?"

Blythe gave him a look, raising her thin eyebrows.

He went on, "This is County jurisdiction, right? Their CID is here, they've got the manpower. How come we're getting involved?"

"Well, it's within County boundaries, but Rookery Bay is a state-run preserve. Technically that water is state water, this reserve is partly state-funded." She was matter-of-fact, her tone flat. "The Sheriff is working it all out with Turnbull. For now, we're here and we're observing."

Tom pulled his pad and pen from his suit coat and jotted some notes.

Blythe said, "So, Susan Libby and the VanCotts are out for their morning paddle. There's an osprey nest, you know, possibility of dolphin sightings. They stick pretty close to the mangrove most of the time, they go down this series of creeks . . . you'll see."

The last words struck him. He'd see? Blythe was expecting him to go out with the body recovery team.

Another vehicle pulled in, a County crime scene van, and the door slid open. Three people piled out, already dressed in wetsuits. They hauled the dive tanks and breathing regulators down to the small beach where they met with Ward and Machado. Tom watched as they spoke with one another and put on their gear.

"Libby and the couple found the body about a quarter mile from here," Blythe said. "They found it floating, sort of tangled up in the mangrove a bit. So we're going to want to get it out of there, keep it as intact as possible."

"Man or woman?"

Blythe looked at him directly for the first time. "Libby said there was a lot of hair floating. But we don't know for sure yet if it's a woman." She turned away from him.

"So they came back to shore and made the call?"

"Susan Libby has a cell phone she keeps in a plastic baggie with her. Once she discovered the floater she dialed 911, who connected her with the Sheriff's Office. That reminds me — whatever you take with you, bag it up."

"There's cell coverage out here, wow." He looked at the sky, pale blue in the morning light, a slight haze burning off. Another mosquito whined against his ear and he swatted at it. He was already feeling hot and wished he'd dressed differently.

"There's some coverage, yes. It's spotty, but phones can work." Blythe folded her arms, finished with the nickel tour and nodded to indicate Machado again.

"Everglades County is covering the statements, including the two people over there. Getting their background, et cetera."

Tom gave the VanCotts one more glance. There was a hollow look in the man's eyes. "And you want me to go out with the divers. And the medical examiner."

"Yes. You're going out." She stepped away and gave him a look up and down. "Not exactly the most appropriate outfit."

* * *

Tom left his shoes and suit jacket in the Jeep and rolled his pants up around his ankles. His toes squished in the muck as he made his way down to the beach. Bottleflies skittered about in the wet, grainy sand, and he caught a fishy smell. Then he was in the water, which wasn't much cooler than the air, like standing in warm milk.

The divers were further out. One of them submerged, leaving a froth of bubbles, then resurfaced and gave a thumbs-up to another diver floating nearby. They both started toward the open water at the mouth of the bay.

A conservation officer in a khaki uniform held out his hand and Tom grabbed it, then stepped aboard. The small boat was wobbly in the water and Tom quickly sat down on one of the benches. He gave the man a nod of thanks. "I'm Special Agent Lange, IFS."

"Randy Ramirez. Estuarine Reserve Officer. IFS . . . that's part of the state bureau?"

"That's right. We handle violent crimes, among other things." They shook hands and Tom twisted around to the other man seated near the front. "Dr. Ward? Nice to meet you."

Ward was lithe, somewhat effeminate, his handshake quick and light. His eyeglasses flashed in the sun as he placed a hat on his balding head. The large duffel bag was now at his feet. Beside him, a woman in an Everglades County crime lab T-shirt with a camera in her lap introduced herself as Katie Mills from the Everglades County crime scene bureau. The last person Tom met was Susan Libby, seated in the center of the boat, looking wary. Libby gave him a warm smile though, the same she probably offered her kayaking guests. Then she looked past Tom at the shore.

Tom glanced at Blythe, standing amid the vehicles and the twirling lights of the County cruisers. There was something powerful in her posture.

Ramirez gave the boat a shove to get it going then hopped in while Tom held on to keep his balance. He wasn't used to boats. He didn't grow up in Florida, on the water, or anything like this place.

Ramirez started the small motor with the push of a button and the root-like tangles of mangrove began to slide past. Tom risked a look over the edge and saw the water rippling away from the aluminum boat.

Blythe receded into the distance as they started on their way.

His first day, his first case, and he got a dead body.

CHAPTER TWO

The sun beat down. Not quite eight o'clock in the morning and Tom could already feel its power, burning against his skin. He thought of all the crime scene workers who would be working the area for hours, examining ingresses and egresses, looking for any signs of passing, trace evidence. It would take days to cover the wetland area, and they could never really scour every inch of it. Hopefully they wouldn't have to try, and the medical examiner would be able to ID the body.

One of the first things Tom wondered was if the person in the bay had suffered a boating accident. A party yacht, maybe, and someone went overboard. Accidentally or on purpose.

"Can't use big boats out here," Ramirez said. He piloted the boat across open water toward a mangrove canal. "Too shallow, for one thing. For another, it's a preserve. Big engines, gas engines — too pollutive, too invasive."

Ahead of the boat, the divers led the way, leaving trails of air bubbles.

"What about in the channel?" Tom could see a couple of buoys beyond a swath of seagrass. One red, one green. There was a large wooden sign in the water that read *SLOW: MANATEE ZONE*. A bird's nest perched atop the sign.

"No. Small motors only."

Susan Libby moved closer to Tom, rocking the boat some more. Tom's stomach felt like putty. "The Florida EPA is partnering with the Reisen Group to help restore two hundred twenty-five acres of mangrove to Everglades County."

"I didn't know that."

"Research into the die-off of the mangrove points to early construction. Nineteen-thirties construction, particularly the development of route ninety-two." She seemed comfortable talking about the reserve in this way.

"Reserve or Preserve? What's the difference?"

Susan smiled. "Potato, po*tat*o. It's protected land, managed to preserve its flora and fauna."

"Is this the kind of stuff you talk about on your kayak tours?"

Susan shrugged, and her smile waned. "Sometimes. Depends on the guests, you know, what they show their interest in. Some like to spot wildlife, some like the exercise, or just the peace and quiet."

"What about the guests this morning?"

"Joe and Linda?"

"Do they have any . . . political interest in the reserve?"

"Joe contributed to the first phase of the die-off research project. Permits, engineering and design, site surveys, excavation and fill removal. Working with the Reisen Group has brought this project international attention. The mangrove system has been in danger, but it's getting better."

"You said he was a contributor . . ." Tom swatted at more mosquitos. "You mean financially."

"A donor. Yes. They come at least twice a year to go kayaking with me."

"And they were the only ones touring with you today? Is that usually the case?"

"Oh no, I can have groups up to ten people. Ten's my limit. But the sunrise tour, not a lot of people are up and ready to go that time of day."

"You always come this same route for the sunrise tour?"

"Yes, pretty much."

"And this is the way you came this morning."

"Yes."

"Do you have more tours scheduled today? Other types of tours, afternoon, sunset, anything like that?"

She made a glum face and Tom noticed her eyes were ringed red. For someone who spent her life outdoors, she was pale. "I did. I've cancelled the whole week. Agent Blythe recommended it."

Tom understood. He thought if anything, though, Paddle Creek Tours would now experience an uptick. Once word got out that a body had been found among the mangrove, people would show their usual perverse interest in such things.

Tom spotted a group of pink birds wading on stick legs. "Flamingos?"

"Roseate Spoonbills," Libby corrected him.

Ramirez said, "They like these freshwater wetlands."

"Freshwater? I thought this was fed by the ocean?"

"It is. The waters are brackish," Ramirez explained. "That's a mixture of salt and freshwater. So we get these wetlands, those yellow-green seagrasses you see over there."

Ramirez and Susan Libby were both eager to display their knowledge, Tom thought. Almost competing a little.

Tom glanced at Dr. Ward, sitting alone at the bow, his back turned, pulling on a pair of rubber pants that went up to his chest. Then Tom watched the birds again, dipping their long bills in the water. The birds moved away as the boat neared, and one by one they slipped into the grass, their pink feathers disappearing.

"And what about those?" asked Tom, pointing up.

High in the sky, a group of dark shapes circled, looking like something prehistoric.

"Turkey buzzards," Ramirez said. "They're attracted by the body."

* * *

The trees arched over the water, forming a canopy. Stopper Creek was a tunnel of mangrove, bushy on top, with one contiguous tangle of roots beneath, giving the whole thing the look of a picture from a scary children's book.

Tom thought he caught the first glimpse of something — a pale fleshy color floating just above the surface. Susan Libby had fallen silent beside him, her hands in her lap. Ward was stretched forward, watching. Tom felt his stomach roll and his pulse quicken. He closed his eyes for just a moment and took another deep breath.

"What about the tide?"

Ramirez said, "Well, we're in April. So we're at about an eleven-hour cycle. At oh-five-hundred, tide was up 0.64 meters. By eleven-thirty, it will be down 0.35 meters, then at seventeen hundred hours, back up 0.82 meters."

Tom wrote it down, the numbers blurring in his mind, and tried to visualize it. The water rose up and fell away by less than a meter, was the gist. "Any current in through here?"

"A little. Ebb and flow with the tide, no real current."

"Could the body have drifted? Or do you think it . . . you know, is this where she died?" Tom leaned away as a branch scraped the side of the boat with a low shriek.

"We don't know it's a *she* yet." Tom turned his head as Ward spoke up for the first time.

The divers reached the body first. Ramirez slowed the tiny motor, then clicked it off. He stood, too abruptly for Tom's liking, and picked up an oar.

"Be careful with that," Ward said. It was as if the man had eyes in the back of his head. The boat drifted, veering toward the vegetation. There was a gentle thump as they made contact with the mangrove roots. The roots further slowed the boat, squalling against the metal.

The three divers broke the surface, one at a time, keeping back from the body, floating around it in a semicircle. Tom strained for a better look. Despite his clumsiness, he rose to his feet, stooped over so he could hold onto the bench. He saw that Ward had also pulled on a pair of latex gloves.

The boat inched closer. A diver stabilized them and, standing, revealed the creek to be almost chest-deep. He gave Ward a thumbs-up and Ward eased into the water. The diver controlled the boat, bringing it right alongside the medical examiner and the floating body.

The body was face down. As Libby had said, there was a lot of hair. One floating arm was starkly visible. Tom could already see signs of decay. He wasn't a doctor, but he knew flesh wasn't supposed to look like that, bluish and saggy, rippling slightly with the water. The other arm was caught in the mangrove roots. The legs drifted beneath the surface, just vague shapes. The dead person was wearing blue shorts and a white T-shirt. The camera clicked as Mills took pictures.

Ward turned to one of the divers. "Is it caught up?"

The diver nodded, then held up a finger before slipping beneath the surface. They all waited for a moment, and Tom slapped at a mosquito stinging the back of his neck. He was sweating in all the humidity, his sunglasses slipping on his nose. He'd seen dead bodies before, but not like this. The body seemed to pull on him like a weight. His chest felt heavy, and as he leaned over the boat to watch, he felt like he was losing his balance.

He caught his sunglasses before they could splash into the water. No one seemed to notice. Susan Libby was looking off in the other direction. Apparently she'd seen enough. Ramirez was watching the activity, his mouth twitching beneath his thick black mustache. He held onto a mangrove branch. Between him and the diver, they kept the boat steady.

The diver broke the surface and pulled the regulator from her mouth. "The legs are free. Just that right arm kind of jammed up in there."

"Okay," Ward said. "Let's see if we can pull it free. I need to roll it over."

"Yep, roger."

Ward took the body by the free arm. Then he encircled his arm around its waist. The female diver came from behind, found the legs, and lifted them up toward the surface. Then Ward started to gingerly work the body back and forth. Tom watched the hair swishing as agitated water slopped against the mangrove roots. A bird called from somewhere close by, and Tom caught the scent of something awful, like rotten eggs. His stomach lurched again.

Ward stopped, holding up a hand. "Whoa, whoa, whoa." The diver ceased. Mills took more photographs while Ward carefully worked his way between the body and the roots.

Tom looked around. There would be no latent fingerprints to lift from the bristling mangroves, no blood spatters to examine on a wall or floor. The entirety of the forensics team for this scene, besides the divers, was able to fit in one small boat.

Ward succeeded in removing the impediment and freeing the second arm. "Got it." He and the diver carefully pulled at the body again. It floated freely a moment, then started to sink. Tom thought the body was going to go under, disappear into the murky brown water, but then it bobbed back.

"Okay." Ward pressed his fingers into the body's upper back, then paused to observe the reaction. Tom couldn't see what happened. Then Ward raised a gloved hand toward Mills and made a small gesture with his fingers. She pulled a tape recorder from the duffel bag, clicked it on and held it for Ward to speak into.

"This is Dr. Alan Ward. April 23, 8.16 a.m. Body located in Rookery Bay, Stopper Creek, about fifteen meters in from open water, fifty meters from the Rookery Channel." He studied the body and then continued. "Water has replaced the air in the lungs, buoyancy now is from the methane, hydrogen sulfide, and carbon dioxide in the gut and chest cavity."

Tom noticed Susan Libby was still looking away, growing paler by the second, wringing her hands in her lap. He touched her shoulder. She startled, then gave him a slight smile. Tom returned his attention to Ward.

"At this point the body does appear to be female. All appendages are intact. The clothing is slightly deteriorated, the flesh does not discolor to the touch. Livor mortis — this is not a refloat. Epidermis of hands and feet swollen, bleached and wrinkled. Only moderate liquefaction of tissues, the beginnings of maceration, early putrefaction. Going to test algor mortis, then bag the hands and get samples."

Ward held out his hand and Mills passed him an instrument. It took Tom a moment to realize it was a special kind of thermometer. Ward waded toward the midsection of the body and stuck the thermometer between the buttocks. Tom looked away. He wasn't disgusted as much as he felt humiliated for the person.

"Body temp has normalized to water temp. Preliminary estimate is that the body has been in the water for three to five days. Death is confirmed."

Ward looked at Tom for the first time, and Tom nodded. He wanted to speak, but his mouth wasn't working. Ward went right back to the body. "Let's turn her over."

Mills clicked off the recorder and put it in her pocket. She brought the camera up to her eye. Ward and the diver got in position to roll the body. Tom watched, riveted, his heart pumping, the sweat pouring down the sides of his head.

With Ward at the shoulders and the female diver at the feet, another diver helped with the midsection. They rolled the body like an animal on a spit. Tom felt his skin pricking hot around his ears and neck as her face emerged. It had been molested by something in the water — fish, maybe. The skin hanging, the lips eaten off, the eyes completely gone. Tom wanted to look away, but didn't.

The air suddenly smelled worse, the sulfuric egg-stink of hydrogen chloride accompanied by the sound of gas escaping the victim's ruined mouth. Tom covered his nose with his hand.

"Oh, God," someone said. The boat vibrated as Susan Libby grabbed at herself. Tom moved to comfort her again, but stopped. He had to see this. He had to see all of it.

Mills snapped more pictures of the body as the female diver turned her head. The diver holding the corpse's midsection arched his back to get his face away.

Ward merely continued with the examination, allowing Mills to take her pictures before she pulled out the recorder again.

Tom heard the thudding of a helicopter in the distance, a welcome diversion from the horror at hand, but he realized what it could mean: the media had learned about the body and were on their way.

"Gross evidence of cellular degeneration," Ward said. "Putrefaction in warm water is slower, but there is a salt content at the location, hastening the process. Facial maceration is likely due to fish or Crustacea. Three to five days remains the preliminary estimate for time of death."

He looked up at Tom again, but Tom didn't think the medical examiner was really seeing him, he seemed to be thinking about something. "Younger bodies putrefy more rapidly, older bodies more slowly . . ."

Ward was seeking to determine the age of the dead person. Tom looked the body over, avoiding the face. He thought the arms and legs and midsection were consistent with someone in their mid-twenties. Then something caught his eye.

"Tattoo, there." Tom took his hand from his nose and pointed. "Inner forearm."

Ward took the arm, turned it outward slightly. Mills snapped some fresh shots. Tom squinted down, mosquitos really swarming his head now. The tattoo was a simple butterfly. Filled in black, like a silhouette. No bigger than an actual butterfly, or thereabouts.

He felt some relief. With a scene as challenging as this one, a body with an unrecognizable face, and no readily apparent cause of death, a tattoo was somewhere to start. Something that felt more in line with his skill set. Of course, according to Blythe, he was only here to observe.

"The decedent has a small tattoo on the right inner forearm, shaped like a butterfly," Ward said into the recorder. Mills had taken to both tasks now, holding the recorder in one hand while continuing to photograph with the other.

"Any more of them?" Tom asked. The body was so close he could reach out and touch it if he wanted — and he felt a strange compulsion to do so. Familiar. Tracing back to his boyhood, and the open casket. Standing beside Nick, who'd swatted his hand when Tom reached in . . .

"Don't see any," the female diver said, inspecting for tattoos.

The helicopter was getting louder, drawing closer. Tom doubted the media would have a pinpoint location — they were just doing a sweep. For now, the team was concealed by the mangrove tunnel. Tom looked up and saw the buzzards had flown off.

"Alright," Ward said with finality.

Mills opened the duffel and pulled out a black plastic body bag. She laid it out along the bottom of the boat, between two benches. Tom had been so fixated on other things it only registered with him fully now that they were taking the corpse back with them.

Susan Libby looked shrunken. Tom got closer to her, their legs touching.

"They're going to put the body in the boat with us."

"I know." She was welling up. "Don't they have to do more, though? Look for more, I don't know — clues?"

"They do. It's best to take the body into evidence. Can you tell me more about Rookery Bay? Give me the basics."

She sat up a little and straightened her hat. "Well, this is one hundred thousand acres of pristine, subtropical forested estuary." The words rolled off her tongue, but without any joy.

Ward gave the divers instructions on hoisting the body. Someone climbed into the boat. Tom focused on Libby, kept her distracted.

"That's a lot of acreage."

"A *lot*. But it's only a start. Mangrove is dying by Marco Island. It's a muddy moonscape of leafless trees over there. Smells just like this. Like rotten eggs." She turned to look toward the body but Tom diverted her attention.

"All of this is mangrove? This estuary?"

"Well seventy thousand acres is the surface area of the open water. Forty thousand acres is primarily mangrove, fresh to brackish water wetlands, upland habitats."

"About how deep is the water?"

"The average is one meter."

"So when the tide is low . . ."

"You see lots of the bottom. When the tide is dead low, that's when the tricolored heron comes to gather minnows. The water flows out, and whole oyster beds are exposed. You can see the white ibis — beautiful bird! And little willets, and they'll be hunting through the exposed bed, looking for any crustaceans."

"Could someone walk to this spot, in Stopper Creek?"

"No, I don't think so . . ."

But she didn't sound sure. Instead she got back to what she was good at, and pointed to the mangrove roots. "You can see those barnacles hanging to dry, even on high tide."

Tom noticed a bluish-white substance that resembled popcorn clinging to the roots. He smiled at Susan Libby, who carried on talking as they loaded the body in the boat.

* * *

The ride back to the beach was even hotter, the sun shining down full-blast, the water sparkling. Two divers stayed behind, searching for personal effects, trace evidence, anything resembling a weapon, any signs of struggle in the mangrove — trampled roots, blood, something. The pulsing of the helicopter had faded, but Tom knew the press would be back.

He had to step over the body bag to get closer to Ward. Ward was cleaning his glasses, gazing over the water.

"So what do you think?" Tom asked.

Ward put his glasses back on. "I need to do a complete histological examination before I can provide any more information."

"Anything strike you, though? Just off the cuff."

Now the pathologist looked at Tom somberly. "Well, I don't know if 'off-the-cuff' helps you."

"It might."

"You're new."

Tom decided not to take offense. "I am new, yes. I understand how this scene is challenging. I'm not asking you to draw and conclusions you don't feel comfortable with."

"Yes, you are."

Tom let it go. He climbed over the body and back to his bench. He was feeling more confident now moving around in the boat. At least that was something.

Ward called over, "I can't even tell you if trace evidence at the scene is consistent with the death having occurred in that location."

Tom twisted around to face him. Maybe Ward wasn't priggish, maybe he was just frustrated. Tom realized the pathologist had a point, too — the water was moving all the time.

They passed into open water where fish were jumping into the air, flashing like lures in the sun. "Mullet," said Susan Libby. Tom watched the fish in their awkward ballet. Katie Mills looked up, too, then returned to previewing the pictures on her digital camera.

Ramirez steered the boat into the next creek and the mangrove tunnel draped them in striped shadows.

CHAPTER THREE

Blythe was gone from the beach. So were the couple who'd been sitting in the emergency blankets. Ramirez brought the boat in close and killed the engine. He splashed into the shoals, pushing it the rest of the way.

There were even more cops around, a senior deputy giving instructions to a group wearing high rubber boots. The forensics van waited with the rear doors open.

Tom approached Machado, who was watching the whole thing with an affable smile.

"How did that go?" Machado asked.

"Great. Nice way to start the day."

She stuck out her hand. "Felicia Machado. Crime scene bureau with County CID." She glanced at Tom's bare feet, toes squishing in the muck. "That must feel nice. Hot today."

"It is."

Small talk over, Tom watched Ramirez, the diver, Mills, and the two techs hoist the body bag out of the boat. Ward stood by the van, directing them.

"No external signs of violence," Tom told Machado. "But her face is a mess. Post-mortem, I guess, being in the water, maybe fish."

"Ugh. Poor thing."

The group carried the body bag to the van and loaded it in. Ward took a brush and swept out bits of sand from the van floor.

"There was a distinguishing mark," Tom said. "Butterfly tattoo on the inner forearm."

"Well, that's something," Machado said. The group closed the doors to the van. Ward got in the driver's side. They pulled out of the lot and onto the dirt road, moving out of sight.

Machado faced Tom. She had to look up at him. "I guess you're off and running."

Tom was confused. "Sheriff's Office isn't going to take this?"

"The people upstairs just told me a half hour ago that this was your show, state bureau all the way."

"Really?"

"Yep. We're here to help, we'll do a lot of the legwork on the scene, doing door-to-doors — or whatever you'd call it out here in Mother Nature. The body will stay with Ward but your crime lab is handling trace evidence. Blythe said chain of custody is yours."

Tom continued to look for Blythe. "Was she nice about it, at least?"

Machado had an easy laugh. She cocked an eyebrow. "Blythe? Be nice? You haven't heard?"

"Not really." Tom got moving toward his vehicle and Machado walked beside him.

"She was in the military. Did three years in the Middle East, then she was a trooper for the highway patrol. She worked her way into a special unit after several years pushing a cruiser. I think she was with the drug interdiction felony team. Then she switched to the FDLE and has been there with you guys since."

"So she's earned her stripes, you're saying."

Machado gave Tom a cunning little look. "Yeah, guess that's what I'm saying."

He took the plastic bag out of his pocket and fished out his keys and cell phone. Ward had custody of the body. Tom felt a little stung that the man hadn't even quickly debriefed before hightailing it, but he supposed time was of the essence. Once the body was out of the water, decomposition sped up.

Tom opened the car door and leaned in. The interior was like a furnace. He turned on the engine, cranked the A/C and searched for a towel in vain. He sat down in the driver's seat with his legs out and cleaned off his feet with a tiny napkin he found stuffed in the door. Machado was waiting.

"Any cameras out here?" Tom asked.

"There are a couple back at the Reserve building. Surveillance on the entrance. Nothing covering the water. It's pretty bush league."

"Any vehicles found?"

"So far, no. We've got a tire tracks specialist coming, but it's rough out here, and we don't know what we're looking for — people drive in and out: kayakers, tourists, conservation officers."

"Well, I guess we can start with the tattoo," Tom said. "Cross-reference with any missing person's reports."

"Sure. I'll reach out to Special Crimes, have them run it through missing persons."

"Maybe domestic violence reports, too."

"Got it. How far back you want to go?"

The napkin he was using was shredded. He chucked it in the back seat. "Just start recent, a week or so, in the immediate area. Battery, assault. We'll start there and see how far we want to widen out." Tom looked out at the water. "No kayak was found floating around out there or anything, right? The decedent didn't just capsize and drown?"

Machado shook her head. She glanced at Susan Libby, who was down at the water's edge with Ramirez and a diver. "None of her inventory anyway. We asked her — or, I think she volunteered the information when we first got here."

"What were their names, the guests she had with her — Joe and Linda VanCott?"

"Yeah. I'm headed in to get their formal statements. Do you want to be there for that?"

"I want to check in with Blythe . . ."

"Agent Blythe is down the road at the Reserve building."

So Blythe was around after all. He found it strange that his supervisor had left the scene — even after word came down it was officially their investigation. The divers were still out in the water, Everglades deputies had been dispatched to comb along the shoreline. Was he supposed to wait? She hadn't left him with much instruction. Maybe he was just overthinking. Maybe this was how the real world worked.

Machado was watching him. "How old are you?"

The question surprised him. He pulled on his socks and shoes. "Me? Thirty-one. Why?"

"No reason. You look young."

Great, he thought. Another person having fun with the greenhorn. And he was just starting to like Machado.

"Where'd you go to school?" she asked.

"Florida State."

"Yeah? Criminal justice?"

"Double bachelor's. Criminology and Sociology."

Her eyes widened. "Well, well," she said. Then she winked.

He supposed he should expect reactions like Machado's. He was new, and he'd been a detective applicant with no prior police experience or military background. He'd gone to school, and he had a mountain of debt to prove it.

Machado said, "So, no external evidence of violence. But nothing like a kayak to signal accidental death by misadventure, or something, either. We're going to need a big brain like yours on this."

"There are no other kayak tours like Susan Libby's? What about people just coming out on their own?"

Machado shook her head. "They had kayak tours which ran November to May up until two years ago. Now they do boat tours only. Libby's little outfit here, Paddle Creek, that's it. She had to jump through all sorts of hoops to be able to do it."

"But people could still sneak in, I mean—"

"Yeah, they could. It's not too heavily guarded, I guess. Rebnar patrols regularly, though."

"Rebnar . . . you mean R-B-N-E-R-R — Rookery Bay National Estuarine . . ."

". . . Research Reserve," she finished. "You got it. Yeah. They're on top of it."

Tom glanced at Ramirez who was now backing his boat trailer toward the water. They weren't *exactly* on top of it, he thought. Not if someone accessed the preserve, either died of natural causes, overdosed, or was murdered — and then floated for three to five days. On the other hand, Susan Libby said the place was a hundred thousand acres. That was a lot of territory to cover. He wondered how many people worked for the Reserve. Probably quite a lot.

* * *

He arrived back at the small building ensconced in the mangrove, turned in and saw Blythe coming down the steps. The camera Machado had mentioned hung over the door, aimed down the walkway. Blythe drew near and got in the vehicle holding a slim, zipped case.

"So?" she asked. "What've we got?"

He gave Blythe the same details he'd given Machado, adding a little bit about Ward's disposition as well as the emotion Susan Libby had displayed during the body retrieval.

Blythe listened, then nodded toward the building. "This outfit is mostly scientists. Biologists, botanists. They get grants, do their research, work to save the mangrove and wildlife. That's the 'research and reserve' part. About twenty of them, but at any given time, there might only be a few working here. Enforcing things are eight conservation officers, two per day shift, twelve hours, one on at night."

"That's it, huh?"

"In addition to patrolling and maintaining they also run the Natural History Museum down the road. There are more employees there, a couple running the administration, selling tickets, and then they have the ornithologist who comes and does the bird show, and the lizard specialist — I forget what he's called."

"Lizard man. And none of the conservation officers saw anything, heard anything?"

"Well we won't know until we talk to each of them." She unzipped the case in her lap and pulled out some papers. "These are the employee records." She handed him the two top sheets. He saw names, addresses accompanied by thumbnail images. He quickly scanned the images, ignoring the males, dismissing older staff. There were three women aged roughly nineteen to thirty, the range he guessed for the woman in the water. He pointed at one of them and looked at Blythe.

"Already checked with all employees while you were out there," she said. "It's not one of them."

"But we're going to talk to them all?"

"Yes. Hank Bloom is going to work with County. He's human resources with the Reserve. Hank is a friend of mine. He knows what to do, and the Sheriff's Office can filter through those." She pulled out a thicker sheaf of paper and passed it to him. "And these are the three-hundred-plus volunteers in addition to the Reserve staff, assisting with all the research and resource management projects."

"Oh, Jesus." He whistled.

"The decedent could be a volunteer." Blythe's gaze was stony. "That would explain how she was in the estuary without drawing attention. Hank Bloom is also getting us a list of ongoing projects and the volunteers assigned to them."

Tom felt overwhelmed as he leafed through the volunteer profiles. So many faces, lots of them women, lots of them young. "Maybe she's homeless," he said.

"Maybe."

"What about her drifting in from somewhere else? With the tide and all that?"

"It would have to be fairly close by."

"Susan Libby indicated Stopper Creek was where she usually takes clients on the sunrise tour. Best views, or whatever. Could explain why she didn't come across the body sooner."

"Let's start in the center, and work our way out," Blythe said, tapping the file.

"What about tattoos?" he asked, looking closer at the pages. There wasn't that kind of detail in the descriptions. Like the employee list, it was just names, phone numbers, addresses and headshots. "There's got to be an in-depth volunteer database, somewhere we can filch through the data, narrow it down."

She shook her head. "By project, maybe, there are better records. Right now there's no big ongoing project — everything is on hold while this relationship with the Reisen Group gets off the ground. In the meantime, volunteers come and go."

Tom looked at the stack of papers, feeling more confused. "So what are we doing with this?"

"*We*, as in you and I, aren't doing anything except passing it to Everglades County."

Tom felt relieved. It would take days to go through all the records. He was glad they were working with a huge law enforcement body like Everglades County. It was also a lot to be in charge of. Typically, the state bureau provided services upon request to law enforcement agencies. Sometimes the FDLE wanted in on something, and such overtures were made higher up by the commissioner, or by regional commanders.

"So the Sheriff let Turnbull turn this over to us?"

Her mouth was a grim line. "They've reached an agreement about jurisdiction."

She seemed reluctant to explain any further. He caught a whiff of her alluring perfume, glanced at her long legs then quickly away. He knew it was ridiculous to be checking out his supervisor. There was something about her, though.

"You, Lange, are going to stick with the body."

Tom must've made a face because Blythe gave him a look.

"Everglades County is used to working with the Medical Examiner's Office which is the closer, better fatality collection point."

"What about Ward? He any good? Seemed a little . . . I don't know."

She glanced away. "He's meticulous."

The district medical examiner handled the biology, DNA, chemistry, toxicology of a body. You'd have to be meticulous.

"We want him to be thorough," Blythe said, "but we don't want to drag our feet. So you're going to be there, keeping an eye on him. Autopsy should take two days, max. External today, internal tomorrow. We'll have the clothing go up to our lab for trace analysis, share the burden."

She checked the mirror. Tom turned around as a van bounced past on the dirt road, going too fast, as he had earlier. He glimpsed "Channel 7" on the side. The media were here.

"I'll talk to them." Blythe got out of the car. "You'd better get going."

CHAPTER FOUR

The office of the district medical examiner looked deceptively pleasant from the outside. The building was a simple concrete structure adorned with palm trees. An entryway extended out toward the parking lot, with a translucent roof that let the sunlight shine through.

Tom walked into the lobby. Threadbare carpeting, industrial gray, led to a long counter. After he'd signed his name on the register, the receptionist handed him a small bag. "Your first time here?" She was young, round-faced, smiling up at him like he was at Disney World.

Tom found a face mask and gloves in the bag. "Yes," he said.

"Great. I'll show you in. Right this way." She led him out of the lobby and back outside into a breezeway.

The breezeway included several small gardens bearing lush plants. There were pipes overhead, and a machine running he first took for air conditioning. The receptionist caught Tom looking at it. "Odor control."

She pointed to the doors on the other side. "The main autopsy room and the infectious morgue suites are there."

Then she nodded at the bag. "You'll want to put those on."

It seemed the facility made every effort to keep death at bay. He slipped the mask over his face and pulled on the gloves.

After the ritual, she gave him a long look. "Got a sensitive stomach?"

"I'll be alright."

"May I?" She fished a small tube out of the bag, scented cream to apply under the nostrils. "These masks are for contamination — they don't do much for the smell." She held the cream up.

"Maybe later if I need it."

"Okay." She opened the first door, inviting him in.

He stepped through.

The smell hit him like a wave, a gag-inducing blend of formaldehyde and decay, and he felt his stomach clench. The receptionist closed the door behind him with a hollow bang.

A row of windows spanned the length of the back wall and his eyes went there, grateful for a view of the outside world. Three separate work stations had fixed dissection tables and sinks. Scales hung beside the sinks, resembling the kind for weighing fruit in a grocery store. In the back of the suite was a stainless steel refrigerated storage room. The floor was tiled like a restaurant kitchen. The whole room, in fact, looked like a kitchen. Only the work lights, suspended over the stations on mechanical arms, dispelled the illusion.

The storage room door opened and Ward walked out, pushing the body on a mobile gurney. He glanced up at Tom but said nothing.

"Afternoon," Tom said.

Ward rolled the body to the middle of the room. The pathologist was wearing a rubber apron, gloves, and a facemask. The body was draped with a white sheet. Tom expected Ward to choose one of the three work stations, but instead he headed for a door. Tom followed him into an adjoining room, much smaller, and windowless — a single autopsy suite. He felt the choke of claustrophobia as soon as Ward closed the door.

"So, the external examination will take us through several steps." Ward rummaged around in a drawer. "We'll inspect and take samples."

Ward handed a packet of papers to Tom. Tom read the first page: *Body Identification Sheet.* He scanned the information — *Name*, *Method of Identification*, *Location Found*, *Time Found*, *Personal Effects*, and so on. The sections had been filled out and the document was signed by Ward.

Tom flipped through to the *Terminal Episode History*, *Decedent Mental Health History* and *Social History*, which were blank.

Right now, he had nothing. Not even a name.

Ward was laying tools out on a tray beside the draped body. Tom thought an assistant would ordinarily prepare the tools, but perhaps Ward was fussy in this way. It would fit with what he'd seen so far. Then Ward paused and looked up at Tom. "Do we know if there is any religious objection to the autopsy?"

Of course Tom didn't know. It was rare, but he'd read about cases where a victim's family balked at an autopsy for religious reasons. Usually, a medical examiner could work around it — it just meant more paperwork, sometimes getting a judge involved — but in this case, the deceased person was a Jane Doe. Tom didn't know if she was Buddhist or Hare Krishna.

"We can't wait for our first post-mortem in case evidence," Tom said.

Ward held a glimmer in his eye, but nodded soberly.

There was a knock on the door and Tom's heart flipped. A dour-looking young woman appeared wearing a white lab coat. "This is Andrea, my assistant and autopsy photographer," Ward said. Andrea closed the door and Tom's claustrophobia tightened.

Andrea clicked on a recorder and placed it on the tray next to Ward while he pulled on a pair of goggles. Then he took the top of the body sheet and carefully rolled it down.

The decedent's face hadn't gotten any better in the past hour. The hollow eye sockets were particularly disturbing, like a mangled doll staring into oblivion. Andrea started taking pictures.

"Estimation of post-mortem interval in water is difficult." Ward continued to remove the sheet. "But temperature is likely to be the more reliable factor governing decompositional changes . . ."

Ward pointed at the woman's hands.

"Palms of the hands show effects of immersion consistent with my initial estimate."

The skin there was wrinkled and looked . . . loose. Tom struggled to not back away. He tried to be clinical, detached. He noted how the hair was falling out. And how the fingernails were close to slipping off.

"Water permeates sweat ducts and alters electrolyte composition . . ."

Tom thought Ward was enjoying himself, the change in demeanor subtle, but there.

"Autonomic nerve fibers in the digits are triggered." Ward took gentle hold of one of the body's hands. "Ah, see here, the vasoconstriction has caused this negative digital pulp pressure." He gently flexed the fingers back and forth.

"What does that mean?" Tom felt dizzy. *Get it together, man.* "It means wrinkles? I need to know if this woman died of natural causes or was murdered."

Ward moved toward the feet, as if he hadn't heard. Tom looked over the bloated and bluish body and took a step closer.

"What about a SAFE kit? Even if any serological evidence was washed away, if she was raped there could be internal cuts, scarring—"

"Patience, Agent Lange." Ward hunched over the feet.

Due to the discoloration of the skin, it was hard to see if there was any bruising, but Tom's eyes kept roving over the body. "What about the head, have you checked the head?"

Ward stood upright and looked across the corpse at Tom, his eyes now obscured by the reflective goggles. He walked to the other end of the body, trading looks with Andrea. Tom should have smeared the damn cream under his nose — the odor was threatening to knock him over, the room was too cramped. He was getting edgy.

Ward started going through the hair and then stopped, beckoning to Andrea who came closer with the camera. He lifted some hair out of the way and she took several pictures.

"What is it?" Tom wanted a closer look but they crowded him out.

Ward answered into the recorder. "Two short lacerations have been identified where the parietal and occipital bones meet." He peered down, pushing more hair aside. Some of the hair was coming off on his gloves. "There is some bruising, a significant abrasion along the Lambdoid suture."

Blunt force trauma, Tom thought. The excitement eclipsed his discomfort. "She was hit in the head." He leaned in, still trying to get a closer look, his revulsion overcome.

"The cuts are old," Ward said. "One should not immediately assume that blunt force trauma is the cause of death."

"But, she was struck."

"Or, she fell." He raised his voice a tick, Tom thought, for the benefit of the recording. "For purposes of death certification, it should be noted that blunt force trauma may be the proximate cause of death. But the immediate cause of death could be a natural disease process."

Still groping her head, Ward's eyes zeroed in on Tom's. Their faces were inches apart. "For example, individuals may die of infections, thromboembolism, or organ failure that occurs as a delayed result of *previous* blunt force trauma. In some cases, the injury may have occurred many years before death."

"You think this occurred years ago?"

Ward retreated, and looked the body over. "No," he admitted. "I don't."

* * *

When Blythe arrived, Tom was sitting in the breezeway next to the gardens, his mask removed, head in his hands.

He looked up at Blythe. "How did it go with the press?"

"Oh they'll be camped there all day, reporters standing in front of the water, swatting mosquitos."

Blythe had a sense of humor after all.

"Are we going to release a statement?"

"Yes."

"When?"

She surprised him by sitting down next to him. "Well, that depends on what we think. We can work with Heather Kibble, the ADA for the twentieth circuit. She's with the Homicide Unit, and she's waiting on our word. How is the autopsy coming along?"

"The victim has bruises and cuts at the back of her head. They did an X-ray and her skull was cracked, probable brain swelling. They did the rape kit and sent it to the crime lab, but it doesn't look like there was a sexual assault. He's not sure though. He's not sure about anything."

Tom looked at the white mask he was holding, turning it around in his hands.

A silence developed and Tom was afraid of how he looked — petulant, even afraid. "You know, I understand that—"

"Forensic pathologists like Ward are specially trained to perform autopsies. Thirteen years of schooling, including a four-year residency in anatomical and clinical pathology and one year in a forensic pathology fellowship. You're not the only one top of his class — like I said, Ward is the best. And the District Medical Examiner's Office primarily handles death investigation."

"Until there's evidence of homicide," Tom challenged. "And I think there is. I think someone hit that woman in the back of the head. Then they dumped her in the water."

"So you don't think the estuary is the primary crime scene."

"No."

She nodded.

"But we have no suspects," he said.

"It's early yet."

Tom looked at her. She was like a different person this afternoon. This morning she'd been icy and all-business, now she seemed almost friendly. He wondered what had changed.

"What do you want to do, Tom?"

She seemed to be testing him. He thought of the way Ward had gently prodded the body in the water. She was prodding him now, seeing what he would do. While this was an investigation, it was also his proving ground.

He stood up. He'd had plenty of time to think while Ward had performed the painstaking examination.

"Well, obviously we need to identify her. No personal effects have been located, no wallet or phone, her skin is mush for fingerprints. So, I want to get a forensic artist here. Have them do a sketch of the victim's face, add the eyes, make her alive. Then I want to get into NamUs and start searching demographics, physical characteristics, distinguishing marks."

NamUs — the National Missing and Unidentified Persons System — was the latest national system, crossing state, county, and municipal borders, reaching between different law enforcement agencies. NamUs was unique because the general public had equal access.

"Maybe someone on the public side of NamUs is searching, too, like her family. So we need to get the victim in there, get the sketch, details, assign a case number."

Blythe seemed pleased. He was about to continue when his phone rang.

It was Machado. Blythe made a nod, indicating he take it.

"Hey there," Machado said. "So, here's what I pulled from the past week. I focused on 10-44s and sexual assault. Demographically, Caucasian women, ages twenty to thirty-five."

"What did you get?"

"A bartender named Darlene DeMerse reported an assault five days ago. Didn't press charges, though, so we don't have a name for the assailant, just her address. Then there is Joan Prentice, a school accountant, and she *did* file charges for sexual assault. His name is Bob Sturgess. That was two days ago. Most recently, a woman named Kimberly Monroe was hospitalized for a concussion, apparently told the medical staff her husband did it, but ended up withdrawing charges. These are all within a three-mile radius of Rookery Bay. That's it, that's what I've got for County. Naples PD might have more."

"Thank you, Detective."

"You got it. I'll send you the info in an email."

He hung up and relayed the information to Blythe. He waited for her to come to terms with the morning, the autopsy, the possibility of blunt force trauma as enough to officially launch the investigation.

"Here's what," Blythe said. "When's the last time you ate?"

"I didn't."

"Okay. Go home, get something to eat. Take a shower. And wash your clothes — the smell is hard to get out."

She handed him a light, black binder, not much in it. "That's your copy of the murder book. You can start your NamUs case from home, or go to the field office. Whichever you want. Keep on it all night. County is working the bay, going through the volunteers and conservation officers. And for those assault cases, we'll have County do some door to door."

"We should look at Kimberly Monroe first," he said. "She was hospitalized for a concussion. We ought to talk to the husband, see where he was last Wednesday through Friday."

"I'll handle it. And tomorrow, eight a.m. sharp, we'll meet at the lab and go over the clothing, alright?"

"Alright."

"We're going to call this a homicide, at least unofficially. I'll tell the commissioner and contact ADA Kibble. We'll give the press conference tomorrow afternoon, with or without an ID."

CHAPTER FIVE

A car blared its horn and Tom realized he was sitting at a green light, lost in thought. He stomped the gas and continued down 41 until the traffic slowed for the Fifth Avenue junction. Fifth Avenue was clogged with more traffic inching along past the ritzy shops. Then it all faded in his mirrors as he drove to the outskirts of Naples.

Tom lived in Lely, a large plot of land subdivided into golf courses and condo complexes and neighborhoods with single-family homes. He wound through the residential streets with tall palm trees brown and brittle in the stolid heat. He turned into his complex, hit the button on his visor and rolled the Jeep into the garage.

Blythe was right: the smell of the morgue clung to his clothes. He could still feel the grit of sand between his toes. He took his copy of the murder book and went inside.

He scrubbed thoroughly in the shower, taking a good ten minutes longer than usual, shampooing his hair twice. He dried, dressed in jeans and a T-shirt and took a seat in the living room. While he waited for the laptop to boot up, he stared at the sign hanging above the wall-mounted TV.

Congratulations, Tom!

The celebration had been Charlene's idea. Charlene was a retired teacher who lived with her ailing husband and tiny Pomeranian a few doors down. Tom mostly kept to himself, but Charlene had special powers when it came to finding out information.

First, in casual conversation she'd learned of his enrollment in the basic recruiter program in Fort Myers. Next, Charlene had intercepted him on the way back from the mailboxes and spied an envelope from the ROC containing the results of his State Officer Certification Exam. After she'd hounded him for the results, in the sweet way she had, he told her he'd passed. He didn't share that he'd gotten a perfect score. He was in, his pending application with the state bureau sure to go through. Charlene had baked a cake, brought her enfeebled husband and their dog over. She'd also invited her friend, Alicia, a single mother with a four-year-old daughter. Charlene was trying to play matchmaker, she had been since Tom moved in eighteen months ago.

His brother, Nick, had got him the condo. It had been an incredible deal, in a buyer's market, and Nick had some decent connections. Fort Myers was an hour away and home to the ROC and crime lab, but there were field offices in Sarasota, Sebring, and Naples. Tom could work from home or drive ten minutes to the Naples field office when needed. Plus, living in the same city as his older brother, he could keep an eye on him.

The laptop was ready, and Tom opened up NamUs and logged on.

The most recent entry had come in just a minute ago.

Case#: 5091702 UP# 6857
Date of Death/Discovery: 04/20/17 (Wooded area at 11431 U.S. Highway 19, Port

Richey, FL 34668) (USA Flea Market)
Law Enforcement Agency: Pasco County Sheriff's Office #09-67244
Physical Description & Other Information: Adult white/male found decomposing and partially burned. Estimated age 39–65, height 5'10", wearing bright colored "Joe Boxer" underwear size L and light colored shirt, also found with battery powered blanket.

Sounded like a homeless person. Florida was full of them, and Everglades had more than any other county. Wherever you had woods, you had people living in them. Tom had considered the possibility that their victim had been homeless.

He spent the next hour searching the missing person side of NamUs. He'd set his parameters for female, aged 20–40, height 5'6", light brown hair. He cached a dozen reports that came close to fitting the description, then initiated a new file for the victim. NamUs assigned it a number and Tom had just started to populate the fields, clicking away at the keys when his phone rang. The incoming number was Nick's.

"Tommy! I saw the news. Are you on this case? Where were you? You weren't standing there — some woman was. Smokin' hot for an older lady. Who is she?"

Nick liked to ask more questions than could reasonably be answered. He also rarely engaged in small talk.

"My supervisor," Tom answered.

"Sweet, bro. Holy shit, pretty big case, huh? I mean, what've they got you doing?"

"I'm working the body. And doing a missing persons search."

"The body? You? Dude, you hate that shit. Did they cut anything open? Pull all the body parts out? Was she raped? I mean, they have tests to determine that sort of thing, don't they?"

"I can't really say."

"Alright, alright. Yeah, I get it. So — what, you're like probably totally swamped, huh? Yeah. Alright I won't bother you. Oh — but hey, did you have a party? I got a message on my phone from Charlene. I was in Tampa yesterday and didn't check my messages. What the hell, man?"

Tom rested his head on the chair and looked up at the ceiling. Already Nick was overwhelming him. Nick had been that type of kid — full of life. He'd been into sports, clubs, anything social. A true extrovert. Nick loved the real estate business for introducing him to wide range of folks. And as an artist, Nick was phenomenal with a pen, he loved doing portraits. Lately, though, Nick's upbeat moods could border on mania. And when he went the other direction, when he got down, the lows were low.

"The party was just a little thing, Nick. Honestly, I think Charlene just wanted to get Alicia over here."

"Alicia, huh? Sounds hot. Sounds nice. How did that go? You lay some pipe?"

"Went okay. No." He quickly diverted the conversation. "Hey, while I still got you on the phone — you ever volunteer for the Reserve again? You did like a year ago, right? You still do it?"

"No, no. I did the one thing, the one project. We picked up all those shells for a week. Fuck, dude. I mean, great to give back and everything, but kinda tedious."

Tom got up and went up to his bedroom. "How's work?"

"Real estate?"

"No, dipshit, aeronautics."

"Hey now . . . Well, I've got a decent property showing tomorrow. Right in your area. Things are okay. Little slow right now. But listen, Tommy, you know, you don't have to beat around the bush. You got a big new case, you just started as a special agent. You've been wanting this since we were kids. I get it. If this weekend is too busy, you know, just tell me."

Tom winced. Nick sounded sincere, but if Tom broke plans, he'd be hurt as hell.

Nick had never recovered from what happened to them as kids. And he'd stopped visiting their shrink, Dr. Camden, before Tom had. For one thing, Nick was two years older and once he'd hit eighteen, the court could no longer mandate him to see a psychiatrist.

Tom walked across the bedroom to grab his cigarettes from the top drawer. As he pulled them out he glanced at the photograph. They were only boys, Nick eight and Tom six, both of them shirtless. Nick had a huge grin, baby teeth missing, jutting his chin for the camera. He had his arm around Tom. Tom smiled softly, a distant look in his eyes. They were standing on the bank by the lake, birch trees behind them.

"I don't know," Tom said. "Yeah, things are busy. So . . ."

"Okay." Nick was abrupt. "Well, good luck with the job, Tommy."

Tom opened his mouth to say something, but no words came out.

"You there?" Nick asked.

"Yeah, I'm here."

Tom suddenly felt like he couldn't stand. He stretched out on the floor. He wanted to say things to his brother, he wanted to ask — was it doing any good to get together each year for their little ritual? Or was it just opening the wound each time? Their parents were gone over twenty years. He could hardly remember them.

"I'll call you tomorrow." Tom lay flat on his back. "Okay? Nicky?"

"Bye, Tommy." Nick hung up.

Tom dropped the phone on the floor and rubbed his face. Twenty years. Twenty *years*. More than twice as long as his parents had been a living part of his life, they'd been ghosts.

But Tom and Nick had made a pact — they would never forget. No matter what had happened with their father, for their mother they would get together each year, on the anniversary of her death.

He rolled his head to look at the phone, thinking about Nick. He had to put this aside now, there was too much to do. He sat up, grunting, and stared blankly into the room for a moment. Then the doorbell rang, snapping him out of it.

Tom rose to his feet. He pulled on his shirt and went downstairs. He wasn't expecting anyone.

He opened the door and saw Alicia standing there, little Gwen in her arms, the girl clinging to her mother.

Alicia had a bloody lip and a bruise on the side of her face.

"I'm sorry." There were tears welling in her eyes. "I didn't know where else to go. I can't do it anymore. I just can't do it."

CHAPTER SIX

Tom ushered Alicia and Gwen into the house, noticing a truck at the far end of the complex, engine idling. He could see the shape of the driver behind the windshield.

The driver revved the engine, and the truck crept forward.

Tom shut the door and faced Alicia.

"I'm so sorry to come here like this," she said.

"What happened?" It was obvious, but he still needed to hear it from her.

"He's been acting crazy all day."

"Who? Is it your boyfriend?"

"We broke up weeks ago."

Gwen had her head on her mother's shoulder, thumb stuck in her mouth. Tom gently put his hands around the girl to take her, but Gwen shrank from his touch. "Alright, well, sit down."

Alicia found her way to the couch in his living room. She was a small woman, mid-twenties, and Gwen was just four years old.

Tom pulled his cell phone out. "I'm going to call it in, okay?"

Alicia hesitated, glanced at the front door, and then nodded.

He dialed the number for the Everglades County Sheriff's Office. At the same time, he heard the engine of the truck drawing closer and walked to the window. He moved aside the curtain and peered out.

The truck rolled to a stop in front of Tom's building. Tom kept watch while he listened to the phone ringing the police station. Finally, patrol division picked up the line.

"Sheriff's Office."

"This is Special Agent Lange with the FDLE."

"How can I help you, Agent Lange?"

"I'm reporting an assault. Victim is Alicia Strong. She's at my house now, I'll give you the address. Can you send a unit to pick her up?" He moved the phone away from his mouth and asked Alicia, "What's his name? Your ex?"

"Josh McDermott."

Tom relayed the information while watching through the window. McDermott was still sitting in his truck. There was a landscaping company insignia on the side, a phone number included. The truck was parked just below the steps down from Tom's condo, blocking their exit.

"Okay," said the officer, "I'll put it out to the shift commander — tough thing is, a lot of patrol in your zone are assisting at Rookery Bay right now. We'll get someone, just might take a bit."

Tom turned from the window, thinking he should've expected it. Everglades County was trying to cover a huge swath of territory. It was a lot of manpower.

The officer continued, "Your Agent Blythe appropriated an additional deputy about an hour ago to look at video from Rebnar's main building. We're adding deputy shifts. Like I said, I'll put out the call — the victim is with you now?"

"Yes. There's got to be a road deputy to come assist. If anyone is in the area, have them swing by, alright?"

"Yes, sir."

Tom ended the call and stared at Alicia for a moment, thinking. He couldn't call Naples Police, either. People with homes along the edge of the ocean benefitted from city police, but where Tom lived inland fell in County jurisdiction. He could call his own highway patrol troopers, but there was no telling how long it would take them to arrive — Troop F was headquartered in Bradenton, and the troopers mainly dealt with traffic safety.

"Be right back," Tom said. He bounded up the stairs to get his gun. He checked the weapon and slid it back into the holster. He pulled on a blazer and went back downstairs.

"Can I use your bathroom? I want to clean my face."

"Don't." Tom shook his head. "We'll get pictures at the hospital." He started toward the window again and stopped. "Josh has done this to you before?"

She nodded, tears brimming again, and turned her face away.

He came a little closer. "What happened the last time? Did you call the police then?"

She shook her head, biting her lower lip and stroking her daughter's hair. "I'm so sorry. I just met you . . . and now here I am, dragging you into this. I should go."

"No. We have to report this and press charges."

Her face contorted in anguish. "Why? What'll it do? Then I'll have to go to court . . . miss work . . ."

He shook his head emphatically and sat beside her. "Not necessarily. Only if he pleads not guilty. But with pictures of your face, your statement . . ." He looked at the little girl, worrying about talking like this in front of her. But the way she clung to her mother, there was no choice. "Did she see it?"

Alicia looked mortified. "No, of course not. She was in the other room."

"Okay, okay." Tom stood up and faced the curtained window. "Does Josh have a lawyer?"

"Not that I know of."

"Then he'll be assigned a public defender. The PD will go for a guilty plea or at least no contest and they'll plea bargain the prosecutor. Does he have any prior domestic violence convictions?"

Again she shook her head.

"Well then, that's still the most likely outcome. Look what he did to you. And not the first time, right? So now you have to fight back. Alicia, he needs to go to jail. This needs to get on his record. Okay?"

She struggled against the tears and at last nodded her head.

"Okay. We're gonna go through that door, down the short steps, and into my garage. We'll get into my Jeep, and I'll take you to the hospital." He helped her stand up.

"I parked in front of your garage," she said.

He hesitated, considering it. "Then we'll take your car." He held out his hand. "Keys?"

"I left them in the ignition."

Shit. Okay, so the only way to get out of there was through McDermott. Who the hell did this guy think he was? Obviously he didn't know this was a cop's home. Well, he was going to find out. And then, if he had any brains at all, he'd get the hell out of there.

Tom moved Alicia and Gwen toward the entrance. He opened the door, urged them outside, and got in front of them. "Stay behind me."

* * *

Before they reached the bottom of the steps, Josh McDermott got out and leaned against his truck, crossing his arms. He was calm and emotionless, his eyes cold as a snake's.

"Let's just go right by him," Tom whispered to Alicia. "Right to your car."

"Leesh," McDermott called. "What're you doin'? Is this the guy?"

Just a couple feet away from McDermott, on the last step, Tom stopped. "I'm Special Agent Lange with the Florida Department of Law Enforcement."

"Oh. Well, I'm Josh McDermott. With Four Palms Landscaping." He kept a straight face and stuck out his hand in greeting.

Tom saw Charlene across the street, walking her dog, headed in their direction. Tom ignored McDermott's offer of a handshake and got moving again, keeping a protective arm around Alicia and her daughter.

McDermott lowered his hand. "Hey now — where y'all goin'?"

Tom opened the rear door so Alicia could deposit the girl in her car seat. He realized they couldn't have taken his vehicle anyway without switching the seat over. Alicia tried to put Gwen in, but the girl resisted.

"No, Mommy. Noooo. I don't wanna get 'rested . . ."

"You're not getting arrested." Alicia pried open the little girl's hands, laced tightly around her mother's neck. McDermott sidled over.

Tom moved to the back of the car and put his hand on his weapon. "That's far enough, Mr. McDermott. Stay back."

McDermott stopped and narrowed his eyes. Tom glanced at Charlene. She slowed her pace. A car drove into the complex, and Tom recognized Jack Vance, another neighbor, behind the wheel. Vance raised his hand in a tentative wave, rubbernecking the situation as he rolled by. Vance was retired Air Force, good at keeping secrets — after eighteen months of neighborly conversation, Tom still didn't know what Jack Vance had actually done while in the service. Charlene, on the other hand, would have everyone in the whole place apprised of the situation within the hour. *So much for my relative privacy*, Tom thought.

But there were more pressing concerns. McDermott turned his attention to Alicia. "She doesn't wanna go, Alicia. Why don't you just let her be?"

Tom held out a hand and released the break snap on his holster. "Stop. We're causing a scene here."

"A scene?" McDermott's eyelids fluttered with incredulity. "What the hell are you talking about?"

"I'm talking about I shoot you, put one in your leg. It causes a disruption." His heart was pounding now and he questioned the threat he made as soon as the words came out of his mouth. But McDermott was either stupid or dangerous or both.

"Hey," McDermott called to Alicia. He pointed at Tom, his finger close enough for Tom to grab. "This the guy here, Leesh? Just tell me, so I know. That's all I want, is to know. You owe me that, don't you think?"

Alicia finally got Gwen in the seat and came closer. "I don't owe you anything," she said through gritted teeth.

Now Tom was in between them. "Alicia, *get in the car.*"

McDermott grinned, amused by it all. "Oh, I see. You takin' orders from *him* now. Does he do all the things you like, Alicia? Is Mr. *Miami Vice* gonna tie you up, put the handcuffs on you?"

McDermott reached out and patted Tom's cheek. "Yeah, I can see you two getting nasty."

Tom jerked his head away and grabbed the man by the wrist. He pinned McDermott's arm behind him and shoved him against the back of the car, grabbed him by the head and folded the man over, slamming his jaw down on the trunk.

Tom's mind raced. He could release McDermott and pull his gun right now, put it to the man's temple, teach him a fucking lesson. He felt the rage boiling. He looked at Alicia and yelled, "Get into the car right now!"

She stared at McDermott, who grunted, but didn't fight back. Somewhat defiantly, she dropped into her seat.

Tom let off the pressure, yanked McDermott to his feet, and shoved him toward the truck. At last he pulled his weapon and pointed it, keeping his finger away from the trigger. "Get in your truck and drive away."

McDermott massaged his arm, more dumbstruck than aggressive for a moment, but then Tom saw the violence brewing in his eyes. McDermott wanted to come back at Tom right now and tear him to pieces.

Charlene was standing on the other side of the drive, staring. He imagined other residents at their windows, watching the whole thing too. Tom took an aggressive step toward McDermott. "I said get out of here. Go home and wait for the police to come pick you up. That's your only option right now."

"You don't tell me my fuckin' options." McDermott had completely dropped the affable act.

"She doesn't want to be with you." Tom adopted a calmer tone. "Go home."

McDermott flinched, as if struck, but continued to sneer, his eyes shining with hate. "That bitch? Fine. She's a fucking slut, she's all yours."

His aspersions carried across the complex. Anyone within earshot was hearing the foul language. *Bitch. Slut.* Charlene finally headed off, walking briskly.

"Alicia," McDermott barked. "It's alright, babe. We're not going to let this get us down. You listening to me? You fucking cunt?"

"Shut up," Tom said. "Get in your truck."

But McDermott didn't budge.

As Tom was deciding what to do, Jack Vance drove back toward the scene and rolled down his window. "Everything alright here, Tommy?"

"Had better evenings."

"Yeah." The older man's eyes pinned to McDermott. Vance put the car in park and opened the door.

"Jack, you should stay in your vehicle. The police are on their way."

Vance's keen eyes devoured the scene. He kept coming, waving a hand in the air. "It's alright. I don't mind." He stopped a few feet from the truck. "Why don't you go ahead, Tommy? Take those two girls where they got to go."

"Can't do that, Jack. I really appreciate it, though."

"No, no," Vance said in that same tone. "I think that's the best thing." His kindly voice was betrayed by the hardness in his eyes. Vance was pushing seventy, but one thing he'd shared with Tom since they'd gotten to know each other was how he'd never lost a fight. He may have been discreet about his responsibilities in the Air Force, but was happy to talk about his days as a young, bar-brawling pilot.

McDermott sized up Vance, then he turned, spat at Tom's feet, and climbed into the truck. He revved the engine and squealed the tires as he pulled away, leaving black streaks on the asphalt. He raced out of the complex way too fast, tires squawking a second time as he turned and tore away into the twilight.

Tom put his weapon away.

"You'd better get going," Vance said. "I'll keep an eye on your place."

Tom thanked him and hurried to Alicia's car.

CHAPTER SEVEN

"Did they teach you that self-defense in police school?" Alicia had climbed into the backseat to sit beside Gwen, trying to calm her down. They were a few minutes away from the hospital.

Tom felt shaky, the adrenaline had yet to settle. "I've never done anything like that before in my life." It wasn't entirely true.

There was no sign of the landscaping truck on their tail. Tom weaved through the sparse traffic, the sky turning dark. "But yeah," he said. "They taught us self-defense. I just, ah . . . didn't expect to have to use it so soon."

"I'm sorry."

He looked at her in the mirror. "It's okay. He . . . ah, thinks you're having an affair?"

Her eyes shined. "He's crazy."

"With me? He thinks you and I are . . .?"

"He's been following me. He knows I came to your house last night."

Tom took the turn onto Rattlesnake-Hammock Road and headed toward the hospital. They were close now.

"It's alright," he said. "Let's just get this on the record, get you looked at." The hospital was at the next intersection. He stopped at the emergency entrance, opened the rear door for her. Alicia unbuckled the child and they all went into the hospital, leaving the car running.

He checked in at the main desk, showed his badge, explained the assault, and that Alicia needed pictures and a full report for the police.

"We'll take care of her," the nurse assured him. "You can wait right over there."

The nurse walked Alicia and Gwen down the corridor toward one of the emergency suites. Little Gwen stared at Tom over her mother's shoulder as she was carried off.

* * *

Tom parked Alicia's car, then spoke to Blythe from the hospital waiting room and told her what had happened. "I want to take a look at McDermott. When County picks him up for the domestic battery, I want to talk to him about Rookery Bay."

"Lange . . ." Blythe sounded doubtful.

"Just a little look. He's a woman beater." Tom had a magazine in his lap he'd been leafing through but not really taking in. He rolled it up now and squeezed it.

"He might be," Blythe said, "but the odds that he had anything to do with our Jane Doe are a long shot, at best."

"Follow every lead, right? They drilled it into our heads in training."

"It's barely a *lead* . . . But alright, I'll tell you what. If and when County picks him up, I won't let you in the room, but you can observe."

"Thank you."

"And I wanted to let you know I followed up with Machado on the domestic battery short list."

"And?"

"Darlene DeMerse gave up a name — Alex Juarez. He worked double shifts at *Lowe's* last week. County pulled his time sheet, he checks out. Sturgess, who assaulted the school accountant, has been in the hospital. He resigned from the school and attempted suicide. That leaves Kimberly Monroe and her husband Frank, who may have given her the concussion, but Frank was out of town at the estimated time of death."

"Well, let's keep looking."

Tom took a deep breath and tried to calm himself. He was off his routine. School and training had kept his life in balance, same thing every day. Swim or jog in the morning, go to class, come home, workout, eat, go to sleep. He'd kept to himself, and he worked the program Dr. Camden had helped him to learn many years before. Now, in a single day, all that had been disrupted. He wished he'd brought the cigarettes from home.

He left the waiting room, went out of the hospital and spied a Quick Mart in the plaza across the highway. He started toward it.

"Where are you going?" Blythe must have heard his movements over the phone.

"Nowhere. What about the couple from the kayaking tour? We never talked about that."

"Not much to talk about. Joe and Linda VanCott. Married for eighteen years, they take a trip twice a year from New York to kayak the bay. They like the sunrise trip."

He'd gotten the same information from Susan Libby. "Yeah, well, Joe is a donor. Supported research on the mangrove die-off."

"So what? You want to take a look at him? What's the motive? We don't know anything yet."

"What about Libby? Anything interesting on her?"

"If dedicating one's life to nature conservancy is interesting. She's practically a nun. Unmarried, no kids, pretty much spent her whole life doing what she's doing today. Grew up in Naples. Never really been anywhere else."

He waited for a break in the traffic then jogged across the multiple lanes to the plaza. "How is it going with the volunteer list?"

"They've gone through more than half of it. Everybody checks out so far. Nobody missing . . ."

He entered the Quick Mart and approached the counter.

"Tom. Stay with your friend, get her home."

"I'm not taking her there. This guy is liable to come back before the Sheriff's Office gets him into custody."

"Then take her to your place. Whatever you've got to do. Listen, I know you're . . . This case we've got is still just shaping up. You're doing fine. The sketch artist was at the morgue for an hour, you'll have an email with the sketch tonight. Tomorrow is a new day, alright? You've got to get into gear, take it slow and steady."

"Alright," he said. He felt a touch of embarrassment but she was right. He wished her a good night and got off the phone. Then he bought a pack of cigarettes from the waiting clerk.

* * *

Back at the condo, he made up the couch for Alicia and Gwen. It was getting late, going on 11 p.m. Gwen had fallen asleep during the car ride back but was stirring as Alicia lay her down on the couch. Alicia petted the girl's hair and spoke softly to her. Tom went upstairs to give them some privacy.

He opened his laptop on the bed and logged onto the NamUs site. He toggled to the Jane Doe case file and felt the hairs on the back of his neck rise. Someone had posted a message.

The way NamUs worked was similar to classified ads. An unidentified person's case was considered a "listing." Anyone on either the law enforcement or public side could post a message beneath a listing. He read what was written by *PublicUser22958*:

> Hello. Not sure if this is the right way to do this? I saw about this site on tv. I'm looking for a frend who has been missing about a week. She fits the descripshin on your site. She has butterfly tatoo. What do I do??

Tom felt wide awake now. He hunched over the keyboard and typed a response:

> Thank you for getting in touch. Please privately message me at the following email.

He left his email address and sent the message. It appeared in the thread beneath the listing, after PublicUser22958's post. Then he logged onto his email through the FDLE server and sat staring at his inbox, waiting. He could hear Alicia moving around downstairs. It sounded like Gwen was crying.

Tom switched back to the NamUs site and reread the post a few times, noting the misspelled words. Sometimes people posted maliciously on the listings. Usually they were identified, and almost always they were kids. A searchable database that was open to the public ran such a risk. The penalty for falsely responding to a record could be stiff, but typically the pranksters were given a harsh warning for their offense, and that was it.

He didn't think this was a hoax. Maybe it was someone young, or someone whose English wasn't great. He also noted the time of the post — 10:22 p.m. As he'd been leaving the hospital and returning to his condo with Alicia and her daughter, someone had been sitting somewhere, typing the message.

He considered the odds. There were an estimated forty thousand unidentified bodies in the United States. They languished in the offices of medical examiners and coroners, or had been buried or cremated as unknowns. NamUs recorded about half of them. And while the demographic search was helpful, there were still a ton of records. It could take someone months to make an identification.

Whoever had posted about the Jane Doe did so only hours after the initial listing. It was fast, but not unheard of. The user had been able to narrow the search because of the tattoo.

Cops loved tattoos as an identifying mark.

He watched his inbox, growing excited, impatient. He flipped back to NamUs one last time and clicked on the link for PublicUser22958.

He found what he'd already expected — when a user signed up to use the database, personal information was protected. This user hadn't made their email or telephone number public, preferring discretion, or control, or both.

* * *

"Tom?" Alicia's voice carried softly up the stairs.

He left the room and went down to the living room. "How we doing?"

"Good." She looked over at Gwen, just a lump beneath the couch blankets, long hair fanned over a pillow. "She's asleep."

Tom's condo was open plan, the kitchen and living room connected without a separating wall. Otherwise, downstairs was a bathroom, a closet, and a screened-in back porch. "Let's go back here and talk." He led her down the hallway.

The backyard abutted on the rough edge of a golf course. Out there was a water trap which doubled as a turtle pond. Over the past months, Tom had seen the turtles come and go while sitting on the porch. He'd also seen a small alligator.

They each took a chair and looked out over the moonlit greens beyond the pond.

"You smoke?" Alicia asked. She'd seen the butt-can in the corner.

"I try not to." He had the pack he'd bought at the Quick Mart in his pocket and brought it out. He offered her one and she took it. Then he got out his Zippo and lit it for her.

"I didn't think you were the type." Alicia squinted against the smoke. "You seem . . . I don't know. Like a health nut, or something."

He smiled and lit one of his own.

"That came out wrong," she said. "Not that you're unhealthy because you smoke. I mean, I know it's not healthy, *you* know it's not healthy. But, I mean, you have that thing in the corner. That little gym — what is that, a Soloflex or something?"

"Yeah. Bowflex."

"Yeah, so you work out. Have to stay in shape or whatever, for your job, right? Did you have to train, or condition, a lot to become a cop? Or, it's agent, right? You're a special agent? Jesus, I'm babbling."

She ran a trembling hand through her hair. Tom could see the bruise around her eye even in the darkness. They'd had to put a single stitch in her lip, and the area was stained rusty brown with disinfectant. She touched it self-consciously.

"You're not babbling," he said. "We're just talking."

"You're not talking. *I'm* talking. You don't talk. Last night at your party thing, you hardly said a word." Alicia quickly switched topics. "That Charlene is something, huh? She's so sweet. She really likes you."

"She's a nice person."

A silence developed, both of them smoking, looking out. The night was fragrant with hyacinth and the air had cooled, but only a little. Tomorrow was going to be another hot one.

"Do you like Florida?" she asked.

"I do."

"We have monsters down here."

He gave her a look.

"For real. The alligators are everywhere. Gwenny is terrified. We're also the lightning capital of the country. Did anyone tell you that? More people get struck by lightning here than anywhere else."

Tom thought about it. "With all the golf courses, people walking around waving iron rods in the air, I'm not surprised."

She laughed, maybe a bit louder than she'd intended, but it broke the tension.

"It's weird living so close a golf course," he said. "You have to wonder if there are lawsuits over people getting clocked in the head with flying golf balls. It's not like where I grew up."

"Charlene says you have a brother?" Alicia flicked her ash into the butt-can.

"I do."

"Any other family? Where are your parents? Back where you grew up?"

He felt the familiar tightening when asked the question. He supposed he should've been used to it after all these years. "They passed away. Nick and I were raised in foster care."

"Oh, Jeeze. I'm sorry."

"It's alright. We had good foster parents."

"What happened?"

Tom debated whether or not he wanted to get into it. For one thing, there was other stuff on his mind. But he'd gotten an intimate glimpse of Alicia's life and ought to reciprocate. He decided on the easiest version of the story.

"Our parents were away for the weekend. Nick hated having a babysitter. He was ten years old and he figured he could take care of himself. He insisted on doing everything — making the dinner, answering the phone. The doorbell rang, and Nick went to get it. Two cops were standing there."

"Oh, God. What happened?"

"They'd died in a fire where they were staying."

She put her hand over her mouth. "I'm so sorry."

"It's okay. I don't really remember them." He shifted in his seat. "Listen, I'd like to talk about Josh for a minute. Is that okay? You mind if we talk about him?"

She finished her smoke, threw it away and clasped her hands together in her lap.

"Josh grew up in Florida. Lake Mary. He was a conservation officer in Big Cypress for a little while, but he was fired. This is before he met me."

"How long have you been with him? Or, *were* you with him?"

"Three years."

"So he's not Gwen's father."

"No."

Alicia didn't seem to want to offer any more on the subject of her daughter's biological father. It seemed they both had their uncomfortable subjects.

"How did you meet him?"

"Not the most romantic thing in the world. We met at a bar. You know, I've had Gwenny all on my own pretty much from the start. And after a while, day in and day out . . . you know, my friends were like, 'You need to get out. You need to do something for *you*.' So, I went out. You know? What do you do? You go to a bar. And I'm not really the Fifth Avenue type, so I went to Ty's. You know where that is?"

"I do. Off Davis Boulevard."

"That's the spot. The first night I got a sitter and went out, I met Josh. He was there. He had his own landscaping business. He was very charming. I let him buy me a drink, we talked . . . the rest is history."

Tom nodded, absorbing the information, thinking through how to proceed. Blythe was right, of course, there were only tenuous connections between Josh McDermott and the Jane Doe. Now that he had the lead with the NamUs user, he could see it more clearly: he'd been desperate, frustrated by the long day at the morgue, the daunting list of estuarine employees and volunteers, and upset by the altercation with McDermott. Furious at McDermott for what he'd done to Alicia, wanting to link him to something big, put him behind bars.

Domestic batterers got shit for jail time. Woman-beaters, rapists, they got a slap on the wrist for their brutal crimes.

But he might as well ask.

"You think Josh would hurt anyone else? Besides you?"

She turned toward him, her eyes widening in the gloom. "You mean like your case? I saw on the news that a body was found in the mangrove preserve . . . That's your case, right?" She seemed to put something together and changed tracks before he could respond. "Oh, shit, Tom. Here I am right in the middle of your work . . ."

He reached over and put a hand on hers. "Hey, it's fine."

She looked at his hand and he pulled away. Then she said, "I wouldn't put it past Josh to hurt someone else." She nodded, pursing her lips. "Yeah, I could see that."

Tom felt instant regret, like he had planted the idea. He opened his mouth to correct the situation, but Gwen's voice floated out onto the porch.

"Mommy?"

Alicia jumped like she'd been shot. "She's been waking up nights. Got to get her back down quick."

Tom turned around and saw the girl in the corridor, just her silhouette in the soft living room light. Alicia scooped her up and headed out of sight.

Tom put his head in his hand. *Stupid . . .*

That's just the old tapes playing, Tommy. Dr. Camden's familiar refrain.

Screw you, Dr. Camden.

He had no business putting ideas in Alicia's mind about her ex-boyfriend being a murderer. The woman had enough to deal with.

Feeling guilty, Tom rose from the chair and walked quietly into the condo, up the stairs, and back to bed.

He sat down and roused the laptop from sleep mode.

The pages were still up. There were two new messages in his inbox. He felt a little thrill and opened the first email.

> Hello Officer Lange, my name is Sasha. I live in Tampa Bay. My frend Carrie has been missing since last Tuesday. That was her last shift. Me and some girls from Hush went looking for her. We checked her apartmint. What do I do? Do I have to talk to the police? I can give you my number. I have to go to work now but you can leave a messige.

Tom read it a second time, then glanced at his watch. It was going on midnight. Who went to work at midnight? Sasha had written that she and "some girls from Hush" went looking for their missing friend. Between those details and the spelling mistakes, Tom formed an idea.

First, he replied to Sasha, then grabbed his phone and dialed the number she'd provided. Her voicemail picked up after the fourth ring. He left a message stating who he was and for her to call him as soon as she could.

Hush. The name tolled vaguely familiar. Someone had mentioned it once, a while back. Maybe Nick? Between the hunch and a hazy recollection, Tom opened Google, typed in "Hush" and added the search terms "gentlemen's club."

There was a hit. Hush was an exotic dance club in Tampa Bay.

She was a stripper. Either that or a bartender.

He checked his email again. The second new email was from the forensic sketch artist. The attachment was a big file, high resolution, and took a few seconds to open on his screen, like a painting unfurling. There she was, the Jane Doe, or, maybe, "Carrie."

CHAPTER EIGHT

Tom called Blythe, getting her voicemail. He hung up without leaving a message. His thoughts were scattered and he needed to focus — what would he even say to her? There was a chance that Sasha, aka PublicUser22958, was talking about someone else. Butterfly tattoos were quite common. Blythe would advise him to sleep on it and follow up in the morning.

No way. No way was Tom going to be able to get any sleep now. He'd written Sasha back, asking more questions, looking for specifics, but she wasn't responding — she'd gone to work.

Alicia and Gwen were counting on his protection. While his condo was locked up and secure, they might take a psychological comfort in his presence. If anything, he was a friend, and it was good to have friends around in a rough patch. Tom could count on one hand the people he considered friends, and they were mostly far-flung. Jack Vance was becoming a real friend, though.

Tom called him up, knowing Vance was a night owl. Vance didn't require much sleep, he'd once told Tom, and had many hours to fill. That was partly why the retiree had a side business checking on peoples' homes when they flew north during the hot summer, to keep busy. But Tom also thought Vance liked to feel of use.

The older man answered on the second ring. "Vichyssoise," Vance said. "I was up making damned soup."

"We'll press charges in the morning, McDermott will get picked up by Everglades County. In the meantime, the girls are here at my place."

"Is she alright? What was her name? Alice?"

"Alicia, yeah, she's going to be alright, I think. Shaken up a bit."

"And the little one?"

Tom thought for a moment about Gwen. About the way she seemed to have two gears: quiet and withdrawn or bursting with emotion. He didn't know what four-year-old girls were supposed to be like, but he was sure that Gwen was affected by her mother's troubles. Kids absorbed everything. He glanced at the picture of himself and Nick over on the dresser and said to Vance, "She'll be alright."

"So what can I do for you?"

"I need to go to Tampa. Tonight. I've got a lead on the case I'm working on."

"The body in the bay?"

Everybody knew about it. The state bureau hadn't released a statement yet or given their press conference, but things got out. The media had scented blood in the water.

"Five o'clock news," Vance said. "Channel 8. They said an unidentified person was found. I saw some aerial footage. You got a lead on who it is?"

"Yeah."

He'd sent the sketch to his phone. He planned to show it to Sasha, confirm Jane Doe's real identity tonight, in person. It sounded like Jane Doe/Carrie was a stripper, too. He wanted the story on Carrie's life leading up to her disappearance. Was she happy, was she worried about anything, who might've wanted to harm her?

He rummaged through his closet and found his shoulder holster. He slipped it on over his T-shirt and snapped it in. The blazer concealed it.

Tampa was normally a two-and-a-half-hour drive, and it was just going on midnight. Florida state law was that bars and clubs like Hush had to shut down by 3 a.m. He had just enough time to make the cut-off if he drove fast.

"I'm on my way over," Vance said.

Vance showed up in under five minutes. Alicia had fallen asleep in the chair in Tom's living room, a blanket drawn up to her chin. Tom thanked Jack Vance again and left through the side door, stepping into the garage. He hopped in the Jeep, setting his copy of the murder book on the passenger seat.

Before Tom started the engine he sat, gripping the wheel again, staring at the garage door.

Was this a rash decision? The state bureau had given him — a brand-new agent — big responsibilities. Now he had to live up to them.

But it wasn't enough for Tom to be adequate, Dr. Camden would say — Tom had to be the best. Top of his class, the most physically fit, the quickest to solve a case. Camden would say it wasn't Tom's fault — the drive to be perfect came from the loss of his parents and he was overcompensating.

Tom pressed the button for the garage door and it rolled open. He'd stopped seeing Camden years ago — it was time to stop listening to the man's voice in his head. There was a dead woman and Tom needed to know who killed her. Anything else was irrelevant.

CHAPTER NINE

TUESDAY

The highway fed into the Jeep's grill, streetlights flashed over the windshield. He made the drive to Tampa in less than two hours — record time. He had the strip club's address plugged into his GPS and could view the location of his vehicle, a blinking green dot, on the screen. He was close.

He found it in a shopping plaza across from a used car lot called Gleason's.

Middle of the night, and the humidity was still suffocating. Muffled music pulsed behind the blackened windows of the club, and a bouncer sat on a stool outside the door.

Tom kept his badge in his pocket. He was just an ordinary guy, here to unwind. He just happened to be strapped beneath his blazer.

The bouncer was around thirty, with olive skin. He pushed a toothpick around in his mouth and looked Tom up and down.

"Ten-dollar cover," he said.

Tom fished out the cash and looked at the club doors. "Sasha here tonight?"

"Who?" The bouncer scowled.

Tom realized Sasha could be the stripper's real name and she might use an alias at the club. Or, the bouncer was playing dumb, maybe nosing out Tom as five-oh. Tom shook his head and offered a shy smile. "Sorry, maybe I forgot her name."

The bouncer ran his hands over his black, slicked hair. He stared at Tom, and Tom stared back.

The bouncer grabbed the money and looked away. Tom took it as his cue to head inside.

The bass became louder, the place blasting with music. There was a central dancefloor surrounded by leather chairs looking like they belonged in an executive board room. Only three of them were occupied.

A woman gyrated against a pole, then thrust out her butt, jiggling it for the spectators.

The lights were red, purple, amber, the walls mirrored. Two gaudy chandeliers hung above the bar. Cushioned bench seats lined the opposing wall. Tom saw bathrooms at the back, and an exit. There was a DJ booth in the corner, squished between two unmarked doors. The place wasn't all that big, more dismal than sexy.

A cocktail waitress with legs everywhere took a tray of drinks over to two men seated together on the benches. Tom sat at the bar, noticing more men at the far end, huddled together. Four of them, young, dressed in expensive suits. One laughed and clapped another on the back. Then he got up and went to the bathroom, unsteady on his feet, while the rest guffawed and pointed at him.

The bartender made her way over to Tom. She put on a big smile and leaned down, her breasts squeezing together. "Hi. What can I get you?"

Tom ordered a Heineken and she moved off to get it. He glanced at the men on the far bench, well-dressed, middle-aged. They stared at the woman onstage. Tom checked out the customers in the executive-looking seats. One, his back to Tom, was wearing a ratty-looking sweater, bald head shining in the syrupy lights. Another, overweight, in a tracksuit, leaned forward with a grin and a bill in his hands. The stripper squatted down in front of him and bounced her ass. The overweight man gobbled it up with his eyes, licked his lips and stuck the bill in her G-string. The last man, bobbing his head to the distorted beats pumping through the speakers, watched the exchange, then his eyes met Tom's.

Tom turned away as the bartender set down the bottled beer. "Hey," he said, "do you know if Sasha is working tonight?"

She pulled back and her smile faltered. She searched his eyes, probably wondering who he was, whether he was trouble or not. He took his badge and palmed it, then grabbed some cash. He set the cash on the bar and then moved his hand away to partially reveal the badge. She looked down and her smiled disappeared altogether.

"She's not in any trouble. I want to talk to her about Carrie." Tom wondered if the bartender could even understand what he was saying beneath the deafening music. *How do people stand it?*

As soon as he thought it, the song faded. The DJ's voice boomed over the speakers. "Alright, gentlemen, let's give it up for Skylar!"

The stripper left the stage and the overweight man put an unlit cigar in his mouth and applauded enthusiastically. The three young suits at the bar whistled and howled. As their intoxicated companion came wandering back from the restroom, he made a sweeping bow, as if the applause was for him. The suits at the bar cut up laughing.

The drunk guy sat down by the stage instead of returning to his friends.

"Alright now," the DJ cooed, "coming on to the stage next, our final show of the night, let's give a big welcome to . . . Destiny!" The DJ drew out the clichéd name so long and loud the speakers rattled. At the same time a new song dropped, bass booming, synth-tones rippling. Tom realized that "Destiny" was already in the room — she was the cocktail waitress he'd seen coming in with the crazy long legs. Destiny had traded in her tray for a horse whip. She took the stage, grabbed a pole and snapped her hair around as she twirled to a squat. She gave each of the men a feral look, hair hanging in her face as she slowly rose and strutted in her stilettos, dragging the whip, wagging her finger at the men in the chairs. They had been bad boys, she seemed to be saying, and she was going to punish them.

The bartender nodded at the woman onstage. "Maybe you should ask her when she's finished her routine." Then she left for the three men in suits, who were waving their money for more drinks.

Destiny was Sasha.

Tom watched the show for a moment. Sasha worked herself up into a frenzy, mock-whipping the men, then slapping her own backside hard enough to leave red streaks on her flesh. The drunk guy in the suit really seemed to be enjoying the show. He moved his body to the beats, then beckoned her over. Sasha got down on all fours and crawled, tossing her hair back.

The drunk guy gave her some cash and then reached for her breasts. Sasha shook her finger in the air, no no. Then she rolled back onto her haunches and spread her legs, giving him an eyeful. Now the guy started to go crazy. He kept looking at the three suits at the bar, egging him on. They whistled and clapped while their friend kept swiping at Sasha, acting like he was going to climb up and get her.

He had a knee on the stage when the door burst open and the bouncer strode in. The man backed away, holding his hands up in a gesture of innocence. The other suits at the bar booed and hollered, laughing all the while. A big joke for them, seeing their buddy dragged out of the joint, blowing kisses at the stripper.

Sasha's number was winding down and the DJ made the announcement for last call. Tom peeled a couple bills from his stack, left a decent tip and walked out of the club.

* * *

It was a relief to get away from the deafening music. He felt like his ears were ringing as he lit a cigarette and kept his eye on the bouncer, talking with the rowdy, drunk man. The guy was putting up a big fuss, whining that he wasn't doing anything wrong, just horsing around.

"You're done for the night," the bouncer said. "Get the fuck out of here."

"My friends are still in there. I need a ride."

"I don't give a shit. Wait for them over there."

Tom saw an ATM machine near the club entrance and eyed the roofline for cameras. Seeing none, he rounded the building, leaving the bouncer and drunk guy behind. He wanted to see if there was a side or rear entrance to the club so he walked along until he found a set of double doors back by the dumpsters. He pitched his cigarette away and returned to the front of the club, noticing the used car lot again, the colored pennants limp in the breezeless night.

The bouncer had taken his stool inside and was gone. The drunk guy was still in the parking lot. He tried the front door, found it locked. Then he spied Tom. "Hey!"

Tom quickly got in the Jeep and started it up. He didn't know which door Sasha was going to leave from and wanted to park over on the side street to have eyes on all possible exits.

The drunk guy knocked on the window before Tom could pull away. Tom rolled it down.

"You got a smoke?"

"Yeah." Tom fished one out and handed it over.

"Got a light?"

Tom gave him his Zippo and the man fumbled around with it before getting the flame to work. He was swaying on his feet. The booze coming off him smelled like apples left to rot in the sun. The man pocketed the Zippo and stared at the club.

"Hey," Tom said. He snapped his fingers and stuck his hand out the window, palm-up.

"Oh. Sorry." The man dug through his pockets, cigarette dangling from his lips. The cigarette fell. He bent to pick it up, mumbling something incoherent. At the same time, the front door opened and the customer in the ratty sweater scurried out. He looked left and right, as if crossing a busy street, then hurried away from the club.

Tom glimpsed more movement along the side of the building. He could just see the back of a car parked there.

The drunk guy stood up, his face flushed with blood. He'd recovered the cigarette but not Tom's lighter. Tom dropped the Jeep into gear and pulled away.

"Hey! Hey, man, what the fuck?!"

Tom spun the wheel and goosed the gas. He was afraid after all this he was going to lose Sasha. He didn't waste time finding the parking exit but drove over the curb onto the side street, the Jeep bouncing.

He slowed in the side street, having caught the attention of a woman — the first dancer, the one called Skylar. She shot him a look then got into her car. He parked and waited, his heart pounding. That was close.

A moment later, the door near the dumpster opened again and Sasha emerged. Tom killed the engine and hopped out.

"Excuse me. Miss?"

She saw him and grew alarmed. He had his badge ready. "Sasha? I'm Special Agent Tom Lange."

She seemed to relax. "Oh . . ." Then her eyes widened and she repeated, "Oh!"

"Can I talk to you? Somewhere we can go?"

She was drop dead gorgeous, the kind of face he saw in magazines. She'd put on a pair of sweatpants and a T-shirt that said *Ralph's Gym*. She threw her bag in the open car door. "How did you find me?"

"Your email. You mentioned this place."

She looked at the building, ugly from this side with pipes rambling up the wall to the roof, the smell of garbage wafting from the overloaded dumpsters. "Oh right," she said. "Yeah, okay."

He flipped to the image of the artist's sketch of the Jane Doe on his phone and held it up for Sasha to see. The recognition in her eyes appeared genuine and she welled up. "Yeah, that looks like her. That's Carrie. What happened to her?"

"You mentioned you went to Carrie's apartment," he said. "Can you take me there?"

"Yeah." Sasha nodded, her expression serious. "Yeah, sure. Bosco is all freaked out about it. She's one of his best girls, he's always saying. But we haven't seen her since—"

"Last Tuesday, you said."

"Exactly. Last Tuesday. It's not like her. We went to her apartment, knocked on the door, looked in the windows, nothing."

"Is it far?"

"Ten minutes, this time of night."

"Great." Tom started away. "I'll follow you?"

"Sure, of course." She gave him another look, as if working out once and for all whether he was alright. Then she made a little nod and got in her car.

"Yo!" Tom heard. "There he is!"

The drunk guy was at the corner, pointing. He'd been joined by his frat boy friends from the bar. "Hey, man," the drunk guy said, "you nearly fuckin' ran me over back there. What's your deal, huh?"

The four men started over. Tom glanced at Sasha, who looked concerned. He held up his hand. "It's okay. Just give me a second."

He approached the four suits as they walked down the sidewalk in a pack, got out his badge again and held it up. As they gaped at it, he pulled open his blazer to reveal the firearm holstered against his ribs.

"Guys, fuck off, alright?"

They stopped, and two of them turned around and started walking away. But the drunk guy stood his ground, holding up the Zippo lighter. "Hey, was just trying to give you this back, that's all."

Uh-huh. Sure.

Tom snatched it out of his hand. He glimpsed the fat man in the tracksuit walking away from the club, crossing the street near the used car lot. The man was talking to himself and chuckling, paying Tom and the others no mind. Tom returned his attention to the drunk guy and his friend, their two buddies lingering a little ways off.

"Alright, get home safe," Tom said.

"Fuckin' asshole pig," he heard the drunk guy mutter. The guy's friend patted him on the chest and hustled him away.

Sasha started up her car and backed out into the street. Tom got in the Jeep and followed.

CHAPTER TEN

It was a five-story mid-rise with balcony walkways. The community pool looked like it hadn't been cleaned for a few weeks, with dead bugs and leaves floating in it. Carrie's apartment was on the top floor. There was a white door marked 36 and a window, drapes obscuring most of the interior. Tom cupped his hands to the glass and peered in.

He saw a simple layout, couch and TV in the living room, beyond it a kitchen with a pass-through window. A dim light glowed in the kitchen, either from a stove hood or a plug-in nightlight. A hallway led from the kitchen out of sight. It looked lived in — a rumpled blanket on the couch and a box of takeout on the coffee table — but otherwise tidy. No immediate signs of a struggle.

"What happened to Carrie?" Sasha's voice was a low whisper.

"I don't know."

He moved to the door and feathered his fingertips over the seam where the door met the wall, searching for gouges or scrapes. He was getting his prints on a potential crime scene, but he could eliminate himself later on. At the moment, exigent circumstances were dubious grounds to enter the apartment. Better way to get inside would be to obtain a search warrant from a state judge and do it properly, with a Tampa forensic team, or his own IFS. Peering through the crack, the deadbolt appeared engaged. He tried the knob anyway, found it immovable. He probed the lock with his finger — no one had punched it out.

There was a worn welcome mat at the door. It could be taken to the crime lab and examined for trace evidence. He took a few pictures with his phone and then let the scene be.

"Please tell me . . . you're killing me." Sasha said.

"Can you show me the parking lot?"

She sighed and took him back down the stairs where they followed a pathway around to the rear of the building. The lot was lit by three lampposts. Sasha pointed out a green Hyundai. "That's Carrie's."

Her vehicle? It was a major score. Tom circled the car, excited, looking for scratches or dents. He switched on his flashlight. There was a disposable Starbucks cup in the center console, some wrappers on the floor. A couple utility bills, it looked like, sitting on the passenger seat. In the backseat, an empty Amazon box. He walked to the rear and took a few more pictures, getting the license plate and a couple angles on the car. He'd work another warrant for the vehicle, have the forensics team give it a thorough examination.

"Alright," he said.

"Alright? What happened to Carrie?"

She was really something, a natural beauty beneath the heavy make-up. Her mouth turned down to a pout on one side. The air around them was fuzzy with humidity, and her skin glistened, her eyes sparkled.

"Now let's find a place where we can talk. And I'll tell you what I can."

* * *

Sasha led him to another part of the city, North Bon Air, not far from Carrie's apartment. It was four-thirty in the morning, the first hint of dawn brightening the sky. Sasha's neighborhood was more upscale than Carrie's. She had her own house. She unlocked the front door and invited him in.

"Nice place."

"Thanks. I haven't been here long." She tossed her gym bag on a plush couch and gave him the tour, only switching on a couple of lights, seeming to prefer the place dim. When they came to a gun cabinet, he asked about it. "You want to see?" She undid a rotary lock and stepped aside so he could look, pride on her face.

Tom gaped at the small arsenal. "That's an AR-15 . . ."

"Yup. Got that beauty at a Georgia gun show. And there's my favorite, the M&P9. That's the same handgun the cops use in L.A. County. Everything is registered, legal. I have no criminal record." She smiled at him, then invited him to sit on the couch and offered him a drink.

"Just water, thanks."

While she was in the kitchen fiddling with the ice machine, she called back, "I know what you're thinking."

"Oh?"

"You're thinking, how does a stripper afford all of this?"

Tom looked around at the framed art on the walls, the statues on the entertainment center flanking a giant flat-screen TV, expensive furniture, guns in the cabinet. *I guess you could say that.*

She came back with a water for him and a bottle of beer for herself. She sat on the adjacent couch, and took a long pull from the beer. "Ah, that's good." She crossed her long legs. "Well, I'm just a girl from Macon, Georgia. For one thing, I know some real estate people. But, I dreamed big. You know?"

"What's your full name, Sasha?"

"Sasha Marie Clay. My momma and I, we had nothing. At one point we lived under a bridge. I used to find green tomatoes in the trash and we'd fry 'em up."

"Wow."

"Yup." She took another swig, smacked her lips and bounced her foot. He imagined she was used to the hours — she seemed full of pep, whereas he could feel the fatigue closing in. He realized time was slipping away — he had an 8 a.m. appointment at the ROC to keep.

"So, about Carrie . . ."

"I just said to myself, Sasha, this ain't gonna be your life. You ain't gonna live like your momma. You know? First of all, you don't need a man. They are just gonna leave you high and dry, like my daddy left me and Momma. So I decided, I'm gonna make that work for me. You know what I mean? No offense."

He nodded, hoping she would finish her story.

"And then I saw what some of these other girls were doing. I mean, some of them — they've built a fortune!" Her eyes widened and she planted her feet, sitting forward. "I mean, this one girl, Theresa, T, she's got *three* houses. Can you believe it?"

He could, though he imagined T, whoever she was, was in debt up to her tassels. People who could afford three houses were hedge fund managers and surgeons and movie stars. Or, they'd been issued subprime mortgages and lost everything in '08. Certainly exotic dancing could pull in some cash, but he didn't see Carrie living that way.

"How about Carrie? She seems to be living a bit more modestly."

Sasha frowned a little and shook her head. "Well, that girl doesn't know what to do with her money. You blow it all on stupid stuff when you need to be investing it, and that's what you get."

"Like what? What sort of stuff did she blow it on?"

"I was telling you a little about myself. You don't want to hear?"

He found himself grinning at her shtick. "I'm sorry. You have a very interesting life story. I just . . . I have an early appointment."

"You made me wait. Acted all cop-like and wouldn't tell me what's happening. I'm not stupid."

"I didn't think you were."

"You're here, means something real bad happened."

"Why would you think that?"

She scowled at him and stuck out her lips for effect. "Gee, officer, are you trying to get me to say something? Such clever tactics."

Tom didn't reply. She sat back and looked away. "Carrie is a pretty private person. No drugs, though — that girl is clean as a whistle."

He pulled out his notepad and wrote a few things down. "So you're friends with her."

"Yeah, you could say that. We went out for breakfast a couple times, back when we had the same shift. But that was months ago."

"You last saw her on Tuesday, you said. Was that at work?"

"Yes. At Hush."

"What time?"

"At seven. During shift change. There's day shifts and night shifts at Hush. Plus bump shifts, midnight to three, which is what I worked tonight. Daytime there's no cover at the door." She winked.

"So it was a Tuesday day shift?" Tom could think of few things as depressing as grown men in a strip club on a Tuesday afternoon.

"That's right. I was coming on to the *night* shift. She was leaving her *day* shift."

She re-crossed her legs and gulped more beer.

"Did you see anyone? Did Carrie talk to anyone?"

"No. We talked by the bar for a minute, then she went out the side door."

"How did she seem?"

"She seemed fine. The usual. I asked how the day went, she said it was slow. I mean, Carrie was never what you'd call — I don't know — spirited? She had this kind of . . ." Sasha made a mopey face. Then she flashed a smile. "But we loved her. She was sweet. Good heart, that girl. Just, I dunno, not much to her."

"Not much to her?"

"Yeah. I mean, pleasant and all, but . . . you know."

"Just sort of average, maybe, you mean."

"Is that terrible of me to say?"

"I don't think so. But Carrie didn't act distressed? Worried about anything?"

Sasha's eyes bunched with scrutiny. "Um, no, I wouldn't say. I mean, but, that's what I'm talking about. You couldn't always say with Carrie."

"Nothing specific?"

"No. Nothing comes to mind." She glanced away from him.

He felt like Sasha had just told him her first lie.

"Did Carrie work anywhere other than Hush?"

"No, not any other clubs. I do, though."

"Where else do you work?"

"At Kronos. That's where I really make my bank. I want to leave Hush. But, you know, the money can be good on the weekends, and I'm still new at Kronos so I haven't gotten any prime spots yet. I will, though." Sasha sniffed and touched her nose.

"Do you mind if I ask — about how much do you pull in a week?"

"Me?" She got a sly smile on her perfect face. "I can easily clear two grand."

"Damn." Tom's starting salary for the bureau was $48,000 a year, which, after a quick mental calculation, he realized was less than half of what Sasha made per week. "I'm in the wrong line of work."

Her eyes lit up and she leaned toward him. "Yeah . . ." She looked him up and down. "Oh, you could totally do it.

They have men's strip clubs you know. Yeah, I could see you. You've got the body for it. Face isn't bad either. Just that little scar by your eye."

Her candor made him slightly uncomfortable and he blushed. He tried to get them back on track.

"So, altogether, Carrie missed — what — two or three shifts?"

"What's today? Monday?"

He glanced at the window, dawn colors turning to blue. "Tuesday. It's been almost a week since she was last seen at the club."

"And she's dead. That thingy online, it just said she was deceased, but not how, or where."

"I promise we'll get to that. Just—"

"Fine," she said. "Carrie should've worked Wednesday night. She was no-call, no-show. Then Thursday, same thing."

"And then you and some of the girls went to her apartment. What day was that?"

"We went by on Saturday. Me and Ricki and T. Ugh, her landlord showed up. He's such a wormy little dude. He hadn't seen her. He ran us outta there, said we were violating her privacy."

"Okay." He wrote down, *Landlord*. "And then you decided to check NamUs, the online thingy. How did you hear about it?"

She pointed a fire-engine red fingernail at the TV. "There's a public service announcement for it. Saw one yesterday."

"So you looked for her as a missing person."

"Yes, sir."

"How about Naples, Sasha? Carrie ever talk about Naples? Have family there, friends that you know about? She ever talk about her parents, or where they might live?"

"Naples, no, I don't think so. She didn't talk about her family. Well, she mentioned her momma once. But I don't think she lives in Naples. In the Midwest, I think."

"Did Carrie have a boyfriend? Maybe someone she visited there?"

Sasha finished the beer, licked her lips and shook her head. "No. Uh-uh. She had an ex though. Ex-husband."

Tom felt a spark in his gut. "Really? How recently divorced?"

"Um, couple years, I guess. Maybe less."

"Where is he? Local?"

She nodded. "Yup. Far as I know. He has the kid. He raises it."

"A kid? Carrie had a child?"

"Yup, uh-huh." Sasha got a distant look as Tom scribbled down the highlights. *Ex-hub. Kid.* Something had changed, maybe it was getting too real for Sasha. Or maybe she was just coming down from a high. She touched her nose again.

"Okay," he said, "does she see the child? Do you know its name?"

Sasha stood abruptly, as if remembering something. "Do you want another . . .? Oh, right." She walked back to the kitchen and fished out another beer. "She doesn't see the kid, no."

"What's her ex's name?"

"Who? Oh, him? He's, ah, Steve. Hobson, I think."

She returned to the couch and drank some more, her playfulness gone.

"Is it Hobson?"

Sasha gave him a look. "Yeah. Steve Hobson. I mean, that's her last name. Carrie Hobson. She said once to me she'd gone through all the trouble of changing her name to his and hadn't gotten around to changing it back after they split."

"Do you know what her maiden name was?"

"No. I guess I never asked."

"Okay." He set down the pad and thought for a moment. The sunlight was spreading in the windows, brightening the room. He put his hands together and leaned toward her. "Listen, thank you for talking with me. I'm really grateful. When we found Carrie — if it is Carrie — she was in rough shape. Not recognizable."

Sasha put a hand over her mouth.

Tom spoke carefully. "I should've asked when I first came in, but I've been enjoying your home, and talking to you . . . Do you have a picture of Carrie anywhere?"

"Oh," she said, as if snapping out of a trance. "Yeah, sure." She bounced up off the couch, her energy restored, and left the room. Tom rose from the couch and looked around some more.

"Here we go." She reentered the room holding up a framed picture of several scantily clad girls, displaying it with the same pride she'd shown for her guns. "Here we all are."

He recognized Sasha, somewhat taller than the rest. And then the woman who resembled the artist's sketch to a tee. He thought of her lying on the medical gurney. Sasha tapped the glass. "That's Carrie. Isn't she sweet?"

She did look sweet, he supposed. Somehow more "wholesome" than the others, though he knew that was a superficial judgment. But where Sasha, for instance, had more angular, model-like features, Carrie was a bit rounder in the face.

"I don't suppose you'd let me take that for a little while?"

Sasha clutched the photo to her chest and looked mortified. "My girls!"

"How about I take a picture of it?"

"Sure . . . Okay."

"Great, maybe over here by the light."

He had her hold it so the glass wouldn't glare, then took several shots with his phone.

"Just don't sell those online, or something. Bosco would kill you."

He put his phone away. "That's the owner? Bosco?"

Her forehead rumpled again with one of her deep scowls. "Bosco? Hell no. He's the bouncer. He was there tonight. He *acts* like he owns the place, though."

"Who does own it?" Tom walked back to the couch to retrieve his notebook.

"Um, he's an Italian guy. Mario Palumbo. Real Italian, you know? With the chest hair and gold neck chains." She flapped a hand near her breasts for effect. "But he's hardly ever there. Bosco actually does the hiring."

"Bosco does? The bouncer?"

"Yeah. He's a real talent scout."

Tom thought of the meathead who'd been at the door. Who knew? Maybe he had the magic touch. "So Bosco hired Carrie. How long has she worked there?"

Sasha set down the photo and picked up her beer. "She started just a couple months after me. So, just about a year."

It was getting extremely late — or early. And Sasha, while briefly rejuvenated by the picture of the Hush girls, was retreating again to a kind of morose distance. Tom promised her he'd be in touch as soon as he knew more. He told her that the police would probably want to talk to her again — this time formally. He just had a couple more questions before he left.

"What was her stage name?"

"Amber."

"And did Amber have any regular customers? You know, men that preferred her?"

"Oh, of course. We all have regulars."

"Anyone that stands out?"

Sasha stood near him in the entryway, her hips cocked to the side, pinching the beer bottle around the neck. She glanced up at the ceiling. "Um, no, no one in particular. But we worked mostly opposite shifts."

"No one who ever got a little rowdy, like that drunk guy tonight?"

Her gaze landed on him. "No — but come to think of it — the man in that awful sweater? He comes in a *lot.* He might've done a one-on-one with her."

"You mean like private dances."

"Yeah."

"Has he asked about her? Like, wondered why she wasn't there?"

Sasha shook her head.

"What about Bosco?"

"Bosco's pissed, yeah."

"He's angry . . . not worried?"

She nodded. He sensed guilt, as if she felt she hadn't done enough. Or, something else, lurking beneath the surface. "Did Bosco have a policy against tattoos or anything like that? Did he have any reason to be upset with Carrie?"

"Well, we're not supposed to have tats. But no, he didn't care. I mean, she got that tattoo like two or three months ago. He bitched her out about it, but that's just Bosco acting like a big deal. Like he owns her."

He circled Bosco's name and then put away his notepad. "You did good, Sasha. Thank you. I'll be in touch."

Tom showed himself out and walked back to his Jeep. The birds were singing in the quiet neighborhood. He looked around at the other nice, upper-middle class homes, imagining the lives of the people in them, what they did for work, the families, children. He wondered if there was any antipathy for the stripper who lived next door. When he glanced at the house, he saw Sasha standing in the window. Then she moved out of sight.

CHAPTER ELEVEN

To get back to the highway he drove through Oakford Park and North Hyde Park. The neighborhoods looked a lot like other rural places in Florida: flat, tangled growth around pale stucco houses with wavy red roofs. Past a small strip plaza declaring DELI MEAT DELI MEAT, he took a ramp onto the freeway and merged with the morning traffic.

Veering past the downtown area, he slipped by office buildings with mirrored walls, blasted-white apartment complexes, and then the freeway aimed south. He'd just missed the morning rush hour traffic but was still going to have to hustle to get to the ROC for his 8 a.m. — it was already past six.

He was buzzing from the long talk with Sasha. He assembled a mental list of potential suspects, including Bosco, the bouncer, first and foremost. Tom could easily imagine an altercation between Bosco and Carrie because he was the controlling type and didn't like her tattoo. Such an altercation could've escalated, and maybe Bosco hit her. Carrie might've fallen back and smacked her head on something hard. Dead on impact.

The ex-husband was the next potential suspect, then the customers at Hush, then perhaps Carrie's Midwestern family. Maybe the ex-husband was jealous and had found Carrie with another man.

But for all these theories, the idea that anyone would pick the estuary as a dumping ground — why? Why risk highway travel with a dead body in the trunk? Or, if Naples was the true death scene, why was she there? Unless there was some connection between a suspect and the state-run estuary, it was just pissing in the wind.

Or a customer could be the killer. Someone like the man in the sweater. Who wore a sweater in Florida, in April? Otherwise, did Carrie have any more family in Naples? Friends? Had she taken a trip? Her car was at her apartment. Tom would have Tampa pull the history on the vehicle, and forensics go through it, but more important — he'd found the car at her home. However she'd gotten to Naples, she'd either taken public transportation or gone with someone else.

Alive, or dead.

* * *

Tom had a full day ahead, and hadn't slept a wink. He stopped at a rest area, got an egg sandwich and a large coffee, and lit a cigarette in the parking lot, watching the cars rush by. The cigarette made him nauseous and he tossed it away. First he would meet with Blythe, fill her in. Then he had the crime lab waiting— hopefully — with a report on the victim's clothing. Ward would be doing the internal autopsy and getting more conclusive results about the head trauma. Blythe wanted him there again. Tom wasn't looking forward to more hours spent in another claustrophobic room, standing by while Ward unpacked the body like a suitcase.

He checked the time — 7:30 — and his mind switched tracks for a moment. Once Alicia gave her statement, Everglades County would pick up Josh

McDermott. Tom was anxious to be looking on when they grilled him. Blythe was right — a connection between McDermott and Carrie was tenuous at best — but he still wanted to see the guy sweat.

He had Jack Vance's number in his phone and called it.

Vance answered quickly. "How did it go?"

"Good. How about you? How did the night go? How are Alicia and Gwen?"

"Good, real good. We're just making some pancakes. I'm telling you, I got the cooking bug. Ever watch that show, *Cutthroat Kitchen*?"

"No . . . Jack, I can't thank you enough."

"I hope you don't mind me rummaging through your cabinets."

"Of course not. Jack, really, thank you."

"Listen, don't mention it. I told you, I'm happy to help. These girls are great."

Tom thought he could hear them in the background — Gwen babbling contentedly, the soft murmur of her mother. Tom lowered his voice. "Did Alicia call the County yet?"

Tom thought he heard the porch door squeak open.

"No."

He felt a sinking sensation. "How did last night go? Anything happen?"

"I don't sleep much. I didn't mean to listen in — I gave the girls your bed after you left. I took the couch."

I should've thought of that. "Good idea. What happened?"

"Well, the prostate is ornery and I frequently get up to pee. That's what happened. I heard Alicia's voice from your room, and I eavesdropped. I'm not proud of it, it's none of my business, but, you know, old habits. And with everything that happened . . ."

"Sure, of course."

"I just heard her talking a little. Talking to a guy on her phone."

Tom set his coffee on the roof of the Jeep and switched the phone from one ear to the other. He liked what he was hearing less and less — something in his gut. "What did it sound like?"

"Like they were patching things up. Lots of *oh, baby* — like she was soothing him."

Shit. "The hospital sent the paperwork to the Sheriff's Office. I can take her myself this morning — I just have to stop in Fort Myers first. Maybe you can . . . talk to her? She needs to press formal charges."

"Tom, I like you. I know your heart is in the right spot here. It's just not my place to intervene."

Tom blamed himself for not being there. He didn't know why, but he thought if he'd stayed home she wouldn't have taken a call from McDermott, let him sweet-talk her. How could she forgive a guy who beat her up? Someone who called her bitch and cunt in front of people? But he knew these matters were complex. He'd been close to it before.

If she didn't press charges, he could potentially sway the County prosecutor to press them anyway. But he didn't want to play that card too soon. It was far better for the victim to push the charges. He also didn't know exactly what they'd said to each other. Vance had said he'd only heard a little bit. He was more or less guessing. Still, Vance had been in some surveillance or top secret shit in the Air Force — he probably knew what he was talking about.

Tom took a deep breath. "Well, thanks again, Jack. I'll be back as soon as I can. Sorry it took longer than I expected."

"Not a problem."

He thought about asking Vance to put Alicia on, but didn't. She would probably call in sick to work today — she had a black eye and a stitch in her lip. "Can you hang out for a little while longer, Jack, just until I get there?"

"Sure thing. We might go over to the pool."

"Great . . . wait, is she going to go back home for bathing suits?"

"Charlene," Vance explained, and Tom understood. He'd almost forgotten that Charlene and Alicia were friends — or at least acquaintances. Tom forgot how, precisely, they knew each another. "She called me this morning, crack of dawn. Wanted to know what had happened. I gave her the rundown. She felt terrible she walked away last night. So we can expect the full Charlene regatta today. Probably be cake and ice cream involved."

Tom laughed but was cut short when another call came in. He quickly thanked Vance again and took the new call, from Blythe.

"Lange, we got an early start. Where are you?"

"On my way. There in thirty minutes."

"Okay. Looks like the scotch pads picked up some trace evidence on the clothing. I'll see you in a half hour."

* * *

Tom hurried through the building to the crime lab and wriggled into the protective gear — hairnet, mask, booties, gloves. Blythe was in the lab with two of the IFS chemists. They brought him into a walk-in freezer where a long table was covered with envelopes, baggies, and jars containing collected evidence from the victim. In the center of the table was the white T-shirt, blue shorts, and a pair of underpants resembling grubby tissue paper.

Tom already knew the chemists, so introductions were unnecessary. The first, a plump, humorless woman named Veronica Morley, identified the collected materials for Tom. Her breath smoked up around her mask.

"These are the exemplars here. The divers brought them in last night. Mangrove bits, some water, soil sample. Nothing there. Over here are the control samples."

She moved on. "These envelopes have the hair and fingernails in waxed paper. DNA processing is underway.

As is the biological sample processing from the Sexual Assault Evidence Collection Kit."

She stepped to another section. "This is from the head hair brushing and pubic brushing."

Tom recalled the painstaking process from the previous afternoon — Ward carefully brushing out the hair, holding butcher paper under each area as he combed through.

Tom waited for the news Blythe had sounded excited about.

Veronica pointed at the clothing. "We used both scotch pads and lint rollers for the clothing. Honestly, we didn't expect much due to the submersion."

Tom looked around, sensing the tour was over. So what was the big revelation? "You said the scotch pads picked something up . . .?"

"It looks like blood. Just a microscopic portion of it on the shirt."

"No shit. So you did ABO typing? Is it the victim's blood or someone else's?"

Veronica shook her head. "It's microscopic. I almost didn't see it. Dried blood is one thing, this is blood that's been submerged for days. A bloodstain contains antigens and polymorphic enzymes which are virtually destroyed after almost a week in the water. The testability is very poor."

Tom looked between the three of them. "So, I don't get it. What do we do?"

"We go molecular."

"DNA," Tom said.

"And not just typical STR typing. Low copy number. Low copy number profiling is an enhanced technique. Cutting edge. But we have to take every precaution against co-contamination. We may be able to pull DNA even though the victim was in the water because LCN typing allows us to use a smaller sample, just a few cells."

Tom felt like his head was spinning. They'd gone over DNA in training, but these people loved spitting out acronyms. Plus, he'd been awake for more than twenty-four hours.

"Walk me through it," he said.

"There are several basic steps performed during DNA testing, regardless of the type of test being done. The general procedure includes, first, isolation of the DNA from an evidence sample containing DNA of unknown origin, which we've done. Next, we isolate DNA from a sample taken from the victim. We then process the DNA, determine the test results — or types — from specific regions of the DNA and then compare and interpret the test results from the unknown and known samples."

"Right. To determine whether the victim is the source of the DNA from the blood.

"Or is included as a *possible* source of the DNA."

"Okay . . . and that's it? You'll find whether or not this is the blood of the victim."

Morley exchanged looks with the other tech, Kurt Bronson, and then with Blythe. "Correct."

Tom opened his mouth but Blythe headed him off.

"Thank you, Veronica." Blythe turned to the other tech. "Thank you, Kurt."

She came around the table and took Tom by the arm, led him out of the freezer. It was a relief to be back in normal room temperature. They stood next to one of the large X-ray machines and Blythe speared him with her gray eyes again.

"You don't look so good."

"I'll tell you all about it. But what did you get from the scene?"

"We're still going through the estuary." She folded her arms. "Jesus, you are a go-getter, huh? You're hoping to solve this thing by dinner, I take it."

"I went to Tampa last night." Tom avoided her sharp eyes.

"Oh?"

"I got a hit on NamUs. Tried to call you."

"I was sleeping. You should try it. What was the hit?"

"A stripper from a club called Hush. So I checked it out. I spoke to her. She took me by Carrie's apartment. Place is locked up, her car is there, everything."

"*Carrie?*"

"Carrie Hobson. That's our Jane Doe."

Blythe took a step away, glaring at him. "Are you out of your fucking mind?"

Tom was taken aback. "I said I tried to call you, I wanted to confirm it."

They left the lab for the bullpen, a large room filled with cubicles where the agents labored over their paperwork, something he'd already fallen behind on. Blythe stalked through the room, Tom trailing. People were looking at Tom like he was a dead man walking. They went into Blythe's private office and she shut the door, pulled the blinds.

"I want every detail."

Tom did his best to summarize the events of the previous night while being thorough. Blythe looked ready to blow.

He asked, "Do we have Tampa pick up Bosco for questioning?"

She shook her head. "Not yet. We'll have them go into the club, pull employee records, talk to everyone, then take it from there. You said this stripper thinks the family is in the Midwest? We need to find them. Otherwise we have the ex-husband do the formal identification if we have to. We want to talk to him anyway, obviously. And I want you looking at the apartment."

"We'll need a warrant to search it."

It was Blythe's turn to be caught off guard. She blinked at him. "We don't need a warrant. The only person with Fourth Amendment standing in this case is deceased."

"But the landlord is still protected."

"Exigent circumstances."

"The emergency exception doesn't apply."

"*Brown v. Jones.* A federal district court said, 'Obtaining a search warrant is pointless when the authorities would have no idea what they're looking for. It would be a sham, since the object of the search is so broad it's meaningless.'"

"With respect, that's for a homicide scene, Agent Blythe. We don't know if this is that scene. This is just the victim's apartment, and it's protected by constitutional law. We need a warrant."

Blythe surprised him by slapping her hands down on the table. "Which is it, Lange? One minute you're rushing off into the night, the next minute you want to bury us up to our necks in paperwork when we could be out catching a killer."

Her eyes were locked on him as she continued to let him have it. "You spent the past several years sitting at a desk in school. Think you can bring your criminal law bullshit in here? Next time something like this happens — you get a major break like last night — you call me until I answer, you come by my house." She stabbed a finger at him. "And don't question my authority again."

CHAPTER TWELVE

Tom located his designated cubicle in the bullpen and sat down with the murder book. The cubicle featured a desktop computer, a jar of pens, a pad of paper, nothing personal. It was his first time that he'd sat at his desk at the ROC.

Blythe's words rang in his head as he printed out the picture of Carrie and her stripper co-workers and slipped it into a plastic sheet. He added the artist sketch and snapped them all into the binder.

Where did Blythe get off? Maybe he'd been impulsive, he could admit that. But Blythe seemed to want to do an end-run around procedure. Maybe she just knew things he didn't.

He let it go and started a SpyFly web-crawl for Carrie Hobson. There were all sorts of hits, none of them pertinent. Facebook, Twitter, Instagram, there were many people with the same name, and none were his girl.

But, Carrie Hobson was her *married* name. Tom needed Carrie's Department of Motor Vehicles info, which would have her maiden name, and he delegated this to

Machado in a text message. Her reply came back seconds later: *I'm on it.*

He called the State Government Office in Tampa and talked to a clerk for a state judge, the Honorable Emily Tapper, who requested he send over all the pertinent paperwork on the case. The clerk promised that Judge Tapper would be back in the office that afternoon. Everything looked good, the clerk assured, and the search warrant for Carrie's apartment should be a cinch. Forensics would scour the place the following day and process the vehicle.

After two hours of filling out forms and making calls Tom felt the fatigue closing in.

His phone rang, bringing him back around.

"Nicky? What's up? I'm kind of—"

"Tom . . ." Nick didn't sound too hot. "Tommy . . . can you swing by my place?"

"Nick, I really . . . what is it? What's the matter?" Tom glanced at the clock: it was past noon.

"It's better if you just come."

Christ. On top of everything else. But he couldn't say no to Nick. He'd never been able to. "Alright, give me a minute. I'm on my way."

* * *

Tom drove to Port Royal, the waterway neighborhood where Nick lived — rivers and creeks ran alongside expensive homes, shored up by concrete retaining walls. Galleon Drive was lush with landscaped palms and orange bird-of-paradise planters. Breezes from the Gulf typically kept the temperature pleasantly warm.

He saw his brother's brand-new Escalade in the half-circle driveway and turned in behind it. Nick's place wasn't as upscale as some, but still impressive, and mortgaged to the hilt. Nick was in worse debt than Tom.

Tom's phone rang.

"Director Turnbull. What can I do for you?"

"How you doing, Lange?"

"I'm good, sir." Tom already had a feeling he knew what this was about. Turnbull had been away on business until the afternoon — he'd been expecting to see Tom at the ROC.

"Listen," Turnbull said, "I know you're busy on this case . . ."

Tom waited for it.

". . . I called Special Agent Blythe to check in this morning. She was unhappy."

"I understand, sir. I'm sorry that I was—"

"Let me talk, please. I know that you're a field agent, and we give you guys sort of free range. But Blythe is calling the shots. Once you prove your mettle, you might just get to run your own ranch. But for now . . . okay?"

"Yes, sir." Tom watched Nick's house, seeing no movement through the windows. He noticed a big black truck with dark windows parked on the street a few houses down. He was about to say goodbye to Turnbull when the man continued.

"Now that I've said my piece, I want to tell you: Blythe doesn't like many people. She's, you know . . . she's very loyal to a select few."

Tom rubbed his forehead, feeling more tired. He knew he had this coming.

"But she likes you," Turnbull said. "Do you hear me, Lange?"

"Yes, I hear you, sir."

"I've never seen her . . . I don't know. She won't come out and say it directly; but she likes you. I can tell. Just . . . you've got to give her her due. Okay? Easy on the Boy Scout stuff."

"Absolutely, sir. Thank you."

"Alright."

They ended the call and Tom walked up to his brother's front door, finding it unlocked. He gave the black truck down the street a final glance, then entered.

"Nick? Hey, it's Tom."

Nick had eclectic taste. The ridiculous statue of armor in the foyer, for instance. The giant framed photograph of a guy kissing a girl while sitting on his Triumph motorcycle was nice, but hanging near a bust of Albert Einstein, just weird. Tom thought he noticed a few things missing, but hadn't visited in so long it was tough to say for sure. Nick had some of his own artwork up, too — seeing it Tom felt a pang of sadness, thinking Nick had squandered his talent, like a lot of other things.

The rest of the place was dark and cool. Some boxes on the floor overflowed with stuff Nick was getting ready to store or sell. Maybe he was moving. With Nick, who knew? Doing a little liquidating, perhaps.

"Nick? Where are you?"

In the backyard was a dock and a boat shed on Haldeman Creek. The water was the color of pewter, the creek fifty yards wide. On the other side were the greens of the Windstar Golf and Country Club. Tom and Nick had sat on the dock and shared beers on muggy nights, swatting at the no-see-ums and watching the mullet jump.

He thought about the waterways around Naples, and Blythe's concession that Carrie could've floated from somewhere, but it had to be somewhere close by. Nick's place was at least five miles from Stopper Creek. Not that he thought Nick had anything to do with it, but Tom realized it was about time he learned the full geography of the waterways.

He went back inside and called out for Nick again. Finally he heard his brother answer, "Up here!"

Tom went up to the master bedroom.

The blinds were drawn and Nick sat in a chair in the corner, his face dark with shadow.

"Nicky," Tom said, stopping in the doorway, "what the hell is going on?"

"Hey, Tom. Come on in! Sit down."

Tom stayed in the doorway. Nick sounded on the verge of mania. It was hard to make out his face, but it looked like he was grinning.

"I'm fine right here," Tom said. "What are you doing? You're freaking me out, man. I'm in the middle of a case."

"I know, I know." Nick patted the air with his hands as if to say *Enough, I get it.* "Sit down, wouldja?"

Like many other people in Southwest Florida, Tom and Nick originated from the nation's northeast, and their New York accents often came out, especially when they were together.

Tom took a seat on the corner of the bed. He could see Nick was in bad shape. It looked like he hadn't slept either, and his posture was strange. Why hadn't he risen from the chair? Nick was usually a live wire, unable to sit still. Unless he was depressed. Then he might spend the whole day in bed. But this was neither.

"I'm in some trouble, Tommy."

"Okay. Well, I can't do anything for you unless you talk to me."

"It's best you don't know too much, alright? Plausible deniability. You're a cop now, for chrissakes."

"Nick . . ."

"I need some money. That's all. I just need a little help."

And there it was. Tom should've figured. Not that Nick was always asking, but it was one of those things Tom just expected would come up sooner or later. Nick was fast and loose with just about everything in his life. Tom might be a bit impulsive at times, but compared to Nick he was pretty square. "For what? Money for what?"

"Let me worry about that. I need ten grand. Have you got it, or what?"

"Jesus, Nick. Ten grand? You think I just got that lying around? What about you? Sell something. Sell that friggin' suit of armor."

"I got that at a flea market for seventy bucks."

Nick fell silent. Tom really didn't like the way his brother was just sitting there.

"What's with you? Get up outta that chair, Nicky. What the fuck? I got school loans, I've got a mortgage . . ."

"The state is helping you pay off your loans. And I got you that place. You were gonna rent some crappy little apartment. You'da been pissing away your money."

"I know, Nick. I'm grateful you found me my place."

Nick grunted as he rose, using the chair to hoist himself upright. He clenched his teeth as he gained his feet, then stepped into the light.

Tom saw the pain on his brother's face. Nick hobbled a few steps and sat down on the bed. He had been a good-looking guy. A square jaw and one of those perfect noses. But his lifestyle had aged him. There were pouches beneath his eyes, which were ice blue and bloodshot.

"I got into it at the dog track."

"The *dog track*?" Tom was relieved that it wasn't something worse, but at the same time, utterly disappointed. "Oh Nick, man. What're you *doing*?"

"Hey," Nick snapped. "Spare me the lecture, okay?"

Tom pointed at Nick. "So this? This way you're walking? What've you got, a cracked rib? This is from owing money? On dogs?"

"They tuned me up a little bit, yeah. Not *dogs*. Jesus, give me a little credit. Poker. Caught me cheating, they said."

Tom rubbed a hand over his face. First Alicia, now Nick. He had his first case, a dead woman, and all these other people kept popping up with more problems. When it rained, it poured. He stood up, angry, and walked to the doorway. "I can't help you, Nick. I'm sorry."

"They hit me with a baseball bat, Tommy. My knees are swollen to like, fucking grapefruits, couple ribs are bruised. Nothing broken, I don't think." Nick grunted some more and pushed himself off the bed. He lifted his T-shirt with one hand, holding the bed for balance.

Nick's torso was covered in tattoos, most of his own design. He didn't have any on his face or forearms, but all over his back — a pair of wings there — and on his chest a Christian sacred heart. There were bruises, purple and yellow. Like he'd been kicked a few times. Probably while on the ground after having his knees busted.

"Well, go to the hospital." Tom pulled his eyes away. "Sell your shit, your giant car, I don't know, sell the house, come up with the money. I gotta go."

"Tom . . ." Nick called, but Tom was already going down the stairs.

Instead of walking out the front, though, he was drawn to the backyard again. He stepped out into the bright sunshine, relieved to be out of Nick's dark house. He watched the water flowing past. Nick had been living in Port Royal for several years and had never bought a boat. "We're land-lubbers," he'd said once while they sat out together. It was true. They were kids who'd never spent any time on the water, and now they lived in a place where it surrounded them — oceans and creeks and bays and estuaries. As if they lived here, but still didn't quite belong.

Nick and his drug problems. Nick and his gambling problems. If it wasn't one, it was the other. And now he had guys beating him up. Probably the juice was running, and that ten thousand was just going to get heavier by the day.

The state bureau knew about the dog track, of course, and betting at the track was perfectly legal — pari-mutuel wagering on greyhound racing was allowed with a permit. But dog racing was a sport in serious decline. Owners had turned to other revenue streams. Poker was in a legal gray area.

The poker businesses at the tracks, like the one in Bonita Springs, were highly profitable. And State of Florida law mandated that in order to keep the poker room open, the dogs had to keep running, even though the racing was losing two and a half million bucks a year.

What it all meant was quasi-legal gambling, frustrated track owners, and crime taking root. Nick had probably lost at poker. Three-card poker or Pai Gow poker or Casino War — he'd lost, then cheated to make it back, and they'd given him a warning.

Tom turned away from the river. He looked up at the second floor, expecting to see Nick in the window. But Nick wasn't there. His older brother, who'd had a bright future in front of him, was getting his kneecaps cracked by gambling goons. It seemed Nick was doomed to a life of abuse.

Tom heard the sound of an engine out front. He thought Nick had hopped in the Escalade and taken off, but it was still there. A different vehicle, the black truck, raced away down the street and turned the corner out of sight.

CHAPTER THIRTEEN

Tom stopped by the field office, an annex in the shadows of the County Courthouse. He needed to get Nick off his mind. But Nick had made him think of something.

The field office was small, a main room with a kitchenette, a bathroom and a supply closet. Tom clicked on the closet light and rifled through boxes of supplies. He came up with various maps, found one he liked and tacked it to the wall beside his desk.

Nick had given Tom the lowdown on Naples' development more than once. Fifty years ago the city wasn't much more than a couple streetlights and a pier. Development had followed the coast north. To the south was swampland. Now the whole area was developing at an incredible rate. It was a mixture of old and new.

The Gulf Coast south of Port Royal was a series of islands and bays, Rookery the largest. The only road access was Shell Island Road. Otherwise the various creeks threaded from the bays toward residential areas.

But the geography meant nothing without the right suspect.

Bosco, the bouncer from Hush, still topped the list of potentials. Carrie's ex-husband, Steve Hobson, was next. Sasha Clay, the stripper, went on it, too. As did the man in the ratty sweater. Tom wanted to know all the regulars from the club, anyone who came in and requested that Carrie — aka Amber — give them a private dance. He also wanted to check in with the tattoo parlor where she'd had the butterfly done, though that was further down the list.

He called Machado this time. "How are things going with the list of Reserve volunteers?"

"Almost done. So far, everyone is accounted for." She paused. "How about you? How are you doing?"

Tom almost wanted to say something about Blythe, how she'd reamed him out. Machado was nice, sympathetic. But he held his tongue.

"I'm good."

"Good."

Tom thanked her and ended the call.

It seemed more and more like Carrie hadn't had anything to do with the Reserve, her body had just been dumped there, the killer needing a place to hide it.

But, had it been hidden? Not exactly. It was right on the route of Susan Libby's sunrise tour. Stopper Creek. That could mean a couple of things. It could mean that the killer hadn't known any better, he'd thought it was a reasonable place to hide a body. The Reserve was, after all, a hundred thousand acres. Or the killer might've thought the body would be found eventually by one of the conservation officers who patrolled the site, or Susan Libby herself.

In the latter scenario, the killer was a type of narcissist, hoping his work would be discovered. Maybe he had some vendetta against Libby, maybe against the Reserve. Could be someone who was anti-environmental. Or even someone who'd been hurt by the new regulations which restricted businesses and development around Rookery Bay.

But that was a stretch — a killer making an environmental statement by dumping a stripper from Tampa in the estuary? Long shot.

Tom stared at the map.

The dump site was over two hours from Tampa, and that remained significant. A person didn't kill someone and then risk the time and exposure by disposing of the body that far away. It was more likely Carrie Hobson was murdered in the vicinity. So the real, primary crime scene had yet to be discovered, where there might be blood from her head wound. Somewhere there might be other personal effects — maybe a bag or purse she'd had with her.

He leaned closer to the map, his eyes roving, taking in as much as he could.

The press conference later that afternoon would issue the number for a hotline. If anyone in Naples knew Carrie Hobson, they would hopefully ring in. Maybe she had friends down here.

He went to the kitchenette and put on a pot of coffee. Then he walked to the window, wondering how Alicia was doing.

* * *

Before returning to the condo he visited the Everglades County Prosecutor's Office and spoke with a prosecutor named Ginny Staithe in the domestic violence unit. Staithe agreed to look at the hospital records on Alicia.

When he got home, the landscapers were out, the big van parked near Tom's unit: *VillaGomez Landscaping and Lawn Service.* It made him think of Josh McDermott's Four Palms Landscaping. One of the crew had the leaf-blower going, the rest were out of sight. Probably hurrying to get the job done before an afternoon storm broke. But Tom checked the sky — a gathering darkness had dissipated. It was too bad because the region needed rain — there had been a bit of a drought that spring.

Alicia's car was gone. Tom opened the garage and parked the Jeep.

"Hello?"

No answer. Vance wasn't there, the mother and daughter were gone. He found a note on the counter in the kitchen.

> Tom, thanks for everything. Sorry to have caused you any trouble.
> Good luck with your new job!

It was signed by Alicia, the dots of the "i"s big and round.

The dishes were done, the couch-bed had been dismantled and the blankets put away. He suddenly felt bad, a mixture of guilt and sadness. Like he hadn't given Alicia the attention he should have.

Alicia and Gwen lived on the other side of St. Andrews Boulevard, in an area called Naples Manor, which sounded swanky, but was a working-class part of the city, mostly Latino. He thought Alicia had some Latina heritage in her — she had dark eyes and dark hair, an olive touch to her skin.

He remembered now how Charlene knew her: not as a neighbor, but because Alicia bartended at the Rivergate Hotel. Charlene's husband, Roger, had worked night security there before he took ill.

His phone rang. Ginny Staithe was on the line.

"Ms. Staithe, thanks for calling me back so quickly."

"My pleasure, Agent Lange. So, we've got an unwilling victim?" She was referring to Alicia.

"Looks that way. I'm still hoping to turn her around. But she's scared."

"I've seen the pictures. That would scare me, too, guy like that around. Well, you know how this goes. If she stays unwilling, it can get ugly if you want to keep pushing. We could threaten her with hindering prosecution. I mean, we've got the physical evidence on record, but these battery cases, we've bumped these up to felonies. We could try to proceed without her sworn statement, but I think you know what's going to happen. It will get held over for grand jury action to see if there's a true bill."

He appreciated that Staithe was a straight shooter and he knew she was right. Unfortunately it all amounted to either Alicia proceeding with the charges willingly, or Tom turning into the bad guy when, because of him, the County subpoenaed Alicia to sit through a preliminary hearing only to have the defense argue against allowing her testimony. He didn't know if he wanted to force Alicia into that tug-of-war.

"I'll keep talking to her, Ms. Staithe. Really, thanks for getting back to me so soon."

"Best thing you can do, you know, assure her that the path of least resistance is her sworn statement. With her written testimony and the photographed, physical evidence, they might plea out."

"That's what I told her."

"She'd still need to be at the preliminary hearing, though."

"Yeah . . ." He thought of Alicia making excuses about missing work, finding somewhere for Gwen to go. No one liked to be in open court.

"And, if worse comes to worse, you can see if she'll seek an injunction."

"Thanks again."

Tom stood in the middle of the living room suddenly feeling like he was fucking everything up. It just hit him, all at once, the idea that since yesterday morning he'd done one wrong thing after another. Was he supposed to pressure Alicia to file charges? Or just let her live her life? Should he help Nick, or was that enabling?

He wondered if Dr. Camden's number was still the same. It had been three years, at least, since they'd spoken. They'd kept up contact by phone (Camden didn't like email). Tom had called every once in a while, mostly to put Camden's mind at ease, to assure him how good everything was going. The psychiatrist had been a big part of Tom and Nick's life after their parents had died.

He tossed the phone onto the couch and headed upstairs. Maybe he'd call Camden later. As he walked into his bedroom an awful smell stopped him in his tracks. He opened his bedroom closet and identified the source — his clothes in the hamper, the suit he'd been wearing yesterday. It needed to be dry-cleaned — no, it needed to be burned. The stench of the morgue filled the small space.

And he had to go back to the morgue today.

He stripped out of his clothes and turned on the shower. The irony of showering before returning to the morgue wasn't lost on him — but he'd been up all night, the day had been hot, he needed to re-set before continuing. He remembered something he'd heard once, that there were two kinds of work — the kind you showered before, and the kind you showered after. His work required both.

* * *

Ward made the Y-incision in Carrie Hobson's chest. The blood flowed into the gutters on either side of the inclined table and went down the collection drain with a sucking sound.

At least they were in the main autopsy suite today.

Tom looked at Carrie's breasts, small pink nipples, and he thought of the many men who'd ogled those same breasts at Hush.

He watched as Ward worked the scalpel, slicing through flesh easily. The whole thing was surreal: taking out her organs, weighing them on the scale, then setting them into special pans. Andrea, Ward's ubiquitous assistant, wrote everything down — how many grams the organs weighed, the coloring, any distension. Every detail. The process was painstaking, and Tom's mind wandered.

He wanted to get back to the club, question the employees and certain customers. But Blythe was meeting with Turnbull and the new prosecutor, Bob Mandi. Since the case now involved Tampa, an entirely different district and jurisdiction, bigger guns were required. Once they had the warrant from Judge Tapper they would return to Tampa, search the apartment and talk to the ex-husband. And they would return to Hush. For now, Blythe considered the body the priority, and she was probably right. So far it was Carrie Hobson's body that had given them the tattoo helping to identify her and the head wound which indicated homicide. What was inside of her could reveal even more.

Tom watched Ward for a while. The pathologist moved with a kind of elegant dexterity, somewhere between a master chef and a professional athlete. He had one speed. Blythe had called him meticulous, but Tom thought she'd meant "methodical." Ward never wavered in what he was doing.

Tom needed to walk around, circle around the room, stretch his legs. He glanced at his phone. Nick had left three messages. But there was no call from Judge Tapper yet confirming the warrant for Carrie's apartment.

Ward snapped off his gloves and ushered Tom into the breezeway. Grateful to be outside, Tom sucked in the fresh air. He glanced up and saw stars in the night sky. The internal had so far taken four hours.

"We've extracted the essential proteins from the liquid stomach pulp," Ward said. "So far everything looks consistent with the estimated time of death. I'm not seeing anything unusual, nothing to indicate internal poisoning. I was informed that your crime lab found trace amounts of alcohol in the blood. But no other intoxicants?"

Tom nodded. "We're working on the full toxicology report."

Tom noticed the way Ward pressed his wrists against his lower back, pale fingers dangling against his blood-spattered apron. He thought of Jack Vance talking about *Cutthroat Kitchen*. The analogy was disturbing.

"If the metabolic capacity of the liver for a given drug is great, bioavailability is substantially decreased," Ward said.

"What now?"

Ward gave Tom a condescending look. "It's called the 'first pass effect.' There are many factors that modify absorption. The victim's metabolism, the type of drug, the site of administration . . ."

"You mean you can't tell if there were any drugs in her system."

". . . molecular size and shape of the drug, solubility at the site of absorption, chemical characteristics, manner of administration, these all affect drug transfer. How long did they give you for the toxicology report?"

"They said a week, maybe."

Something flashed in Ward's eyes and he folded his hands in front of the bloody apron. "There you have it. People expect everything now, now, now."

"Are you saying there are drugs in her system, or aren't there? What about rape?"

"I'm saying I can't make that assessment, Agent Lange. Not clinically. For the reason I just explained. Blood and DNA take time. You want to know about rape. Determining signs of sexual abuse is considerably more difficult because of the superimposition of post-mortem modifications. Tissue modifications that can be mistaken for traumatic lesions."

Ward had kept telling Tom what he couldn't say for sure, and why. The doctor didn't want to commit to anything. He wanted to spout off medical terms and criticize society. Normally there might be lawyers present at an autopsy like this. But the police had no suspect, had made no arrests. There was no one to defend. The Office of the State Attorney had entrusted them with overseeing the autopsy. Tom was alone to handle it.

"Okay, thank you, Doctor. I'll be back in a few minutes."

Ward gave Tom another snide look and went inside, leaving Tom pacing the breezeway. Drugs, no drugs, Ward couldn't say. Head trauma as cause of death, he couldn't say. Tom thought the pathologist would spend another month cutting and probing if he could. Poking and prodding, sending things up to the ROC, just to prove to everyone what a head-scratcher it all was.

"Fuck!" Tom muttered. He was holding his goggles and he threw them in the ferns. He wanted to hit something, anything. The sudden frustration was on him so intensely he felt like a wild animal. His brother, Alicia, the painstaking autopsy — all he could do was keep pacing. Then he stopped and pressed his palms against the cool stucco wall. He stared at the ground between his feet. "Fuck," he said again, just a breath.

He fished his goggles out of the ferns and decided to go for a walk.

* * *

Machado called after he left. The driving abstract on Carrie, based on her license plate, had come through. Her maiden name was Gallo. She was Carrie Anne Gallo to the Department of Motor Vehicles.

"She has a Facebook page, but it's been inactive for over two years. Lots of pictures of her dancing at what look like big shows. She's like an extra dancer, whatever you call it, sort of off to the side. And pictures of her sisters, I think, and her mother — you can see the family resemblance. Two sisters, is what I found. I'll send it all over to you. But, like I said, not active for more than a couple years. No Twitter account or Instagram or anything else I found except for a Match.com profile."

"Match.com? Do people still use that? I thought it was Tinder now, or something."

"Like you don't know," Machado joked.

"Haha. I don't."

"Uh-huh. Alright, I'll send that to you also."

"Thank you."

Machado had cheered him up, and he had another piece of the puzzle. He realized he'd walked a fair distance from the Medical Examiner's Office and didn't quite know where he was. Somewhere between Goodlette-Frank and 10th Street. Small, simple houses. Lots of rhododendron, ficus trees, bougainvillea shrubs. A little girl rode her bike up the street, giving him a look. He was a white man who'd wandered into one of Naples' only African-American neighborhoods.

He found his way back to the morgue. The internal autopsy wouldn't be done, but the press conference would begin at six o'clock, broadcast live on the evening news. Murders were rare in Naples and the case was drawing attention.

Tom changed into a second set of clothes he'd brought, using the bathroom at the morgue. When he left, he swung the Jeep past the building's dumpster, took the clothes he'd had on, and threw them in the garbage.

It was time to tell the world about Carrie Anne Gallo.

CHAPTER FOURTEEN

Bob Mandi was a big man with a round stomach. He shook Tom's hand gruffly then bent over his phone. Apparently he was the type of person who left the button tones active — they bleeped and chimed as he pecked at the keys. Perhaps more importantly, Mandi worked beneath the attorney general and was able to prosecute crimes that impacted two or more judicial circuits.

They had gathered in the antechamber to the press conference room along with a police-media liaison and ADA Heather Kibble, who had little to do now the case had gone multi-jurisdictional. There was an excitement surrounding the broadening scope of the investigation.

Blythe spoke. "Agent Lange contacted a co-worker of the victim through NamUs. Lange then met the woman at her place of employment — a strip club called Hush, in Tampa. You have that information. Lange tells me he has learned some new things since we spoke earlier. Lange?"

Tom cleared his throat. He went through the DMV information and social media. They now had Carrie's maiden name.

"Well done." Mandi put away his phone.

Tom stressed the importance of the apartment and vehicle search. He could feel Blythe watching him.

Mandi looked at Blythe. "You want me to reach out to Tampa, get them ready, or did you already talk to them?"

"We made the call, but a follow up from you would help." She cut a quick look at Tom after she said it.

Mandi nodded and addressed both agents. "Let's talk to everyone. All the strippers, bartenders, this guy Bosco. Tampa can really help you there, get all the statements. Where are we with the victim's family? And what about a formal ID?"

"We have witness identification of the victim," Blythe said. "Forensics is almost there. I've spoken to the decedent's mother, explained that due to the investigation, the press conference was urgent."

The police-media liaison made some notes, and showed them to Mandi, who nodded. Then they all shuffled into the conference room.

The large room bristled with cameras and outstretched microphones. There was a mult-box feeding more mikes at the podium for the bigger broadcast channels.

The press spent the first part of the conference focused on the relationship between the law enforcement bodies. The state typically worked big cases, often involving the investigation of other law enforcement. A recent FDLE audit of the Clearwater Police Department was still in the news. The Rookery Bay case was a bit outside the norm, and the press had a lot of questions about the state bureau working with Everglades County. They were used to the FDLE being involved in malfeasance investigations, fraud, missing guns — not dead bodies.

Mandi worked the media with aplomb, deftly avoiding any controversies and sticking to the facts. He reminded them that the state bureau had a violent crimes division.

Tom stood off to the side with Blythe, neither of them required to say anything.

"The state has taken this case due to its jurisdictional nature," Mandi said. "The Everglades County Sheriff's Office is working with the FDLE in a fully cooperative manner."

"Weren't there state agents present at the scene yesterday morning?"

Several sets of eyes and a few cameras turned to Tom and Blythe.

"Yes," Mandi said. "As the estuary is partly state run, the FDLE has had a presence since the beginning."

"Do the police have any suspects?"

"We have several promising leads. We're urging anyone who knew the victim, Carrie Hobson, to come forward."

Mandi offered the hotline number and Tom glanced at the picture of Carrie. It was a blow-up of her driver's license photo. In it, she smiled brightly, her eyes vivacious. She might not have been as conventionally beautiful as the other exotic dancers she worked with, but she was certainly alluring. Tom thought Nick would call her "the girl next door."

* * *

After the press conference, Blythe surprised Tom by inviting him for dinner to catch up with how things were going. She told him which restaurant to meet at and they both went home to change.

At home, Tom looked in his closet and all he could find was a flower-print shirt hanging from the rack. A gift from Nick. He hadn't done a wash in weeks and dirty laundry was heaped on the closet floor. He sniffed the shirt to make sure it didn't reek of the morgue. It smelled like a department store, good enough, so he pulled it on and stepped into a pair of jeans then looked at himself in the mirror. Hey, it wasn't a date.

Near where 41 changed from east–west and elbowed to run north–south was a collection of touristy restaurants and a mall called "Tin City" along Naples Bay. It was a tourist trap filled with shops selling bric-a-brac — seashell necklaces, wall art with phrases like *Since I Retired Every Hour is Happy Hour* — couched in a working-class, seaside aesthetic. It was also the mini-mall that housed his brother's realty office, *Lange Real Estate.*

Tom parked the Jeep and walked around inside the mall, stopping at Nick's office, which was closed up for the day. The glass front featured a monitor displaying properties. Toward the end of the slide-show was a picture of Nick grinning hammily. Seeing his brother stirred regret. Nick's plight had been bothering him all day, interfering with his concentration.

He left the mall and headed for the Dockside Restaurant at the far end of the complex. His timing was good. Blythe was talking to the hostess. They greeted each other and were shown to a table beside the wharf.

Blythe ordered crab and Tom got the sea scallop special. They waited for their food, each nursing a drink — Tom a beer and Blythe a vodka gimlet. It was like they needed the food before they could break the ice and start talking, so they watched as boats moored in the harbor bobbed in the black water.

On the other side of 41 from Tin City was the Bayfront Inn and Condominiums. You could cross from Tin City to the condos via an underpass alongside a creek flowing from Naples Bay. Thick, concrete bridge supports were stained rust-colored from high tide. The tide was low now, water purling over the rocks.

Blythe finally spoke. "Nice shirt."

"Please. I need a housekeeper."

When the food came, she got down to business. "Good job today."

He didn't know exactly what she was referring to — maybe how he'd been with Bob Mandi — but he didn't fish for more compliments.

She cracked open a crab leg and suckled the meat. "So, what are you thinking?"

He liked this version of Blythe. "I think Carrie Hobson was nobody remarkable. And I don't mean that as a character judgment, but maybe it was part of the killer's motive."

Blythe nodded, but said, "Her family thinks she's someone remarkable. Her mother is Eileen Gallo. She's in Idaho, and she's trying to get a flight down. Maybe tomorrow, maybe Thursday we'll have her do the formal ID on the body. The two sisters I haven't been able to track down yet. But we know they're far-flung. One in New York, one in California."

"What about the father?"

"Deceased. She alluded to cancer."

Tom got back on track. "Of course she meant something to her family. I meant that as a cultural characteristic, Carrie being unremarkable. As something her killer thought about her. Maybe why her killer chose her."

"You don't think a stripper is remarkable?"

"She was a dancer who didn't make it big. Kind of a cliché, really. She became a stripper out of necessity."

"She has a family, an ex-husband."

"Right. She's not completely isolated. That's kind of hard, this day and age, to be a total loner. But even among the dancers at Hush, she's the one who you kind of pass over . . ." He gave Blythe a quick look, catching himself in a possibly sexist or objectifying remark, but she was listening impassively.

"I think . . ." He paused, looking out at the harbor. "I think that maybe the killer feels that way, too."

"Feels invisible?"

"Maybe passed over. Under-recognized. Unappreciated."

"You're making a leap here . . ."

"Maybe. I'm thinking of someone in a visible position who feels inadequate, even rejected. Someone with something to prove. Or maybe that's my years-sitting-at-a-desk-in-school talking."

"Touché." She smiled lightly, and he felt his skin flush. "But you do realize it sounds like you could be describing yourself."

She'd hit a soft spot, but she wasn't insinuating he'd had anything to do with Carrie's death, only that his profile could describe a lot of people. It still threw him off guard and he tried cheap humor. "Yeah, well, you think I'm good shit — it can't be me who's the killer. I've got my high praise." He took a showy swig of his beer and grinned at her.

Blythe laughed. It was the first time he'd heard her laugh in two days. A throaty laugh, genuine, contagious. Somehow she'd found him funny.

"You've been talking to Director Turnbull," she said after a moment.

"No, I can just sense it." He cut his eyes back to her and found her smiling. Damn she was attractive. "Do you even have a first name?"

"I do. It's Lauren."

"Hi Lauren, I'm Tom."

He stuck out his hand. She took it, smiling, then she looked away. No wedding ring on Blythe's finger. He wondered if she'd ever been married, if she was in a relationship now. If anyone had ever hurt her.

A thought struck him. "What if our guy never had sex with her? Ward hemmed and hawed about post-mortem modifications, but he would've seen *something* by now. The colposcopy shows nothing. And I'm sure you've seen the email from the lab, initial sampling is negative for semen, negative for any trace evidence, really."

"She was in the water a long time."

"You're right. She was. I'm just playing out a theory. That *maybe* it wasn't about possessing her, or being with her. Maybe it wasn't about sex. I mean, it could be, in the broader context — lust of the eyes, love of the world, that sort of thing — it could be a statement. But without the act as part of the crime."

"Are you going biblical on me, Agent Lange?"

His foster family had been religious. "'For everything in the world — the lust of the flesh, the lust of the eyes, and the pride of life — comes not from the Father but from the world.' First John, 2:16."

She watched him a moment, the subtle smile still on her lips. "Maybe it's not about obsession at all." Then she wiped her mouth, set her napkin aside and grew serious. "Alright. I'm going to let you in on something. I've been talking to Sergeant Danny Coburn, vice narcotics."

"With Everglades County?"

Blythe nodded.

"They think this is drug-related?" He'd certainly considered it, but for him, it hadn't fit. For one thing, Naples wasn't really a strategic point for drug trafficking. True, Everglades City, further southeast, was once a major smuggling point. Weed, coke, brought in by boats, was then hauled up I-75 and into Tampa. I-75 passed through Naples, but Naples was nowhere near the market Tampa was. And Everglades City had been hammered by the DEA and the Sheriff's Office.

Still, it was possible.

And maybe this explained why she'd been so scarce lately. She'd been in talks with vice narcotics. From what Tom knew about the VNB, they set their own rules. They wore street clothes, drove unmarked vehicles, spent months building cases.

"They're interested. But they're real tight-lipped about what they're working on. They don't want to educate anyone."

Tom understood. The narcotics guys didn't even like to talk to other cops about what they were doing. And in certain cases, they were legally prevented from it.

Blythe said, "They busted this guy in Immokalee last week buying a nine-piece. Had the interdiction officers pull him over, and, you know how it is — they act like they don't know anything, like it's a random stop so the bad guys don't know how far up their asses the VNB has actually gotten. And the vice guys hang back, stay out of sight."

"And?"

She shrugged. "They didn't say where it led, but Sergeant Coburn, Coby, called me today and asked me some questions about our vic."

"That's it? Just some questions?"

"We opened a dialog."

"I'm sure they wanted to know why we took it over, right? I mean, as long as jurisdictions are willing and able to cooperate, we're not really needed. Just like Everglades vice narcotics works with Tampa vice narcotics, and they don't need us to hold anyone's hand."

She picked up her drink, looking into it, and didn't answer.

"I mean, it went to County CID, then we hopped on and took it over. I already heard the answer that it's a state preserve, but I think we both know County could have handled it. Why did Turnbull step in, get us involved?"

She pushed her plate aside, the meal finished, then turned and looked out at the harbor, sucking at something in her teeth. "Turnbull is . . . well, you've met him. He's taciturn. He might talk for five minutes but not tell you anything. There's always changes in administration, and what we do, you know, what we cover, it's not static."

Tom sat back, thinking Blythe had just given him her own taciturn, non-answer. When the waiter came around, he ordered another beer. Blythe abstained, and he got the sense that the conversation was winding down.

He got back to the victim. "Hopefully we'll find something at Carrie's apartment. And we'll talk to the ex-husband. I'm just glad the autopsy part is over."

He looked at her, hoping maybe she'd pick up on his cue and say something more about why he'd spent so much of the past two days with the body. But it had already proven to be time well spent, and given them the evidence to proceed with Carrie's death as a homicide. Blythe said no more about it.

The waiter returned with his drink and cleared their plates, asked if they wanted anything else, and Blythe requested the check.

They made a bit of small talk about the boats in the harbor, and then Blythe excused herself for the evening. Tom was relieved. It had been a good talk, but he had more to do. The night was calling.

CHAPTER FIFTEEN

He swung past Nick's place first, but his brother wasn't home. He sat outside the dark house, thinking about Nick and Alicia. Pushing them aside wasn't getting rid of the nagging sense that his help was needed.

He called Alicia. She answered right away. "Hi, Tom. I was just thinking about you."

She sounded sleepy. Maybe even a little drunk. He wondered where Gwen was, and hoped she was okay.

"Oh yeah? What were you thinking about?"

"Just how it's nice to have a guy like you around."

Yeah, definitely sauced, her tone flirtatious.

"I'm glad you feel that way."

She laughed, and said, "Plus, you're cute. You know you're cute, right? Well, not *cute*. A lotta guys are *cute*. You've got that former-high-school-jock thing going on. Were you a high school jock, Agent Lange? I don't think so. I think you were quiet and shy."

"Alicia, are you alright? How's Gwenny?"

"She's fine, Tom. We're fine."

A heavy silence developed. Tom figured he needed to come right to the point. "Alicia, I think you're scared. I can understand that. But I think if you meet this thing head on—"

"Jack is nice," she interrupted. "He took us to the pool. You have a great pool over there . . ."

"Alicia, did Josh call you last night?"

There was a long pause. When she spoke again she sounded a bit more together. A bit colder, too. "Tom, I'm really sorry for what I did. I shouldn't have gotten you involved. I'll leave you alone now."

"Alicia, that's not what I want. I want to help you."

"You want to help me? The best thing you could do for me is forget you ever met me."

"I can't do that. I want to help, but . . . I don't know the right thing. Have you seen Josh since you were at my place?"

She was silent for so long he wondered if she'd hung up. When she finally spoke, he could barely hear her. "Yeah. I saw him."

The quality of her voice — everything was clear to Tom. "What did he do?" His voice was rising. "Alicia? What did he do?"

"It's best to just let it go." She was crying now. "Goodbye, Tom."

"Alicia? Hello?"

She was gone.

* * *

Tom found Josh McDermott's address in the Yellow Pages, and ten minutes later he turned the Jeep down an unlit road. He drove until he found a plant nursery, several vehicles parked around the yard. In the darkness he could just make out *Four Palms Landscaping* on the sides of two vans.

He slowed almost to a stop, looking down rows of potted ferns, baby palms and thin pines ready for planting. There didn't seem to be anyone around. He got out with his flashlight and checked the premises. The humidity was thick, the air moving with tiny insects, crickets singing.

After a little walking around, Tom found a single-story house behind the plant nursery, the windows dark.

All manner of junk was piled around the house — hubcaps and busted tables, discarded boxes, a jet ski converted into a four-wheeler, large empty planters and bags of potting soil and mulch. McDermott's pickup was nowhere in sight. The man was not home.

Tom circled the house. More stuff out back — pallets piled up, stacks of sod, an old boat on a rack, half the paint scraped off. Tom had to push through the undergrowth to get around to the front of the house. By the time he did, the anger was flowing, the sweat coursing down. He stood there for a moment, mosquitos circling, and decided it was time for a drink.

* * *

Ty's was typical, a business within a plaza of businesses — a box within a larger box. Tom cruised through the parking lot until he saw what he was looking for. McDermott's landscaping truck gave him a nervous thrill. He found a spot and parked, his mind raising all sorts of objections.

There was no ostensible connection between McDermott and the murder. His domestic dispute with Alicia was really none of Tom's business. Tom was a professional, he needed to operate within the bounds of the law. He was a brand-new agent for the FDLE — behavior like this could either tarnish his burgeoning career or get him fired altogether.

He stepped out into the muggy night air and walked toward the bar, deciding he was just going to talk to the guy, nothing more. Alicia was a friend. McDermott had beat her up repeatedly, and she was too scared to press charges, or too reluctant to go through the red tape of the justice system, or both. But the abuse was ongoing.

The inside of the place felt just as humid. A few alkies were belly-up to the bar, a couple of them watching the KINO with half-lidded eyes. AC/DC's *Highway to Hell* played in the background. One of the booths was occupied by a trio of Mexican men with a pitcher of beer and a mess of shot glasses. In the back were two pool tables, a juke box, a couple more booths. Josh McDermott was chalking his pool cue. The big man knocked in one of the solid balls.

Tom approached, his pulse quickening. He'd had the advantage of surprise yesterday, grabbing McDermott's arm when the man probably hadn't seen it coming, and doing a quick takedown on him. McDermott would be on the defensive for this encounter. Tom had to handle it just right.

The guy playing pool with McDermott was short and muscular. They both had on grubby white T-shirts bearing the *Four Palms Landscaping* logo. McDermott's back was turned, but Tom caught the eye of the shorter man. Then Tom sat down at the end of the bar and waved for the bartender's attention.

As the bartender shambled over, Tom kept watch on McDermott and his employee, reflected in the mirror behind the liquor shelves. Tom ordered a beer as the muscular guy got McDermott's attention. The guy nodded his head toward Tom, whose back was turned, and McDermott looked over.

Bingo.

Tom pretended to be watching the TV as McDermott set down his pool cue and started over. Tom hadn't been in the field very long, but he'd spent years studying criminal behavior. McDermott would either come on strong, or he would act innocent and unassuming, even friendly.

"Hey," McDermott said amicably.

He'd chosen option two.

Tom looked around, acting surprised. "Oh, hey. Josh McDermott, Four Palms Landscaping. Tom Lange, Florida Department of Law Enforcement." He made the introduction with a big grin.

McDermott put on his own fake smile. "That's right. That's right. What're you doing in here?"

Tom took a sip of his beer and looked back at the TV screen for effect. "I thought we could talk."

"Talk? What're you, playing hard-to-get sitting over here? Come on, yeah, let's talk. I got nothing to hide. Hey, Sandy . . ." McDermott rapped his knuckles on the bar. The bartender had already been watching them. He hobbled over, raising his eyebrows.

"Set my man Tom here up with another beer. And let's have a couple of shots. Tommy? You got a preference?"

"I'll take a tequila."

"A tequila man! I like that."

McDermott made a big show of ordering the drinks, flashing a wad of cash. Tom noticed the man's dirty fingernails, the deep tan to the skin of his hands and forearms. Tom glanced in the mirror again, this time at the trio sitting in the booth, who showed an interest in the proceedings. Tom hadn't been sure at first, but now figured they were also McDermott's employees. It was after ten, and McDermott probably worked them until dark. That meant they had a couple hours of drinking under their belts.

He didn't think they would be much trouble — there was a good chance they worked illegally and would avoid police involvement at all costs. Even if they were documented workers, though, they wouldn't want to tangle with a state special agent. Still, McDermott might use them to intimidate Tom, if he could.

The bartender poured the shots — just two of them — and set down fresh bottles of beer. "Come on,"

McDermott said. He jerked his head toward the back. "Step into my office."

Tom drained his beer, collected the reinforcements, and followed McDermott to an empty booth, smiling at the pool player as he passed. The man didn't smile back. Tom slid into the booth across from McDermott, who immediately raised his shot glass.

"To new friendships."

He was really laying it on thick. Tom downed the tequila, feeling the heat warm his stomach and the fumes rise in his nose. He chased it with a swig of his beer. This was his fifth drink in a couple hours. He rarely drank and was starting to feel the effects. He warned himself to be careful.

Tom tried to act casual. McDermott was wearing that letterbox grin.

"So," McDermott said, "let's dish."

"You talked Alicia out of pressing charges."

McDermott's expression morphed into something meant to convey a grievous misunderstanding in their midst. "No, no, bro. I didn't talk her out of anything. We spoke, yeah. We had a disagreement, you know, but we got it all settled."

Tom waited for it. Was he going to deny it or justify it?

"A disagreement?" Tom goaded him. "Is that what you call it?" Tom pointed to his face, thinking of Alicia's wounds and any more recent damage.

"Yeah. What else am I going to call it?"

"Domestic violence."

McDermott looked deeply wounded. Sorrowful, even. "Aw man, it's not like that, bro." He shook his head, looking down for a moment. "It's not like that at all."

"What's it like?"

Head still lowered, McDermott raised his eyes to look across the table. He pulled on another grin. "You know, man. Come on. You know how it gets, right?"

Tom stared back, feeling his pulse quicken. Now McDermott was goading *him*, it seemed. McDermott wasn't going to admit anything. Why would he? He was sitting across from a cop. Outside the condo, Tom had wondered if McDermott was stupid. He didn't think so anymore. This close to the guy, talking with him, he found McDermott was stone cold beneath the yah-bro facade.

Tom fiddled with his beer bottle, moving it between his hands, the glass sliding on the condensation.

"I looked you up. This isn't the first time someone has reported you. Happened six years ago. A young woman called the cops because you beat her up, then she didn't want to press charges. Two years ago, same thing."

McDermott's grin held, but the expression grew humorless. He sat back against the wooden booth, then gave a dismissive shake of the head. "Ah man, they Baker Act-ed that one. She was crazy — she called the fucking cops every other *week*, bro. About all sorts of things. She was a meth head, man. I'm lucky I got away from that bitch when I did."

The Baker Act stated that a civilian could inform on another civilian who seemed to be in trouble, mentally unstable, drugs, otherwise. Police could use the Baker Act, too, and send someone to treatment instead of incarceration. McDermott had used it as his own get-out-of-jail-free card.

Tom forged ahead, ticking off the years on his fingers. "Six years ago, two years ago, yesterday. These instances are getting closer together, women calling the police because you kicked the shit out of them."

McDermott grew sarcastic. "Oh, come on now, man. That's a bit dramatic. Anyway, Alicia didn't call the cops on me, bro. *You* did. How's that work, anyway, cops calling other cops? Do they like, look down on you after that? Like, 'Hey, why can't you handle your own shit?'"

"My area is not domestic violence. I handle cases for the State of Florida. Like right now, I'm working a murder case."

"Is that right?" McDermott took a healthy gulp of his beer and looked away. Tom glanced at the pool table. The muscular guy had moved over to the table with the three other landscapers, just at the edge of Tom's sight.

"Yeah. That's right. Woman found, back of skull cracked, sort of your M.O."

"My M.O.? What the fuck are you talking about?" McDermott's front was crumbling, things getting too personal for him. "That woman on the TV? That body in the bay? That's you, huh?"

"That's me. Along with another special agent, and Everglades County's finest. We've even been up to Tampa and worked with them."

Tom didn't take his eyes off of McDermott, hunting for any giveaway — just in case.

"Tampa, huh? That where she's from?"

"What makes you think that, McDermott?"

Silence for a moment, the air filling with tension. McDermott narrowed his eyes. "Aw, fuck, man. Are you kidding me? I thought you came here to talk about Alicia. You're in here — what? You think I've got something to do with that shit?"

Tom stopped playing with his bottle and finished what was in it. Then he stood up. "One more shot? I'm buying." He could really feel the alcohol buzzing now, charging him up. *Easy now. Go easy.*

McDermott stared up from the booth. "You for real? I mean, what? Because you think I tuned up my girlfriend, now I'm a killer? Lookit you, in your Tommy Bahama shirt. You're a real piece of work, huh?"

Tom let the remarks slide off and tipped his empty bottle at McDermott. "Another round, or not?"

"Shit, man, I don't have time for this . . ." McDermott started to slide out of the booth and Tom blocked him. He leaned down so they were eye-to-eye.

"You come in here a lot? To this bar? Alicia said she met you here."

"Get out of my face."

"I've been here before, too, once or twice. It's a good place. You usually bring your guys here?"

"I'm telling you—"

"Like, a week ago, say, last Wednesday night — you were here?"

McDermott looked like he was ready to explode, but was still weighing the consequences of doing so. "I don't know, I can't remember. Probably."

"What about Thursday? Can you give me an account of your whereabouts each night last week?"

"Fuck you."

Tom gestured toward the men at the booth. "I start asking your guys questions, you think they're going to like that? What if I want to see all their paperwork? I get a forensics team down at your nursery, turning over all your plants, going through your house, maybe have the Everglades deputies doing a little door to door, talking to your customers about what kind of guy you are, how's that going to work out for you? For your business?"

He watched McDermott stuff his anger behind another phony smile. Tom decided to let off, and stood back up. McDermott slowly rose, and squared his shoulders with Tom.

"Go ahead."

"Don't ever talk to Alicia again. Don't ever go to her house. Don't call her. Let her think you fell off the face of the Earth. Or you're going to have a team of cops so far up your ass you'll shit badges."

McDermott laughed, but Tom could see the fear behind the man's eyes.

"Whatever, bro," McDermott said. "I think our conversation is over." He pushed past Tom, their arms brushing. McDermott walked over to the four men at the table, whistled, said something in Spanish. The guy McDermott had been playing pool with rose and the two walked back to their game, McDermott acting like he didn't have a care in the world.

Tom headed for the door. The guys at the table averted their eyes as he passed.

He was glad to leave the bar, and let out a rushing breath as he moved into the night air. McDermott was acting tough, but Tom thought he'd gotten through. He thought McDermott would leave Alicia alone. But he didn't think McDermott was Carrie Hobson's killer.

CHAPTER SIXTEEN

WEDNESDAY

Tom's hangover lingered on the drive north to Tampa, beating a steady rhythm in his temples. He drove into the parking lot for Carrie Hobson's apartment building and spotted an unmarked police car beside a patrol cruiser. He was supposed to meet with a Detective Gomez, from Tampa PD.

Tampa felt even hotter than Naples, the tarmac wavy with morning heat. Tom knocked on the window of the unmarked car. After a moment, it came down.

"Detective Gomez?"

The man in the driver's seat was smoking a cigarette, loud Latin music on the stereo. He looked up at Tom, eyes half-lidded with boredom. "Uh-huh?"

"Tom Lange." He stuck his hand through the window.

Gomez snubbed the cigarette and pushed the door open with a jerk. Tom had to yank his arm before it got bent in the door. Gomez stepped out in his snakeskin boots. He was dressed in a charcoal gray suit that looked a size too big. He hitched up his pants and gestured to the two Tampa patrolmen who ambled over, looked Tom up and down, and gave their names and quick handshakes.

Tom figured the Tampa cops would react coolly to him, but Gomez was looking off like he was lost in a daydream.

"So this is the residence of Carrie Hobson, nee Carrie Anne Gallo," Tom said. "Twenty-six years old, from Boise, Idaho. The Medical Examiner's Office has contacted the next of kin, my supervisor spoke with her, too. Hobson is survived by a mother and two sisters, both older . . ."

Gomez flitted his fingers in the air. "I read the report."

"Great. And you ran the victim, correct?"

"Yes. We ran Hobson through our system and came up with a single hit. Indecent exposure — she was stripping at a party in the city that got busted up five months ago. She got written up, paid a fine by mail. That's it. No prior record."

"And the others?"

Tom opened the murder book and took out photos while Gomez spoke.

"Raymond T. Bosco, twenty-nine, has had several misdemeanors, including reckless endangerment and drug possession. Are we really rehashing this information while we stand in the fucking burning hot parking lot? We've had phone calls and emails galore."

Tom glanced at the uniformed officers. "Are you two familiar with any of this?"

They traded looks and shook their heads, no.

"Continue," Tom said.

Gomez gave Tom a nasty look. "Fine. Steven R. Hobson, thirty-eight, one DWI nine years ago, out of state. That's it. Okay? Where's your crew?"

"They're right behind me," Tom said. He addressed the officers next, distributing photos of Raymond Bosco and Steve Hobson.

"I'd like you two questioning neighbors while the team processes the apartment, okay? It's Wednesday morning, lots of people at work. If they're not home, make a note of it and we'll follow up this evening. There's forty units, but here's what — for now, stick to the units on the ends which have views on the staircases. That's twenty units. You're just asking if anyone has seen either of these two men. Anyone says yes, you come get me. Okay?"

They looked less than thrilled.

Gomez muttered something and walked away, his snakeskin boots sticking to the tarry pavement.

* * *

Carrie Hobson's landlord was a jittery type, a short, wiry man who kept looking at the cops like they were going to beat him up and steal his lunch money. When they came to Carrie's locked door, the landlord dropped the keys. Finally he fumbled the door open and stepped back.

Tom entered first. He wore latex gloves, as did the three IFS techs who followed in after him, and Detective Gomez after that. When the landlord started scurrying away, Tom called him back. "Hey, sir? Hold on."

The landlord skulked back.

"Your name is Derrick Massey?" Tom asked him.

"Yeah?"

"How long has Carrie Hobson rented from you?"

"Less than a year. She was coming up on her eleventh month."

"Okay, I'll need to see her rental application. Her list of references, previous residences, that sort of thing."

Massey only jerked his beady eyes around.

"You do have that paperwork, right?"

"Hey," Massey said. "I give people a break. Alright? Everybody has something they do to try to help out. I don't ask questions. I let people in provided they got cold, hard cash. Sometimes, all someone needs is quick and easy."

"Anything on her at all? Tell me you at least made a photocopy of her driver's license."

Derrick Massey scrunched his nose in a look of defiance. "Like I said, I don't give my tenants any trouble. There's no law says I have to—"

Tom held his hand in the air. He wasn't about to get into state law concerning property rentals with this guy. He didn't need the driver's license, he already had the basic information — he'd just hoped the landlord would have something else of interest.

"So you ever go into her apartment?"

"No. Well, yeah, okay, twice. Once when she first rented it, then one other time when her toilet was running, I let the plumber in. Carrie was at work."

"When was that?"

"Um. Six months ago, maybe. I don't know."

"Well, an officer will be along and we can get your full statement, okay? You're in Unit 1, correct?"

"Yeah."

"And I understand you have just one security camera?"

"That's right. On the pool. I've had all sorts of shit happen in that pool. Now I've got it on video."

"Okay. Well, you can turn that over to my techs when we're through."

"Turn it over? That's my video."

Tom stared at him.

Massey broke eye contact. "Jesus. I don't keep it forever. I have a week's worth at a time. I'm just looking for punks who sneak in. Someone puked in the pool and that's why I got the camera."

Nice place, this apartment building.

"You ever see anyone with Carrie? Coming or going?"

Massey switched looks between Tom and Gomez. "I don't poke my nose in people's business."

"Just at the pool."

"I'm very clear with my tenants — only people living in the apartment, or using the *pool*, are the people pay me money. No sublets, nothing."

"A friend? Anyone you might have seen her with? Doesn't mean you're spying, just means they happened to walk past your field of vision."

Massey lowered his voice. "You know, those women came by this weekend. They're strippers, I think. Could tell by how they dressed and talked."

"How about a man? Ever see a man here?" Tom held up the photo of Steve Hobson first. "How about him? Have you seen him?"

Massey squinted at the picture and shook his head. "No."

Tom switched to the one of Bosco.

"How about him?"

Something. A little tic in the corner of Derrick Massey's already twitchy eyes. "No. I don't know. I got forty units, sixty-eight tenants. I have a life. I can't see all the people coming and going."

Tom nodded sympathetically. "I hear you. Maybe, though, if my associate here, Detective Gomez, takes you down to the police station, you have a cup of coffee, think about it, it might relax you, help you remember."

Massey snorted, an angry little sound. "I said no. I never seen that guy."

Tom decided to let it go for now. He slipped the pictures back in the book and zipped it up. He'd started away when Massey said, "I noticed those girls, though. You know? I mean, who wouldn't." He got a look in his eyes like he had some nasty fantasies tucked away. "You should check into them."

"Thank you, Mr. Massey."

Tom walked back into the apartment where the techs were already spreading the black, magnetic dust around, flipping on their special lights, snapping pictures. Massey called from the exterior walkway. "Hey, what happens to all her stuff? I mean, what if no one claims it?"

"We'll be in touch."

Tom nodded at Gomez, who took Tom's meaning and closed the door, shutting Massey out.

"What a little sleazebag," Gomez said.

"We'll need his prints."

They stood on plastic laid out in the doorway while they slipped booties over their shoes. Gomez grunted and swore as he struggled. Tom looked around the room, then moved to the windows. The curtains were closed most of the way, like they had been the night before. Not much of a view, just the exterior walkway and the parking lot below. The door hadn't shown any signs of forced entry, neither did the windows.

Massey never saw anyone with Carrie, but that didn't mean anything, or he was lying. She could've had a boyfriend. Most women, looking like Carrie, didn't go long without one. Maybe someone had a key.

Massey had a key.

Tom picked his way through the apartment, Gomez trailing behind in his oversized suit. There wasn't much to the place. Single bedroom, walk-in closet. Tom looked in and found it full of clothes. He pushed some aside, checking out the wardrobe. A couple of sun-dresses, a more formal-looking dress in a plastic garment bag. Blouses and tops and jeans — a couple designer brands, nothing outlandish. There was a suitcase on the top shelf, the kind with wheels. Unpacked.

He moved to the bureau where he took a pen from his pocket and pushed through the underwear and G-strings, feeling a bit like a pervert. He wondered if Massey had let himself in here during Carrie's absence, done a little luxuriating in her underwear drawer.

He found it odd that there were no photos in her home. One framed picture hung on the bedroom wall, the kind of "corporate art" that looked like it came with the place. Flowers in a field, suggestions of lavender mountains in the distance. There was a paperback copy of *Cujo*, spine well-creased, on the bedside table. The bed was unmade, though one side was neater than the other.

"What are you looking for?" Gomez had drifted so close his voice gave Tom a jolt.

"Evidence of sudden departure, evidence of anyone else besides Carrie in this apartment." Tom fanned the pages of the paperback before setting it down. "And, a box."

"A box?"

"Yeah."

"I don't get it."

"It's human nature," Tom said, looking under the bed. "People tend to keep a box with things in it." It could be anything, one of his psychology professors had said, sometimes valuables, or drugs, but often keepsakes such as photos, letters, other mementos.

Carrie Hobson didn't have a landline or an answering machine. Maybe Everglades County would eventually find her cell phone in the bay, but it might be useless by then.

Nothing beneath the bed but dust bunnies and a worn pair of slippers. He wandered out of the bedroom, determined, Gomez still ghosting him.

"You been with the Tampa CID long, Detective Gomez?"

"Seven years."

They entered the kitchen and Tom opened the fridge. Not much in it, just a few sports drinks, yogurts, a bluish-looking head of broccoli in the crisper, condiments in the door.

"And that's the major crimes bureau you're with?"

Gomez scowled. "I'm SIB."

There were a few unwashed dishes in the sink. Tom looked through kitchen cabinets and drawers. "SIB? What's that? Undercover ops?"

"Right. Strategic investigations bureau. Narcotic and gang enforcement."

In a drawer beneath an unused coffee maker Tom found a wallet. Inside was sixty-eight dollars, a bank debit card, a Dunkin' Donuts gift card, a few receipts, and Carrie's driver's license. He put all these in a baggie and took the baggie to the evidence box in the living room.

"A wallet," Gomez said. "No shit."

"I think between the wallet and the clothes, the unpacked suitcase, we can pretty much rule out that she took a trip on her own to Naples. She was either killed in Tampa, deposited in Naples, or she only expected to be in Naples briefly. Leaving her wallet behind . . . I'd say she was with someone who promised to take care of things."

Gomez nodded like he was thinking all these things, too, though Tom sensed Gomez was out of his element. He had no clue why Tampa would deploy an SIB detective to a homicide case.

The living room was a simple set-up. A small flat-screen TV, a couch and chair set, a coffee table. Sasha had indicated that Carrie spent her money foolishly — Tom didn't see any extravagant buys, just normal stuff. On the coffee table was an old box of Chinese food. He gave it a sniff from a safe distance. Highly unpleasant, but compared to the morgue, it was begonias. The box contained the remains of a single serving of sweet and sour pork. Maybe Carrie had been in the middle of a meal when she'd suddenly left the apartment, leaving her wallet and ID. Or, maybe she was just a bit messy at home.

He checked the carpet. Noting a few specks, fibers well-matted, he guessed it hadn't been vacuumed for a month or so. There was a rumpled blanket on the couch.

Carrie wasn't a drinker or druggie from the looks of it. She was fairly healthy. She'd been a dancer, but only an extra. She was from a small Midwestern town and looked like the girl next door. She read popular fiction, ate Chinese food. When her place got messy, she didn't fret.

Tom thought it again: She was anybody.

She was nobody.

About the only thing that was remarkable about Carrie Hobson was that she was a stripper. Though in Tampa Bay, that wasn't very unusual at all.

"Well?" Gomez asked, lingering in the kitchen doorway.

Tom glanced at Gomez, and down at the man's feet again, seeing the sharp points of his boots tenting against the blue booties like weird erections. Then his eyes drifted to the baseboard along the bottom of the wall. Tom looked around at the rest of the trim in the room, crown molding that abutted the ceiling, simple trim framing the doors. The place was in decent shape. But a section of baseboard next to the kitchen doorway bore dark smudges along its upper edge.

"Hey," Tom said to one of the techs. "Help me with this."

He got on his knees next to the baseboard, the tech beside him. The tech seemed to know what Tom was after, and the two of them probed the seams with their gloved hands. A piece of baseboard wiggled fairly easily, and they pulled it away from the wall.

Behind the section of baseboard, the wall had been cut away, forming a long rectangular compartment. Tom took his flashlight and got low to the ground.

Just a small space, in between two framing studs, a couple inches deep, sixteen inches wide. Not a box, but something.

He turned to Gomez.

"Let's get the landlord back in here."

Gomez was staring into the hole, but he nodded and left to fetch Massey.

* * *

Derrick Massey stood in the living room, twitching, looking at the baseboard gap.

"Ever seen that before?" Tom asked.

"No. Huh-uh." He bent and stared in at the empty space. "You pull something out of it?"

"No. But there's room to store something in there, even stack something behind the drywall."

Massey stood upright. "Somebody's got to pay for that damage."

"Well . . ." Tom tucked his flashlight away and glanced at Gomez. ". . . That's what security deposits are for."

Tom looked at the tech lifting the prints from the baseboard, using the coffee table as a bench. It typically took between forty-eight and seventy-two hours to process elimination prints, so it would take at least that long to find out whether they belonged to Carrie, or if they were latents — unknowns. If they were latents even a priority response could still take a while.

The hidey-hole in the wall was very interesting, but just another piece of the puzzle for now.

* * *

He left the evidence techs to their work and consulted with the Tampa officers. They'd covered the twenty units and spoken to nine tenants, and no one recognized either Raymond Bosco or Steve Hobson. Only one had ever seen Carrie, and that was a month ago. She'd been alone, coming back from the grocery store.

"Keep up the good work, now the middle twenty units," Tom said, and the cops looked like they wanted to throw him off the balcony.

He headed for the strip club, wondering if this was the same route Carrie would have taken to work. He thought of her driving her green Hyundai along the Tampa streets. He thought of her about to dance for men who hooted and hollered, men like Derrick Massey, maybe, envisioning themselves taking her, devouring her. Was there pleasure in that? Did Carrie — or Sasha, or any of the rest of them for that matter — derive pleasure, knowing that they had something the spectators so desperately craved? Was it ever thrilling? Or degrading? Or just a job like any other?

Ahead of Tom, Gomez's unmarked car made a turn and Tom saw a familiar sight: the used car lot, strings of colored pennants flapping in the breeze. Across from the dealership, the plaza with the bakery, hair salon, and strip club. A bouncer, not Bosco, was sitting on the stool.

A Tampa cruiser parked in front, blocking the entrance. Tom found an available spot and parked more like a customer would. A second Tampa cruiser carrying two more uniformed officers pulled in and stopped near Gomez's car. Gomez had called in reinforcements. They all gathered in the parking lot, the bouncer glaring at them like it was business as usual.

Gomez said that the police visited the club regularly. There was at least one drunk and disorderly per week. Every month or so, a fight. Tom thought about the group of businessmen who'd acted like frat boys on Monday night. Tampa was rounding up some persons of interest for questioning.

"I want to pull any surveillance video from last Tuesday," Tom said. "And that includes any of these surrounding businesses, like the car dealership. Let's get basic statements from each employee, including the DJ. We're doing two things here — we're clarifying our timeline, and we're also wondering about anyone who might've taken a special interest in the victim. I'm going to look at employee records and Carrie's time sheet."

The quartet of Tampa cops went inside. Tom hung back for a moment while Gomez spoke with the bouncer. Jimmy was the day shift. Tampa PD had Bosco's phone number and would give him a call, ask him to come down to the club. Jimmy said he thought Bosco would be at home. "He sleeps most of the day cuz he's up all night."

Inside, everyone looked uncomfortable in the presence of the police. The music was thumping, a stripper doing her routine onstage, skin wet and glistening. Another was writhing over a man seated at the benches, his eyeglasses fogged up. The stripper threw her hair, arched her back, and thrust against the man's pelvis. But the man had clocked the cops. He spoke to the stripper, who turned, hands plunged into her voluminous hair, and stopped.

Sasha.

The girl on the stage had halted mid-routine, too. Jimmy had followed the police into the club and hustled over to the bartender. They spoke, heads together, and then Jimmy moved on to the DJ.

The DJ turned the volume down and made an announcement — the police had a few questions for the staff. The customers were asked to come back later.

Tom had the DJ show him to a cramped office where the time sheets were kept in a file cabinet. Carrie's file was right up front. He noted her last clock-in and clock-out and skimmed over her previous shifts. It was all as Sasha had reported.

While the Tampa cops gathered statements, Tom checked the bathrooms. The men's room was grimy, pungent with urinal cakes. The ladies room was nicer, smelled better.

He opened the side door where Sasha had emerged two nights before and peered out, noting the dumpsters, the quiet side road.

He returned inside and circled the room. He caught Sasha looking at him over a Tampa cop's shoulder.

Checking behind the bar, he stopped when he found a shotgun tucked up underneath. He waved Gomez over and pointed it out.

"Yeah, we're aware," Gomez said.

"Did you reach Bosco?"

"No answer. I sent a black and white over to his place."

"Good."

Tom hung back and watched the exchange between the Tampa officer and Sasha. He observed her body language — she became agitated. At one point the cop reached out and grabbed her arm.

"Hey, hey," Tom called. He started over as Sasha disappeared into the dressing room. Before she slammed the door, she flashed him an angry look. Like he'd betrayed her somehow.

The cop approached Tom with his hands in the air. "Relax, relax. She's agreed to a formal interview. She'll come downtown tomorrow and give us a full statement."

There was a star on the door, the kind you get backstage at a Broadway show. "Can you do me a favor?" Tom asked. "Follow her from here and see where she goes tonight. But leave her alone. I want to see what she does, who she talks to. Keep me updated."

CHAPTER SEVENTEEN

It was getting late in the afternoon as they drove through Tampa Heights, a working-class neighborhood. The house on North Morgan Street was quaint, surrounded by a white picket fence. An American flag hung from the front porch. There was one bushy palm tree in the yard, a large ficus beside the short dirt driveway where a white Honda CRV was parked.

Gomez stepped onto the porch and rapped on the front door, Tom behind him.

A warm breeze rustled the palm fronds overhead. Tom heard footsteps and the door opened. A short bearded man stood there. He was older than his picture, heavier, and wore glasses.

Gomez pulled his badge. "Steven R. Hobson?"

"Yeah? What's going on?"

Apparently Steve Hobson didn't watch the news. "Sorry for the late hour. I'm Detective Gomez, Tampa Police, this is Special Agent Lange. Were you married to Carrie Hobson? Carrie Gallo?"

His eyes flashed recognition. Then, concern. "Yeah . . . What is it? Is Carrie okay?"

"Can we come in, Mr. Hobson?"

Hobson tossed a look over his shoulder. Tom leaned in and saw a set of wooden stairs leading up to the second story. Hobson turned back to the cops. "Um, yeah. My son is napping, so . . ."

"We'll keep it quiet," Gomez assured.

Hobson hesitated, then pushed the door open the rest of the way. He brought them to a small kitchen, all yellow and white and old-fashioned. Tom thought the floor was canted at an angle. "Is this alright?" asked Hobson.

"This is great," Gomez said. They sat down at the little table by the window. There was a view of the next house and the car in Hobson's driveway.

Tom wanted Gomez to lead the questioning, and had said so before arriving. Gomez began, "This is your house, Mr. Hobson?"

"Yeah. I mean, I rent. What's wrong with Carrie?"

"Do you live here with anybody else?"

"It's just me and my son."

"How old is your son?"

"He's almost four." Hobson's eyes kept flicking between the cops.

"Just a couple more questions and then I'll explain. This isn't a formal interview, okay? You're not in any trouble. We're just looking to get some information on Carrie."

Gomez wore a pleasant, if detached expression. But Hobson was quick, intelligent. "Oh, I get it. Something happened to her, right? You're shaking me down."

Tom shared a glance with Gomez. "Why would you say that?" Gomez asked.

"Well, you're not telling me what happened because you're waiting to see if I give something away."

"Mr. Hobson," Gomez said, "let's keep calm."

"I'm calm. What happened to her? Shit, I knew something like this would happen someday." He rose from the table.

"Something like what? Sit down, please, Mr. Hobson."

Hobson glared at Gomez, then returned to his seat. "Something like whatever it is that brought you here. Whatever it is — and it's probably bad — and now you're jacking me up."

Tom wondered where Hobson had heard terms like 'shaking him down' and 'jacking him up.' Probably on TV, but you never knew.

Gomez leaned in. "When is the last time you spoke with your ex-wife?"

"Five months ago."

"You didn't have to think about that very long. You're sure?"

"Yeah, I'm sure. She needed money. That's why she called. It was just before Christmas."

"Did she say what she needed the money for? Presents, maybe?"

"No."

Tom did the calculation. Five months ago, Carrie had picked up the indecent exposure charge and had to pay a fine. Maybe that was it.

Gomez asked, "Did you give her any money?"

"No. And we haven't spoken since."

Tom made some quick notes, while Gomez continued, "What do you do for work, Mr. Hobson?"

"I'm a stay-at-home dad. That's my first job. And I do some online consulting."

"Can you explain that?"

"Marketing. I help people with their businesses. I got my BA in Marketing at Columbia. You can look me up. I'm on LinkedIn, Facebook, all of those. I do a little consulting, I also do a little bit of graphic design."

Tom had already looked him up. LinkedIn was where Tom had found the image of Hobson for the cops to shop around Carrie's building. Whatever work Hobson was doing, it didn't seem especially lucrative. The house they were sitting in probably rented for a thousand dollars a month, the car was an older model, affordable.

Tom set his notebook aside. Gomez settled in his seat, as if the Tampa detective knew what was coming. Tom thought they'd seen enough from Hobson to let him in.

"Carrie's body was found two mornings ago," Tom said.

Hobson absorbed the shock, at first only staring blankly, then looking out the window. His lower lip trembled for a moment, and he touched his face to stop it. He nodded, subtly, as if coming to terms with the cold fact. "Where?"

"Before we get into that — did Carrie ever tell you she was worried about anything? Confide in you that she had . . . I don't know, been the recipient of unwelcome attention? Or even that she had a stalker, anything like that?"

"My ex-wife is a stripper," Hobson said coolly. "I think that's welcomed attention, getting paid to have men look at you naked."

"Was Carrie in that line of work during your marriage?"

"No."

"So she never said anything to you, that she was worried, anything like that?"

"I told you, we haven't spoken in five months."

"What about before that?"

He shook his head. "We have talked exactly three times since she left. Once was about where to meet to sign the divorce papers. We did the online thing — the quick and easy. There was one other time she called me after that, and then the last call, five months ago, asking for money."

"And how about your son?" Tom asked. "Arranging custody? Placement?"

Hobson shook his head again. "Harley is my son. From another woman. Carrie was his stepmother."

Tom leaned back, considering this. He'd assumed the child was Carrie's biological offspring. He realized he'd been judging her, a little bit, thinking she'd abandoned her own child. But now that he found out he was her stepchild, his feeling changed, which he wasn't proud of.

"Okay. So, you met Carrie, where?"

"We met online. Match.com."

"Online," Tom repeated. Everything about this guy was online. But, Match.com tolled significant.

"I moved to Tampa from New Jersey four years ago. Well, a little over four years ago. I moved with my girlfriend at the time, who was pregnant with Harley. She got a job down here at the work release program in St. Pete's."

He meant St. Petersburg, which was next to Tampa, in Pinellas County. There was a State Work Release Program over there, a correctional facility.

"She's a case worker," Hobson explained. "Her name is Donna Pitt."

Tom took down the info. "You lived in this house with her? With Pitt?"

"No. We lived in Youngstown, about ten miles from her work. Look . . ."

Tom picked up on Hobson's tone. The man seemed increasingly uncomfortable.

". . . this is my personal life, okay? I'd really appreciate it if you could tell me a little something. Carrie is dead? Where was she found? What happened?"

Tom got the feeling there was infidelity in the background, perhaps Hobson meeting women on Match.com while he was still with Donna Pitt, or that Donna Pitt had been seeing someone while still with Hobson. Hobson was becoming nervous the closer they got to airing his dirty laundry.

"Did your ex-girlfriend, Pitt, did she ever meet Carrie?"

"Did they ever meet? Yeah, they met."

"How did they get along?"

Hobson gave Tom a look like he was crazy. It wasn't such a wild idea, Tom thought — people could behave like adults. There were amicable break-ups and healthy co-parenting examples all over. Just maybe not in this case.

"Donna gets Harley on the weekends. She'll be here Friday afternoon if you want to talk to her. You can ask *her* how she felt about Carrie."

"So you do have a custody arrangement? Just not with Carrie. But with Donna."

"Right. Donna works five days a week, and I have Harley. Then she gets him on weekends."

Tom considered the whole messy scenario. Maybe Carrie had left because of Donna. The biological mother resenting the stepmother. Something like that. But for now, he wanted to get back to Carrie working as a stripper. "You said she wasn't an exotic dancer when you were together . . ."

Hobson shifted in his chair. "She wasn't."

"So . . . what did she do?"

"Um, she was a dancer-dancer. She'd been in a few things, big shows. She got work for a little while at Disney World, in Orlando. But then, you know, things weren't so hot."

"How did you know she was working at a strip club?"

Hobson got a shrewd look. "She told me. When she asked me for money I said, 'You got a job?' And she said, 'Yes, for your information, I'm dancing.' And I said, 'You mean stripping,' and she was silent. I knew."

It was an interesting leap, inferring Carrie was a stripper when she'd said dancer. "Had Carrie worked as a stripper before?"

Hobson looked nervous. "No. Maybe. I don't know."

"Okay."

"I just had a feeling."

Tom let it rest, and shifted the inquiry. "Did Carrie use any drugs?"

Hobson tensed up again. Tom would bet there was a small stash of weed somewhere in the house — he'd caught the sweet scent of marijuana upon entering.

"Not to my knowledge."

"Did Carrie get along with her family? Was she close with them?"

"She wasn't. Not really. She showed me a birthday text from her mother once."

"When was that?"

"I dunno. Over a year ago."

"So, you met online — Match.com — and that was . . . how long ago?"

More tension — a runlet of sweat tracked down Hobson's cheek. "Three years ago. We were married for ten months. Okay? No-fault divorce. I spoke with her a couple times after it was final, that's it. Now will you tell me what happened to her?"

Tom gave Gomez another look. Neither man thought it was the right choice to give up the details just yet — Hobson could still hang himself, if he was culpable. He had something to hide, Tom was sure. Maybe about Carrie's past. Perhaps about her murder.

"Did she have a computer when she lived here? Her own personal laptop?"

Hobson threw up his hands, frustrated. "No, okay? Carrie hates computers. She lives for her phone, though."

The atmosphere grew awkward as Hobson realized he'd referred to Carrie in the present-tense. Embarrassed, he lowered his head.

That wasn't what interested Tom. He asked Hobson to excuse him and Detective Gomez. "Sit tight," Tom said.

* * *

They spoke in the hallway, whispering.

“The phone could be in the house,” Tom said.

“Could be.”

“If the phone is here, now that we’ve questioned him, he might get rid of it before I can get a crew to search. So I’m going to ask him about it, get the make and carrier.”

Gomez just stared, Tom’s own doubts reflected in the man’s wide face. “Or,” Gomez said, “You keep him talking while I have a look.”

“Won’t work. This guy is paranoid. Guilty conscience, weed in the house, or something.”

“Or he’s a murderer.”

“You find something, we arrest him, it’s not ‘search incident to arrest,’ it’s the other way around. He lawyers up and the phone data could be inadmissible in court.”

“You state guys . . .” Gomez rolled his eyes.

Tom walked back into the kitchen. “So was Carrie’s phone a smartphone? All the bells and whistles? Know what brand?”

Hobson seemed grateful the cops were done with their secret powwow. “Oh, she had the latest. I mean, she was a total technophobe with computers, just couldn’t figure them out. But her phone . . . I think the interface is more, I dunno — female friendly? I don’t mean to sound sexist.”

Tom waved his hand in dismissal. “Do you remember the carrier?”

“Well, she had AT&T when we were together. I don’t know if she changed it.”

Gomez retook his seat at the table.

“Great,” Tom said to Hobson. “What about her email? Do you have her email address?”

“Sure, yeah, I remember it.” He gave Tom the address, and got a certain look in his eye.

Now it was time to cut to the quick. “Where were you last Wednesday and Thursday nights?”

Hobson blinked. “I don’t know — here?”

"Can someone, maybe Donna Pitt, maybe your son, corroborate that?"

Hobson glanced between Tom and Gomez. His face reddened with anger. "My son? Yeah, my four-year-old son is going to tell you about a week ago? And Donna? Why would my ex know anything?"

They would dig into his alibi later, at a formal interview.

Hobson turned to look out the window again.

"Last question," Tom said. "Do you have a key to Carrie's apartment?"

Hobson's head snapped around. "No, I don't have a key. Look, I'm not stupid. You say informal interview. But you want to talk to me anymore, you want to snoop around, I want to see a warrant. And I want a lawyer."

* * *

Tom drove back to Naples, the sun setting over the Gulf. It had been a long day in Tampa. The faces of Sasha and Steve Hobson drifted through his mind, snippets of conversation replayed on a loop. Hobson was hiding something, and Sasha definitely knew something, too. The cops needed to talk to Bosco, but he wasn't home or answering his calls, and Gomez seemed reluctant to press harder, like his hands were tied. And Gomez was with a department which prioritized gangs and drugs over homicides.

Tom finally arrived home in the dark, and saw something sitting on the ground in front of the garage door. It was a large Tupperware with spaghetti and meatballs inside.

Charlene.

Tom brought the food inside and ate it cold. When he was finished he called Blythe and debriefed her. Then he hit the pillow, and fell into a fitful, dreaming sleep.

Tommy . . . Tommy help me.

CHAPTER EIGHTEEN

THURSDAY

The early heat hammered down like a blowtorch and the sweat broke his skin. It was now seventy-two hours since Carrie's body had been found in the bay. Tom hurried into the field office.

Blythe was waiting inside. She dropped the murder book on the table with a loud smack. It had grown considerably thicker. She went about fixing some coffee while Tom leaned over the desk and reviewed their progress.

"We're going to talk to Coby," she said.

He looked up. "Okay . . . I want to talk to you about Gomez, too."

She turned and folded her arms, coffee burbling behind her. "Where did you go the other night?"

It didn't follow, but he knew exactly what she was talking about. He decided to stall, anxiety creeping up his neck. "What do you mean? You mean after we had dinner?"

She nodded, staring across the room at him. "Tuesday night."

"Nowhere. I went home."

He felt like she already knew the truth. He blushed. "I talked to McDermott," he admitted. How the hell had she known?

"Your friend's boyfriend."

"Her *ex*-boyfriend. I just had a talk with him."

"Uh-huh. Well, Agent Lange, people see things, people talk. Some deputies go to Ty's. Sandy, the bartender, knows them all. He talked about a cop who came in, apparently, and had some choice words with McDermott."

"God. It's like a fucking sewing circle . . ."

She cocked an eyebrow. "Did you threaten McDermott?"

"We talked over some beers."

Her face was inscrutable. The coffee wasn't finished brewing yet, but she turned her back and poured a cup anyway. He imagined bitter black sludge. Blythe drank it up and smacked her lips. "Anything you want to share with me, Lange?"

"I talked to the State Attorney's office about my friend, Alicia."

Blythe raised her eyebrows. "Who'd you speak to? Staithe?"

"Yeah. She advised me to have Alicia seek an injunction."

"But Alicia doesn't want to."

"No. She doesn't want anything to do with it."

"Well, if she's scared, an injunction for protection is the best thing she can do." Blythe tipped her mug at him. "You, Lange, are not such protection."

"I know."

She took another sip, her eyes locked on him. She set the cup aside. "I'm thinking of having Turnbull reassign you."

He felt struck. "What? Why?"

"Look, I expected a little impatience. Everybody comes into this game thinking they're going to get the bad guys the next day."

"I don't think I'm gonna—"

"Shut up and let me talk." She pushed away from the countertop and paced the small room. "If you did what I think you did the other night — if you threatened this guy to stay away from your friend and used this case to do it . . . you could lose your job. Like *that*." She snapped her fingers, the sound loud in the small room.

Tom felt his stomach twist but he kept quiet.

"This case has gotten too personal for you. You stepped over the line with him. Just like you stepped over the line running up to Tampa before you consulted with me."

She stopped pacing and fixed on him. "I don't know whether you feel you've got something to prove — to me or yourself — but you've got two big strikes. One more, and I'll get you reassigned to Governor Protection. That seems to be what you want to do anyway — put yourself in harm's way. What I want to do is solve a case."

He felt trapped by Blythe here in the field office. He'd been the one running around Tampa all day yesterday while she did God-knows-what. She was talking about getting him transferred — demoted, really — and what did Coburn have to do with any of this?

"Good. Let's solve the fucking case," he said. "You can start by telling me what you've been doing all this time. Or why Tampa sent me a narc instead of a homicide investigator who acted like I was keeping him awake. If there's something going on with drug trafficking, why am I out of the loop?"

She stared at him for a moment. "A guy was pulled over late last night by the Sheriff's Office. Deputies served a warrant on his Dodge pickup. There was a suitcase in the truck bed. Inside, deputies found 45.9 kilograms of cocaine."

Tom felt his mood change. "Holy shit. That's a street value of — what? A million and a half?"

She nodded. "1.6 million."

He whistled, the reprimand from Blythe temporarily forgotten. "How did they get him?"

"Press conference will be later this morning. They're going to say what they always say. 'It was a random stop.' Probably illegal tint on the windows, busted taillight, something like that. I haven't seen the report."

"But it's bullshit."

She shrugged, sipped her coffee, looking over the rim at him. "A narcotic-sniffing dog alerted on an area in the bed of the pickup hidden by a tonneau cover. That's where they found the case with the drugs. What do you think?"

"I think vice narcotics was working a drug op that pinpointed this guy."

Her look lingered, and he knew she agreed. Or maybe she knew. What he didn't understand was how it connected up to Carrie Hobson, so he asked, nicer this time.

"A bust of this size will have a ripple effect," Blythe said. "When this much cocaine is taken off the street, price goes up, quality goes down. And the pickup driver, guy named George Parsons, he's looking at a hard stretch. And he's old, with priors."

"You think he'll talk."

"Maybe, maybe he'll just take it and die in prison. But it's going to shake things up. Coby's team will monitor that like a hawk."

Tom felt like Blythe was evading his question, still withholding. She didn't trust him — and could he blame her? Yet he dared to press her. "If it's drug-related — and you still haven't told me what the connection is — why was Carrie Hobson killed with a blow to the head? Why not shot?"

"I don't know. Because the criminals are educated? Repeat offenders, they adapt, get smarter. They even learn from TV cop shows. So maybe by blunt force trauma they avoid the chance of ballistic fingerprinting matching a gun? It could be anything."

Tom walked across the small space, grabbed a mug out of the chintzy cabinet above the counter and poured himself some coffee. It was still bitter, but he needed to clear his mind. Blythe was right, he'd been impulsive and unprofessional with McDermott.

"I'm sorry," he said.

They were silent for a moment.

"There was a high speed chase," Blythe finally said. "This was back when I was a trooper. Everglades County was involved, Lee County, FHP, all of us. Two suspects tearing it up, doing a hundred-plus miles an hour. One of the deputies from Lee County was this guy I didn't like. I'd had words with him in the past. He was Zone A in Lee County, District Three. And that was around where I was usually stationed. So we'd butted heads. Anyway, this deputy, he claims he gets a visual on the bad guys. Says they appear to be juveniles. So we had to give up chase."

Tom understood. He listened to Blythe intently, realizing it was the most personal she'd gotten with him since they'd met.

"And then the bad guys ended up colliding with another car, T-boning it, killing the passengers." Her eyes alighted on him. "The passengers included one thirteen-year-old boy."

"Oh man . . ."

"That was twenty years ago," Blythe said. "Seven years later, I moved from the highway patrol and into the agency. That deputy from Lee County had risen through the ranks and was a captain. There was an investigation. The captain was keeping drug money, dealing, even involved in two murders. That's when I met Coby, during that investigation. It took us six months to build the case. And we put him away."

Tom tried on a smile. "Bet that felt good."

"Point is, I wanted that son of a bitch for almost eight years before I got him."

Tom dropped his gaze and nodded soberly. She was telling him, once again, to be patient. The wheels of justice were slow to turn. He knew she was right. If she wanted to bring Coburn in and entertain a possible drug connection to their Rookery Bay victim, she had the experience and he needed to trust her, even if he didn't know the why. Maybe she didn't, either, and was working off a hunch.

"And that's why we've got Gomez," Tom said.

"Gomez knows the drug scene. If there's anything to it, he's the guy to spot it. But you're the homicide investigator on this, not him. It's your show."

Tom nearly told her Gomez hadn't spotted diddly shit in Carrie's apartment, namely, the hidey-hole in the wall, exactly the type of place someone would hide drugs, but he thought it best to keep it to himself.

He set down his coffee and ran a hand over his face. Something else crossed his mind and he asked, "What color was Parsons' truck?"

"What *color* was it?"

"Yeah. With the coke in the back."

"Blue. Why?"

"Nothing."

Blythe watched him a moment, then sat down at her desk. She feathered her hands over her MacBook keyboard. The screen blinked on with her prompt.

"They've had George Parsons' phone contacts for a while." She brought up her email and Tom leaned in to read the message. She continued speaking as he scanned it — a note from Coburn.

"I made a request to Coby after Parsons' arrest, asking him for Parsons' contact list. Coby's team refers to any cellular customer they're tracking as a 'subscriber.' So, there are several subscribers in the Tampa Bay area. But these guys get tricky, and don't use their real names, just aliases — Daffy Duck, Elmer Fudd. Real creative stuff."

Tom pulled the chair over from the next desk. "They know they're being watched."

"Well, they protect themselves, but they don't always know. In fact, one of them was tracked to this location just a week ago." She opened another window, a map of Tampa, with an arrow pinpointing the location. Tom looked closer, envisioning the used car lot, the plaza, the strip club and the dead-end street.

"Holy shit."

"Coby doesn't have the subscriber's ID yet. The alias for this one is Wile E. Coyote. We don't know if it was a customer yet or an employee, but we know someone Parsons was talking to was at that club."

"What are the times?"

"They're not always tracking every subscriber. So it could be multiple times. But they were getting ready to move on Parsons a week ago, then something happened — Coby hasn't said what — and they backed off. At that time they were actively surveilling Coyote and had his location at Hush. We know he was there last Sunday, from six thirty-two to eight forty-four in the evening."

Tom thought the times made it more likely to be a customer than an employee. But, like Blythe had said, drug gangs were getting smarter. They swapped phones frequently.

Or, it could be as simple as an employee — he was thinking about Bosco, maybe even Sasha — who was there for a little while, then left.

"Where did Coyote go after that?"

Blythe turned to face Tom. "This is where it gets dicey. These are very quiet operations."

"I'm sure any vice narcotics operations are protected by court order."

"Exactly. Vice narcotics operate under the Sheriff, who is the law of the land, a servant of the people, authority protected by the Florida constitution. We start poking around with our murder case, questioning people based on data we got from a large-scale narcotics operation, it could blow the whole thing for them. Coby was reluctant to share even this much. We have to use what we can and go it alone for now."

Tom soaked this in, thinking Blythe had the unquestionable lead here. She'd already deferred to him on a few things, like having him observe the autopsy and taking point in Tampa. She would ferret out the possible drug connection, with Gomez's help. For now, she was looking at Tom to get back on track, make the right moves — his first week and already his career was hanging by a thread.

"We need Carrie Hobson's data," Tom said. "I want to subpoena AT&T, her carrier. And she has a Gmail address, and a Match.com account."

Blythe nodded, a subtle glint in her eye. "Right. That's the route we can go for now. Get to work on it."

* * *

Tom walked out into the bright sunshine and took a path through the landscaped trees towards the County Courthouse. The freshly planted palms had structural supports around the base and were yet to develop fronds — just green shoots sprouting for now. One thing he'd come to notice about Southwest Florida was the lack of shade trees. People planted palms to give the place that tropical look, but it was otherwise a concrete world baking in the heat.

He slipped inside the courthouse and endured the process of entry through the metal detector. A security guard ran a wand over his body while Tom stood like a scarecrow.

Police could get phone records without a warrant thanks to *Smith v. Maryland*, a ruling which found the Fourth Amendment protection against unreasonable search and seizure didn't apply to a list of phone numbers. That was very helpful for someone like Coburn, with large-scale drug ops requiring wiretaps and all sorts of surveillance. It also greased the wheels for Tom, who wanted the phone data for a homicide victim. But it still required mounds of paperwork.

Tom opted to take the stairs up to the County prosecutor's third-floor office suite, to keep his train of thought uninterrupted. His footsteps echoed in the cool stairwell as he ascended.

The courts hadn't issued a definitive ruling on social websites, but most were stringent about warrants, and Match.com was one of them. Tom could view her public profile, but he wanted Carrie's private messages, and that meant data from other, living people. The same privacy laws protecting people under Coburn's surveillance protected people on dating sites. And unlike subpoenas, warrants and court orders required judicial review.

He gathered the forms he needed with the help of a young clerk and found a quiet spot to sit and get to work.

Gleaning location data from Carrie's phone would be the hardest of all. Every U.S. cell phone was required to have some type of location-based technology. The technology enabled emergency dispatch centers to find a 911 caller's real-time location and number. And all cell phones registered their locations with the cellular networks several times a minute. But, phone carriers tended to use one of two methods: using satellites, or, triangulation based on cell towers. Steve Hobson said Carrie had used a smartphone, which accessed a Wi-Fi network and could disclose more or less precise information about the phone's location depending on how the ISP provided the wireless connection. It was a toss-up which kind Carrie's phone had used — which meant double duty for the subpoenas.

All this paperwork and nothing would come of it for at least twenty-four hours. Tom wanted the files in Carrie's phone that could reveal her past communications as well as her locations. He wanted to see her private messages on Match.com. But the law would make him wait.

CHAPTER NINETEEN

By one o'clock in the afternoon, Tom was ravenous. He felt edgy after spending the morning pushing papers. There was a plaza two blocks from the County Courthouse with a Mexican restaurant called *Amigos*. He slipped in to the dimly lit room, found a booth, and ordered the special — shredded beef empanadas. He devoured the complimentary tortilla chips, and stared out into the bright street.

When the food came he wolfed it down. Halfway through the meal he started to feel human again and took out the murder book.

He hunched over it, starting with the timeline. Steve Hobson moved from Jersey to Tampa four years ago, with his girlfriend Donna Pitt, who was pregnant with their son, Harley. Three years ago, Steve Hobson met Carrie on Match.com.

Tom pulled out his phone, found the dating site and searched for Carrie Anne Gallo. There she was, Midwestern-fresh with sandy hair. The picture was tasteful, showing her from the waist up, modeling a frilly teal blouse. Her smile revealed rows of white teeth.

He browsed her profile. *Just a small town girl who loves to dance, looking for fun and adventure with a companion.* That was it, short and sweet. She listed her interests as reading, hiking, swimming, snorkeling, and kayaking.

Tom grew still.

Kayaking.

He closed the browser and made a quick note, then called the Sheriff's Office and asked to speak to Katie Mills, with the County crime scene bureau. A deputy forwarded the call to her cell phone.

Mills answered, the connection scratchy.

"Katie, it's Tom Lange."

"Hi Tom. Been expecting to hear from you."

"Yeah. This case has moved in about ten different directions at once. How's things on your end?"

"Good. We're getting ready to fold up our tent here at the estuary." Tom could hear the wind blowing around her.

"What's the story down there?"

"Not much to tell, I'm sorry. We can't even disinfect the site where the body was found." She gave a small laugh. "First, it's protected. Second, you know, it's water."

He chuckled. "Yeah, kind of tough for clean-up. Listen — what's the word on the kayaks? Any other boats found, anything like that?"

"The word is the same. All Susan Libby's boats are present and accounted for. No one else had any boats go missing."

"And nobody's found a missing kayak paddle, nothing like that."

"No, definitely not."

"Alright, thanks, Katie." He hung up and went back to Match.com. One thing his criminology professors had driven home was that there were no coincidences in investigations. Everything always meant something.

He wondered if someone had lured Carrie to Rookery Bay, promising a kayaking trip through the mangrove canals.

"Anything else?"

The waitress made him jump. He smiled. "No, thanks." She took his plates away and he handed her his debit card before she left.

He turned his attention back to the timeline in the murder book.

Steve Hobson and Carrie were married for ten months. According to Steve Hobson, the couple had divorced eighteen months ago. Hobson had the divorce certificate to prove it and said Carrie had moved out that same month. But Derrick Massey, the shifty landlord, had records indicating Carrie began renting twelve months ago. That left a six-month gap.

Tom flipped to the copy of Carrie's DMV abstract. According to it, Carrie's address was in Tampa Heights. She hadn't updated her driver's license with her new address, and Derrick Massey hadn't required Carrie to list her previous residences.

Tom didn't know where Carrie had been living in between the rented house in Tampa Heights and her apartment in East Tampa. Maybe she'd gone home to Boise, Idaho, for a few months.

He grabbed the tab for the section marked "Family" and opened it up. Eileen Gallo, Carrie's mother, had booked a flight for ten that morning. Tom glanced at his watch — it was one-thirty now. Eileen Gallo would be flying in any moment, and making her way to the Medical Examiner's Office. Like any grieving family member, she would want answers. She would also want her daughter's body released to her right away. And chances were, she'd be upset an autopsy had been conducted without her knowledge.

He pulled some photos of Carrie's body at the death scene, then looked at some from the autopsy. Ward wouldn't confirm it yet, but the death looked to be from blunt force trauma to the base of her skull. Someone had hit her with something from behind, killing her.

Like a paddle, Tom thought.

He couldn't get the kayak scenario out of his head.

Or the stain found on Carrie's clothing — just a tiny splotch of blood on her shorts.

The kayaking concerned him, Carrie's finances also concerned him.

Back to the timeline: Sasha claimed that Carrie had been working at Hush for a year. That was consistent with what Massey said and confirmed by Carrie's employment records.

Sasha said Carrie did well working at Hush — just that Carrie blew her money on frivolous things. But Tom hadn't seen anything flashy in Carrie's apartment. Steve Hobson said Carrie asked for a loan five months ago. Tampa had arrested Carrie at the same time and charged her with indecent exposure. It was highly probable that the money she'd asked Steve for was to pay the fine, but Tom couldn't be certain.

The monthly payment on her sensible car was two hundred a month, her apartment cost eight hundred, not much for city living. Yet she'd taken an extra job stripping at a bachelor party. And such parties happened all the time. Tom bet Carrie had done more than one gig. She was earning this extra money, no signs of big expenses, and yet she asked her ex-husband for cash and her co-worker said she was broke?

So where was the money going?

A drug problem was one answer, but nothing circumstantial so far pointed to drug abuse. With the blood toxicology report still in the pipeline, however, Tom couldn't know for sure.

"Here you go." The waitress was back with the receipt. She was giving him a strange look. He realized some of the crime scene photos were showing and quickly closed the murder book.

"Do you kayak at all?"

The waitress just stared, then blushed and shook her head.

"Sorry," he said clumsily. "Thanks."

She moved off, and he drummed the table with his fingers, thinking. Carrie's last shift at Hush had been the previous Tuesday. Now Tom and Blythe had this new information from vice narcotics — Wile E. Coyote, or his phone, at least, had been at Hush for approximately two hours the Sunday evening prior to Carrie's final worked shift.

Then, after that Tuesday shift had ended at 7 p.m., Carrie disappeared. According to Ward, she was murdered sometime between Wednesday and Friday morning.

Tom grabbed his things and left. On his way out he rang the ROC and asked for Kurt Bronson, who had headed the forensic team deployed to Carrie's apartment the previous day.

"Was just going to call your office," Bronson said. "We're analyzing all the prints — should have that later today. DNA will take longer. But what I can say now is that there is no evidence of a crime committed in the victim's apartment. No blood, nothing broken, everything peaceful and quiet."

"Thank you," Tom said.

Blythe called while Tom was hurrying back to the field office. "Eileen Gallo just arrived at the ME's office. We're going over. Where are you? I'll pick you up."

CHAPTER TWENTY

Eileen Gallo was a frail-looking woman, her eyes bunched with sorrow. She wore pleated white slacks and a flowery blouse and had short, bleached-blonde hair. Tom could see her resemblance to Carrie in her nose and cheekbones. She sat with her hands clasped together, across from Tom, Blythe, and Dr. Ward in a special room used for just such sad, but necessary conferences.

At first she was quiet, as Ward explained that the investigation into her daughter's death was being conducted by the Medical Examiner's Office, the Everglades County Sheriff's Office, and the FDLE.

"Is that what you call a task force?" Eileen Gallo asked, her big eyes going back and forth between the three of them.

Blythe smiled politely. "Something like that. Mrs. Gallo, I understand you lost your husband?"

"Yes. He got the cancer. Died two years ago."

"I'm so sorry to hear that. Is there anyone else you'd like here? Have you been in touch with your daughters?"

"Well, sure I have. Catherine is tied up at work but she's going to try to get here. Cindy is . . . well, I have trouble talking to Cindy sometimes."

Ward jumped in, explaining in general terms that the autopsy had been necessary, and Carrie was being treated with the utmost care and respect. "Everything is being done to find out what happened to her." Tom noted how Ward omitted the words *homicide* and *killer*.

Eileen nodded at Ward's remarks. She seemed shocked, somewhat uncomprehending. "So I'll see her now? I don't want to just look at photos. I was very clear on the phone, I want to see her in person."

"Yes," said Ward. "But we ought to discuss the funeral arrangements."

Eileen stood up. Her forehead knotted in a frown. "Well, I'll be taking her home to Boise. No need for that here . . ."

Ward looked at the agents, and Blythe rose to her feet. "Mrs. Gallo, your daughter is still part of an ongoing investigation."

"I read about this," Eileen said. "Performance of an autopsy does not interfere with having the body on view at the funeral. That's what it said. Carrie was my beautiful girl. My youngest baby. Her friends and loved ones have a right to see her, say their goodbyes." The woman's lower lip was trembling, her eyes shining with grief and determination.

"Of course. Do—"

"Mrs. Gallo. Are you prepared for such a transportation?" Ward cut Blythe off. "Grieving family members like yourself often don't even know where to begin, and can make the mistake of relying upon their local funeral home, who may not be versant with the complexities of mortuary shipping."

Tom felt like saying something — Eileen seemed so vulnerable standing there, clutching her purse, lip quivering.

"You have every right to take Carrie home," Ward intoned. "But it is an ordeal and you shouldn't have to do it alone. On your own, you'd need to contract a funeral home in the area for ship-out service and then you'll also need the services of a funeral home at the destination airport that can handle collection, import protocol, and manage the ongoing funeral arrangements . . ."

It was an ambush. Eileen Gallo looked flustered and upset. Tom stood up, feeling his temperature rise.

"If you work with us, Mrs. Gallo," Ward rushed on, cutting Tom a glance, "together with the dispatching funeral home we will coordinate everything on your behalf — collection and removal, embalming, filing of documents, a combination-shipping unit and delivery to the departure airport. The service we typically work with is well established and has expertise in mortuary shipping, and will have a funeral contact in Boise."

Tom felt increasingly sympathy for the woman as she sat back down. Ward, who'd never gotten out of his chair, had subdued her. With his flat expression, Tom couldn't help but feel the medical examiner derived some perverse pleasure from this. Like being in control got him off. Tom and Blythe took their seats again.

"Well, sure we can do all that after I see her?" Eileen asked. She took a wadded tissue from her purse and wiped her nose with it, hand shaking.

"Of course," Ward said. "Just one more thing first. These officers need to ask you a few questions."

It was about time.

Eileen Gallo reluctantly turned her attention to the agents. She took a deep breath. "Okay."

Blythe began, "When did you last speak to your daughter, Mrs. Gallo?"

"About two weeks ago. On a Wednesday."

Tom figured the woman had had plenty of time to recall that final conversation since learning of her daughter's death, playing it over and over in her mind. It reminded him of something — he had yet to listen to the 911 call. Everglades County had listened to it and the transcript was in the murder book. But he'd yet to hear if for himself.

"And what was the nature of that conversation, do you remember?"

"Sure I do. She asked me how I was doing. She was always concerned about me." Eileen Gallo's lip quivered.

"What else?"

"We spoke about the weather. How hot it was in Florida. We had a late snow in Boise. I had the neighbor's boy, that's Finn, come over and shovel the driveway. I pay him ten dollars."

"Good to have that help. So Carrie seemed alright? Did she talk about anything in her life? Anything specific?"

The tears fell, but Eileen Gallo didn't seem to notice. She shook her head. "No. Carrie didn't talk about herself. She was more concerned with other people. With me."

"It sounds like she was a wonderful daughter."

Now Eileen Gallo's chest hitched with a sob, and her word was nearly lost — "Yes."

"I know this is hard," Blythe said. Tom thought Blythe was something else. Her tone was smooth and genuine, real empathy on her face. "Did you know what Carrie did for work, Mrs. Gallo?"

Tom had been wondering the same thing.

Eileen Gallo's forehead rumpled again. "Well, yah. She worked as a dancer. Big shows, and that."

Tom looked at Blythe, who kept her gaze on the older woman. "Where did she dance?"

"She traveled all over. She worked in Disney World off and on. But she did other shows — concerts, you know." The frown deepened and Eileen looked between the agents. "You don't know what she did for a living?"

Tom waited to see how Blythe would handle this. Blythe went straight for the unvarnished truth. "She also worked as a dancer at a gentlemen's club called Hush. It's in Tampa."

The room fell silent. Tom glanced at Ward, but the man's face was unreadable.

Eileen Gallo seemed to be stuck, not knowing how to accept this. "A gentlemen's club?"

"Yes," said Blythe, not faltering. "A strip club."

"No. You're mistaken, there."

"We have her employee records. It was actually thanks to one of her co-workers we were able to first identify Carrie."

Tom thought Eileen Gallo took it rather well. After her initial incredulity, she seemed to resign herself to the idea. "I didn't know."

Blythe moved right on to the next question. "Mrs. Gallo, do you know Steve Hobson, Carrie's ex-husband?"

The woman's face darkened. It happened so suddenly Tom was surprised. Eileen Gallo's tears dried up. Her mouth dipped down at the corners as she spoke with a quiet, conspiratorial tone. "Yes, I know Steve."

"According to Steve Hobson, Carrie hadn't spoken with him in five months. Is that consistent with the information you have?"

"Carrie was not the type to talk poorly of other people, you know. But she didn't have to. I knew that Steve Hobson was no good."

"How did you know?"

"He didn't treat her right. He was always on his computer. I think he met women that way." Eileen wrinkled her nose. "I don't think much of that. Computer dating, or whatever you call it. Carrie never said, but I think that's how she met Steve. On her *phone*, if you can believe it. Using it as a computer, I guess. I think she was lonely. Her life on the road, all the coming and going. But you can get involved with some real bad eggs that way."

"And you think Steve Hobson is a bad egg."

"I think he uses that son of his, that poor boy, to attract kind-hearted people like my daughter. He acts like he is the . . . well, see, now I'm speaking ill." She shook her head.

"Had Carrie talked to him more recently than five months ago, to your knowledge?"

"Not that I know of. But she didn't say a lot about herself. And I tried not to pry."

"Mrs. Gallo, do you think Steve Hobson might've had something to do with what happened to Carrie?"

The woman looked mortified by the thought, but there was still that hard glint to her eye. "I think you need to ask him that."

"I know you don't like to speak negatively about people, Mrs. Gallo. I think that is very noble of you. But I really would like to hear what you think, just plainly. Is Steve Hobson capable of hurting someone, of hurting your daughter?"

"Who isn't capable?" Eileen said, taking a turn for darker territory. "We all have it in us."

Blythe leaned back and gave Tom a look. He took it as an invitation to ask his own questions and cleared his throat. "Mrs. Gallo, I'm so sorry for your loss. I only want to ask one thing, and then Dr. Ward can take you to your daughter."

Eileen glanced at Ward, who was still sitting there like some kind of chaplain.

"This is a personal question," Tom said, "but it's important. Was Carrie sending you any money?"

Eileen blinked at him, hesitant. Her thoughts seemed to clear and she said, "Yes. Carrie was always concerned about me. Clifford — that's her late father — he struggled. He had a temper . . . it wasn't his fault. He had a tough career. Then when he got the cancer . . . We had a lot of trouble with our insurance." Eileen dropped her eyes. "There are a lot of bills left still, even two years later."

"About how much was she sending you?"

Her head came back up, and he could see it wounded her to talk about. "A little here, a little there." She got to her feet again. "I want to see my daughter now."

* * *

The four of them entered the viewing area, where they were joined by Andrea. The storage area was connected to both the main autopsy suite and the viewing room, the door laden with heavy locks on the viewing room side. Tom and Blythe waited with Eileen Gallo while Ward undid the locks and disappeared into the storage vault.

Tom looked around the room, which was appointed like a funeral parlor. Threadbare carpet, a potted plant on an alabaster plinth against each of the two side walls. A pair of wing-back chairs, pastel pink, a table between them, magazines fanned out. A long chest of drawers against the opposite wall, various vases and urns for decoration. He saw a directory of funeral services and a brochure for one in particular — *Young & Sons*. Tom bet that was the "well-established" mortuary service Ward had spoken of. Ward had been like a salesman in the conference room. Tom figured it came with the territory. Still, the guy continued to irk him.

"I thought Ward was going to ask for her credit card right then and there," Tom whispered to Blythe.

She seemed distracted. "Yeah."

"What's with you and Ward?"

Her eyes focused on Tom. "What do you mean?"

"I just . . . You two remind me of people waiting for the divorce papers. Hardly ever in the same room, and when you are, you don't talk."

There was music playing faintly through speakers in the wall, classical, Tom thought it was Mahler. Blythe just looked at him, then moved away.

Tom's phone vibrated in his pocket. It was Nick. Tom had continued to ignore Nick's calls but he was getting worried. Blythe nodded her head at the door, indicating he could leave, take the call. He apologized and stepped into the hallway.

"Nick, I'm at work. I can't talk."

"Bro," Nick said.

"What is it?"

"I need a ride, man."

"You gotta be kidding . . . Why? What's wrong with the Escalade?"

"I sold it. Well, you know, I'm using it to—"

"Jesus, Nicky . . ." Tom figured it out. Nick was turning over his luxury SUV to pay down his poker debt.

"Hey, it was either that or liquidate the office. And I love that office, man."

Despite the grave circumstances, Nick sounded upbeat, almost cheery. That meant he was either having one of his manic episodes, or he was using, or both. Maybe drinking, too. Tom looked at his watch. It was going on three in the afternoon. "I can't do anything for you right now, Nick. How about tonight? I'm in the middle of this thing . . ."

"It's gotta be today. Bonita Springs, six p.m. That's when I gotta meet the guy, turn over the vehicle. I need a ride back, Tommy."

"Take a bus. Call a cab. I'm up to my ears in a murder case."

"Please, Tommy."

Tom closed his eyes and massaged his temples. Taking care of Nick was enabling him. That was what Dr. Camden would say, anyway. But, Tom couldn't help it. Nick could've called a car service or made do with public transportation, but he hadn't. He obviously needed support. Tom opened his eyes.

"Alright. Give me a few minutes to get free here and then I'll be at your place."

"Oh man, thanks, Tommy. Really, tha—"

Tom hung up and stared at the door to the mortuary viewing room, debating whether he was going to tell Blythe the truth or make something up.

The second he stepped through the door, he sensed his presence was an intrusion. Ward, presiding over the body, gave him an annoyed look.

Carrie was draped in a cloth, only her face visible, her skin waxen. They had combed her hair, but it looked terribly thin and dried out. Eileen stood beside Ward, racked with tremors, tears falling.

Blythe escorted Tom out of the room and closed the door softly behind her. "We can give her a few minutes."

"I need to go."

Blythe raised her eyebrows.

"It's my brother," Tom said, and left it at that.

Blythe studied him. "When will you be done?"

"Should just be a couple hours."

"The meeting with Coby is eight o'clock. We've each got to read the full affidavit in order for vice narcotics to share anything with us. Then we might find out who Coyote is. If it's Raymond Bosco, I'm going to want to move on it right away. Have Tampa pick him up for questioning, tell him it's follow-up, routine questions about Carrie."

"I hear you, loud and clear. Two hours."

He hustled away.

Outside, the day was darkening as an afternoon storm rolled in. Tom wondered if it was another pump-fake, or if this one would finally unleash.

Jumping in the Jeep he thought, if it turned out Bosco was working with George Parsons, and was part of the cocaine trafficking out of Everglades City, then they would have to seriously consider Carrie's death drug-related. It lined up easily enough — cocaine being distributed from the strip club, maybe the dancers doing some of the selling, a dime bag here or there to a gentleman customer. Guys like those young execs who'd caused a stir.

CHAPTER TWENTY-ONE

Tom pulled up to Nick's house. The sky was heavy with thunderheads. The Escalade was in the driveway. Thunder rumbled and Tom beeped the horn. When Nick didn't come out right away, Tom wandered into the backyard. He stared out at the creek, remembering how all the waterways were connected. He could get in a boat right now and make his way to the open ocean from Nick's backyard. He could also make his way from here to Rookery Bay.

"Tommy?"

Nick was calling from out front. Tom walked around the house.

"Hey man," Nick said. "You ready?"

When Tom wore a suit, he looked like he belonged in a board room. When Nick dressed up, he looked like some kind of gangster. The brothers stood sizing each other up. Then Tom moved to the Jeep, feeling sour. "Yeah, I'm ready."

"Look, if this is going to be a big problem for you . . ."

Unbelievable. Tom slammed the door and crunched across the gravel driveway to Nick. The thunder growled again, louder, closer. "Get in your fucking car, Nick. Let's go."

"Listen to you." Nick was smiling, but his eyes were wild. He was definitely hopped up. Jesus, here was Tom, working on a murder case possibly involving cocaine trafficking, and his own brother was zooted. "Mister big time," Nick said. "All bent out of shape because I need one fucking favor. You know what? Forget it. I'll take care of myself."

Nick opened the door and Tom caught it in his grip. "You kidding me right now? You call me up, you get me over here — I just left a woman with her dead daughter — and, what? If you just wanted to pick a fight, Nick, you could've done it over the phone." Tom was almost yelling.

"Pick a fight? I wasn't the one to pick the fights, Tom. I tried to stop them."

Tom felt sick. "You're going to play that card now?" He knew it embarrassed Nick to ask for help like this. He was selling his beloved SUV, the symbol of his self-made success. Nick was an addict. Drugs, women, gambling. Trying to fill a hole inside himself.

"You know," Nick said, "it's like you're still locked in that fucking closet. Right where Dad put you."

The remark hit hard. "You tell me you can take care of yourself," Tom fumed, "and yet here I am, helping you out . . ."

Nick surprised Tom when he started laughing. "You're just like him, in a way."

"What? What are you saying to me?"

Nick jerked his head toward Tom's Jeep. "Driving around in that old piece of shit. You know Dad had a Jeep Cherokee, right?"

Tom looked at his vehicle. He'd gotten the Jeep, used, his senior year in college.

"Dad was cheap as hell," Nick said. "He drove that shitbox Jeep up until the day he died."

It made Tom anxious to talk about their parents with Nick. Nick knew things Tom didn't remember.

Despite his grin, the sadness in Nick's eyes was deep and unsettling. "You're driving the same make of car Dad drove. Right up to the end."

Nick took a step closer and Tom braced for a punch. But Nick put a hand on Tom's shoulder. "You say you don't remember, or you put it all away somewhere. Fine. I get it."

Tom was trembling. "I *don't* remember, Nick. I was just a fucking kid. Seven, eight years old."

But he did. He did remember some things. He remembered his father shoving him in the closet. Maybe his father just didn't want him to see. Maybe Tom, the way he saw the world, even at that tender age, was different, and his father knew it.

A fresh kettle drum boom of thunder tumbled across the sky. The air was electric. Tom felt incensed, and stepped away from Nick. "Are you really leveraging Mom and Dad to make me . . . what? Feel guilty? I already feel guilty, Nick. I feel guilty about everything. You tried to stop Dad from hitting her. He kept hitting her . . ."

Tom bent over forward, suddenly feeling sick, flashes of his father punching his mother, viewed through the crack in the door. Nick stepping in between them.

Nick squeezed his shoulder.

"I feel guilty that you waited for me before you came down here," Tom said. "That you've taken care of me, helped me get set up. Guilty that I don't know how to help you."

"You can help me by following me to Bonita Springs. Giving me a ride back home. That's it. You know, without the big tough-guy attitude."

Nick let go of Tom and jumped in the Escalade. He rolled down the tinted window. "And you didn't stay in the closet, Tommy. You came out and tried to help me, to help Mom. That's how you got that scar right there. That's who you are."

Emotions still churning, Tom wandered back to the Jeep. He followed the Escalade out of the driveway in a daze.

They made for the interstate, and were speeding north to Bonita Springs when the skies finally opened up, dumping buckets of rain.

* * *

As they approached The Bonita Springs Greyhound Track, Tom saw the second story, walled in glass, hanging over the concrete stands. The dirt race track was just out of sight.

Tom followed the Escalade around to the side of the building where a sign declared "Clubhouse" and "Heroes Lounge." Nick parked the Escalade off to the side, blocking access to a double set of dumpsters.

Tom maneuvered into a nearby spot. The storm pummeled the Jeep, loud as a bucket of coins dropped from the sky. Nick came running over, holding an arm over his head. When he jumped in the Jeep he was soaked.

He pointed at the lounge sign. "I'm going in there," Nick said. "Shouldn't take long." There was a walkway in the shadows toward an unmarked door.

"I'll come in with you."

"Nah. Not a good idea."

Tom looked at the steel gray door beyond the deluge of milky rain. "Where does that lead?"

"Don't worry about it. Goes into the kitchen. There's an office in the back. Hey, I got this, bro. Easy-peasy. Just got to hand over the keys and the title."

Nick gave the Escalade a forlorn look.

"You gotta give 'em that whole vehicle? I thought you were only in it for ten grand?"

"No, I'm gonna cut the car into quarters, give them a fourth of it," Nick said with a straight face. He slapped Tom on the leg and opened the door. Tom watched him go, running through the storm in a hunch, before disappearing through the gray door without looking back.

Tom sat watching the rain drumming down. The few imported palm trees were bending almost sideways as the wind ripped over the flat land. He didn't know how long Nick was going to be and his patience was already running thin.

He banged out of the Jeep and jogged to the main entrance, passing a sign: *Poker Room, Open Daily 9:45 a.m. to 2 a.m.* Next to it was a cheesy photo showing four dogs, dressed to the nines, sitting around a poker table, cards fanned out in their paws. Rain pelted and coursed down the sign, melting the whole thing into surrealism.

Tom ducked inside.

He stood a moment, drenched, looking around. The ugly drop-ceiling felt too low, and a couple of fluorescent light-squares flickered with bad bulbs. A few old-timers, one wearing a classic, banded fedora hat, were queueing between velvet ropes. A distorted voice blared over the P.A. system, and Tom could hardly discern the words.

Even if he wasn't going to place any bets, he still needed to queue for entry. Tom sluiced the rainwater off his blazer, drawing a look from the attendant as it pattered to the floor.

The attendant was a buxom middle-aged woman who asked him if he wanted to become a VIP card holder. Tom declined. A dirty desk fan twirled in the attendant booth. It was warm in here, the AC turned low. The track was keeping their costs down. He could've just showed his badge, but he coughed up the two bucks for entry.

She handed him a schedule and he passed through the turnstile. Thursday featured "Poker High Hand" and dog racing post times at 11:45 a.m. and 6:30 p.m. He stuck the schedule in his back pocket and went to the next floor.

The rain thrummed like white noise, but it was tapering off at last, the wind dying down.

He bought beer in a plastic cup from a vendor and continued to wander until he had a view of the dog paddock and kennel. A couple dog-trainers were out in the mud, dark-skinned guys in white polo shirts, getting dirty. They surrounded one lone dog who was curling around in a circle, barking.

The men spoke softly to it, and one of them got a hold of it and stroked its short coat. The other man fitted a racing jacket over the dog with the number 8 on it. The storm having passed, it looked like a post-time was imminent.

Tom checked his phone to see if Nick had texted or called. He hadn't, and it was after six o'clock. Sipping the half-gone beer, Tom headed for the betting booth and placed ten dollars on number eight, who was three-to-one odds. He was handed a slip of paper with his betting info on it and took a seat on one of the wet benches.

The stands were nearly empty, the track and infield choked with weeds. The numbers on the dog gates were tattered and sun-faded. The place looked like it had been through a war, and the storm hadn't helped.

His phone rang before he finished the rest of his beer.

Blythe.

"Lange, they got him. This thing could be over. You need to get to Tampa. I'm already on my way." She sounded excited, out of character.

"Wait, they got him? Coyote?"

"Yeah. It's Raymond Bosco, just like we thought. He's been distributing narcotics out of the strip club. He's got some of the strippers peddling to customers. They do a private dance with them, ask them if they want a little blow . . ."

"What about Carrie?"

"Well, we don't know for sure. But Coby gave up another name: Sasha Clay. She's in the network."

Tom had thought Sasha made her money stripping, he knew it could bring in lots of cash. Sasha wasn't the only stripper in Tampa to be living high on the hog — it was a whole subculture. But having extra drug money possibly helped her to live the dream. There was one problem.

"Sasha Clay was the one to do the NamUs search. To try and *find* Carrie."

"So? She was looking for Carrie. So what?"

"Well, bit weird if they're part of the same drug network. You'd think Sasha would keep a low profile." He'd told Sasha he was police from the get-go, and she had still been willing to meet. She'd even taken him to her house. If it hadn't been for Sasha, the police could've struggled for a lot longer to identify Carrie.

"Listen," Blythe said. "I'm going to observe when they interview Bosco. You can join me or you can follow up with Eileen Gallo. She was still with Ward when I left the ME's office."

Tom looked around, hoping he'd catch sight of Nick coming up from the kitchen, or wherever the hell he was. The trainers were getting the dogs into place behind the starting gate. The sun was back out and a few people were wandering into the stands. No sign of Nick, though.

"I want to be there," he told Blythe. "But I'm still doing this family thing."

An announcement blared over the speakers that there was a fifteen-minute warning until post.

Blythe was incredulous. "You're at the *dog track*?"

"It's my brother . . ." Tom didn't know how to explain.

"Forget Tampa," she said. "You stay the hell away."

Tom struggled to find the right words but after a few seconds, realized it didn't matter. Blythe had hung up.

"Shit!"

Someone glanced over and Tom put his phone away. He got up, chucked his empty beer cup in the trash. Blythe had told him he had two strikes. That was doubtless the third.

He headed for the parking lot. Fuck this. His brother could find his own ride back to Naples. He pushed through the exit turnstile. As he legged it over to the Jeep he heard footsteps running up behind him.

"Hey," Nick said. "Sorry, bro."

Tom wheeled around on his brother, ready to give him holy hell. He stopped when he saw the way Nick was moving, limping along and holding his side.

"What did they do to you?"

"Nothing, Tommy. Pushed me around a little bit. I fell."

"Bullshit."

Nick started to argue, but coming out of the alleyway by the dumpsters were two heavy-hitting guys in flashy shirts. They headed for Nick's SUV, sloshing through the puddles. Tom left Nick and started toward them, seeing red.

"Tommy!" Nick's voice was an urgent whisper. He got in Tom's path. "Tommy, Tommy, Tommy . . ." Nick was a bit smaller than Tom. Sometime in their teens, Tom had sprouted and ended up topping his older brother by three inches. Tom outweighed him, too. But Nick was strong, and dug in his heels, holding Tom back.

"Don't. Don't, bro."

The heavies got into the SUV. The one slipping into the driver's side looked across the parking lot where Tom and Nick were standing. Then he disappeared behind the tinted windows and started up the vehicle. The wheels barked against the blacktop as the driver made a tight U-turn and roared off.

Tom watched them go, furious. He turned away from Nick and walked back to the Jeep. Nick hobbled along behind him.

CHAPTER TWENTY-TWO

Nick refused to go to a hospital so Tom dropped him off at home and went to the District Medical Examiner's Office. He didn't know for sure Blythe was going to reassign him, but he didn't dare call her up to find out. He figured the best thing was to proceed with the option she'd given him to follow up with Carrie's mother.

But Eileen Gallo was gone. The receptionist said she'd left fifteen minutes earlier. Ward was gone, too.

Tom thanked the receptionist and turned to leave, when he saw Andrea, Ward's mousy assistant, hustling toward the entrance. He caught up to her outside, as she was climbing into a tiny Geo Prism.

"Hi," he said, startling her.

Andrea barely stood as tall as his shoulder — and looked even paler outdoors than she had inside. He wondered if she ever saw much sunlight.

"Is something the matter?" she asked.

"No. I like hanging out here. It's grown on me."

She didn't smile.

"How do you like working here?" he asked.

"It's fine."

"Yeah? Where did you go to school?"

Andrea glanced back toward the medical office. "University of Florida, where Dr. Ward went."

"Yeah? Hey that's cool."

She blinked at him impassively. "That's why he hired me."

"Oh. I see. He likes to stick to his own. What's it like, working for him?"

"It's fine."

"What do you think about this case? About the woman from Rookery Bay? Anything strike you? Stand out?"

"No."

Tom had run out of road. And the longer she stood there, the more awkward it felt. "Alright, well, take care. Thanks for all of your hard work."

She slipped into the driver's seat without another word. She seemed to fumble for the keys. Tom leaned against the adjacent vehicle and watched as she pulled away.

Then she stopped the car with a jerk and rolled down the window.

Curious, Tom stepped closer.

"Listen, Agent Lange." Andrea peered out of the car with glassy eyes. "I measure a person based on their work. Dr. Ward is a brilliant pathologist. I believe in him in and I support the decisions he's made. People get too caught up in scandals and need to look at what he's done."

Tom began to reply but she rolled up the window and took off without a second look.

Huh.

He drove back to the field office. The sun was just about gone for the day, a few of the usual inland clouds low on the horizon, dark underneath, puffy on top. He went into the office and set the murder book on his desk.

He called the ROC and spoke to the officer who had been handling the hotline calls since the press conference.

"Yeah, Agent Blythe checked in, too. We've had twenty-six calls. Eight of them were from reporters digging for more on the story. The other eighteen have been followed up but they led nowhere. Someone called about a body floating in the water in Immokalee, but it turned out to be a dead dog. That's it."

"Alright. Thank you."

Tom flipped through the binder until he came to the section with the 911 transcript. He'd already read it, but he wanted to hear the call with his own ears.

Everglades County had sent across an audio file of the call, and he found it in the shared network folder on his computer.

"*911, for what city?*"

"*Ah, for Naples.*"

"*And do you require the police, fire, or ambulance?*"

"*Um, I'm not sure. Maybe an ambulance. But she looks dead.*"

"*Okay, what's the address of the emergency?*"

"*This is Rookery Bay.*"

"*Rookery Bay?*"

"*Yes.*"

"*Okay, what's the number you're calling from?*"

Susan Libby, with a trembling voice, gave her number. Tom imagined her in her kayak, Carrie Hobson's body floating in the mangrove tunnel, Joe and Linda VanCott looking on, likely horrified.

"*Okay, tell me exactly what happened.*"

"*I'm a guide, I give kayak tours in Rookery Bay. I'm giving the sunrise tour this morning. I have two customers. We are on Stopper Creek right now . . . there's a body in the water.*"

"*A body? Do you mean a person?*"

"*Yes, I mean a person. I'm sorry.*"

"*It's okay. Is he or she conscious?*"

"*I think it's a she. No. She doesn't look conscious. She looks dead.*"

"*Is she breathing?*"

"No. She's floating face down."

"How close are you to this person, ma'am?"

"Um, just a couple yards away. I don't want to touch it. She looks very dead, you know? Like she's been in the water a while."

"Do you think you could give me an approximate age for the person in the water?"

Susan Libby sighed, a sound like radio static on the digital audio file.

"No. I mean, could be twenty, could be forty. No older than forty, I don't think. Can you send someone? I need to get my people back to shore."

The emergency dispatcher continued to follow protocol and Susan Libby grew increasingly agitated. She really wanted to get out of there, and Tom couldn't blame her. But she agreed to meet the Everglades County deputies who would arrive shortly, and assist them with locating the body once they were on scene. Tom listened to the entirety of the call, which lasted another five minutes.

He sat back, thinking. The call stirred two concerns, hard to say how minor or major. One was the sex of the victim. For certain, Susan Libby had made a guess, but by the conclusion of the emergency call, both Libby and the 911 operator were using the pronoun "she." Prior to arriving on scene, Ward would have been given a quick overview, and chances were good such an overview would've referred to the body as being that of a woman. Yet Ward had initially insisted the sex was unknown. Tom felt bothered by it. Ward acted like he was the only one capable of making any evidentiary determinations. But maybe that ego came with the territory.

The other concern circled back to the jurisdiction issue. The call for service had gone to Everglades County first, as protocol dictated. At what point had Turnbull intervened? At whose behest? Tom thought it was unlikely the Sheriff had been the one to call. For one thing, Tom thought, most cops didn't like the FDLE. The agency often investigated other police.

He paced the field office waiting for some fresh coffee to heat up.

He'd been kept out of the loop from the beginning. He didn't even know what Blythe had been doing these past few days. This thing with Coburn's drug op — she'd let him in, but not completely. She was controlling what he knew, how much he was involved. Follow up with Eileen Gallo? Ward had already importuned the woman while she sat wracked with grief. And they'd asked her their questions. Tom had already found out what he'd wanted to know — Carrie had been sending her money, and that's why she'd been hard up for cash.

Spending more time with Eileen Gallo was a fool's errand.

"This is bullshit," he said. Blythe may have told him to stay away, but he couldn't. He left the office with the coffee still brewing and sped north toward Tampa.

CHAPTER TWENTY-THREE

Tom slipped into the monitoring room. Blythe glanced over but said nothing. Gathered around a large screen were Sergeant Coburn and two vice narcotics officers, the Tampa Police Captain, and the statewide prosecutor Bob Mandi, watching Raymond Bosco being questioned by Detective Gomez. On a second screen no one was watching, Sasha Clay sat alone, slumped in her chair.

Gomez was just finishing up with Bosco. He gathered some papers and put them into a file, rapped his knuckles on the desk and said to Bosco, "Thanks very much. Sit tight for just another minute."

Blythe leaned her head toward Coburn. They spoke in low voices until Gomez stepped into the room. Gomez made a nod toward Tom, then approached the other officers, tapping the file against his open palm.

"That's one slippery fucker," Gomez said.

Coburn turned to the Tampa captain. "You gotta kick him loose."

Blythe held out her hands, opened her mouth, as if betrayed.

Gomez said, "You heard him. Bosco's at Hush six nights a week. Comes on at seven o'clock, works until four a.m. Confirmed time of death for Carrie is between eight and nine p.m., Wednesday afternoon. It's a no-go."

Tom realized the more precise time of death must have come from Ward, probably while Tom was dealing with Nick.

"Bosco runs the club," Blythe said, sounding unhappy. "He could have written up his own time sheet." She glanced at Tom again, her eyes like hard jewels.

"Sasha Clay corroborates it," Gomez said. "She was on a shift at the same time."

"She could be covering."

"She's not even in the system. Zero record. She's pretty clean for a stripper."

They all looked at Sasha on the screen. She had spruced herself up to talk to the police, wearing a white, frilly Southern Belle-style blouse, but she looked desultory, her face partly covered by her hair.

Blythe pointed at Bosco on the screen. "This is our guy."

Bob Mandi cleared his throat. "What do we charge him with if he's got an alibi? Right now neither of them have requested a lawyer, because they're both here under the assumption that this is a follow-up on Carrie Hobson, and nothing more."

Tom wished he'd seen the interviews. He made a mental note to watch the recordings later.

"Well," Blythe said, "we can let *her* go, but we've got to keep *him*. Come on, Bob. Coby . . . We can hold him for forty-eight hours . . ."

Coburn seemed to think about it. He was a big man, over two hundred pounds, with a salt-and-pepper beard. He wore a dark blue T-shirt with the Everglades County Sheriff's Office insignia on it and a pair of jeans, sunglasses perched on his head. The gun on his hip was a 9 mm Beretta.

Blythe said, "We hold him, we get the evidence we need, we charge him."

"He gets charged with murder," Coburn said, "and everything we've been doing, for months, is in jeopardy. What I gave you wasn't supposed to be actionable intelligence, just intelligence. You need to develop your case on your own."

Blythe looked offended. "You don't want us to arrest him at all."

"Arrest him, and his first phone call is gonna scatter everybody. We lose the element of surprise."

"He would be pliable. He'd talk to you and he'd turn on Palumbo. That's what you want, isn't it? I thought that's why you called me."

"Whoa, whoa." Mandi tutted. "Not everyone here has read the affidavit and Sergeant Coburn can't divulge any more information or he's in danger of jail himself! We're talking about two very different cases here, and we need to keep them that way . . ."

"How do you have the element of surprise after George Parsons?" Blythe said to Coburn, ignoring the prosecutor. "I mean, Bosco's got to know that forty-six kilos of coke weren't seized because Parsons had tinted windows . . ."

"He didn't have tinted windows," Coburn said. "He had a gun rack that was obscuring his rear view."

Coburn said it straight-faced, but the vice narcotics officers grinned. Still, the tension of the room was still palpable.

"Well, there we go," Blythe said. "He's no dummy. He's 'Wile E. Coyote,' and he's been doing this for years. He knows the heat is around the corner, Coby. He knows that's why we're here. And he probably even knows he's protected, because *you're* protected. He's banking on it."

They all looked at Raymond Bosco again, fiddling with his empty coffee cup. He tipped it to his mouth to get the last few drops. Tom noticed a discoloration along

Bosco's hand, but it was hard to see it clearly on the monitor. Then Bosco turned and looked right at the camera. Like he was watching them.

"See?" Blythe said. "He already knows. I bet he knows what you're thinking, right now. That he's going to slide right out of here because you don't want to rock the boat. But the boat is already rocked. You need to let me keep him. And take him down."

Coburn stayed glued to the screen, sucking at something in his mouth, a hard candy. Tom heard it rattle around the big man's teeth.

"I'm telling you," Coburn said at last, "the only reason you're looking at him for Hobson's murder is because of what we gave you. We've cooperated, we've shared what we could share, and that's it. He has an alibi for the time of death from the wiretap and from his co-worker stripper there."

"Coburn is right," Mandi chimed in. "Right now we've got nothing to prosecute. No murder weapon, no opportunity, no motive."

"Opportunity is he works with her at the same club!" Blythe was exasperated. "Motive is she screwed him somehow on a deal. Either she pocketed the money or something else happened. He could have passed the phone to anyone. Coby, you didn't have eyes on him, right? No surveillance was close enough to actually *see* Bosco there at the club."

"True . . ." Coburn admitted.

"We're going to need to show where the money is," Mandi said. "You've been to her apartment. No drugs, no money. If she's a facilitator, where's the evidence? You said she's got a mother who maybe she was sending money to for medical bills?"

"We're working on the bank stuff. We'll get Eileen Gallo's bank statements, show the checks cashed."

"What about Carrie's bank account? What's in it?"

Blythe gave Tom another quick look. "Not much. Two hundred and eighteen dollars."

Mandi shrugged. "I'm telling you, it's a hard sell."

They fell silent again. Bosco was bouncing his knee now. He kept checking the clock on the wall. Sasha had barely moved.

Tom drifted closer to the screens, really studying Bosco's hand. He pointed at it, knowing he should probably keep quiet, but he couldn't help himself. "What happened to his hand?"

They all stared at Tom for a moment. Then Gomez answered. "He just had stitches out this morning."

"For what?"

"Ah, he sliced it. Cutting limes or some shit. You know, slicing them up for the bartender, prepping for the night shift."

"How long do stitches stay in?"

Gomez looked around at the others in the room, like *Get a load of this guy*. "I don't know, Lange. A week? Two weeks? Should we factor that in?" It was sarcastic.

"Coby, this is Agent Lange," Blythe said, sounding displeased.

Coburn turned to face Tom.

"Can I make a suggestion?" Tom asked.

"Okay . . ."

"Let me talk to Sasha. One-on-one. But not here . . . I'll go to her. She works the other club tonight."

Coburn's frown deepened. "What club? Caliente?"

"Kronos." Tom looked between Coburn and Blythe, feeling the room getting smaller. "Sasha went looking for Carrie. *She* was the one who checked NamUs. And I have a rapport with her. I'll find out if she's covering for Bosco. If she is, then we've got reasonable grounds to charge him, because he lied."

No one said anything. Coburn and Blythe traded long looks, then the lines on Coburn's forehead cleared. "Sounds okay to me."

"Good idea," said Mandi.

Blythe was stone-faced a moment longer. Then she looked away, swallowing her pride. "Fine, alright."

CHAPTER TWENTY-FOUR

Kronos was in the heart of the city, surrounded by dazzling skyscrapers and long bridges. Tom took the Dale Mabry Highway past the football stadium to the red-light district known for its strip clubs. He left the Jeep in a parking garage and walked the streets which teemed with people in skimpy clothes. Hush had been all male customers, but Kronos was more fashionable with as many women as men waiting to get in. He waited in line and paid a thirty-dollar cover charge to enter.

Kronos had two floors and several private rooms. The lights were as bad as the music, neon glaring, a red wash over everything. Velvet chairs and leather booths. It was early, only ten o'clock, but the place was already half-filled. More customers streamed in through the doors.

He found an empty table in the corner and sat down, his back to the wall, facing the door. A cocktail waitress sauntered over, dressed in a shimmering silver bikini and high heels. She looked like she'd stepped out of a modeling catalogue, her sinewy body perfectly plucked and tanned, hair long and lustrous. Probably a weave. He ordered a Heineken and watched for Sasha.

As he waited, he imagined someone from Coburn's vice narcotics team posing as a Hush customer in another part of the city. Coburn would be all over Hush. They had the line on Bosco and knew he was selling in the club. Tom bet Sasha would go down, too, when Coburn finally pounced. Tom was operating under strict guidelines not to reveal any of this.

The DJ announced a new girl taking the main stage, which was twice the size of the one at Hush. The surrounding lights twisted into a new pattern, the musical number opened with a flourish of drums, and the dancer flung her hair back, kicked out her leg, and took the pole. She flipped herself inverted then slid down, landing on her shoulders. She arced backwards until her feet touched the stage, then spread her legs, flexible as a gymnast. The crowd whistled and cheered.

The dancer got back to her feet and teased the crowd, unclasping her top with a deft move and holding the fabric against her breasts as she leaned toward a trio of men. She wagged her finger at them, taunting, and they howled and elbowed each other with delight.

The cocktail waitress came back with Tom's beer and he pulled out his wallet, dropping a couple of bills in her palm. He caught sight of another waitress holding a tray of drinks. Sasha. He slid out of the booth and headed over.

As he crossed the room something soft hit him in the neck. The dancer onstage grinned and made a coy face, touching a finger to her lips. The customers cheered as Tom placed her top on the stage. Down on all fours, she picked it up with her teeth, her breasts dangling, and cocked her head. He dug out his wallet again, and, feeling clumsy, set a ten down in front of her.

She rose to her knees and playfully shook her head, no. She pushed her hips toward him, slowly gyrating with the music. Tom glanced across the room and realized Sasha had seen him. She watched as Tom picked up the ten-dollar bill and put it in the stripper's G-string.

He caught up with Sasha at the crowded bar, where she was loading drinks onto a tray. She knew he was there, he was sure, but she avoided looking at him. He got in step with her as she walked away.

"Hey, can we talk?"

"I'm working."

He trailed her through the crowd. Once she'd delivered all the drinks, she turned to him. "You want a dance, or something?"

"I just want to talk."

She wore glittering earrings, hair done up high like the others, eyelashes made thick. "I'm on shift. I can step off the floor if you want a private dance. Otherwise I'm done at three."

There was no way he was hanging out here for another four hours, so he leaned in, speaking close to her ear. "Alright."

She took his hand and led him away from the main room, stopping at a waitress station to drop off her tray. As she pulled him along, people clapped.

Sasha took him down a hallway which fed several rooms. A huge man in a suit occupied a stool in the hallway and they stopped there. He was so big he looked like a circus bear on a beach ball. Beside him was a narrow desk with a laptop, six images split on the screen. He spoke to Sasha as he moved toward Tom. "How we doing tonight, honey?"

"Good, Brett. This big stud here would like a one-on-one."

"Of course he would, look at you, you're gorgeous." Brett smiled at Sasha and she winked at him. Then Brett turned to Tom and the smile dropped. "Raise your arms."

Tom pushed aside his blazer, revealing the holstered weapon. "This is all you're going to find. And it's not coming off."

"No guns in the one-on-ones. I need it, or you're not going in."

Tom pulled his badge. "It stays on."

Brett eyed the badge, licked his lips and looked at Sasha.

Sasha shrugged. "It's okay with me."

Another girl was leading a man into the private area. He was red-faced, wearing a starchy dress shirt and glasses, like an accountant. He looked embarrassed. They waited for entry and Brett glowered at Tom. "Okay. Whatever. Keep it. But I'm cutting you short. You two have got fifteen minutes. One simple rule: No touching. She can touch you, you can't touch her. Got it?"

Tom nodded.

"Okay, you guys are right here. Room four."

The room was tight, walled in mirrors, a bench rail running along three walls. There were small drink tables and a riser in the center of the room. Sasha took his beer and set it aside. She touched his chest, lightly pushing. He followed her lead and moved back until his legs bumped against the bench and he sat down.

The music started — low, deep beats. Sasha climbed onto the riser and moved slowly at first, undulating her body in sync with the music, dragging her fingers over her skin, up from her thighs, her buttocks, further along her rib cage, then grabbed the back of her head.

"Sasha . . . You don't have to do that."

"Yes, I do."

Tom glanced at a camera mounted in the corner.

"I don't think you told me everything about Carrie."

She threshed her fingers in her hair and swayed back and forth. Then she stepped down off the platform and came closer.

"I think she was involved in something . . ." Tom said.

She touched his knees, moving in and out. Then she stood, removed her top and came back again, grabbing his legs, tossing her hair back. She climbed up and straddled him, her breasts inches from his face, his mouth.

"You need to talk to me," he said. "If you're in trouble, I can help you."

Sasha curled into Tom as she continued to grind into his pelvis, and her lips grazed his ear. "You smell like him," she whispered.

"I smell like who?"

She rocked against him, raked her fingers through his hair.

"Tell me what you know!"

She stopped. She stared into his eyes a moment, then pouted her lips. "Carrie's a small town girl. Just like me. Small town girl with big dreams."

"Did Bosco do something to her? Did he hurt her? You don't have to protect him."

She caressed the sides of his face. She brought her lips so close to his he could almost taste her.

"Bosco is all bark and no bite."

She nipped his ear and resumed her gyrations. It was everything he could do to keep focused. Even though he was here for a reason, even though he'd been in a room this size with a dead woman for an entire day, his body was responding. He gripped the leather seat, trying to ignore the way her legs felt straddling him, the way she was undoing the buttons of his shirt.

"If you know why Carrie was killed, please tell me."

A spark of defiance in her eyes. "This wouldn't be because of that bust down in Naples, now, would it?"

And there it was. Blythe was right — Bosco and Sasha and whoever else was involved in drug-dealing at Hush were no dummies. They knew the cops were closing in.

"I don't know anything about that," he lied. "I want to find out who killed Carrie."

"Well. . ." She came closer again, pressing against his chest, legs squeezing his hips. ". . . Carrie had nothing to do with any of that." Her breath was warm in his ear.

He moaned involuntarily as she slid back and forth on his waist. Fine, he was going to let the cat out the bag.

"No? She had nothing to do with it? She didn't steal any money from him?"

"No. She didn't steal any money."

"And you would tell me if she did?"

She nodded. He let go of the bench a moment and feathered his hands over her naked back, not touching, but wanting to. Wanting to grab her.

He knew this was all a part of it. He'd only been to a strip club once as a civilian — Nick had brought him to a dive in Fort Myers for Tom's thirtieth. It hadn't really impressed him. Nick liked the clubs, but Tom knew what could happen at places like this, what went on in some of the VIP rooms. Coercion. Forced prostitution.

Tom turned away from Sasha. He couldn't touch her, couldn't even push her off, unless he wanted Brett banging in the door and throwing him out on his ass.

She relished his resistance and played into it. "Would I tell you if Carrie was involved in something? Yes . . . yes, I would. I like you."

She licked his lower lip, then kissed him.

"Come to my house tonight. Come over after I'm done here."

The words suddenly excited him more than anything else. He knew he wanted it. But there couldn't be a worse possible mistake. "I can't."

"You can trust me. I cared about Carrie. I went looking for her, remember?"

"I know you did."

"She was my friend."

She kissed him again, so quickly he didn't have time to get out of the way. He kissed back, arcing his spine, close to wrapping his arms around her.

The door opened. Brett stood there. "Alright lovers, time's up."

Tom shared one more look with Sasha. Her emotions were masked, but he glimpsed what was genuine, hidden beneath her persona — a real person seeking a real connection. Then it was gone. She swung her leg and stood up, picked up her top from the floor and snapped it on, brushed the hair from her face. "Thanks for the dance." And she sauntered out of the room.

Brett remained, filling the doorway. Tom got off the bench, a little embarrassed about what might be showing.

"That's one hundred," said Brett.

Tom dug the money from his wallet. This case was going to clean him out. He only had a twenty and a couple of ones left after he paid Brett. He grabbed his beer from the table and Brett stepped aside, letting Tom through.

Brett followed him into the hallway. "She's something, huh?"

"Yeah."

"Sasha's my favorite."

Tom detested the look in the man's eyes, like Brett thought they shared something now. Tom headed straight for the exit, but looked for Sasha as he made his way. He spied her back by the bar again, but she wasn't watching.

He drank the rest of the Heineken, taking the empty bottle with him as he left.

The street was even busier, the line outside Kronos longer. Tom headed toward the parking garage through the balmy air, his head ringing from the music, pulse still running high. He pulled a plastic baggie from his back pocket, dropped the Heineken bottle in the bag and sealed it up.

CHAPTER TWENTY-FIVE

FRIDAY

Tom awoke in the hotel room. He could still feel her hands on him from the club, her body heat lingering.

He kept the water cool in the shower and let the powerful jets beat down. He shaved, dressed in the fresh shirt and slacks he'd had the intern drop off when they picked up the beer bottle. He set himself up in a corner of the room overlooking the Gulf.

He had an email from the First Bank of Florida with data on Carrie's deposits and withdrawals. He scanned through these and made a few notes. Then he called the ROC crime lab and asked for either of the IFS chemists. Veronica Morley came on the line. She sounded her usual grouchy shelf.

"We received the bottle you sent down last night. We'll lift the print and check it against the two distinct sets from the baseboard piece."

"Thanks. Listen, do me a favor . . . Have you searched the system yet for a match on the baseboard latents?"

A pause. "What do you think we do here? Yes, a search is ongoing."

"Okay."

"Good times last night, Agent Lange? The intern said you were near the red-light district. Sounds like fun." Her voice dripped with sarcasm.

"Not really." He wanted to hang up on her but thought better of it. "Hey, Veronica, I know we can't rush the toxicology . . ."

"It takes as long as it takes."

"I know. But I also know you're a good chemist."

She hesitated, and he thought the hook was in. "Yeah . . .?"

"You've got to have a feel for the results, something preliminary. I want your honest opinion. It's not for the prosecutor, it's nothing I'm going to act on directly, it just—"

"Clean." She cut him off. "At this point it looks to me like Carrie Hobson's blood toxicology is going to come back clean. Just the minor traces of alcohol, no drugs. Not prescription, not illegal. Clean. Does that answer your question?"

"Yes." He ended the call.

He was about to phone Blythe when Detective Gomez's number flashed on his screen.

"Lange. You asked for video."

"I did." Tom felt a rush.

"Hush has no cameras, as you know. But, we pulled video from Gleason's, the car dealership next door. It's pretty bad, not much on it of use, I don't think. But we also found there's a camera just down the street, at a mattress warehouse. Haven't pulled it yet. What do you want to do?"

Tom opened the door to the terrace and looked out over the water. "I want to come in and see the video from Gleason's. I can be there in twenty minutes."

"Twenty minutes? What're you taking, a helicopter?"

"I stayed in Tampa. I'll come to you, then go to the warehouse myself."

"Alright. We'll be here."

Gomez hung up and Tom gathered his things, strapping on his shoulder holster, checking the weapon.

Down on the main floor he used the hotel's wireless printer to print out Carrie Hobson's bank records. The hotel offered a free continental breakfast in the main lounge and Tom scarfed up a bagel and grabbed a coffee on his way out.

* * *

Gomez was waiting for him at Tampa headquarters. He walked Tom through the main detectives' room, a bullpen divided into cubicles, similar to the ROC. Plain-clothes detectives and uniformed officers milled about, chatting, phones ringing.

Gomez led Tom down a corridor to a room filled with video screens and all manner of playback devices. A young woman sat at a screen, using a dial to scrub through fuzzy-looking footage. She had the AC cranked high and the place was like a refrigerator. Gomez made quick introductions and said he had somewhere to be.

Tom called Blythe and could tell by the tone of her voice he was still on thin ice with her, thin as it got. One false move and he would plunge into the abyss.

"How did it go last night?" she asked, and he could hear her getting in her car to head to the station. She had stayed overnight, too, elsewhere in the city.

"Good. I lifted her prints. We can see if they match any latents found at Carrie's apartment. Specifically the two sets on the baseboard. And we got the prints without needing a court order or arrest, so Coburn should be happy."

"Fine."

"So we're keeping Bosco, or aren't we? His prints are already in the system. They could show up on the baseboard."

"No. He was let go." Blythe sounded annoyed.

"Listen," Tom said, "as far as the whole drug thing . . . just letting you know I asked Veronica Morley about the impending tox results. A preliminary analysis from the chem lab."

"And?"

"She says it's looking like a clean screen on Carrie."

Blythe was silent for a moment. "Proving?"

"That she wasn't a user."

"So what. Smart dealers don't use. Oh, I see what it is — in your mind, not only is Carrie uninvolved in the drug operation, her blood's clean, so she's a good girl. A stripper with a heart of gold."

"She sent money home to her mother every month." Tom felt provoked. The officer in the room glanced over her shoulder. Tom pulled out the material he'd printed at the hotel. "I got the banking info this morning. Carrie was sending thousands to Eileen Gallo to help her pay down the hospital bills leftover from her father. That's not a character assessment, Agent Blythe. That's a fact."

He thought she might explode at him at last, break this icy wall she'd built, but instead Blythe was calm. "I guess I can't argue that."

"Good, because I don't understand why you're pushing back so hard against this."

"Am I pushing back so hard?"

"Yeah, yeah you are."

"What did Sasha tell you about Bosco's alibi?"

"She didn't give me an indication she was covering for him."

"And you believed her."

"Yes. I think I'm building something here, Blythe, based on the evidence."

"Is that what you're doing?"

He excused himself and stepped into the hallway. He knew he was getting riled up, but hated the way Blythe was patronizing him. "Yes," he said, keeping measured. "That's what I'm doing."

"Because I thought maybe . . ." She kept her own voice even ". . . you might have gotten your dick stroked a little bit last night. I'll see you in ten minutes."

* * *

"You're looking at Tuesday evening," Tom said. "The end of Carrie's last shift at Hush."

Blythe sat down in the cool, dark room. The Tampa officer had been relegated to a chair in the corner, Tom now in command of the playback.

The video image showed a line-up of cars, pennants flapping in the breeze. Beyond the cars, the plaza across the street was partly visible. Hush was on the corner. The front door was out of view, but the side doors near the dumpsters were in frame.

A time code ran on the bottom of the screen. Tom looked from the time code to the side doors. Everything was tiny, pixelated.

"Okay," Blythe said, "I'm watching."

"Hang on. Coming up at 19:13."

He waited patiently, watching the numbers, feeling his heart knock against his ribs. Then the door opened and a figure stepped out.

"That's Carrie," he said. "Blue shorts, white top."

Carrie started for her car. The doors reopened and a man leaned out.

Blythe bent closer to the screen. "Who is that?"

"I think Bosco. But hold on. There's someone else."

Carrie appeared to speak to the guy in the doorway. Then the guy made a gesture, like a wave, and retreated inside. Carrie started to get in her vehicle.

"Here he comes," Tom said.

A second man walked into frame, from the direction of the parking lot. Carrie was in her Hyundai. The man took a few more steps and then halted.

Tom's mouth felt dry even though he'd already watched it through three times. This was the same way he'd met Sasha earlier in the week — around the side of the building, after her shift.

"This is video from Carrie's final shift?" Blythe asked to confirm.

"Yes. And this man here, this could be someone who'd been at the club."

The man made a gesture and Carrie got out. She approached him, but kept a distance. Tom scrutinized the image but the man's face was a small mass of shifting, colored pixels. He was in what looked like jeans and a white dress shirt. No ratty sweater. He could've been anybody.

"This is no good," Blythe said.

"There's other video," Tom said in a quiet voice. "From a warehouse two blocks from the plaza."

"Did we pull it?"

Tom glanced at her. "Not yet."

"Let's pull it. Maybe they drive by."

Tom felt a wave of relief. The excitement was catching — Blythe was on board.

They watched as Carrie and the stranger continued to converse. Then the man turned and walked out of the frame, and Carrie went back to her car. A moment later, she drove off.

"Could be Steve Hobson," Blythe said.

Tom had wondered the same thing, but doubted it. "Steve Hobson is a bit on the heavy side. That guy was svelte."

"That guy was the size of a little plastic army man," Blythe said. "You could tell that?"

"I'm into fitness." He knew it sounded stupid, but it was true. Even the micro-movements of the figure from the video, the posture, it wasn't someone like Steve Hobson, who was short and stout. Still, Hobson could've visited Carrie after work, pledging to make amends, maybe even asked for her back. She might have agreed to meet him, and when he didn't like what she had to say, bashed her head in, before driving her as far away as he dared, dumping her in Rookery Bay.

"But, yes," Tom said, "could be him. We need to have a good look at his house."

"Agreed."

Tom sat back from the screen — his neck hurt from staring so intently. Blythe was watching as he picked up the phone and dialed a number.

"Calling the warehouse?"

"Yes."

She nodded. "I'll scramble the forensics team."

Their argument was over. They had a fresh lead.

CHAPTER TWENTY-SIX

A young guy with very pale yellow hair fumbled through the DVDs in an attic office at the warehouse. While Tom was waiting, he looked through the windows at endless rows of mattresses stacked twenty high in the cavernous main room below. A forklift cruised along, its orange light twirling.

"We record over the DVDs each month. You said this was last Tuesday, right?"

"Not this past Tuesday," Tom said. "The Tuesday before that. The seventeenth."

The guy went through the file box again. It wasn't very well organized, the system outdated. Compared to the video room at Tampa headquarters, it was the dark ages. But Tom wanted to have a look right away.

The display monitor was small, but at least it was color. The camera feeding it was mounted outside the front door. Right now it showed the entryway, part of the small parking lot, and the street.

"I keep telling Neil we need to update the security system," the warehouse worker complained, "record directly to hard drive. But he's cheap as hell, and you've got to get one of those converter things . . . Okay, here, I got it." The guy, who Tom thought must be albino, opened the DVD tray in the recorder. He popped in the disk he was holding and pressed play.

"We're looking at around 7:13 p.m. to 7:15 or 16," Tom said.

"7:13 p.m., got it." The guy hit a button on the remote, which jumped ten minutes at a time. He stopped at 7:10 p.m. and slowly advanced to seven-thirteen. Tom crowded in and watched.

For about ten seconds, nothing happened. Then a vehicle passed, a pickup truck, heading south. A few more vehicles went by. Tom wasn't blinking. He didn't want to miss it.

Just after 7:16, a green Hyundai drove by in a southerly direction. Tom felt a twinge of excitement. He leaned closer, breathing shallowly, counting in his head, even though the time code kept track to the millisecond. Just a few of those milliseconds shy of 7:16, a second car passed.

"Stop, stop it, right there."

The guy fumbled for a second, then hit pause. He was late reacting, and just the rear bumper of the vehicle was showing. The image jittered in pause-mode.

"Can you back it up? I want to see that car."

The guy hit the button, and the image jumped back a few frames. Too far — the car disappeared.

"Don't you have a . . .? Here, let me see that." Tom took the remote. He was sweating, it was hot as hell up here even though air blew from an overhead duct. He found the frame toggle on the remote and advanced the footage, one frame at a time, until he got the clearest picture the DVD could render.

He stared at the car, at the human shape behind the wheel.

It sucked that it was a white car. Half the cars in Florida were white. Even his own Jeep was white. People chose white because it reflected the sun.

This was just a basic DVD image, and the camera had recorded a side view of the street. He toggled a few frames forward, then back, but there was no chance of getting the license plate number. And it was impossible to verify whether this was the person Carrie had been talking to outside the club.

But he knew it was. He just did.

Blythe had gone to see the Tampa judge about a warrant for Steve Hobson's home, getting a full forensics team in there to search for signs of Carrie, or anything else. Tom wanted to know for sure what sort of car Steve Hobson drove, but he could check his notes in a minute. If memory served, it had been a white Honda CRV. This vehicle was different.

Tom pointed at the screen. "What kind of car would you say that is?"

"Um, that's a Lexus."

"You sound pretty sure."

"I know my cars. See those headlights? They're angled, narrow, like cat's eyes. There's actually three little bulbs in each. And you can just sort of see it there, the black here in the front of the car. That's the spindle grille. What it looks like to me, anyway. Lot of people hate the spindle grille."

Tom manipulated the footage back and forth again. Only eight frames of video included the car. The best frame was at the beginning as the Lexus entered from the right. "Yeah, okay, I guess I can see that."

Part of him felt like he was grasping at straws. The other part of him thought he was looking at Carrie Hobson's killer, and the killer was driving a white Lexus with a spindle grille.

"You know the model?"

"Um, well, if it's got the Triple-L headlights, which it looks like, and the spindle grille, then I'd say that's an RC F Sport Coupe. That's a high roller car, dawg."

Tom wasn't a car guy. To him it looked like most other cars, though he could see that it was fancier. "I'm going to need to take that DVD, okay?"

"Ah, yeah, okay . . . I got to clear it with the boss." The young man looked up with his eerily pale eyes.

"You're already cleared. We talked to Neil."

"Alright then." The guy ejected the disk and the screen reverted to the current image.

Tom slipped the disk into his pocket, thinking. A little after seven on Tuesday evening, Carrie is in blue shorts and a white top. She finishes work, talks to the man in the Lexus. She leaves, he follows her.

They go to her apartment so she can drop her car. Does she even go upstairs? Tom didn't think so. She's found dead in the same clothes. If she was going to pick up her wallet, she probably would have changed her outfit, too.

Whoever was in the Lexus convinced her to leave with him. Drop her car, get in with him, and — what?

Go down to Naples together. Do a little kayaking. Something. And he was in a hurry, too. No time for Carrie to shower, change, get her things. *Let's just go, baby.*

That could mean Carrie either knew him, or was extremely trusting. All Tom had was the CCTV, no discernible faces, and the make of a car he was taking on the word of a kid from a mattress warehouse.

He stood there a moment, then moved toward the door. "Thanks for your help."

* * *

Idling in his Jeep in front of the warehouse, he could just see the edge of the plaza and the used car lot beyond it. He rolled on until he pulled up outside the strip club. The alternate bouncer was at the door, looking sleepy.

Jimmy perked up when he saw Tom coming, and glanced nervously around. Tom raised his hands in a gesture of peace.

"Hey. Just a quick question. You sit out here all day, you see the customers come and go. How about a guy in a white Lexus RC F? You know what that is?"

"That's a sixty-thousand-dollar ride."

"Does anyone here drive a car like that?"

Jimmy cracked a smile, revealing gold-capped teeth. "They wish."

"But have you ever see one here? Someone who works here?"

"No, no one who works here."

"Not the owner, maybe, Palumbo?"

"Nah man. He drives a Hummer."

"A customer's car, maybe?"

Jimmy licked his teeth. "What's it to you?"

"What's it to me? The question is, what's it to *you*? You get to maybe help solve a murder. Go to bed at night feeling like a hero."

The bouncer just stared, then he cracked another shiny smile. "Is that right?"

Tom changed tactics. "Where you from? You don't seem to me like a Florida native."

"Me? Jersey Shore. You?"

"Yeah my brother and I are from New York. Yonkers."

"Sure, I know Yonkers."

"So, how 'bout it, man. You seen a car like that?"

Jimmy looked into the distance, hawked and spat. "Yeah. Couple times."

"Get a look at the driver?"

"Not really."

"What's that mean, 'not really'? You were at the door here when you saw the car? We're talking about Tuesday, the seventeenth, around 7 p.m. Maybe earlier. Guy left around 7.15 p.m., he coulda gotten here, I dunno, an hour earlier, give or take."

Jimmy's eyes flew open and he jerked his head back. "You for real? That's like, two weeks ago? What do you think, I got one of those photographic memories or some shit?"

"You were here, at the door, right? Around six p.m.?"

"I don't know man, shit. Bosco sometimes gets here early, late, whatever. I have no fuckin' idea."

Tom felt exasperated, excited — he needed to calm down. "Alright. Okay. But you saw the guy in the Lexus. You're not sure when, but you saw him. You were sitting here when he came in."

"Look man, I already talked to all y'all. Right? I gave them all my info, when I was here, all that."

"Fine forget the time. Just tell me what you remember. What he looked like."

Jimmy glanced at the sky, sighed loudly, like it was all a huge imposition. "Think it was a little guy, yo. Alright, I mean, skinny. Glasses on. Looked sorta . . . you know. Like a puff-tart."

"You mean effeminate."

"Right, right. Whatever. You know, we get all types." He held up his hands. "Hey, I don't judge."

"But you saw his face. Can you remember it?"

"I don't know man. All you white people look alike."

"How tall?"

"Tall? Shit. Five eight? Five nine?" Jimmy spat again, annoyed.

"What if I were to ask you to come down to the station and look at a photo array?" Tom had the picture of Steve Hobson with him, but things were getting dicey now. Jurisprudence mattered here, and eyewitness identification procedures were rigid. One false move and a good defense lawyer would tear up case evidence in court.

Jimmy looked at Tom like he was insane. "You outta your mind, you think I'm gonna go shop photos with you?"

"How about a sketch artist? You don't have to look at anything, you just talk. Describe what you saw."

"I just did."

Tom held up his hands again. "I'm no artist."

"Man, I gotta work. I ain't going to the police. You for real?"

Tom could force it, but then Jimmy might wind up even more uncooperative. "I'll have someone come to you. Where will you be tonight?"

"Right fucking here. Working."

"Bosco's not on?

"Nah, man."

"I'm gonna send someone. Okay? You can sit right on that stool. You describe this guy from the Lexus, best you can, we'll get a sketch done. You think you could do that?"

Jimmy stilled, and raised an eyebrow. "What's in it for me? Don't tell me about being a hero."

"You're looking for a little incentive?"

A wry smile. "Yeah, you know." Then he rubbed his fingers, indicating money.

"I'll see what I can do," Tom said, thinking he could grab the guy by the neck right now and give him some incentive. He backed away toward the Jeep. He pointed. "I'm counting on you, Jimmy. Alright? This is huge."

Jimmy cupped a hand to his ear, as if to better hear. "What about the incentive?"

"Take care of it, then I'll get you squared away."

"Yeah?"

"Yeah."

* * *

He drove back to the Tampa police department, adrenaline cranking. Blythe wasn't far away, in the State

Attorney's office next door. Gomez showed Tom to a room used for morning briefings.

"I need you to run a search for a white Lexus," Tom said. "Can you do that?"

Gomez blinked. "Um, you don't have the tags?"

Tom shook his head.

Gomez looked doubtful. "How about the model? Lot of white Lexuses . . ."

"Looking for an RC F Sport Coupe."

"Okay. Well, we can submit an offline search to the DMV admin. Turnaround could take a week or more." Gomez started away.

Tom caught up with him. "Can we push it a little?"

Gomez stopped and gave him a look that said, *You're already pushing it.* "You're going to wind up with all the issued license plates and their associated registration information. Not sure about you, Agent Lange, but at my department, it's very difficult to get someone to approve an offline search. I'm not sure why, except maybe that no one wants to take on all the fucking work chasing down those leads."

"Not if it's just Tampa and Naples . . ."

Gomez was solemn for a moment, his thin mustache twitching. Then he shook his head and laughed, presumably at Tom's tenacity. "Alright, man. Alright." He walked off, calling to another detective. "Hey, Seaborne, get me the DMV, alright?"

Tom jogged back beside him. "And I need something else."

Gomez rolled his eyes. "I don't fucking bel—"

"Save it," Tom said, shutting Gomez up. "Get a sketch artist with Jimmy Kendall, at Hush. He saw the driver. Do it now."

Gomez looked stunned and Tom hurried away.

He slipped back into the conference room and shut the door on the many watchful eyes in the bullpen. He sat at the big desk and called the state troopers. He issued a

Be-On-the-Lookout, or BOLO alert, for the Lexus. Without a plate number it wouldn't do much, but it was something. Then he called Everglades County and was transferred to the vice and narcotics bureau. He asked for Sergeant Coburn.

"This is Coburn."

"Sergeant, Special Agent Tom Lange."

"Afternoon, Lange."

"You got a minute?"

There was nothing from Coburn for a few seconds but the sound of him sucking on one of those hard candies. "Okay."

"I met with Sasha last night. I got her prints. I'm testing them against the loose baseboard from Carrie Hobson's apartment."

"How did you get those? She's got a clean record. You pull from the Feds?"

"Beer bottle she touched. I had it analyzed."

Coburn fell silent again. He'd even stopped rattling around the candy. "We don't care about Sasha Clay. She's small potatoes. You want to know anything else, you come in, read the affidavit that releases us. It's two hundred pages. You'll love it."

Tom felt a relief he knew was ridiculous. Coburn's operation wasn't interested in Sasha and for some reason that felt good.

He could hear Blythe in his head, though — *Maybe you got your dick stroked.*

"I can't right now," Tom said. "But, I will. I just need to know if you're looking at Carrie Hobson as a facilitator. Was she holding for anyone? Cash? Drugs? Dealing out of her apartment?"

Coburn chuckled. "Boy, you don't quit. Look, I can't tell you if Bosco was at her apartment or not. I can't tell you any of that. The *only* thing I can tell you, and I told Blythe already — your vic, Carrie Hobson, is not one of the subscribers we've traced. She's nothing to us."

Another bombshell. Carrie wasn't on their radar either. They were after bigger fish, apparently.

"I got a confession to make, sir."

"Sir? Who is 'sir'? My father is 'sir.'"

"Talking to Sasha last night, she acted like she knew your operation was closing in. And while we were talking, I asked her if Carrie had stolen any drug money. She said no, but I just wanted to be straight with you that it came up. It slipped, and I'm sorry."

A long silence. Tom tensed, ready for the blowback.

"I appreciate the disclosure, Lange. Blythe know you're talking to me?"

Tom let out a breath. "She's with the State Attorney. We're going to have another look at Steve Hobson, the ex-husband of our murder victim. I'll bring her up to speed as soon as she's out."

Coburn surprised him with another chuckle. Then the laughter faded and the clicking of the candy against his teeth resumed. "Don't fuck with Blythe, man. She's got claws."

CHAPTER TWENTY-SEVEN

The sun lowered toward the horizon as the forensics team scoured Steve Hobson's house.

Tom felt like the clock was running faster.

Techs poured into the house wearing white jumpsuits with "IFS" stenciled on the back in black. The street was choked with police vehicles, several uniformed officers milled on the lawn and the commotion had attracted attention. People were on their porches and in their yards, watching from windows.

Steve Hobson was livid. He'd been shown the warrant and let the techs in, but insisted on staying at the house with his son. Tom could have him removed from the scene, but instead convinced him to sit on the porch, and let the investigators do their work.

Hobson gripped his four-year-old boy like someone wanted to take him. Tom watched the kid goggle at all the people going through the house, interested in what they were doing.

"What do they think they're going to find?" Hobson took a seat at last, and Harley squirmed in his lap.

"What do you think they might find?"

"I told you I wouldn't talk to you again without my lawyer."

"Alright." Tom nodded. "You don't have to talk to me. That's your right. Just like I don't have to arrest you."

"For what? What would you possibly arrest me for?"

Tom was glad the kid's attention was focused elsewhere. "How much marijuana do you have inside? Tell me now, and it will all go much smoother for you."

Hobson grew bright red. "Nothing. There's nothing in the house."

"Listen," Tom said. "You got an eighth in there, maybe?"

Steve pursed his lips but Tom figured it was about that much. A personal supply.

"What I want, is for you to answer me some real easy questions. If you've got nothing to hide, you don't need a lawyer."

He cringed at his own shopworn line. The funny thing was, it was true. He didn't give a shit about Steve Hobson the casual pot smoker. He cared about Steve Hobson, ex-husband of Carrie and potential killer.

"Fine," Steve said, looking constipated. "Ask. But if I don't like the question I'm not answering."

"Do you own a Lexus RC F Sport Coupe?"

Steve's expression changed so radically it was almost comical. "Are you kidding me? No."

"Know anyone who does? Have any friends? What about Donna Pitt?"

"Donna? No. She drives a piece of shit. No one I know drives a Lexus . . . whatever you said." His brow furrowed with curiosity. "That car has something to do with what happened to Carrie?"

Tom dodged it. "Never mind. You and Carrie divorced eighteen months ago. Twelve months ago, she started renting her apartment. I don't know where she was for those interim six months. I was hoping you did."

Harley spoke before Steve could answer. The boy cocked his head at his father. "Daddy, can I have a popsicle?"

"No. Get down now. Play with your truck over there."

"I want a popsicle!"

Steve set Harley on the porch and the boy whipped up a tantrum, collapsing onto the floorboards and howling. Hobson reached for him but the boy batted his hands away. A dark vein swelled in Hobson's forehead as he tried to calm the kid down.

Hobson raised his voice to Tom. "Am I a suspect?"

"Did you visit Carrie at Hush on Tuesday the seventeenth?"

"What? No. I told you, I haven't spoken to her in five months. Listen, if you want proof that I was here that Tuesday, you can talk to my neighbor." He pointed to the house next door. Tom saw a woman's face looming in the window.

Tom glanced at the uniformed officers who'd been close enough to overhear. Two of them headed toward the house next door as the woman disappeared from the window.

Harley was really wailing and Hobson couldn't calm him. "This is bullshit," he panted. He grabbed the boy up who screamed and tried to wriggle free.

Tom felt for the guy. He beckoned a remaining Tampa officer over and whispered to her. The officer nodded and put on a big smile as she approached Harley. "Hey, buddy . . . you want to check out my police car? Turn on the lights?"

Harley gave a big nod, the tears already drying on his cheeks. Hobson looked skeptical but he let the cop lead Harley by the hand to one of the squad cars.

"Do I know where Carrie was for those six months, or whatever? No. I have no idea. Probably some shitty motel. Or she found some dude to shack up with."

They stood watching little Harley climb into the police car. He was all smiles and questions as the officer flicked on the lights. The headlights and taillights strobed white and red.

"You think she would've gone back home?" Tom asked.

"No."

"Stayed with one of her sisters?"

"She didn't want anything to do with them. Or, they didn't want anything to do with her."

"How come?"

Hobson shrugged. "Bitches be crazy." He stepped from the porch and called to the boy, "Hey, Harley, be careful in there . . ."

Hobson moved off to collect his son and Tom let him go.

The two officers returned from next door. One of them said to Tom, "Neighbor claims Hobson and his son were here all day Tuesday the seventeenth, car was parked, and the boy came over to play for a half an hour — she has a dog, and the kid likes the dog."

"Think she was telling the truth?"

The officers exchanged looks. The same officer said, "Yeah. Seemed legit to me. She's like seventy. Watches the street all day long. She's willing to give a statement when Hobson was home or not, all last week."

"Good. Let's get it."

Tom's phone rang. He asked the officers to keep Hobson and his son from going in the house a little longer. Then he stepped off the curb and walked down the street, finally answering the ringing phone.

"Bad time?" Blythe asked.

"All good. How did the interview go with Donna Pitt?"

"She didn't like Carrie very much."

"Big surprise."

"Yeah. Pitt had even less nice things to say about Steve Hobson."

"Hmm," Tom said. "Interesting that Steve Hobson has placement of the kid." He turned and looked at Hobson's small house.

"It is interesting, until you talk to the judge. Pitt apparently got physical with Steve Hobson. She attacked him in front of the kid. Gave him a black eye, cracked one of his ribs."

"You're kidding me."

"She caught him cheating."

"With Carrie?"

"That's the name of that tune. Pitt is a case worker, you know, but she acts like she's a cop. You should've seen her. The woman had more swagger than Elvis."

Tom laughed, maybe a bit too eagerly. It was good to have Blythe in a companionable mood again.

"Pitt started snooping on Steve Hobson after she suspected him of some online rendezvous. She wanted to see if he was making it with any of these women in real life. He had, at the time, plans to meet up with Carrie Anne Gallo. They'd met each other on Match.com, according to Pitt."

"Okay . . ."

"So, Donna Pitt goes into Hobson's computer, finds all this stuff, confronts him on it, and they, you know, they break-up. She tries to get custody of her son, but Hobson has the police report, pictures, everything, on the beating. So she gets stuck with weekends and he gets primary placement."

Tom considered all of this. No wonder Steve Hobson didn't want the cops poking around in his business. Not just because of any marijuana. He was a cheater whose girlfriend had kicked his ass when she found out. Then he'd married the woman he'd had an affair with . . . for ten months. He had *The Jerry Springer Show* written all over him. "So what do we think of Pitt going after Carrie?"

"She claims she's had no contact with Carrie Hobson since Carrie's divorce from Steve. They'd seen each other sometimes when Pitt picked up Harley for weekend custody."

Tom felt the late afternoon sun beating through his clothes.

"She works all week," Blythe said. "She was at work for the TOD. So what about Hobson? We have nothing to verify his alibi, right? Just his kid. And his car is white, correct?"

"Yeah, white car, but not the same. And Hobson's neighbor can verify the seventeenth — she's still giving a statement to Tampa. Honestly I think Hobson goes over to the house to sell her weed, or something. Regardless, the neighbor says Hobson was home all day, came over with his kid and played with the dog for a couple hours on Tuesday afternoon. We'll check Wednesday, but . . . I don't know. I don't see it. I don't see Steve Hobson as our killer."

Blythe fell silent, it was clear they were both thinking the same thing: Steve Hobson and Donna Pitt were looking like dead ends.

"Did you ask Pitt about the six-month gap?" Tom asked. "Maybe she knows where Carrie was, following the divorce from Steve?"

"I did ask her. She says she has no idea . . ."

Tom waited, sensing a change in Blythe's tone.

"What?"

"Pitt says she's pretty sure Carrie was a pro."

Tom rejected the idea. Carrie was straight — there was no evidence of any drugs, any illegal activities. She couldn't be a prostitute. She was just a girl whose dreams of being a professional dancer had met with reality and she'd gotten practical and turned to stripping. He thought about her Match.com profile. It was sweet and innocent. Just a country girl looking for a nice boy.

"Yeah, but Steve Hobson married her," Tom said. "If he was hunting for a pro . . . you don't end up marrying the woman you pay for sex."

"Maybe Steve Hobson is sentimental. Maybe he thought he could 'free her of the life.'"

"So she was on the street for six months?"

"She could've been. Yeah. She could've been homeless after the divorce. Steve Hobson doesn't have much, financially, and they did the divorce online, no-fault split."

Tom lit a cigarette. If Carrie was a pro, it didn't really change much. If anything, it just added to the pool of unknown people who had encountered her. It also suggested the possibility she was still working as a pro while stripping at Hush.

"Well, this is all just on Pitt's word? A disgruntled, violent ex-girlfriend of Steve Hobson's?"

"Well, Pitt is a supervisor at the work release program in St. Pete's. She sees prostitutes almost every day. And pros have been known to use Match.com, even craigslist, to advertise. Most of the time it's fake profiles. Web cam solicitations, or escorts seeking 'companionship.' If it's an individual, and they use the word 'companion' in their copy, certain men know what that means, and they bite. They can pass back a coded phrase, and if they get one of those little winky faces, the deal is on."

Tom could remember Carrie's profile easily enough. She'd used the phrase "looking for fun and adventure with the right companion." He walked back toward the house, moving quickly. "I'll ask him."

He hung up and pitched the cigarette away. Steve Hobson was chasing his son around on the lawn, looking none too happy about it. The boy made a dash for the squad car, and the Tampa cop, good humored, let him climb in again.

"That's enough, Harley," Hobson said. He glanced at Tom.

Tom pushed him, firmly but gently, into the driveway.

"Hey," Hobson protested. "Hey, what the hell? Police brutality now?"

Tom saw the Tampa cop look over and then return her attention to the kid.

"Did you know Carrie was hooking? Is that how you met — you solicited her?"

Hobson's lips moved soundlessly for a moment, then he dropped his eyes and turned his head away. His body language confessed it all.

"Take him in," Tom said to the Tampa cops. Then he growled at Hobson, "I've had it with you. You've withheld critical information, and you've solicited a prostitute. Maybe we'll let you out when the search is over. Call Pitt and have her pick up your son. Otherwise he can stay with DCF."

Hobson's lip trembled at the same time his eyes brimmed with anger. "Not in front of Harley," he whispered.

"Fine." Tom walked over to the boy and picked him up. "Hey, pal. Come with me a minute. Can you show me the dog next door?"

Tom carried Harley off as the Tampa cops put the cuffs on Steve Hobson.

* * *

Tom and Blythe watched on the monitors. They had grilled Hobson and now he sat alone in the room looking deflated.

"His story is sticking," Blythe said.

It was true. No matter how they phrased the questions, Hobson came back with the same answers. Tom had talked to the neighbor, and she was willing to swear Hobson was home on Wednesday, the eighteenth, too. That was the date of death. So he had an alibi, and his phone and email data — which he'd turned over to computer forensics willingly — was consistent with his story. He hadn't been in touch with Carrie other than the times he'd already mentioned. Carrie's phone had not been found in his house, and he didn't own a Lexus. The only question left was what to do about his pending charges.

Blythe had an answer. "A guy frequents a prostitute, marries her, divorces her and she's later killed, probably by someone else. I can't even think about a solicitation charge for this poor schmuck."

"Whatever," Tom said. "Kick him loose."

"You sound tired."

He shrugged.

"This really bothers you? That Carrie was a pro? Are you a moralist or something, Agent Lange?"

He thought about it. He'd gotten rough with Hobson. "It bothers me that I didn't see it."

Blythe fell silent a moment. "How's your brother?"

Her comment surprised him. Before he could respond, she said, "Look, I know I came down on you about it. But, I get it. Family is important. I have a brother, too . . . I look out for him. There's always *one*, you know?"

"Thanks. I like it when you do this human thing."

"Does it make you feel warm and fuzzy?"

"It does. I'm not going to lie, Blythe. I like warm and fuzzy."

She laughed. He thought when she laughed, she really meant it.

"So where does this leave us?"

They were alone in the viewing room. Blythe pushed back from the desk, rolling in the swivel chair. They faced each other.

"I like Bosco for it. You know that. It's just been tricky with Coburn's operation. I also think Sasha Clay could be involved. We just have to play it cool, wait for Coburn's word."

"We're not afraid Bosco is going to run?"

"No. They have eyes on him. He's not at work, but he's still in Tampa. They're waiting to see what he does.

But, it's close. We'll move as soon as we can." She paused. "You really don't like Bosco for this?"

"It's not that I don't like him for it — he fits, but the location doesn't. Why Naples? And then there's the video, the Lexus, and the other guy. I told Gomez to get a sketch artist with Jimmy Kendall. Jimmy says he saw the man in the Lexus."

Her good humor dissolved. "You did what?"

"He saw the fucking driver, Blythe."

She stood and scrambled for her phone. She dialed a number, Tom watching. "What are you doing?"

"Calling Coby."

"Why?"

"Jimmy could be in the net. We ran him. He's had two possessions and a DUI. I think he may be an informant. I need to run it by Coby."

Tom stood too, cursing under his breath.

He watched the monitor a moment. The door to the interview room opened. Harley ran to his father and they embraced. Hobson squeezed the boy tight. It looked like he was crying.

CHAPTER TWENTY-EIGHT

Tom drove south through amber streetlights. The long, flat drives between cities were wearing him thin. This convergence of cases was a real problem. Now they were waiting until tomorrow to decide whether to send a sketch artist to Jimmy because of his informant status. No wonder cops grew sick of procedure.

He opened the glove compartment and took out a bottle of pills. They were over the counter, non-prescription, in the natural remedies section of the drug store. They were supposed to help a person relax, quiet their mind. He doubted they even did anything except on a psychosomatic level. But he shook two out and popped them in his mouth anyway.

It didn't help matters that Blythe thought she had the case solved. Bosco was all she could see. But Tom thought there were people they hadn't looked at yet, possibilities unexplored.

Waterways, connecting to Rookery Bay.

The victim as incidental, the killer meaning to satisfy some other craving or need besides sex or murder per se, but to prove a point, make some kind of statement. These thoughts were like an itch that Tom couldn't scratch.

His phone rang, interrupting his train of thought, and he pulled off into a gas station.

It was Veronica Morley from the crime lab.

"We matched the prints to the baseboard. One set belongs to Raymond T. Bosco. The other we've matched to Sasha Clay, thanks to your beer bottle."

That clinched it. Bosco and Sasha had been in Carrie's apartment and had removed whatever had been tucked away in her wall space.

"Thank you, Veronica."

"Yeah. I'm going home. Been here eighteen hours straight today. Gonna go watch some Netflix and pass out."

"You do that. Thanks again."

He hung up, and tapped his cell phone against his knee.

Sasha and Bosco in Carrie's apartment . . . But Carrie wasn't someone that Coburn's team was interested in — Coburn didn't consider her part of the network. If Sasha and Bosco had been using her apartment as a stash house, it made Carrie a facilitator. But what if Carrie hadn't known? Her prints weren't on the baseboard. Maybe she had arrived home early one day, and busted one of them. Probably Bosco. And since she'd discovered what he was doing, he'd killed her, then had someone else drive the body to Naples? Such as the man in the Lexus, part of the same damned drug operation Tom wasn't allowed to touch.

He understood the legalities of Coburn's op as well as the emotion — vice narcotics had run on overtime for months, building their case. A murder charge brought against Bosco was a wrecking ball that would scatter the network. Coburn could lose the whole thing unless they all made just the right moves.

Coburn would try to get Bosco to flip, and take Palumbo down, close his clubs, shut down the drug traffic. Somewhere in there they could get Bosco to confess to the murder of Carrie Hobson, if he had done it.

Tom wished it felt right, but it just didn't.

He pulled out of the gas station and drove the rest of the way into Naples.

When he got back to the field office, no one else was there. It was dark outside, mercifully cool in the small space. It was late, and he figured he should take Blythe's advice and pace himself. Go home, sleep in his own bed, start fresh the next day.

But he couldn't. Not yet. That itch was there.

He booted up his computer. With no one else in the office, he decided to sneak a cigarette, ashing in a paper coffee cup while he checked his email. He'd been copied, along with Blythe, on an email about Carrie's car. IFS had worked the car and analyzed a few clothing fibers, hairs, and stains — possible sweat secretions. What they'd determined was that Carrie had had a couple different people in her car over a period of weeks, but no flags were raised. Still, they suggested that all employees at Hush submit to DNA tests so they could match the trace evidence, wherever possible. Tom ran a hand over his face and groaned. Such a process would be tedious, and cause Coburn more trouble.

He drummed his fingers on the desk, waiting for the courage to listen to his gut. Thinking about someone with something to prove.

Someone who'd seemed to revel in the ambiguities of post-mortem evaluation. Someone whose socially awkward assistant had blurted out something about a scandal.

It had been bugging him since talking to Andrea the previous afternoon.

Tom pecked at the laptop and opened up the website for the District Medical Examiner's Office.

Like Blythe said, Dr. Alan Ward had done extensive schooling to get where he was. He'd gone to school at the University of Florida and William R. Maples Center for Forensic Medicine and graduated near the top of his class. Then he'd gone on to Miami to complete a residency training program in anatomic and clinical pathology. After residency, he'd trained as a forensic pathologist under noted forensic consultant David Albrecht.

Educated, indeed.

Tom stared at Ward's picture, thinking of the way he'd been on Monday morning, snippy and standoffish. He considered the way Ward had seemed to bully Eileen Gallo into using the mortuary service he probably received referral fees from.

I'm being silly, Tom thought. Grieving relatives probably needed a firm hand to guide them through such a horrific ordeal. Still, he flipped through his notes and found *Young & Sons*, the service Ward had prescribed, then found their website online.

The images of shiny caskets and floral arrangements stirred memories of his parents' funeral. One funeral, two caskets. His father's body had been badly burned and the casket was closed. His mother had died more due to smoke inhalation, and hers had been open. He'd reached out to touch her, unthinking, just drawn to her, and Nick had grabbed his hand . . .

Tom looked at more pictures of Ward.

The pathologist had bothered him since day one. But just thinking Ward was an asshole wasn't grounds to be suspicious. It was Andrea's mention of a scandal that had really done it. What was she referring to?

There were some shots of Ward with a group of other doctors, posing in their laboratory. Tom analyzed the pathologist's posture. He was slender, always unsmiling, his hands delicate.

One lab picture accompanied an article from the *Tampa Bay Herald.* It described a lawsuit filed by Ward, dated five years ago.

> An official of the Tampa Medical Examiner's Office sued the city on Wednesday, claiming that he had been forced from his job for raising questions about the office's use of a novel form of DNA testing whose reliability had come under question.
>
> The lawsuit is likely to add to a growing debate over the office's use of new techniques to analyze trace samples of DNA, a practice that other public crime laboratories have shied away from because of concerns over reliability.
> Such critics say that while DNA profiles analyzed from a drop of blood or a semen stain are the gold standard of forensic evidence, the "low copy number" method involves too much subjectivity and even guessing, and could lead to wrongful convictions.

Tom lingered over the words "low copy number" for a moment before continuing.

> The former employee, Dr. Alan Ward, 46, served for nearly a

> decade as director of the office's Forensic Toxicology Laboratory, which conducts post-mortem examinations to determine the absence or presence of drugs, and what role they may have had in causing someone's death.
>
> But Dr. Ward claimed in the lawsuit, which was filed in Federal District Court in Tampa, that he fell out of favor with his superiors because he had sought more transparency about the office's research into the novel technique.
>
> The Medical Examiner's Office said on Wednesday that it was "committed to fairness and providing the highest standards of service for the people of Tampa." It added that court had "recognized that our DNA techniques are reliable and generally accepted by the scientific community."

Tom sat back after reading, reminded of multiple interactions with Ward wherein the pathologist warned against making evaluations too soon.

He searched for an article describing the outcome of the lawsuit, but there weren't any to be found. The press wasn't as interested, perhaps, only the sensation of such a filing in the first place made the news. He scanned for more headlines and found articles on Ward being involved with several homicide and death investigations for Everglades County. All pretty standard stuff.

The lawsuit was very likely what Andrea had been talking about.

Tom did one last search, on Dr. David Albrecht, Ward's former mentor during his fellowship program, recently retired. He found a phone number.

The time was just before 10 p.m. — a bit late for a phone call.

On impulse, he dialed anyway. The phone number was for a landline. Albrecht didn't answer, but a machine picked up. Tom left a quick, general message that he was with the FDLE and had a couple questions for Albrecht about a case.

Tom hid the evidence of his smoking, rinsing the paper cup before trashing it, washed his hands, and left the office.

* * *

Ward's home address was in the Everglades County personnel and contact file. He lived ten minutes from the field office in Central Naples, on Malaga Way. Tom kept watch on the house numbers then pulled over when he found Ward's one-story home with stucco siding and a red clay roof. There were a few lights on inside and a light-brown Toyota Rav 4 sitting in the driveway.

Ward was unmarried. At least, Tom had never seen a wedding ring on the man, and there was no mention of a wife or children on any website or police contact information. His house was modest, the vehicle he drove inexpensive. Yet, as chief medical examiner for the county, with all his credentials and experience, Ward had to be making a very comfortable living. By all accounts he ought to have had a home closer to the ocean, and he could've driven a much nicer vehicle.

Tom saw a shape move past the window. Someone was home.

Suddenly Tom's suspicion collapsed, and reality poured in. He had nothing solid on Ward at all. He'd gone digging around in the past of a respected pathologist, and now he was sitting outside the man's home, evaluating his lifestyle.

It was ridiculous.

Tom pulled away from the curb and headed home.

CHAPTER TWENTY-NINE

SATURDAY

Tom swam his morning laps in the pool. It was still early enough that a mist skimmed the surface and the water felt like warm silk. He tried to concentrate on his form as he plowed through, but his mind kept drifting. It was now five days since Carrie Hobson's body had been pulled from the bay.

He reached the shallow end for the twentieth time and rose up out of the water. He came face to face with a pair of shoes and looked up at Agent Blythe.

"You weren't answering your phone," she said.

Tom got out, grabbed his towel. It wasn't even seven thirty, with the sun just breaking over the condo rooftops. "What's wrong?"

Her eyes were hidden behind dark glasses. "Get dressed. I'll tell you in the car. You can ride with me. Hurry up, though, okay?"

Tom jogged back to the condo. Normally he would've showered off the chlorine, but he dressed quickly, opting for a pair of slacks and one of the button-downs he'd had the intern buy for him. He ran the toothbrush hastily over his teeth, and returned to Blythe, sitting in her department-issued Crown Vic.

He drew the seatbelt across his chest, looking at her. "The suspense is killing me." He was trying levity, but Blythe's expression was slack, her mouth a wry line.

She rolled out of the complex. "Just sit back. Okay? Relax. When we get there, let me do the talking."

Her tone of voice, her hidden eyes — it was starting to get to him. He could feel the old anxiety creeping up his neck, like a heat. Something terrible was just around the corner.

"Where?"

"Downtown. We've got another body."

* * *

Naples PD was everywhere — they were up on the bridge, having closed down both an eastbound and westbound lane of route 41 traffic, and in the Tin City parking lot. A uniformed officer waved Blythe through and she parked the vehicle. An ambulance sat nearby.

Three nights ago, Tom had been sitting with Blythe near the harbor, able to see this spot where the creek flowed out of Naples Bay beneath the bridge. Now he followed Blythe toward the same underpass, his stomach tightening as they slipped into the shadows.

The water was low, the thick, concrete legs of the bridge — spaced every few yards — were stained that rusty color from high tide. A long scree of rocks broadsided the concrete walkway.

A body lay on the rocks, face down, dark hair fanned out.

Several detectives surrounded it, standing on cardboard laid out to protect the ground. Naples PD had erected barricades on both sides of the underpass. The lamps along the walkway were unlit, everything gray in the bridge shadow.

Blythe and Tom climbed over the berm and onto the rocks, following the cardboard path. The closer he got to the body, the more his stomach knotted. He already thought he knew who it was.

"Morning," Blythe said to the group.

"Morning," said a man with a trim goatee.

Blythe held up her badge. "Special Agent Lauren Blythe, and this is Special Agent Tom Lange."

The other law enforcement officers returned introductions. Detectives Bill Reddy and Angelo De Sauza with Naples PD, and Lieutenant John Haylock with Everglades County, who wore the goatee. Katie Mills was also there.

"What've we got?" Blythe asked, looking down the rocks toward the dead woman.

Bill Reddy answered. "A jogger called 911 from her cell phone at 5:38 this morning. We got the call for service, and 911 sent the bus."

Someone else was approaching. Dr. Ward climbed over the berm and down onto the rocks.

They waited until he reached them, and everyone greeted. Mills started taking pictures. "My team is on the way," Mills told Ward. Everyone fell silent as she took more shots and Ward, down on his knees, absorbed the scene. Finally, Ward motioned to one of the cops standing by. De Sauza bent down and helped turn the body over. Tom braced himself. When he saw the woman's face, he exhaled.

Haylock snapped a look at Tom. "Know her?"

"Sasha Clay. From Tampa."

Haylock glanced at Blythe. "Your Rookery Bay case."

Blythe nodded, studying the dead woman's face. Blythe was probably thinking, *Coby's case, too.* At least Sasha appeared intact — nothing had eaten away at her. Tom noted the high-water marks on the bridge supports again, then glanced upriver. Sasha had wound up on the rocks, but maybe only after the water settled and left her there.

Suddenly Tom bent over and clutched the edge of the berm, gagging. He remembered Sasha touching him, pressed against him, her hair dusting over his face.

He felt a hand on his shoulder.

"I'm alright." He wiped his mouth. He saw concern on their faces, or disgust. Except for Ward, who wasn't looking.

Haylock put his hands on his hips. "Alright," he said to Blythe, "so, how are we handling this?"

"Ward and the district medical office — it's his crime scene. Your CSB on the documentation, processing and evidence recovery. We'll work alongside you to see what it turns up in relation to the Rookery Bay homicide and take it from there."

Haylock nodded, seeming pleased. Tom heard another vehicle pull up in the parking lot, an Everglades County Sheriff's Office van. The doors opened and the evidence techs got out, gathered up their gear and trotted over.

"See what it *turns up*?" Tom muttered.

He kept seeing her face, her eyes. *You smell like him*, she'd said. Then she'd invited him to come back to her home.

Blythe cut Tom a sharp look. "Excuse me, Agent Lange?"

He was getting his strength back and he felt a swelling wave of anger. "See what it turns up in relation to the Rookery Bay case?" He pointed at Sasha. "This has everything to do with our case, and you know it does."

The tech crew climbing down the rocks were giving the cops nervous glances.

Tom was on a roll, knowing where it was heading, no longer caring. "And we tiptoed around, God forbid we encroach on Coburn's precious drug op—"

"That's enough, Agent Lange," Blythe said, her face flushed. Her eyes jerked to Haylock, who looked baffled.

Tom knew how it probably appeared — the new guy was mouthing off, couldn't handle his shit.

"A sketch artist. A fucking *sketch artist*, and there's red tape . . ."

"Lange, get out of here," Blythe said.

Ward spoke from the edge of the water. "I'd say time of death no more than twelve hours ago."

Tom's head whipped around. He was seeing red now. He started toward Ward, his footing unsteady on the rocks. "And *you*. What's with you, huh? This get you off, does it? You like this?"

Ward just looked at Tom as if he were watching some animal at the zoo. Curious, but detached. Safe.

Blythe shouted, "Lange. Stand down. Get out of here *now*."

Tom growled at Ward, "What do you think happened to her? Huh? How did she die?"

Ward's eyes were dark knots behind his glasses. He looked down and touched a gloved hand to the back of Sasha Clay's head. When he pulled his hand away, his fingertips were spotted with blood. "You know how I feel about premature determinations, Agent Lange . . ."

"Yeah. Oh yeah, I do."

". . . but it looks like she sustained damage to the back of the head, and it killed her."

"That's what I thought," Tom said. He climbed back to the underpass, stumbling along the way. He could feel everyone's eyes on him, and knew Blythe was following behind.

* * *

"You're done, Tom."

"Yeah, yeah," he said, waving his arms. He dimly realized it was the first time Blythe had called him by his first name. They stood a few feet apart in the parking lot by Blythe's Crown Vic. The heat was stifling.

"I gave you every chance. I don't know what you think this is . . ."

"Drive me back home, please."

"I'm not leaving this scene, are you nuts? Seriously, Lange, do you have some . . . oh forget it. You're just done. You need a fucking shrink." Blythe turned and walked back to the underpass, her shoes making flat claps on the blacktop. Tom watched her disappear into the shadows beneath the bridge. He could see the shapes of people moving around. He tried not to think about Sasha Clay, but he could practically smell her perfume.

He turned and steamed across the parking lot to one of the Tin City entrances, enflamed, trembling with emotion. He found the doors locked and pulled on them, rattled them, cursing. He kicked the doors, then kicked them again.

"Tommy?"

Tom shielded his eyes to see in the bright morning sun — Blythe had picked him up so quickly he'd left his sunglasses back at the condo. Nick was walking across the lot, coming down from 41.

"Tommy? What's going on? I had to park next door at the marina . . . Hey, you alright, bro?"

"It's Saturday — you're working?"

"Yeah, just on my way in. No rest for the wicked. What's happening here?"

Nick looked pretty normal, Tom thought. He wore slacks and a short-sleeve collared shirt that revealed one of his arm tattoos. He had a briefcase and his hair was combed. Tom got up close to his brother. He didn't smell like alcohol. Tom pulled Nick's sunglasses off and stared. His eyes were clear.

"Jesus, Tom," Nick said, taking his sunglasses back. "What the fuck is it?"

Nick followed Tom's gaze beneath the bridge. It was hard to make out, but it looked like half the cops and techs down there were staring back this way, probably talking about Tom's outburst. "Who's down there?" Nick asked. "Who is it?"

"Let's go into your office."

Since Nick had arrived, Tom felt some of the emotion subside. But he was in a fishbowl out here. Even some of the uniformed Naples cops holding the street were watching.

"Alright," Nick said. "Alright."

Nick got out his keys and opened the wooden doors. Tom followed him in.

* * *

It was cool in the mini-mall, the shops dark. Tom followed Nick, trying to calm down, worried he was going to have a full-on nervous breakdown. It wasn't about the job, or losing it. It was about seeing Sasha dead under the bridge — that was a big part of it. It was Ward, too, it was everything. Tom needed to unload.

Nick stopped in front of his office and Tom watched pictures of houses scroll by on the monitor as Nick opened the front door. For a moment, one looked familiar, then it was gone.

Nick's office was a single room with a bathroom in back.

"Tommy." Nick took a seat at his desk. "Tell me what's going on."

Tom left out the names, but he filled Nick in from the beginning — a kayak tour guide and her two guests finding the body — up to the trip to Kronos and the lap dance, before Nick interrupted.

"So who's under the bridge? Another stripper?"

"I can't say, buddy. Sorry." He realized he was parched. "You got anything to drink in here?"

Nick gave him a look. "Bit early for that."

"No, dumbass. Water."

Nick smirked and took a couple bottles of spring water out of his mini-fridge. Tom felt better now that he was with Nick. He became sidetracked for a moment, sipping his water. "Where did you go? I tried you a few times yesterday."

Nick looked thoughtful. "I'm sorry, man, I just needed a couple days to get my shit straight. And I had to rent a car."

Tom had to admit, Nick did look better. Tom knew about addiction, though. There were ups and downs. Promises went unfulfilled. But he felt — he hoped — that things could be different this time.

Nick frowned, thinking. "So you think it's this bouncer guy who did it? To the first one? The main victim?"

"That's the obvious choice," Tom said. "And there's evidence to build a case against him. He's tied to both victims — they worked with him at Hush. He's also tied to this drug network I can't say too much about."

"Does this guy have a record?"

"Yeah, but they didn't let me see much because it's a sensitive op."

Nick grimaced. "That's bullshit. You're trying to solve a murder."

Tom shrugged and guzzled the rest of the water.

"So it sounds like your partner there, or supervisor, she's going to be able to wrap this up, pin it on this bouncer guy. I mean, from what you're telling me, it sounds like he's the bad guy, doesn't it?"

Tom played with the empty water bottle for a moment.

Nick cocked his head. "What?"

Tom told him about the video footage and the mystery man seen talking to Carrie outside of Hush.

"I don't think the guy was the bouncer. For one thing, I'm pretty sure the bouncer stuck his head out of the club seconds before the stranger showed up. This stranger talks to her for almost a full minute, then follows her on her way home. Driving a White Lexus Sport Coupe."

"The Lexus is definitely not the bouncer's?"

Tom shook his head. "The one thing I could get from Coburn was the make and model of the vehicle registered to the bouncer. It's a Camaro. I also checked to see if the club owner has a Lexus, and he doesn't."

"Can't you just find out who owns this Lexus if you can do all that?"

"You have to do a Boolean search. It takes a little time. Tampa hemmed and hawed about doing it. I should've just done it myself. Now . . . shit. I don't know, maybe they'll come through."

"So then you'll know." Nick raised his eyebrows. He looked so youthful in that moment, Tom's heart stung with nostalgia. Sitting across from him was the kid with big dreams, the natural athlete and born leader Nick had started out as.

"*Maybe* I'll know. Identifying the car and its owner from the warehouse video won't necessarily prove anything. It could give us opportunity, but we'd still need motive. And it could be stolen, registered to someone else, who knows."

Nick shook his head, woeful. The youthful look drained away and he appeared older again, his more seasoned self.

Tom lowered his voice a little. "So, you're off the hook with those guys from the track? Free and clear?"

Nick soberly nodded his head. "Yeah, we're square. And I'm all done with that."

Tom must've been smirking because Nick said, "What? Come on, Tommy . . ."

"Hey, I hope so, Nick. But, you know. It's a hard road. You might need some help."

"Oh spare me the AA bullshit, please. I tried it and it didn't take. I'm not using, Tommy."

Tom believed him. He was happy for his brother, but he felt empty now that the storm of emotion had passed.

He stood up. "Hey, I know you just got to the office, but would you give me a ride home?"

Nick didn't rise, he only looked up at Tom. "Really?"

Tom felt a flash of the recent anger resurging. "What — I can drive you to Bonita Springs but you can't—?"

"Tom, no. Jesus. I'll fucking drive you home. But you're just giving up? Just like that?"

Tom pointed at the door, thinking of Blythe chewing him out in the parking lot. "Nick, my supervisor just told me I was over. I was already on thin ice with her. Now I just puked at a crime scene, yelled at her and the chief medical examiner. They're right — I'm off my fucking rocker."

Nick looked mournful, but he finally got up. "Well, you sound better to me than you've sounded in days. But, what do I know? Fine, let's get you home."

CHAPTER THIRTY

Tom stepped out of the shower and his cell phone was ringing. He winced when he saw the incoming number — it was Turnbull, from the main office.

"Lange . . ." Turnbull's voice was thick with disappointment.

"I know, sir. I'm sorry."

Turnbull breathed heavily into the phone, then launched into his spiel about how an agent should conduct themselves, both in the field and in life. He talked about the complexities the FDLE faced when handling investigations that were multi-jurisdictional. But he didn't fire Tom.

"The Internal Affairs Bureau will be in touch. I've recommended three weeks suspension, with pay."

"Thank you, sir. May I ask, who issued the complaint? Ward or Blythe?"

"I issued it, Tom. Wrap up what you're working on, contact your rep. I'll speak to you later."

Tom hung up and finished getting dressed, feeling like shit. Part of him thought it would've been better to be fired. He had no feel for this, apparently. Here he'd considered himself a stickler for procedure and it turned out he was all emotion. Maybe it was finally time to call Dr. Camden.

But the phone rang again. Tom didn't recognize the number.

"Is this Agent Lange?"

"Speaking."

"Agent Lange, it's David Albrecht. You left a message — you wanted to talk about Alan Ward?" Albrecht sounded apprehensive. "I almost didn't call back . . ."

Tom searched for his notepad. "No, thank you, sir. So glad you called back." He hurried downstairs and sat at the kitchen table. "You trained Ward as a forensic pathologist after his residency?"

"That's right. Is he involved in something?"

Tom found the question telling. "Well, as you may know, he's the chief medical examiner here in Everglades County. He's doing the pathology work on a victim in a murder case investigated by my department. I'm just doing a little background check. There have been some things that . . . well, to be honest, I'm just looking to confirm his credibility."

"Oh boy," Albrecht said.

"Is there something I should know, Dr. Albrecht?"

The man hesitated. "Maybe we should meet. Where are you located?"

"I'm in Naples, sir, just outside the city in Lely."

"Okay. I'm in Bonita Springs. Do you have time today?"

"I do, absolutely. How about right now?"

"Alright. That's fine. I'll give you my address."

* * *

David Albrecht's lavish home was a few blocks from the beach. There was a widow's peak which probably viewed the ocean. Albrecht was a man of about seventy, with silvery hair. He greeted Tom at the front door and took him through the house, which was bright and cheery. Two shaggy Golden Retrievers plodded alongside the men. Albrecht's wife was in the backyard, sitting by the pool. She smiled as Albrecht introduced her — Winnie — and offered Tom something to eat or drink.

"I'm fine, thank you, ma'am."

She took the dogs inside while Tom and Albrecht sat down at a shaded table tucked up against a rambling wall of bougainvillea. Albrecht had a half-smoked cigar sitting in an ashtray and lit it. He squinted against the smoke and looked at Tom. "Would you like one? They're Nicaraguan. I don't bother with the expensive stuff."

"Thanks, I'm alright. Mind if I smoke one of these?" He pulled out his cigarettes and Albrecht nodded it was fine.

"You know about the lawsuit?" Albrecht asked.

"I read about it. Ward worked for the forensic toxicology lab in Tampa. He didn't like some of the new tech, is that right? A novel form of DNA test."

Albrecht nodded, then got a distant look. "Ward was very meticulous. Very meticulous. That's the trait of a good pathologist. And Ward is definitely a good pathologist."

"What was he like? On a personal level."

Albrecht blew out a boll of smoke, his gaze wandering. "He was different, for sure. People expect pathologists to be eccentric, but mainly, they're not. They're normal people, just able to stomach things most others can't, or won't. But Ward, he really tucked into the work."

"Did he have any sort of social life?"

Albrecht paused a moment, as if reflecting. He eyes seemed to darken. "No. That much I can say for sure. He spent every hour in the lab. I think we talked about women once, just in an offhand way, and he got down in the mouth."

"Can you tell me a little more about that? What did you talk about?"

Albrecht gave Tom a long look. "What did you say this is in regards to? Checking on Ward's credibility?"

"I'm sorry, Dr. Albrecht, I really can't say any more than that. I know this is unfair to ask . . . I just need to know your honest opinion of him. You said you talked about women. Please."

Albrecht searched Tom's eyes, then studied the tip of his cigar. "Well, let me put it this way. When you spend significant time with a person, as I spent with Alan Ward, you get to know them a bit. But Alan was very private. Practically a monk. He hardly ever socialized, almost never drank. But, yes, there was one time, I think it was around the holidays, we were at a party together. He'd had a few drinks and said something. It was hard to tell if he was joking or not. But he alluded to all the cadavers . . . that working with the dead had ruined him."

"Ruined him . . . ?"

Albrecht said nothing, and dragged on the cigar.

"Do you think he meant spiritually, or something else? Maybe physically? Sexually?"

"I don't really know."

Tom switched topics. "Can you tell me a little more about this lawsuit?"

Albrecht's eyes cleared and he blew out another plume. "Have you heard of 'low copy number DNA'?"

"I only know the basics."

"It was developed in the UK," Albrecht said. "What it means is, a profile can be obtained from only a few cells. We're talking one millionth the size of a grain of sand. Just a few cells of skin or sweat, maybe a tiny drop of blood."

Tom thought of the blood found on Carrie's clothing, then refocused on what Albrecht was saying.

"The controversy is over whether it's reliable. There are methodologies to increase sensitivity of detection to enable LCN typing, modifications during the polymerase chain reaction. But when processing a small number of starting templates, exaggerated stochastic sampling effects will occur."

Tom opened his mouth to ask for clarification of the medical jargon but Albrecht went on a moment longer. "And you also have to consider the possibility of contamination from a laboratory source. It's called 'low copy number' but actually you're copying the DNA sample more times, so that's more room for error. Normal STR typing requires seventy to a hundred and fifty diploid — those are human — cells. LCN typing can be as few as fifteen."

Tom tried to make sense of it all. Basically, Albrecht was saying that this type of testing was tricky because it made more copies of smaller DNA samples. From the article Tom had read, it seemed Ward had been against such a method — it didn't jibe with his meticulousness. And because he hadn't gone along with it, his superiors had given him a hard time, and forced his resignation. A few months later, Ward had filed a lawsuit.

"What was the outcome of the lawsuit?"

"Ward lost. The court found that there were no grounds for what he was asking — money to recompense his loss of income."

It was taking shape. Ward had an axe to grind. But how it related to Carrie's death was unclear.

"One thing I don't understand," Tom said, "Ward worked for the tox lab. Determining drugs in a body, things like that. How did the low copy number DNA come into play?"

Albrecht shifted, crossing his legs. He seemed to be growing more comfortable with Tom now that they'd veered from Ward's personal profile.

"Well, the lab is just one part of the Medical Examiner's Office. That office performs about twenty-five hundred autopsies each year, sees lots of cases. They developed novel techniques and procedures for analyzing trace quantities of DNA left on touched objects. There was a case Ward was involved in, several bodies turned up after a drug deal gone bad. Police recovered a handgun at the scene, believed to have been passed among several people. The office felt it could reliably discern DNA profiles from such a sample."

"They used the low copy number technique."

"Correct. That's when Ward balked. He was doing the tox screens on the bodies. He became very vocal that the LCN results should not be introduced in the courtroom."

"Why? Based on some moral principle?"

"Sure. It's possible he was worried it could lead to wrongful convictions, an erosion of criminal justice, et cetera. But, I don't think Ward's any kind of human rights crusader, he just believes in his way of doing things."

"I've encountered that."

"He's in it for himself. I mean . . . who isn't, to some degree. But Ward . . . Put it this way, Ward didn't like one of the cops who was working the case. They'd come to loggerheads before and this cop was really pushing for a conviction through the low copy number data. I know, because Ward was talking to me while this was going on."

"Who was the cop?"

Albrecht took another pull on his cigar, then stubbed it out in the ashtray. When the smoke cleared, he stared across the table at Tom.

"Her name was Lauren Blythe. Do you know her?"

* * *

Tom sped along in the Jeep toward the County Courthouse. He'd continued to grill Albrecht, getting earfuls of forensic jargon, but essentially it kept coming back to the same thing: low copy number typing was controversial. Cops and prosecutors loved it, because it added more to their arsenal taking down the bad guys. Sometimes all there was for evidence were a few microscopic scraps. With LCN, those scraps could mean putting a criminal behind bars.

But not everyone was aboard. Ward may have been against the technique on principle, but he'd seemed to dig in his heels for more personal reasons.

Blythe . . .

She'd been working this case that Ward was a part of. The two of them had gone head to head over whether or not to use LCN to aid in the prosecution of a big case.

Then, Ward had resigned. He'd been ostracized, Albrecht said, his pushback against LCN profiling construed as helping criminals. They'd said Ward had "gone Indian," "gone native," empathizing with the bad guys.

Blythe had a history with Ward she'd never mentioned. And now here he was, chief medical examiner in Everglades County, and he was the pathologist on the Carrie Hobson murder case. It seemed like a huge conflict of interest. And Tom had felt unsettled about how and why the FDLE had gotten involved. Maybe Blythe had spoken to Turnbull. Maybe they knew Ward would be handling the death investigation and Blythe wanted to keep an eye on him.

Tom glanced at his phone sitting on the passenger seat, rattling around with the vehicle's vibrations. He should call Blythe right now.

But, how could he trust her? And what would he say? That she'd lied to him, withheld critical information? That he thought Ward was — what? Involved in Carrie's death?

Instead, he picked up the phone and called Veronica Morley at the crime lab. Morley wasn't there, so Tom asked the tech who had answered the phone to grab the files on Carrie.

"You're using low copy number DNA typing on the Carrie Hobson case. Blood found on her shirt. Right?"

Tom was close to shouting and the tech seemed flustered.

"Correct, Agent Lange. What can—?"

Tom lowered his volume. "Anybody call you? Anyone from Everglades County hounding you for results? Vice narcotics, maybe?"

"Um, no, no one called me. I'll check the log, see if Veronica—"

"Tell me how you worked it."

"I'm sorry? Tell you how—"

"You make millions of copies of the sample's telltale DNA regions. Then you look for a match, right?"

"Well, we focus on Short Tandem Repeats, which vary widely from person to person. But essentially, yes, we look for a match."

Tom remembered his schooling — to convict a suspect, his or her STR repeats must match all thirteen STR regions in the crime scene sample.

"So where did you get your suspect samples from?" he asked. "Are you using CODIS?"

The tech seemed confused. "No, sir. We're testing a single sample right now."

Tom felt a lump in his throat. "And where did you get it from?"

"From Agent Blythe, sir."

"Name?" Tom asked. A car blared its horn as he swerved into the next lane and made a turn at the streetlight.

"The name is Raymond T. Bosco."

I fucking knew it, Tom thought.

"And how many STR sites match so far?"

"Right now we have eleven out of thirteen."

Tom put it all together. When all thirteen STR sites matched perfectly, it was virtually guaranteed you'd gotten your culprit — the odds of fingering the wrong person were about one in a billion. A single STR mismatch, however, was enough to exonerate a suspect, and the LCN typing was what made the whole thing dicey.

"Thank you." Tom hung up.

He reached the County Courthouse, grabbed a spot and jogged across the parking lot. Many cops would be wrapped up in the new Sasha Clay case, but Machado hadn't been at the crime scene. He didn't want to be seen in the main building so he called Machado and had her meet him at the field office. He told her to bring the list of volunteers from the Reserve.

She showed up at the office ten minutes later. Tom had the lights off and was sitting in the gloom.

Machado came in, looking around, a worried expression on her face. "What's going on?"

He grabbed the file from her and flopped it down on the desk. The volunteers had been alphabetized and he flipped through the pages until he came to the letter W.

Tom stared down at the thumbnail picture of Dr. Alan Ward.

Machado was nervous. "Lange? You're freaking me out a little bit."

Tom pointed at Ward's image, reading the caption beside it. "Ward volunteered for two months, two years ago. On the mangrove restoration project."

"Yeah? And? There's hundreds of volunteers. I think we counted at least thirty who are active medical professionals, law enforcement, or retired . . ."

Tom looked at her. "What did Ward have to say about it?"

She seemed to shrink from his intense gaze. "What did he say? He didn't say anything, because we didn't ask him about it."

Tom thought about it, and registered the look in Machado's eyes. She was clocking him like he had gone nuts. And, maybe he had. Tom sat down heavily in the desk chair. His eyes were drawn back to the picture of Ward. Then he turned away as Machado settled into Blythe's chair at the other desk.

"Lange, what's going on?"

He didn't know if he should say anything. He was under IAB review, for one thing. For another, the ideas forming were just an inchoate swirl. Anecdotal, still nothing solid.

"Hang on a minute," he said. "Can you just stay here for a few minutes?"

"Sure . . ." She reminded him of those child-protection workers years ago. Looking at him like they felt sorry for him.

Tom picked up the phone on the desk and called up to Tampa. He asked for Detective Gomez.

"Lange, what do you want?"

"Did you hear back on the vehicle check?"

"No, not yet. Maybe tomorrow."

"How about Jimmy Kendall? The other bouncer? I asked you to get a sketch artist to him."

Gomez was silent.

"Pick him up for me. Get him with an artist. We need the driver of that Lexus. We need the sketch, we need the reg. And we need it now."

Tom hung up before Gomez could be cute and say anything else. Then Tom looked over at Machado, who raised her eyebrows. "Boy, you're hot, huh?"

He needed to trust someone, he needed help. Blythe hadn't been upfront with him, Gomez was a narc. "Ward had some kind of falling out with the District Medical Examiner's Office in Tampa a few years back. Did you know about it?"

She shook her head.

"I talked to a former mentor of Ward's, from where he did his fellowship, a guy named David Albrecht."

"Sure, I know Albrecht. He wrote the book on forensic chemistry. He was on one of those shows . . . oh, what was it? One of those cop shows."

"Albrecht said Ward had no friends, never a girlfriend. I think Ward might've had some sexual issues. And he worked in Tampa until this case. There were multiple vics in a drug deal gone bad. A highway chase, car crashes. Ward was working the toxicology for Traffic Homicide Investigations. And Blythe was involved."

"I didn't know that."

"When you and I first met, you said you thought Blythe had been with the Drug Interdiction Team. You were right. I checked and she was definitely on that case. The whole thing hinged on DNA obtained from the car wrecks. The cops closed their case but Ward raised a racket. I think he fouled the case for the prosecution somehow. Ward claimed they forced him to resign and he filed a lawsuit. He lost."

Tom could see Machado putting it together. She searched the gloom for a moment. "You think Ward is involved in the Carrie Hobson murder? Last I checked your crime lab was closing in on matching DNA from trace evidence to Raymond T. Bosco."

"I know," Tom said. "I know . . ."

Machado narrowed her eyes. "So, what've you got? You got Carrie Hobson mixed up in a drug operation — wittingly or unwittingly — and you've got Bosco likely your killer. Sasha Clay talks to you the other night, she winds up dead, too. Ward is just the pathologist. So what if he's got a past? We've all got a past."

"Yeah, but who's the guy talking to Carrie Hobson on the tape from the used car lot? Who's the guy following her home in the white Lexus?"

Machado blinked. "You lost me."

Tom opened his laptop and plugged in the flash drive where he'd copied the Gleason's car lot footage.

Machado stood up. "I gotta get back, Lange."

He opened up the video file and beckoned Machado closer. She acted like he was contagious, keeping her distance.

"I'm not gonna bite."

She relaxed a little and stood over his shoulder, watching as the video played.

"This is from what? The Gleason's car dealership?"

"Right."

They fell silent as the scene played out. They watched Carrie exit the side door and then someone after her leaned out. "There," Tom said. "Does that look like a bandage on that guy's hand?"

"Pretty hard to tell. I can't even make out his face."

"Bosco had some stitches removed the other day. He cut himself slicing fruit at the bar. I see a big bandage there on his hand. That guy is Bosco, I know it. Alright, here comes the second guy. Look, see how he moves? Does that remind you of anyone?"

Machado leaned down now, at last intrigued, her apprehension dissolved. He could smell her perfume and felt her hair brush his ear. It remind him of Sasha Clay.

"Yeah," Machado said. "Huh."

"Huh what?"

Machado stood up and said nothing else until the video ended. Tom was tempted to show her the warehouse video with the street view, but he sensed Machado getting edgy again. He spun around in his chair and looked up at her.

"What do you think?"

She was pale. "I don't know what I think. What did Blythe say?"

"Nothing. This video wouldn't hold up in any court. You could only make an ID on someone at a closer range."

"Any way to enhance it? Don't you have people for that?"

"You just watched the enhanced version. There's one where the video is cropped, but they're just bigger pixels. You can't add resolution."

Machado absently rubbed a finger on her lips, staring at the last frame of video on the screen. She didn't have to say it, but Tom knew she thought the person on the screen could be Ward. It was subtle, it was in the gait, the posture, but it was there.

"I gotta go, Lange." She headed for the door.

"Machado," he called before she walked out. "Can you do me a favor? Just keep this between us for now."

She hesitated in the doorway, looked down and nodded. "I can do that." Then she left.

* * *

He called Gomez again.

"Were you on the case a few years back, multiple collisions after chasing down possible drug traffickers?"

"What? What case? You better quit it, Lange. This thing will turn around and bite you." Normally Gomez was a bit smug. Now he sounded cold. "Listen, guy, Blythe called. She said you're off the case and we're not supposed to consult with you on it anymore."

"I'll call the DMV myself."

"The DMV is no longer running the offline search. It's dead." Gomez hung up.

Tom stood up and grabbed his files and his jacket. He headed out the door.

CHAPTER THIRTY-ONE

Tom slipped into the County Courthouse feeling like a fugitive. When the prosecutor's clerk asked him what he was doing, he told her he was following up on an order of protection for Alicia Strong. It had been days since he'd spoken with or seen Alicia, but he doubted she'd changed her mind.

She hadn't. There was no record of Alicia getting the injunction against McDermott, nor had she pressed any charges. His heart sank.

But he had another purpose in the courthouse. He spent the next hour drawing up a subpoena for the company which owned the ATM located next to Hush. Gomez was supposed to have done it, but now Tom doubted it. Once he'd submitted the paperwork he hurried away, taking the stairway down to the ground level. He jumped into the Jeep and headed straight for Tin City.

* * *

It was just after 5 p.m. as Tom pulled in. Naples Police were still on scene — two cops tidied up the sawhorses and spooled crime scene tape, the road block gone. Crime scene techs crawled over the rocks and Tom edged closer to the spot beneath the bridge. He recognized Katie Mills. When she saw him she raised her gloved hand in a tentative wave.

The body was gone. By now Sasha Clay would be in Dr. Ward's hands. Literally. He would be touching her, prodding her, examining her wounds. Tom knew the head wound itself wasn't enough to link the two victims, but they were connected in so many other ways — both strippers at Hush, both associates of Bosco, both found in Naples though they lived and worked in Tampa. The fact that they'd each succumbed to blunt force trauma (whether Ward, Mr. Meticulous, felt comfortable making that call or not) was just icing on the cake.

It was like the killer was mocking the police. Saying, *Look what I can do. I can take two lives, right in the same way, and still leave you scrambling.*

If anything it only emboldened the cops against Bosco. They knew Tom had talked to Sasha at Kronos. They would say Bosco knew it, too, and killed her. Blythe and the others were tightening around Bosco like boa constrictors.

Tom stared at the scene (the Naples cops were watching him now, drawing closer), then turned and headed into the mini-mall to see his brother.

Nick was just packing up for the day. He suddenly struck Tom as so professional, the way he placed his papers neatly in the briefcase, lost in thought.

Tom knocked on the open door and roused Nick.

"Oh, hey bro."

Tom glanced at the paintings on the wall. "Hey. You have any of your art stuff with you? Charcoals, paper, whatever you use?"

Nick raised an eyebrow in sarcasm. "You want me to do your portrait?"

"I need a favor from you. I'm calling on my marker."

"So soon?" Nick snapped his briefcase closed.

"Yep. Time to cash it in. But rest assured, it involves a strip club."

"Tell me more."

Tom told Nick about the call from Turnbull, and his pending suspension.

"So this is, like, some private detective shit," Nick said.

"You're going to do a sketch for me. Based on a description. Think you can do that?"

Nick considered it. "I'm rusty. Haven't drawn or painted for a while . . ."

"It'll be fine," Tom said. He didn't tell Nick about Ward. He didn't want Nick to think about Ward, or know what he looked like. It needed to be an uncontaminated effort. They headed for the parking lot and Tom suggested they take the Jeep. But Nick was parked at the marina and he didn't have a pass to park it overnight.

Tom sat in the Jeep looking out at the boats while Nick got into the rental. Sailboats and yachts and a few smaller fishing boats bobbed in Naples Bay. There was a tourist ferry chugging along in the near distance. One of these days he was going to have to get out on the water. Get his own boat. Maybe even live on it.

He followed Nick to his home in Port Royal and on the way got an unexpected call.

Blythe was curt, emotionally detached. "Thought you should hear it from me first. We're going to arrest and charge Raymond T. Bosco with the murder of Carrie Hobson."

No surprise there. "When?"

"In the next hour."

"Where?"

"What does it matter where?"

"Just Bosco?"

"Just Bosco. Strictly a murder charge. Coby and I are working together on the other stuff."

"Who's getting the collar? Tampa?"

"I am, Lange. I'm going to personally arrest Raymond Bosco myself. We have eyes on."

"I'm surprised he hasn't already run."

"This is why we do what we do, Lange. If we'd moved too soon, he might have. But he's sitting tight."

Maybe that's because he knows he's not guilty of murder, Tom thought.

But here came the barrage of evidence. "We've got Bosco's blood type on Carrie Hobson's clothing," Blythe said. "We've got his fingerprints in her home. Derrick Massey, the landlord, admitted to us he's seen Bosco at Carrie's apartment. What's more — we've found that Bosco had a *key* to Hobson's apartment. We've got statements showing several large deposits in Eileen Gallo's bank account, probably from money Carrie found in the baseboard and decided to keep."

"No. It's from money she saved and money she made while hooking. That's why—"

"Stop it, Lange. Coby and Mandi will show how Carrie was an unwitting facilitator in the drug operation. She found out, confronted the situation, and paid for it with her life."

He felt the adrenaline crawling all over him and wanted to scream. Carrie hadn't found money. Carrie was killed by someone else and then Bosco got his shit out of her apartment to protect himself.

Blythe's case sounded pitch-perfect, but it was bullshit. If Carrie had found the money in the wall, why weren't her fingerprints on the baseboard? Had she used gloves? Doubtful. Where did Bosco kill her? If it was in the apartment, why hadn't forensics found a spot of blood? Only on her clothes. Bosco was at the club working — time sheets showed it, and he was on video leaning out the door. With a cut on his hand he'd gotten from slicing limes — a story so dumb it had to be true. And he could have easily bled on Carrie by accident.

"Most important of all," Blythe said, almost gloating, "we have Bosco's DNA on the victim. It's over."

Or, the low copy number DNA could simply be wrong. Eleven out of thirteen STRs wasn't an incontrovertible match.

Just like Ward would surely say. But, the cops were going forward with it. The rest would be up to the lawyers now — plea deals or a trial.

Tom turned down Nick's quiet street, driving slow, waiting for Blythe to say more. He could sense she wanted to. She wanted to tell him, *You had so much promise, Lange*, or something to that effect. Let him know he'd screwed up. He'd let everyone down. But she didn't.

"You'll need to be at the arraignment. I'll let you know." She hung up.

Tom set his phone aside and pulled into Nick's driveway. So much for heading to Tampa to get the sketch. The cops would be swarming all over Hush.

Nick jumped from the rental and ran into the house, holding up a finger. He needed a minute to get his art supplies. Tom didn't bother to tell him to stop yet, just nodded. He found the number for Jimmy Kendall, and called. There was no answer.

"Shit."

He didn't know where Jimmy was. They said Jimmy was an informant, and it was possible vice narcotics had tipped him off to Bosco's impending arrest to keep Jimmy usable. He could be anywhere.

Tom got out of the Jeep, started for Nick's door and stopped.

He had to let it go. He was about to be suspended. He was off the case. Blythe was compelling, the theory was sound, holes or not. Bosco had opportunity and, cooperating with Coburn and the statewide attorney, they would show motive through the drug stuff. Tom wasn't omniscient. He might be wrong. And even if he was right, there was nothing he could do

He found Nick in his studio, gathering his art stuff into a black bag.

Nick glanced up. "Alright, I'm ready."

"Change of plans," Tom said.

"What? What do you mean?"

Tom shrugged. "You got anything to drink?" He wandered out of the studio, headed toward the kitchen, trying to escape the sense of defeat. Only after he left the room did he realize his brother was trying to be sober — there would be no consuming alcohol in Nick's presence. Tom turned back to apologize.

"Hey, sorry. I didn't mean . . ."

Nick was standing in the door, pissed off.

"What're you doing, Tommy. You giving up?"

"Listen, Nick, there are things that—"

"Look at you. Why're you such a baby? I saw you on the phone — did your supervisor slap your wrist again?"

Tom flinched. "Yeah, that was my supervisor. Letting me know they're going to arrest a guy for the murder. They're on their way right fucking now."

"One little thing, you know, you get one little road-bump, one little bruise of your ego and you just fold up."

Tom was baffled. "Road-bump? Nick, this is done. It's out of my hands. There's other shit going down, stuff you don't know about. I decided, you know, I'm compromising an investigation like this. And I'm already in enough trouble. Alright?"

Nick just stared. Every time they argued, Tom felt the fear kick in. Like they were going to fight. And they'd never fought, not really. But it was always there, this potential for violence. Just like their father.

After a moment in their stalemate stare, Nick threw up his hands and pushed past Tom. "Alright. Whatever."

"Hey." Tom made a grab for his brother, who jerked away.

Nick disappeared into the other room.

A pressure built within Tom.

"I should've given you the money!" Tom called after Nick. He'd been thinking it for days but only in the deeper parts of his mind. No, he didn't make much money. But he'd taken what little their parents had left to them and saved it. "I'm sorry . . ." he said quietly.

Nick stayed hidden, unresponsive. Tom thought about following him but decided to just let things cool off. He felt angry at his brother — Nick was acting like Tom was chickening out or giving up, and maybe he was. Maybe if Jimmy saw the number and called back Tom would see if they could meet up tomorrow.

In the meantime, he knew how to occupy himself. Maybe Tampa wasn't the right move, but there were other things he could accomplish right here in Naples.

CHAPTER THIRTY-TWO

The sun had just set, turning the western sky purple. The District Medical Examiner's Office sat beneath the swaying palms. Tom found the front door locked. He cupped his hands and peered through the glass — the lobby was dark, the receptionist gone home for the day. It was for the best — better no one knew he was here. The door to Ward's office was open a crack, light spilling through. He'd seen Ward's Rav 4 in the parking lot and figured the pathologist was around, working late.

Working on Sasha.

Tom headed back to the Jeep, and pulled out onto the road so he was partly obscured by a drooping willow tree but still had a good view of the Rav 4.

He waited, cracked the window and lit up a smoke, wishing he'd brought a cup of coffee to go with it. After a few minutes he snubbed the smoke in the Jeep's ashtray and called Alicia. As the line rang he thought about how much time he spent on the phone. It was no wonder outfits like Coburn's based their intelligence on cell phone surveillance. Life seemed to revolve around it.

"Tom?"

"Hey, Alicia, how you doing? Sorry I've been out of touch."

"I'm good. How are you?"

She seemed genuinely pleased to hear from him. It edged out some of the guilt he was feeling. Just like with Nick, Tom felt like he hadn't done enough. These people needed him and he'd turned his back. Some part of him thought that it was better this way — sometimes people had to take care of their own business — but it was still tough.

"I'm doing okay," he said. "How's Gwen?"

"She's okay. A little bit sick, though. Got a cold or something. How's the case going?"

Tom leaned back, his gaze wandering over the Jeep's ceiling. "Just about wrapped up."

"That's great. Wow. You know I hear how these cases can go on for months. Years, even. You guys do good work."

"Thanks. You, ah . . ."

"I haven't seen Josh." She picked it up before Tom could ask. "Not a text or a phone call, nothing."

"That's good, right?"

"At first it freaked me out a little bit, to be honest. He's sort of gone silent like that before. But, you know, it's stayed quiet."

"When was the last time you heard from him?"

"Not since . . . you know, that night. After your place." Tom thought there was a hint of embarrassment in her voice.

"Well, that's great." He decided not to say anything else, or try convincing her to file the injunction. Things seemed to be working out. His talk with McDermott, while wildly inappropriate, had apparently worked.

The conversation faltered. He realized that they barely knew each other — he didn't even know where she was from. He thought about asking her to dinner, but hesitated. He wasn't in any position right now, and probably she wasn't either.

He looked out the window and saw a figure moving through the parking lot. Ward.

"Alicia, I gotta go, okay?"

"Alright." She sounded disappointed. "Be careful . . ."

Ward was getting into his Toyota. Tom put the Jeep in drive. "I'll call you."

Ward took off out of the parking lot and Tom had to quickly get up to speed, round the corner and floor it in order to keep on his tail.

He caught sight of the Rav 4 at a stop sign, red taillights flaring in the dusk. Ward made a right turn. Tom reached the stop sign and hit the brakes, squawking the tires.

Easy. Go easy.

He made the turn and kept on Ward, moving slower, until they reached highway 41. Then Ward surprised him, turning left instead of right. Tom had been to where Ward lived in Central Naples the night before. That was north. Ward was heading south.

Tom thought maybe the pathologist was going to get a bite to eat downtown, but then they passed Fifth Avenue and all the restaurants. Ward followed 41 as it curved east and drove over the bridge where Sasha had been found dead on the rocks. A crime scene van was still parked in the Tin City lot.

Ward made a lane change beyond the bridge and gained speed. Tom kept a few cars between them. Now they were passing Lely, where Tom lived. Further southeast, away from the city, away from pretty much everything, toward Rookery Bay. Nothing beyond this point but swamps and alligators. Tom started to get excited. What was Ward doing way the hell down here?

The Rav 4 came to a stop light. There were no cars in between them now and Tom grit his teeth as he slowly drew up behind the Rav 4. It was almost fully dark, and

Tom had the headlights on. Ward wouldn't be able to make out Tom's face, and it was doubtful he expected a tail.

The Rav 4 blinkered for a right hand turn. The streetlight changed green and Tom waited, letting the pathologist get ahead. Ward pulled onto Barefoot Williams Drive. Tom had never been down Barefoot Williams before, but knew it was one intersection away from the road to Rookery Bay.

He fell back even further. They passed a trailer park, and then Ward made another right turn.

The road was dark, no lamps, but the moon provided some light. The first couple houses were in decent shape, the properties well-tended. Further along, grass was overgrown and the yards got a bit junky. Tom passed a sign marked *DEAD END*.

Ward drove to the very end, then seemed to make a turn directly into the jungle. Either that or he'd come to a driveway.

Tom shut the headlights and pulled the Jeep to the shoulder, killing the engine. The silence was stunning, only the ticks of the cooling motor and the thrum of blood in his ears. He walked until he reached where Ward had turned.

The home in the woods looked like a giant treehouse. A lamp-lit walkway revealed the creeping fig overtaking the walls and rambling front porch. Enormous trees flanked the home.

The Rav 4 was parked in the dirt driveway. By now Ward might've gone inside but Tom stayed out of sight, waiting. He heard a sound like metal being dragged over metal, and then nothing.

A light came on inside. Tom hid in the woods off the driveway. A second light turned on upstairs and Tom heard the muffled thump of footfalls.

He wanted to check out more of the place but it was too risky with Ward there. And he didn't have a shred of evidence with which to confront the pathologist. Maybe the ATM next to Hush would show Ward's debit card, but that was a long shot and didn't prove anything on its own. The video was unreliable — no jury would convict based on a blurry image. Ward's past with the Tampa case, and Blythe, and the low copy number controversy was circumstantial. Coincidence, really.

Tom didn't believe in coincidence, but there was nothing he could do. Ward had a second home, so what? It was ramshackle and creepy, but not illegal, not signatory of criminal activity.

Beneath the singing of the cicadas and the occasional whine of a mosquito, he heard something familiar, so blended with the nightscape he'd almost missed it.

The sound of running water.

He went towards the sound, back out of the driveway and toward the dead end. The road stopped at the woods, but beyond a shabby gate was a trail. Tom trotted back to the Jeep, passing the driveway, glancing at Ward's house in the woods. He fished a flashlight out of the glove box.

The trail wound through tangling vines and shrubs. Tom cut through the brush, sweeping the beam of light. He waved away clusters of gnats, thinking of the mosquitos buzzing in Rookery Bay.

Thinking of the turkey buzzards circling high above Carrie's bloated corpse.

At the trail's end was a creek, the brownish water slow and sluggish. He shined the light across to the other side. Nothing there but more woods.

He remembered the map. There was every chance this creek connected up with Rookery Bay.

He checked Google maps on his phone to confirm what his gut was already weighing in on: not only did this creek connect with Rookery Bay, it flowed into Stopper Creek, which was less than a mile away.

"Holy shit," Tom said in the darkness.

He put his phone away and played the light beam over the water, his heart thumping. He thought about the tide ebbing and flowing throughout the day. Ramirez had said it was on an eleven-hour cycle. At the right time, a floating object, such as a dead body, could conceivably drift from here into the bay, pulled with the tide.

He started back for the Jeep, moving faster, breaking through the brush like it was no longer there.

* * *

He eased his pace as he got back to Ward's house, but he boldly headed down the beachy driveway, staying in the shadows, then made a wide circle of the house, mindful of his footing.

Ward's place was loaded with boat stuff. Two Grumman canoes — big old aluminum bastards — a small fishing boat with an outboard on a trailer, a wooden rowboat sitting on a rack. And then there were the kayaks. Three of them, propped against the side of the house, their primary colors pale in the moonlight.

Tom's heart beat harder. The dirt driveway where Ward parked the Rav 4 continued around the house and led to a shed. Tom rejoined the driveway, tossing glances over his shoulder at the house. So far he hadn't been spotted. He hoped.

As he neared the shed he made out a large shape in the gloom. The shed was big enough to hold a vehicle, and it looked like there was one hiding beneath a large blue tarpaulin. Another boat, maybe.

Maybe not.

Palms sweating, head buzzing, Tom lifted a corner. The monstrous grille of the Lexus Sport Coupe was unmistakable.

Tom pulled his weapon. His heart felt like it was going to rattle out of his rib cage but his hands were steady. He swallowed several times — no spit — and headed back toward the house. Suddenly one of the lights winked out and Tom froze. Had Ward seen him? He waited a moment, breathing, trying to quell the adrenaline. He didn't want to kill Ward, he wanted him alive.

The second light turned off, the one downstairs. A door opened and closed. It sounded like Ward was leaving.

Tom sprinted round to the front of the house. As he ran, he heard the Rav 4 engine ignite.

He could only watch as Ward backed the vehicle out of the driveway. Tom made a quick decision — rather than run after Ward with his gun out, which would do nothing but cause Ward to panic, he hid in the creeping fig so the headlights wouldn't reveal him. Then he peered out through the vegetation as the headlights swung away, Ward put the car in drive, and took off.

Tom ran to the road and watched Ward's taillights receding in the distance. They brightened as he stopped for the intersection and turned left, out of sight.

Tom hustled to the Jeep, knowing Ward would have seen the vehicle. Even if Ward didn't know the Jeep was Tom's, the pathologist would wonder who was pulled over on a dead end street at nine o'clock on a Saturday night. He'd be on alert now.

Tom swung the Jeep around in the road and raced down the street. He stopped at the intersection and had to wait for a truck rumbling by before turning. He slammed his fist into the steering wheel, blowing the horn and cursing.

Then he stomped the gas and floored it to the stoplight at 41, which was turning red as he arrived. He considered running the light, but Ward had a big head start. Tom came to a stop and shook his head, saying *fuck fuck fuck* under his breath.

It didn't matter. He could get Ward later — he'd seen everything he needed to see. He'd seen the Lexus in the shed — there could be no doubt that car was the one in the video. Ward had been to Hush. He was the guy in the video seen talking to Carrie Hobson, then, moments later, following her car as she drove away. It had to be him. Any prosecutor would see that as opportunity. When the ATM records came through and showed that Ward had been stupid enough to make a withdrawal, they had him.

Ward owned kayaks. He had a second house just a short way from the water, from a creek that easily connected up to Rookery Bay. He'd been a volunteer at the reserve. His former teacher, Albrecht, called him a loner, odd, obsessive. Once he got something in his head, he didn't let it go.

This was their man.

Tom was so excited that when the light turned green he squawked the Jeep's tires, burning a bit of rubber as the vehicle shot forward. He raced down 41, trying not to double the speed limit. His condo was close. He was going to stop and call Blythe from there. If he called her from the road he was liable to kill somebody, he was so worked up.

He took the turns through Lely and toward his condominium complex like a Formula One driver. Then he slowed, reminding himself there were children in the neighborhood, elderly people who sometimes took evening walks. But he again beat the dashboard with a fist, gritting his teeth and grinning.

He hit the button for the garage door and pulled in, barely able to wait for the thing to roll open. He jumped out of the Jeep and fumbled with his keys, stabbed the lock, and opened the door to his place.

The blow to his head came out of nowhere.

CHAPTER THIRTY-THREE

When he came to, he was on the ground, hands tied behind his back, duct tape over his mouth. His gun was gone from his shoulder holster. He blinked some blood from his eyes — and stared up at his own ceiling. Then a person's head, in a black balaclava mask and sunglasses, loomed in Tom's view.

Gloved hands reached around his armpits and hoisted him to his feet. There were at least three men. Two behind him, with the guy in the mask just watching, arms folded. There was something in his hand. Some documents.

What are you doing? Tom's words were muffled by the duct tape, incomprehensible.

The men dragged him into the kitchen and sat him down on a stool by the island. The kitchen light was the only one on in the entire condo — Tom left it on when he was away. The man in the mask, lingering back by the door to the garage, was all but lost in the dark, just that kitchen light reflected in the sunglasses. Then he came forward, almost casually, and held up one of the pieces of paper.

Tom read what was written in black marker.

YOU FUCKED UP.

Tom tried to speak again, his words obscured. *Hey, hey. Who are you?*

For a fleeting moment Tom thought these could be guys from Bosco's drug gang, angry that his murder investigation compromised their operation. But that was unrealistic. Going after Tom wouldn't solve anything.

I'm an agent with the FDLE. You better let me go.

As if to counter it, the man switched to another sheet of paper.

I DON'T CARE WHO YOU ARE.

Was he someone hired by Ward? But how, when? Things had happened too fast for Ward to have already thugs. Tom sized the man up. About six feet tall, two hundred pounds. The guys holding him back were smaller and smelled of a hard day's work . . .

It could be Josh McDermott standing there. He was the right height and build. He was someone Tom had humiliated in front of his crew. That same crew was now holding Tom on the stool. Had to be.

McDermott, Tom groaned. *Don't do this. Whatever you're thinking* . . .

McDermott, if it was him, switched to a fresh sheet.

NOW WE'RE GOING TO DO THIS MY WAY.

Tom felt icy chills of fear. At first there had been the shock of getting hit, disorientation, trying to figure out what was going on. Now the realization sank in — there were men in his home, dressed in black, not saying a word. They wanted to stay anonymous, even if he thought he knew who they were. Anonymous, because they meant to harm him.

Tom felt the cool touch of a blade against his arm. He braced for the plunge of the knife, his mouth moving futilely, tasting the glue of the duct tape. Then the knife slid between his wrists, and made hard, downward motions. It cut through the tape and his hands were free.

One of the men now slipped an arm around his neck. There was a new sensation — the pressure of steel against his temple. Just one man holding him, keeping the gun to his head, while the other moved around front. Tom glimpsed him for the first time, also wearing black clothes and balaclava mask, sunglasses concealing his eyes. The man crouched and sliced the tape at Tom's feet.

Now Tom was free at his wrists and ankles, but didn't dare to move. Their actions made it clear: try anything and we'll blow your head off.

McDermott switched to the last sheet.

PUT 'EM UP.

Tom stared at the words, uncomprehending. At the same time, someone gave him a hard shove to his feet.

Tom looked behind and came face to face with the business-end of his own Glock 37.

In the living room, McDermott raised his fists in the air. He even started flexing a little on his legs, like a boxer.

This was about Alicia. This was about Tom intimidating McDermott. First Tom had pulled his gun on the guy, then he'd threatened him with police intervention and investigation of his workers if McDermott didn't leave Alicia alone.

They must have come in through the front door. Jack Vance was always telling Tom to get an alarm system, but Tom had been too busy with school and training.

Didn't matter now. McDermott wanted to fight him.

Tom kept his arms relaxed. He shook his head, slowly. He wanted to talk to the guy, reason with him, but his mouth was sealed shut.

Tom sat down on the stool, still shaking his head. Then he felt the gun press against his scalp, and he grew still. The gunman gave a savage push with the gun barrel, forcing Tom to his feet again.

Had the landscaper-turned-gunman ever been in a situation like this before? Tom doubted it. Who knew what McDermott had threatened them with. Maybe their jobs. They might be loyal workers, but that didn't make them criminals. Tom gave the gunman a look, trying to convey a message with his eyes: *It's not worth it, walk away now.*

Christ, just being here, doing this, these guys had racked up hefty potential charges. Breaking and entering, aggravated armed assault, and all against a state cop. They were wearing masks and hadn't spoken, as if that was going to save them. Tom would get them, and McDermott had to know that.

The big fuck was still standing there, rolling his fists around in the air. He suddenly came toward Tom, two quick, big strides, and punched him right in the mouth.

Tom stumbled back and fell. It was like being hit with a rock. He saw stars.

He picked himself up and lunged for McDermott, driving into his midsection like a linebacker. The hit knocked McDermott off balance and the big man stumbled back and fell into Tom's glass coffee table, shattering it.

Fortunately, Tom had slipped McDermott's pawing grip just before the guy went down. Show over, thought Tom, that was it. He rose to his feet and ripped the tape from his mouth.

"Guys," he said to the two men in the kitchen. They looked frantic, the gunman spreading his stance, aiming the thing, his arms visibly shaking. "Put it down, man. You don't want to—"

McDermott tackled him from behind.

Stupid, Tom thought as he hit the ground. Shouldn't have turned his back. He flipped over and McDermott pounced again. He hit Tom so hard that Tom's vision turned black.

Then McDermott grabbed Tom by the feet. He seemed to be done screwing around. He was breathing hard and grunting. Tom's head lolled as McDermott dragged him across the floor, muttering curses. McDermott pulled him right through some of the shattered glass and the shards bit into Tom's back, his arm.

The side door to the garage opened. Tom was dragged down the three steps, his head and shoulders slamming against each stair tread. McDermott let go of his legs and Tom lay wrecked on the concrete floor.

Hands groped at his pants. Someone took the car keys from his pocket. The Jeep door was opened and the engine fired up. What were they doing with the Jeep? Were they going to shoot him?

He heard a loud bang. A moment later there was a bright white flash, like sparks. Then two of the men bounded back up the stairs into the house. McDermott was last to go — Tom knew it was him, looming in Tom's view again in his balaclava mask, because McDermott said, "Fuck you, pig."

Tom heard the click of the lock to the condo door. His head throbbing, his back and arm smarting with embedded glass, he sat up.

The Jeep was running. The garage door was closed. The control box had been torn away, just the wires poking out of the drywall. That had been the bright flash.

He began to understand. They weren't going to shoot him — they had trapped him. McDermott wanted him to asphyxiate. Maybe he wanted it to look like a suicide. Or, he just wanted Tom to suffer.

Tom got shakily to his feet and steadied himself against the Jeep. His nose felt like it could be broken, his jaw ached. Blood dripped from his face and landed in splotches on the concrete. He grabbed the Jeep door handle and pulled.

The door stayed shut, locked.

Tom heard the rumble of another engine. There were no windows on the garage door, but he was sure if he could see out there, McDermott's pickup truck would be roaring past. He cursed himself for not seeing it when he pulled into the lot.

He'd been too hopped up on discovering Ward's secrets and had completely dropped his guard, ready for the big win. He'd never thought McDermott would go to such lengths. He'd expected maybe a threatening phone call, or that McDermott would keep harassing Alicia. But not this.

This was bad.

And to top it off, now Blythe and the others were making the Bosco arrest. Taking him down for the murder of Carrie Hobson despite the risks to Coburn's drug op. Tom had the evidence on Ward, and there was nothing he could do about it. He patted his pockets for his phone, but it wasn't there, of course. Probably inside, along with his gun. Or maybe McDermott's guys had made off with the items. He doubted it — they seemed determined to remain anonymous, and stealing a cop's gun, or phone, both of which could be tracked, would work against that inspiration.

Tom tried the passenger door of the Jeep. Locked. He tried the rear doors and the back hatch and couldn't open any of them. He grabbed the garage door, gave it a hard tug, but did nothing more than trigger fresh blasts of pain where the glass punctured his skin. The manual pulley had been smashed — the loud bang he'd heard — so it was bent to the side, effectively locking the door closed. He jumped for it and could touch it, but without something to stand on and some real leverage there'd been no way to bend it back.

He looked around for something to bash in the door to the condo. He sifted among the few items he had in the garage — a beach blanket Charlene had given him as a gift, a plastic ashtray, a Styrofoam cooler with half of a six pack left inside, a stack of old magazines, and a broom. His bagged suit from the first day at the morgue sat in the corner. Nothing he could charge the door with. He'd just have to kick it down.

He climbed the stairs, coughing from the rising fumes. The air was turning blue, the stench acrid and gagging. There were two problems with kicking the door down.

One, it was elevated three steps from the ground. He tried getting on the middle step, bracing himself against the back wall of the garage, and kicking, but he had no torque this way. The second and bigger problem was that the door opened outward, not inward.

The panic was settling in.

* * *

"Hey!"

Tom continued to shout, irritating his lungs, gagging. He pounded on the garage door, pulled at the handle some more, and screamed at the top of his lungs. His complex was in a quiet area, no one really out after the sun went down.

The face of his watch had been cracked, but he could make out that it was after ten o'clock.

Bosco would be in the back of a Tampa squad car by now, or maybe Blythe's own Crown Vic. She'd said herself she was making the collar. Meanwhile, Ward, who'd surely seen the Jeep, could be making a run for it. Something in his hurried movements had already suggested he was planning something. Maybe an exit. Albrecht could have told Ward the cops were poking around. Or Ward might have seen Tom outside his house in Central Naples the night before.

Tom fell against the door as he thought about it. The fumes made him woozy. He took off his shirt, triggering the worst pain yet. His entire back was slicked with blood. He almost passed out, but propped himself against the door. He stuck his shirt over his mouth and breathed through it.

The room turned blurry to his watering eyes. The panic choked him like the fumes choked him.

Easy, a voice said in his head. *Go easy, Tommy.*

It could've been Dr. Camden, a memory of one of their many sessions together. It could've been Nick, who, when he wasn't a total mess, could be a cool head in a crisis.

But Tom thought the voice was his foster father's.

He had a memory of being on the sidewalk, looking down at his scraped and bloody knee. He remembered how he'd gotten back up, angry at the bike. He'd kicked at it, yelling. His foster father's words had been calm and patient, in his ear:

Go easy, Tommy. You got time. You'll get it.

Tom looked around the garage again. It wasn't so much that he needed to escape — that was the panic talking. A trapped animal just wanted out. Sometimes it wanted out so bad it killed itself in the process.

What he really needed to do was stop the Jeep pumping out the carbon monoxide.

He went to the items in the corner and unbagged his soiled suit. He tore the shirt to shreds, then formed a ball with the fabric and stuffed it into the Jeep's tailpipe.

For a moment, it seemed to work. Then the exhaust blew the shirt out in a black plume.

Plugging it up wouldn't work. He needed to kill the damned motor.

Tom shuffled back to the front of the vehicle, holding himself against it as he went. The only way to pop the hood was from inside the vehicle. He didn't have a crowbar or anything else. He got his fingers into the seam and tried to pry it up. Not a chance. He felt for the latch, but he couldn't get the seam wider than a quarter inch.

He was no gear-head, he'd only ever had a basic knowledge of cars, but he realized that beneath the car were various pipes and tubes constituting the fuel and electrical systems.

Tom shimmied under the vehicle. The powerful motor thundered above, mostly covered by a protective under-shield. He kept thinking about the fuel. The tank was too full to syphon out the gas, and he didn't have a hose anyway. But cars had fuel pumps. The Jeep had one.

Only if a vehicle had a carburetor, you couldn't turn off the fuel. Nick was right, this was the same vehicle his father had owned. Tom had bought it without realizing at the time. Now he searched his memories. He closed his eyes, the engine roaring in his ears, the shirt to his mouth, and he thought back.

His biological father had tinkered with the family Jeep when he wasn't high or yelling at the boys or their mother. He remembered his father saying he'd gotten one of the first Jeep Cherokees without a carburetor, the last time a Jeep had used them was in the mid-eighties. Then they'd converted over to something — what the hell was it? It had an acronym like TMI, but that wasn't it.

TBI, Tom thought. *Throttle-body Injection.*

He opened his eyes. He'd remembered something, but he still had no idea what he was doing down here. He stared up into the thundering, clattering darkness of the engine. Metal and hard plastic fixed with massive bolts and pins. He saw some lines running but they could be brake lines. Tom started pulling at everything. Stretching and reaching and yanking and tearing. A few things popped loose, hot liquid spurted in his face. His hands were black now, fingers bleeding. He thought of Bosco's bleeding, cut hand. He thought of Alan Ward with the Lexus in his shed. Luring Carrie down to Rookery Bay. He'd solicited her, brought her to his house, taken her to the river with his kayaking boats, and killed her. Brought the boats back home and she'd washed deeper into the bay, just like he'd known she would, just like he'd known the state bureau would be likely to pick up the case.

That Blythe herself, the agent for the region, would pick up the case.

Ripping and tearing at the Jeep like this, Tom cried out. It was a primal sound, something he didn't recognize with his own ears.

The Jeep's engine started to sputter.

* * *

Though the engine finally quit, the small, enclosed space was filled with fumes. Tom could hardly see. He hacked into the shirt covering his mouth. His blood was everywhere — smeared on the concrete floor along with blackish fluid oozing beneath the Jeep. Like the vehicle was bleeding, too.

He'd stopped the car running, but the lingering fumes smothered. There wasn't a lot of ventilation in the garage, not much space to move around. The claustrophobia was back, and with it, fresh fear.

He kicked and pounded the garage door, his mind growing wooly, the air acrid and stiflingly hot.

Someone banged back on the other side.

"In here! I'm in here!"

He heard a muffled response. For an anxious second he was sure it was McDermott — he hadn't left at all, but was sitting out there, waiting, enjoying Tom's struggle against death. But even McDermott, brazen as he was, wouldn't risk that.

"You have to go in the front door!" Tom called. That could be dangerous, too. It was unlikely McDermott was waiting outside, but still possible he'd remained in the condo, waiting for Tom to drop.

"Hello?"

Tom no longer heard or sensed someone on the other side. He hit the door, the big stupid thing rattling. He sat down in the smoke and foulness. Like a taste of hell.

Maybe he'd only hallucinated someone outside.

Then the door to the condo opened, and Jack Vance stood there. The old retired Air Force pilot waved a hand at the air, came down the steps and rushed over, helped Tom to his feet and hustled him out.

* * *

Tom drew deep, ragged breaths in his condo. The fumes from the garage were sneaking in, but Jack Vance slammed the door closed. Tom fell on the couch as Vance looked around the room, seeing the shattered coffee table, the messed-up kitchen, the blood on the floor.

"Tom, what happened?"

"Need your phone . . ."

Tom didn't like what he saw in the old man's eyes. Vance looked worried, and Tom knew not much worried Jack Vance. "I'll call it in," Vance said. "You want me to call it in?"

What Tom wanted was Blythe. Something about the way Ward had been acting, something stirring in Tom's gut . . . Even if Bosco was arrested, he could be released after they cleared things up, and who gave a shit about Bosco anyhow. He was a drug-dealing asshole who was going to go down for distribution anyway. It wasn't that.

But it would have to wait. Tom nodded at Vance.

"Tell them it was Josh McDermott who did this."

Vance was already on the phone. He paced the room as he spoke to the police, and Tom realized he was trampling evidence.

"He's banged up pretty bad," Vance said. "Multiple cuts and bruises, head wound . . ."

Tom thought about the head wound. He'd been bashed upside the skull when he'd walked into the room, but it hadn't killed him. You had to know right where to do it. Right where to strike.

Two small lacerations have been identified where the parietal and occipital bones meet . . . Ward had said so himself when he performed the external examination on Carrie's body. He'd been reluctant to classify Carrie's death as blunt force trauma. And yet he'd known. He'd been grandstanding, showing how skeptical a pathologist had to be. He'd taken a victim to prove what a challenging prospect a cause of death diagnosis was. That was part of it, anyway, Tom guessed.

His eyelids fluttered closed and his thoughts swam away for a moment.

He envisioned himself in the bay, moving slow along the surface through the endless mangrove canals, the buzzards circling overhead, the brambles of mangrove closing around him, tightening into a narrower tunnel, thatching together, blocking the sun.

Something floating there, in the silvery water, just up ahead.

CHAPTER THIRTY-FOUR

SUNDAY

"Tom? Tom . . ."

He opened his eyes. Detective Machado was standing beside the hospital bed. He could see Jack Vance outside the room, talking with a deputy.

"Tom, you with me? There you are. Hey pal. You look like shit."

He coughed, and his lungs felt like they tore open. He clutched his chest and groped at Machado, wanting to sit up, get some water.

She helped him elevate the bed and handed him a cup with a straw. As he drank he looked down at himself. A blanket covered his legs but his upper body was bare, fixed with more bandages than he could count. He set the empty cup on the edge of the bedside table and it fell off and hit the ground.

Vance looked around at the sound and came into the room. "Hey, there he is."

"Blythe . . ." Tom said to Machado. He realized he had no voice, just a croaky whisper.

She leaned down to better listen. "What's that, hon?"

"Get Blythe. The killer is not Bosco."

Machado must've understood because she got that look on her face again, like she'd gotten at the field office when he'd shown her the video of the strip club and the Lexus. Like she either didn't believe him or didn't want to. Vance was looking between them, forehead lined with concern.

The talking irritated Tom's throat and he coughed some more. Vance picked up the cup and refilled it in the bathroom while Machado just looked uncomfortable. Tom drank greedily and handed Vance back the empty. He cleared his throat and found he could talk a little better.

"I went to Ward's place. He has a second home. Lexus was there beneath a tarp. Kayaks on the property. We need people there, and at his place in Central Naples, on Malaga Way. Bring him in. He's the killer."

"Carrie Hobson's killer?"

"Maybe Sasha Clay, too. Just put out the call, okay? Or get me Blythe. Please. Can you do that?"

Machado looked Tom over and nodded. "I'll be right back." She started to leave the room, pulling out her phone.

"What about McDermott?"

She stopped by the door, and glanced at Jack Vance. Tom looked at Vance, too, hovering beside the bed.

"They found him."

"Where?" Tom's heart was already sinking.

"With your friend. Alicia Strong."

"She was at his house?" Tom tried to sit up straighter and the bandages pulled. He felt something tear. "Is she alright?"

"At her house. Yes, she's fine. Tom, Alicia says McDermott was with her all night."

"Bullshit!" It was loud enough that the deputy leaned into the room. Vance held up a hand toward the deputy.

Machado left to place her call.

"It was McDermott," Tom said in a quieter voice. He implored Jack Vance with his eyes. "What did the cops find at my house? Those papers? Anything?" He looked at the clock on the wall and it was going on one in the morning. "Did they find my gun?"

"I haven't heard yet about your place. But County is all over it. If there's anything there, they'll find it. Detective Machado will take care of it."

Tom glimpsed her in the hall, on the phone. She looked in and winked at him.

He eased back and stared at the ceiling. He couldn't believe Alicia was lying about McDermott, giving him an alibi. But, then, he understood it, too. People wondered why the abused stayed with their abusers, but it was always easy to judge from the outside. It was a far different thing to be in it. His mother knew that, Nick knew that.

The doctor came into the room and picked up Tom's medical chart.

"How are you feeling, Mr. Lange?"

"I'm alright."

"Well. Just over a hundred stitches. In your head, your back, and arm. But we're not out of the woods yet. I want to run further tests to determine the extent of the damage to your lungs from breathing in the fumes."

Tom wanted to get the hell out of there, but he stayed quiet.

"I'm going to write you a prescription for Vicodin for the pain. And I'll be back." She smiled at him and left.

Jack Vance sat down in the chair in the corner.

Tom looked over at his neighbor. "Now you can tell me what you did for the Air Force."

Vance smiled lightly. "Classified."

"Come on, Jack. You heard the doctor. After all I've been through . . ."

"Ha. Sorry, no can do. Besides, maybe all I did was clean the aircraft. Maybe I pushed a mop."

Tom was exhausted, but couldn't stop thinking about Ward. When Machado returned, it was 2:30 a.m. Agent Blythe was right behind her.

Blythe looked concerned by Tom's condition, but, as ever, she got right to the point.

"We went to Ward's place — both of them. No car, no Lexus at the house on Price Street. Saw the kayaks though."

"It was there, I saw the car . . ."

"I talked to Gomez. We lit a fire under the DMV and they came back with the vehicle search. You were right. The Lexus is registered to Alan Ward. But both Ward and the vehicle are gone."

"You didn't find him?"

"He's gone, Lange. He's in the wind. We're looking."

They stared at each other. Despite everything, Blythe was poised. Tom wanted to ask her about the lawsuit filed by Ward. Why she hadn't mentioned her history with him. What she and Turnbull were up to when they wrested the Carrie Hobson murder from the hands of Everglades County, pushing their state jurisdiction.

Instead his mind swung to a related concern. "What about Sasha Clay? Ward was doing the autopsy on her. He could've killed her, too. Maybe she knew about him. What was she doing down here?"

Blythe lifted her hand in the air, putting the brakes on him. "We don't know that Ward killed anyone." Her voice was very low, almost a whisper.

"Are you kidding me? He *ran*."

"We have Raymond Bosco's blood, his DNA, on Carrie Hobson's clothes. He had a key to her apartment. They worked together. They argued. They—"

"Blythe, fucking quit it. This is *exactly* what Ward wanted. You're falling right into it. This is all about that case you rammed through with the low copy number DNA profiling as your evidence. I think this is Ward trying to prove how LCN typing can lead to a wrongful conviction."

She spoke at him through gritted teeth. "I thought this was about 'lust of the eyes,' Lange. Moral rectitude. Wasn't that your theory? A killer with a compass out of whack?"

"Yeah. Bent on revenge. I spoke to the pathologist from his fellowship who'd trained him. Ward is an obsessed loner. He took what happened in Tampa way hard. Who were you trying to take down? Someone was exonerated because of Ward, weren't they? Who was it?"

"That's irrelevant."

"It's irrelevant?"

She turned to Machado and Vance. "I'm sorry, would you two mind excusing us for a moment?"

Machado raised her eyebrows but said nothing, and left. Vance shuffled across the room. The poor old hardass was finally showing fatigue. "Time for a coffee," he said cheerily enough, and followed Machado out.

Blythe closed the door and locked it. She crossed the room, her shoes making those crisp sounds on the hard floor, and took the seat by the window. Outside, dark palm trees stirred in the Gulf breeze.

"Alright, Lange. Here you go. There's an auto wreck involving two cars. This is several years ago. State police investigate. I'm one of them. We find drugs scattered on the highway. Suitcase open, packets of coke broken and fanned out like snow. Six people involved. Three people in one car, three in the other. And all three people in one of the cars are dead."

She paused, perhaps to let this sink in, and Tom remembered Blythe's story about the high speed chase which had also resulted in a death. How she had played the long game, how she never forgot, and then got her man.

Unless she got desperate, Tom thought, and then she sought to prosecute on questionable evidence. Or ram through apartment searches without a warrant.

"In the other car, one person died. All three had records and were known drug offenders. Small timers, though. The suspects denied the drugs had anything to do with them. We drug-tested, found them clean. But then forensics searched for DNA on some intact packets of cocaine, a suitcase, and an unregistered handgun recovered from the scene."

Blythe glanced out the window, as if finding herself back in the memory.

"DNA was scarce, but they used low copy number profiling and matched the samples to the two living suspects."

Her head swiveled back, slowly, and she glared at him.

"Ward balked, saying it was an unreliable method. He was deposed for the defense. He testified."

"Shit," Tom mumbled.

"The court convicted only one man, who got fifteen years, the other was charged with reckless endangerment and released on probation. That was Raymond Bosco."

And there it was, Tom thought. Blythe had had Bosco in her sights for years. She burned to take him down. Despite her otherwise cool demeanor, that was where the desperation came from.

"The case was closed. Ward was accosted and urged to resign. After the trial, I switched from the state troopers to the FDLE. Ward eventually took a new job in Everglades County. About a year ago, Coby launched a drug operation that included Bosco in the network. And a few weeks ago, Coby was getting ready to move on George Parsons, who was operating in that same network out of Naples and believed to be supplying, among other places, several Tampa strip clubs with cocaine that strippers sold to customers."

Parsons — the guy with all the coke in his pickup. Tom could guess the rest. When the body turned up in the bay, and Turnbull wanted it for the FDLE, Blythe made sure that trace evidence went to the state crime lab. The same DNA profiling was used again. She'd had Bosco's DNA in the system already.

When Tom finally spoke, he tried to be empathetic. "Blythe, can't you see it? Ward figured you'd use LCN typing again. And you've burned to take Bosco down all these years. Ward knew you'd make it work, even if the DNA profiling was questionable, and the wrong man would go to jail. You can see that, can't you?"

She stared, unblinking. God, she was tough.

"Ward didn't choose Hush at random," Tom said. "He picked it because Bosco was the bouncer. Ward patronized Hush intermittently, not enough to be noticed. And then Bosco cut himself, sliced his hand. I believe that gave Ward his inspiration, or maybe the last bit of courage. It's my best theory anyway — Bosco gets some blood on Carrie's clothes, just a tiny bit, and Ward sees it happen, there at the bar. He follows Carrie when she leaves. My guess is he'd seen her on Match.com. Maybe they even corresponded. We'll know soon enough. She included kayaking as one of her interests. And, you said it yourself, Blythe — you think she was a pro. So, he solicits her in the parking lot. He takes her to his place. Keeps her in the same clothes — hey, guys are into all sorts of kinky shit, right? They go kayaking together, at just the right time. He knows the tide schedule — he was a volunteer for the reserve. And he hits her, hard, in just the right spot, probably with one of his paddles, and dumps her in the creek. Her body drifts into the bay."

Tom finished, and had to catch his breath. He couldn't tell if he'd convinced her or not.

There was an excited knock on the door. Blythe didn't object when Tom said, "Come in!"

Nick looked harried and wild. His suit was rumpled, his hair messed up, tattoos showing, and Tom had never been happier to see someone.

Nick charged the bed and looked Tom over like a worried mother. "Jesus, Tommy. It was that McDermott dude? That's what the old guy said. What's his name, Vance? Shit man, you look like you've been chewed up and spat out."

Nick was doing that thing, talking faster than an auctioneer. Tom hoped he wasn't drugged up. Christ, not in front of Blythe.

Nick realized someone else was there and offered his hand to Blythe. "Hi. Nicky Lange, Tom's brother. I'm an artist and I sell a little real estate. You must be Blythe?"

She shook his hand, unsmiling. Nick lingered a moment — Tom figured he was either evaluating Blythe's cold demeanor or checking out her legs — then spun on his heel, waving his arms. "Tom, I woulda been here sooner. Man, I'm sorry. But, don't kill me, alright? Don't kill me."

"What are you talking about?"

He made a move for his briefcase. "Just don't kill me, man."

"Nick . . ."

Nick popped it open and pulled out a sheet of paper. He held the paper against his chest, whatever was on it facing in. The gesture gave Tom a flashback of McDermott standing with his own sheets of paper. But Nick was grinning, his eyes shining.

"I went up. To Tampa. I went up to Tampa, Tommy, I hated to see you that way . . ."

Blythe moved to the edge of her chair, looking interested, if unhappy.

Nick rambled on. "I mean, I thought I was going to have to really work this Jimmy guy, you know? You watch these cop shows and everyone has something to hide. I figured, he was going to take some convincing, but he was like, man, he was all ready to tell me about this guy, what he looked like—"

"What guy?" There was a sharp edge to Blythe's tone.

"Ward," Tom said without looking at her. He realized now what the hell Nick was talking about and he felt better.

Maybe it was the Vicodin.

"He wanted me to pay him, but I said no way. But we got to talking about Yonkers, Jersey, how both our dads liked to beat the shit out of us—"

"Nicky, show me."

Nick flipped the page around. Tom stared at the image. The likeness wasn't perfect, but it was damn close.

"Huh? Yeah?" Nick was hoping for praise. He looked from Tom to Blythe, more excited by the quality of his artwork than anything else. "What do you think? Is that fucking *banging* or what?"

Blythe was out of the chair. She crossed the room in a lick and snatched the page from Nick's hands, studied it. "This was from a description the bouncer gave you?"

Nick nodded, his grin so big it almost made Tom laugh. Fucking Nick. He wasn't high at all, he was manic with excitement.

Blythe drove into Nick with her molten stare. "Do you know who this is?"

Nick was temporarily flummoxed. "Huh? You mean the dude there?"

"Yes, I mean 'the dude' there. You know who it is? Anyone show you a picture?"

Nick understood, shook his head with emphasis. "No. No, ma'am." He glanced at Tom, then back to Blythe. "Does that look like someone? A suspect or whatever?"

Blythe had nothing to say. Tom could sense she wanted to deny it, but couldn't. She could barely look at him, but when she did, he saw it register in her eyes. Someone who didn't know Ward, had never seen him before, had rendered a picture of the guy based on a description offered by some bouncer at a strip club. A strip club Ward had been to.

Blythe left the hospital room without another word. Nick watched her go. He flinched when the door slammed.

CHAPTER THIRTY-FIVE

Turnbull called several hours later. The sun was up and streaming through the windows. Tom was dopey from the pain meds and lack of sleep as he listened to Turnbull's trite praise.

"That's the kind of initiative I knew you had, Lange . . . That's the Boy Scout I saw in you . . ."

Tom wished he was at home, slipping into the pool. The swimming set him straight for the day. Well, straight as could be said for him, lately. He'd been all over the place. During the night, half dreaming, half awake, just the beep of the machines keeping him company, Tom had come to some decisions about his life.

"I had my thoughts about Ward," Turnbull continued, "after the debacle in Tampa. I didn't know if I wanted Blythe and Ward on the same death investigation. But Blythe seemed to have ideas from the get-go."

I'm sure she did, Tom thought. She'd had a bone to pick with Ward, and that was why she had Tom witness the autopsies, she didn't want to be around the pathologist. Tom recalled the way they seemed like divorced parents, avoiding eye contact or speaking.

"We've got a problem, though," said Turnbull.

"Sir?"

Tom sat up a little, feeling stiff and sore. He looked around for his water.

Turnbull was quiet for a moment. Tom heard the usual chatter in the background. Turnbull liked to keep a scanner in his office, monitoring emergency calls. "I want you to interview Raymond Bosco."

"I don't understand, sir, he's already been charged . . ."

"Correct. Charged on information. Bob Mandi filed the criminal complaint last night. Bosco is at Hillsborough County Jail. He wants to talk. I would have Blythe do it, but . . . obviously there's a problem with that."

Tom looked at himself. He was in a hospital bed, half his upper body bandaged, his nose bandaged, painkillers circulating in his bloodstream — Turnbull really wanted him to interview someone?

"Mandi is not going to like it."

"I don't give a shit," Turnbull said with a spark of ferocity. "This thing is . . . well, with everything you've uncovered, I want you there, Lange. Can you do it? I'm rescinding the personnel complaint against you as of this moment."

Tom was already getting out of the bed. He realized he couldn't go far because he was hooked up to an IV and a drug drip. "Alright."

"I can have an agent pick you up this morning."

"That won't be necessary, sir. I'll have my brother drive me."

Turnbull was quiet. "I'm not sure that's a good idea."

"Sir, with respect, you want me in Tampa, I'll have my brother take me."

"Fine," Turnbull said at last. "Let me know when you're en route and we'll set it up."

"Thank you, sir."

When Nick came in the room he was carrying a box of powdered donuts. Despite the late nights and his own fading bruises, Nick continued to look like a new man. He stopped in his tracks as Tom shuffled across the room, dragging the IV pole.

"What the hell are you doing?"

"Going to the bathroom."

"You need help?"

"That's debatable."

Nick watched as Tom moved along, grinning at first, then laughing. Tom frowned at him. "What?"

Nick shook his head. "Nothing."

Tom kept going and opened the door to the bathroom, Nick still watching.

"Tommy Lange," Nick said. "My little brother."

The doctor warned against it. The nurses just stared. Tom and Nick left the hospital, Tom imagining they made quite a pair, both of them beat to hell.

* * *

They rode the highway north, Nick doing most of the talking. Tom realized that while his brother jabbered more than anyone he knew, Tom still didn't have a clue about Nick's personal life. Nick talked a lot, yeah, but it was mostly bullshit. He talked in circles, and Tom realized it was his defense. But today was different. Nick mentioned a woman he'd been seeing. He said he thought he loved her, but she'd been unwilling to sit by as he drank and drugged himself to death. She didn't approve of the gambling either. When Nick first got beat up for not repaying his debt, he'd called her, but she wouldn't get involved.

"She cried on the phone, man. She felt so bad. But she just couldn't stick with me, she said."

"Smart woman," Tom commented. Nick gave him a look, but didn't argue. "I don't like what happened to you,

Nick. I don't like what's going on at the dog track. When this is over, I'm talking to Turnbull. I'm opening a case."

They left the subject there, stopping at a rest area to get something in their stomachs besides donuts, and then they were back on the highway.

"You know what today is?" Nick asked after a period of silence.

"Yeah, I know."

Nick surprised Tom by slapping him on the knee. "Here we are together, just like we said we always would be. We survived. You know it? That's all I ever wanted, Tommy — for us to get together on the anniversary of their death, to remember that we're survivors, maybe even to forgive them. They made us who we are."

Tom thought he saw a tear in his brother's eye.

* * *

Raymond Bosco looked afraid. The first time, they'd questioned Bosco at the Tampa police department. This time, he was at Hillsborough County Jail, dressed in the DOC orange jumpsuit, bracelets cuffing his hands, anklets on his feet, linked by a chain. Hillsborough Jail didn't fuck around.

Corrections brought Bosco into the interview room where Tom was waiting. They sat him down and left, but Tom knew they would be outside the door. Also outside of the room, watching the monitor, were Turnbull, Coburn, Gomez, and Mandi. Blythe was not there, and Turnbull had yet to fully explain her absence.

"Afternoon," Tom said.

Bosco had a hard time meeting his eyes, and just nodded. His lawyer sat beside him, a young woman in a snappy suit who looked like she wanted to be somewhere else.

Tom settled in his seat, trying to get comfortable. His bandages were hidden beneath his suit, but Bosco grew interested, like he sensed Tom's pain. "You get tuned up?"

Tom ignored him. "Raymond, I'm here because you wanted to talk."

Bosco sat back, cocky. Now that he was in a room with a wounded officer, he acted tough. His beady eyes gleamed in his pock-marked face, beneath his slicked hair.

"I already talked to the drug cops about using her apartment as a stash house. I admitted it."

"Okay."

"But that's it."

"That's it? You ever pimp her out?"

Raymond angled his head like he didn't understand the question. Tom knew he did, but he rephrased anyway. "You ever offer her for sex to paying customers, Raymond? Then take your cut?"

"No."

"No?"

Bosco shook his head and then grinned. "You don't understand Carrie, man. That girl was her own. You know what I'm saying? She wasn't one of these bimbos needs a pimp. She handled her own shit."

"You're saying you knew she was soliciting sex on her own."

Bosco shrugged, and glanced away.

Tom persisted. "You ever sleep with her, Raymond?"

Another grin, like he was getting a real charge out of this. "Occasionally."

"Occasionally. Like, once or twice a week?"

"What the fuck you think occasionally is? I don't know. Maybe four or five times."

"And that was it."

"Uh-huh."

"Did you care about her?"

"Did I . . .? What does that mean?"

Tom unfolded his hands and touched his chest. "Feelings, Raymond. Emotions. What people have. Did you have any for Carrie?"

Another shrug, and he seemed to study the floor.

"Did you ever get jealous of her johns?"

Bosco's head snapped up and he narrowed his eyes. "Her *johns*? Nah, bro, I didn't know any of her *johns*. Like I said, she was her own person."

"But you had a key to her apartment . . ."

Bosco leaned forward, getting serious. "I didn't kill Carrie."

"I didn't say you did." Tom opened the file in front of him and pulled out a glossy photo of Ward. He rotated the photo around and slid it toward Bosco. "You recognize this man?"

Bosco leaned in again and studied it. "I don't know. Yeah, maybe."

"Maybe? Or yes?"

"Hey, I see a lot of fucking faces, okay? So, *maybe*, like I said. Maybe he was there a couple times."

"Couple times. Think you could say when the last time you saw him at Hush was?"

"I don't know. A week or two." Bosco turned away once more, looking sick. Like he wasn't happy to be naming someone.

"Let the record show that Raymond Bosco has identified Alan Ward as a customer at the gentlemen's club, Hush," Tom said for the benefit of the recording. He showed Bosco a picture of a Lexus Sport Coupe next. "How about this car? Ever seen a car like this parked at the club?"

Bosco seemed to really resent the questioning now, and gave Tom a long, sideways look before finally glancing at the photo. "Maybe."

Tom put the pictures away. He chose a different tack. "You're on the hook for this." He tapped the file. "And you know it. Your blood, your *DNA*, is on Hobson's clothing. You were one of the last people to see her alive. Her landlord said he saw you. You had a key to her apartment. Now, you asked to talk, you say you didn't do it. Why should anyone believe you?"

"Because I didn't fucking kill her!"

Bosco was enraged, but there was also pain in his eyes. He just stared for a moment, then his lower lip trembled. He turned to hide his emotion.

"You cared about her."

"Yeah. Yeah, I fucking cared. Alright?"

"Alright. Well, listen to me. The guy I just showed you a picture of, we're looking for him. But we're not looking hard enough. If you—"

Bosco jerked his head around. "Yes, I saw the motherfucker." He faced the glass. "Okay? I saw that fucking weirdo. He came in the club, and he was watching everyone. He watched me, too. I thought maybe he was one of these, I don't know . . . that he swung both ways, or whatever. The way he was checking me out, you know what I mean? Like he knew me. I got cut, I cut my hand, he's fucking staring at me. But I don't sell women, okay? I had nothing to do with it if she hooked up with him."

Tom looked at Bosco's hand. It was healed up now, no more bandage, but there was a scar. Bosco had gotten blood on Carrie, Ward had made his move. And Bosco, just like Ward had planned and expected, was arrested for the murder. Thanks to the miracles of modern forensic science.

Tom leaned back, feeling satisfied. But that sense of closure was fleeting. There was still a big loose end.

"Okay, Raymond. What about Sasha Clay?"

"What about Sasha?"

"You know she was found yesterday morning. In Naples."

"Yeah, I know . . ."

There was a knock on the door. Tom scowled at the corrections officer coming into the room who whispered that they wanted to see Tom in the viewing area. Tom rose, glancing at Bosco. "One minute, Raymond, okay?"

* * *

The group of men in the next room wore hangdog expressions. Mandi looked furious. Coburn seemed lost in thought, Gomez embarrassed.

Turnbull spoke. "Lieutenant Haylock just called. The CSB took over the Sasha Clay autopsy early this morning, in light of your revelations."

Tom looked at their grave faces. "And?"

"The clinical toxicology found cocaine in Sasha's stomach, undigested, and in her nose and mouth."

The results were quick, but Tom knew the difference between clinical and forensic toxicology. Clinical was what emergency room doctors might perform in cases of a possible drug overdose. When a death was recent, chemicals were more readily detectable, unlike with Carrie, who'd been dead for days.

"And they believe the head trauma was from when Sasha either pitched herself over the bridge, maybe fell, coulda been pushed," Turnbull said. He looked down at his hands for a moment. He was a big man, dark-skinned, just over sixty but today he looked older. "This is . . . ah, man . . ." He stared at Tom. "You feel strongly about Ward for Carrie Hobson's murder?"

"Yes. Solid. Don't you? We've got witnesses, the Lexus, his second home location, even a sketch . . ."

"I know, I know. But, what about for Sasha Clay?"

"I'm not sure. It depends, sir. Like I said, I think for Ward, this was about payback for his forced resignation, the lawsuit he lost, the humiliation."

"Explain that," Mandi barked.

"Ward set out to show that this controversial technology, LCN typing, could lead to a false conviction."

"But the DNA is a *match* for Raymond Bosco. It's not false, it's *his* DNA."

"It's not a perfect match. The point, for Ward, I think, is that the police tried to use this method in the past. Ward vocally disapproved, and it cost him his job. This is his revenge, and a way of saying, 'Look what can happen.

The wrong man goes down for a murder, put away largely due to DNA profiling.'"

"How does he prove this point to anyone if Bosco goes to prison for Carrie's murder? Who would even know it's a false conviction?" Mandi was getting loud.

"Ward would. And who knows, maybe eventually he'd show up and say he did it. Ward's not right in the head. I spoke to someone who spent years with him. Ward might have some serious issues. He told this person all his work as a pathologist had 'ruined him.' This is the kind of person who might see people — women — as if they're already dead. Someone who's impotent, sexually dejected. For someone like that, murder would be far too easy."

Tom wondered again why Blythe was missing. He also thought they should've had someone here from the original Tampa case involving Ward and Blythe. It was like Mandi and Turnbull were trying to contain it. Tom realized the whole thing would be bad for Blythe, such errors in judgment could constitute her early retirement. Maybe Turnbull was protecting her. But Tom sensed there was more.

The men in the room exchanged looks.

Mandi pointed at Bosco on the monitor. "Bosco's arraignment is in two hours. We announce the formal charges to the judge. And now we're talking about his innocence? There's a *mountain* of evidence. This is an open and shut case. I just can't . . ." Mandi stormed out of the room.

"We've got confirmation on the TOD for Sasha," Turnbull said. "Midnight."

Tom stared at the door, thinking about Sasha's time of death. Midnight on Friday night, Saturday morning, Tom had been sitting outside Ward's house in Central Naples. Ward had been inside — Tom had seen the man's shape moving behind the curtains, and his Rav 4 was parked in the driveway. He told this to the other investigators.

Turnbull nodded, as if he'd already known, or been thinking along these lines. Tom, too, had come to doubt putting Sasha's death on Ward. "Killing Sasha doesn't fit Ward's M.O.," Tom said.

"I agree. So where does it leave us?"

Tom looked at the monitor. Bosco sat beside his lawyer, both of them looking miserable.

"Bosco?" Tom asked.

Coburn spoke for the first time. "We've had eyes on his every move for the past four days. He was nowhere near Naples on Friday night."

Tom hesitated. "You found Sasha's car?"

"We did. Parked in the marina."

"The marina?"

"Yeah."

"Next to Tin City?"

"Correct."

Tom's mind suddenly leapt to Nick, sitting out in the jail's waiting room. Nick had parked in the marina the morning before, due to the emergency vehicles clogging the Tin City parking lot.

Tom suddenly felt light-headed, nauseous. The painkillers in his system were taking a toll. He'd left the hospital too soon.

The men in the room were all watching him. Tom found a chair and sat down. He didn't like the way Coburn was looking at him. Gomez, too.

Turnbull put a hand on Tom's shoulder. "You alright?"

"What else?" Tom asked.

"Well, like I said, cocaine in Sasha's system, concussive, possibly fatal, blow to the head when she went off the bridge, probably from hitting the rocks, that's all CSB has got."

Tom turned to Gomez. "What about her house?"

Gomez stepped away from the wall, raising his eyebrows. "Yeah, there's a few red flags there."

"Like what?"

"Like, she had a safe, and we found it open, empty. Other girls at the club say Sasha was often talking about how much she was making. She was doing well."

Tom remembered first talking to Sasha in her home, her story about being homeless with her mother in Macon, Georgia, living under a bridge. How she'd come from nothing.

"But no money or valuables were recovered from her vehicle?" He looked between Gomez and Turnbull.

Turnbull answered, "No wallet, no phone. Just a backpack, and we're going through that."

Tom let it all sink in. Sasha Clay had emptied her safe. She'd driven herself to Naples. And, bombed on drugs, fell into the river either deliberately or accidentally.

Or, she was pushed.

Coburn stayed back, rolling a hard candy around in his mouth.

Tom kept thinking about Nick.

Nick worked just a few hundred yards from where Sasha had been found. Nick said he had a girlfriend, but hadn't given her name. Nick had been deep in gambling debt, and Sasha was loaded. Nick had also said he'd been in Tampa the previous week, for a realtor conference.

Nick sometimes went to strip clubs.

No, Tom thought. *No, no, no.* It was just his mind, overworked and searching for answers. He'd just been through a crazy trauma with McDermott. He was on drugs, for chrissakes, painkillers to keep the torture of two dozen glass cuts at bay, a busted nose, suffused lungs, bangs and bruises. It had been a week in hell, a case twisty with potential abuses of power, corruption, jealousy, revenge. He was just grasping at straws now, he told himself.

You smell like him.

Sasha's body, on top of him. The way Sasha had responded to Tom, her familiarity with him.

You smell like him . . .

Tom rose unsteadily to his feet. He needed some air. He needed something. He made a hasty exit, mumbling excuses about his condition. He walked the hallway outside the viewing room in a daze, then realized he was trapped. He was in a jail — every which way was locked. A corrections officer started toward him.

"I need to get out." Tom coughed, like the fumes were roiling again, enclosing him. "I need to get *out*."

Turnbull had followed him out of the viewing room. "Lange?"

Nick. Nick, Nick, Nick . . .

He had to see his brother, right now. Had to look him in the eyes. There were too many questions. Too many coincidences. But it couldn't have anything to do with Nick. It couldn't.

"I'll be right back," he said to Turnbull.

"Lange, wait!"

CHAPTER THIRTY-SIX

When Tom entered the waiting room, things got worse. Blythe was there, along with a couple plain-clothes cops Tom didn't recognize and several Hillsborough County deputies. Blythe was on a walkie-talkie. She addressed the group gathered around her.

"He's in the parking lot."

When Tom neared, Blythe made eye contact. Tom felt his throat close up. He couldn't swallow, his fingertips tingled. Blythe turned and jogged for the door, the rest of the cops following.

"What is it?" Tom called.

Blythe held the door as the cops rushed out into the bright day. "He's running," Blythe said. "Nick is running."

Tom sprinted after her. Outside, the sun glared off the vehicles, the heat was a weight. The cops scattered to their cars. Tom followed Blythe to her Crown Vic, feeling like he was hallucinating. She dropped into the driver's seat as he tried the passenger door, found it locked. He pounded on the glass.

She just looked at him, blankness in her eyes, then she unlocked the door. With Tom in the seat beside her, Blythe hit the gas and screeched out of the parking lot.

They had to sit and wait in the queue at the guarded entrance. Blythe was craning her neck to see ahead in the line of cars. "He's already through. He saw us coming."

Tom continued to feel out-of-body. He tried to gather himself, to make sense of things. "What is happening?"

"Your brother, Lange. Coby has been running a case on Mario Palumbo, the owner of Hush, for months. Nick is involved. He's been dealing, working with George Parsons."

"No way. Nick's clean. He never dealt any drugs."

She cut him a severe look. "Oh no? Not to try to pay down his enormous gambling debt?"

"He didn't owe that much. He sold his Escalade. Well, he turned it over . . ."

"Uh-huh," said Blythe, watching the line of vehicles again. Just three cars ahead of them at the gate now. The guards were basically just waving the cops through now that they understood the situation. Up ahead, a deputy cruiser switched on the light bar as it tore away from the gate. This couldn't be happening.

"Why would I be allowed to work on a case connected to my own brother?"

But he already knew. It was that invisible wall surrounding what vice narcotics worked on. The state bureau hadn't known.

"I only read the affidavit last night," Blythe said.

"Where is Coburn now?"

Blythe glanced in the mirror. "Two cars back. Those are his guys in the black truck."

Tom turned to look, his muscles in mutiny. The big truck behind them, jet black, looked just like the truck outside Nick's house earlier that week. Tom tried to speak, but the words eluded him.

"Nick owed all over the city," Blythe said. "Over two hundred thousand dollars, according to the intel. Maybe more we don't know about. He was in deep, Lange. Sorry."

She stopped at the gate. A guard with a rifle slung over his shoulder gave them a look and then waved them through. Blythe hit the gas and caught up to the convoy of deputy cruisers with their emergency lights flashing.

Blythe's Crown Vic was rigged with its own lights. She flipped a silver toggle on the dashboard and the headlights and brake lights went crazy. The walkie-talkie burst with static, then a voice said, "Suspect seen headed south on 75."

He was running home.

Oh Nick.

Tom still couldn't accept it. He only had pieces. How could Nick be involved with people in the Carrie Hobson murder case? The areas — Naples, Tampa — were just too big, the odds too great. But it couldn't be coincidence. Coincidence did not occur.

The big V-6 engine of the Crown Vic thrummed as they sped along the service road, preparing to merge onto 75 at the next ramp. Tom saw the streetlight coming, and the deputy cruisers blew right through the red, civilian vehicles hitting the brakes, pulling over. Blythe piloted the Crown Vic through the intersection and they blasted up the ramp. The city skyline came into view, the scattered sunlight bright as diamonds.

"You think Nick killed Sasha," Tom said.

"Nick is how Coby's team got George Parsons. They had Parsons, they knew his moves, but his stop in Naples was known because Parsons contacted Nick. It may be a big world, but the drug scene is tight. You and Carrie Hobson, well, you guys got trapped in the net."

"Bullshit, Blythe. Nick wasn't dealing!"

"How would you know? You see your brother, what, once every couple of weeks? Time goes by, right? A month or two?" She had a fierce grip on the steering wheel. "Coby has him contacting you last Monday, the day we found Carrie's body. I've heard the conversation. The anniversary of your parents' death — that's what you talked about."

Tom was furious, feeling invaded, blindsided. They were doing ninety miles an hour, approaching a hundred. The whole thing felt like a dream. Like he was going to wake up in the hospital. He couldn't see Nick up ahead, just the lights of the Hillsborough County deputies, the traffic slowing in the right lane, pushed off nearly onto the shoulder as the cops threaded their way through. He thought at his brother, hoping somehow, by some miracle, Nick would get the message: *Stop, Nick. Slow down. Pull over. Whatever it is we can work it out.*

"Parsons got knocked out of the game by Coby," Blythe said. "Bosco sent Sasha Clay down to pick up something directly from Nick."

"Nick didn't kill her."

"We don't know *what* happened. But you've heard the autopsy results — she ODed on the same shit Nick was peddling."

"That shit is *everywhere* . . ." He tried to stay vigilant, to defend his brother. But Nick was running. Innocent people didn't run.

Nick wasn't the only one on the lam. "We should be going after Ward."

"I admit my oversight." Blythe calmed her voice a little, though she was still tearing along the highway in full pursuit. "I spoke to you about patience, and then I got greedy. I didn't see Ward for what he was. You did." She gave him a look. "But while you saw Ward, you didn't see your own brother."

"I still don't," Tom said, feeling stubborn and scared as hell for Nick. Whatever was going on, this wasn't going to end well. You didn't run from the cops and not pay for it, even if there was misinformation somewhere along the line.

"Coby's phone tap — and we're talking about a stingray, here, Lange, and the stingray surveillance doesn't miss — shows Nick then tried to call you several times on Tuesday. And his phone was pinging off of Tampa towers. He was at Sasha Clay's house."

Tom gripped the door handle with one hand, braced himself against the dashboard with his other palm. Blythe was really going hell for leather, the needle now pinned to a hundred miles an hour. Top speed for a pursuit. Any faster and they'd be in excess of safety regulations.

"Hobson's murder happened to be smack in the middle of one of the bigger Southwest Florida drug ops," Blythe said. "Ward didn't know that. He chose his victim because of Raymond Bosco. You've shown that, Lange. The drug op, the Naples end of it, it goes through a crime family involved with the dog track. Guess who? Mario Palumbo. Maybe that's why Nick got involved — he owed the lion's share to Palumbo. That's who Coby is after. That's why he's working with us on it."

Tom felt like he was growing heavier, pinned to the seat by the G-force of Blythe's driving, weighed down by the truth.

"We didn't know who the body in the bay was," Blythe said. "But Coby took an immediate interest. The Sheriff knew. The Sheriff and Turnbull spoke. We felt right away there was a chance it was drug-related. We were wrong in one way, right in another."

Tom filled in the rest on his own, giving over to it at last: Nick owed money to Palumbo, ultimately. Nick entered into the chain of drug distribution to pay off his debt. He worked with George Parsons, who brought coke smuggled in from Columbia up out of Everglades City into Naples, Fort Myers, and finally to Tampa where Palumbo owned his strip clubs. Sometimes the strippers sold coke to customers.

Nick made his own choices. But he'd needed Tom, and Tom hadn't been there for him. Tom hadn't really listened. He'd ignored Nick's phone calls.

Because he had a case. Because Alan Ward had murdered one of the strippers from Hush in a bid to show the police the error of their ways. Or maybe just because Ward, despite all of his accolades, felt like a nobody with something to prove. If Ward hadn't murdered Carrie Hobson, Tom was sure he wouldn't be here right now. He would've had more time for Nick, he could've helped, and prevented this. This was all because of Alan fucking Ward, a sexual reject with no respect for the living.

"Oh shit," Blythe said.

Tom saw it, too. A plume of smoke on the horizon. The smoke was followed by a thunderous boom and a terrible shriek of metal. Blythe slammed on the brakes and Tom jerked forward. He kept his eyes on the road. He saw a car — a little compact vehicle — go skidding off into the grass. There were more sounds of cars cracking bumpers, and the four lanes were red with taillights and smoking brakes as vehicles careened to a frantic stop.

Someone had gotten into an accident, and it was causing a chain reaction.

Another car hit the Crown Vic from behind and Tom and Blythe were thrown forward. But Blythe maintained control and kept going, veering off the road and into the grass, where the car came to a halt. Then they both got out and ran.

Tom ran so hard his already punished lungs burned in his chest. He sprinted along the edge of the blacktop toward two unmoving vehicles.

Nick's rental car had come to rest on its side, half on the road shoulder, half off. It looked like he'd collided with a minivan that was a few yards away, the driver standing outside the dented car door, looking dazed but okay.

Tom reached Nick's rental, slamming into it to slow himself down, and rounded to the front so he could see in through the glass. Nick was inside. He was conscious, his face contorted with pain, trying to undo the seatbelt. Blood ran down the side of his head.

A tractor-trailer blew its horn. Tom watched as the monstrous vehicle jackknifed in the road, slamming into other vehicles, people screaming and scattering. Unable to stop, the tractor-trailer swept the vehicles along the highway, everything shrieking and smoking. It was headed for Nick and Tom.

The brothers locked eyes through the glass. There was no time. Nick just stared out at Tom, as if he knew, as if he understood.

And then he closed his eyes.

Tom leapt away. He ran and rolled into the grass as the tractor-trailer plowed into the rental, crumpling the front of it, pushing it along. Tom watched from the shoulder as the whole mess came to a shuddering stop.

Suddenly Blythe was there, and she had her arms around Tom. She held him tight as he tried to return to the vehicle. Gas was leaking, there was an electrical fire. Her grip was strong, her words loud in his ear. "The whole thing could blow, we have to get out of here!"

A few stunned motorists stumbled from the road and into the grass with blind desperation. Tom kept walking, pulling Blythe along with him. So close now, he was so close to the vehicle, to Nick . . .

Blythe took him down.

Lying face-first in the grass, Tom felt nothing. He rejected everything that had happened. He was just a boy, and Nick was his big brother. He was just a boy, and Nick was there for him. *Nick, God, I love you so much.*

Nick.

CHAPTER THIRTY-SEVEN

MONDAY

An early storm broke, and rain hammered the cars in the parking lot. Tom watched out the window.

People he barely knew came up and offered condolences, eyes shining. Their lips were moving, but Tom barely heard the words.

They touched him on the arm, or the shoulder, and their voices were muffled, and he didn't know where he was.

Tom blinked, took in his surroundings. This was the ROC in Fort Myers. He understood that Turnbull was taking him into a secluded area in the compound. Tom was shown his seat and Blythe and Coburn joined them. They talked about Nick. They talked about Ward. They said that Ward had been picked up by the Coast Guard. In addition to the Lexus, they said, Ward had a sailboat. He'd been trying to leave the country, but they'd caught him.

The Everglades County crime scene bureau had ripped Ward's house apart. They'd found further evidence of his involvement with Carrie Hobson — her phone was in a box in Ward's bedroom.

The box, Tom thought distantly. It was one of the few things he really registered. *Everyone has a box.* It was what he'd told Gomez in Carrie's apartment — everyone had a place where they kept their precious things.

But he'd never checked Nick's house for such a place. He'd known his brother was a user, a troubled soul, but kept him at a distance. Now other cops would pour over Nick's life, dig into his past and confirm his connections. Tom would never be looked at the same. He'd gone from the new guy to the brother of a dead criminal. He'd lost his parents as a child and now his brother.

The ATM company had come back quickly with their records, showing that Ward did in fact take out cash on two occasions outside Hush. Tom listened with half an ear. Carrie Hobson's data had come through as well. Carrie hadn't stolen any of Palumbo's money hidden in the wall at her apartment where Bosco was keeping it. The large deposits in Eileen Gallo's bank were Carrie's own earnings, along with money from Ward himself, who'd been buttering Carrie up with big tips at the club.

Carrie Hobson didn't necessarily have a heart of gold, but she was a hard-working woman, a good daughter who looked after her mother when her other sisters couldn't be bothered. Carrie's body was going to be shipped back home to Idaho later that day.

At some point Tom realized the room had grown quiet. The others were waiting for him to say something, to make some move, but Tom was done. When he sensed the debriefing was over, he simply got up and walked out. Blythe followed him outside and offered to drive him — she'd brought him to the ROC in the first place that morning, though he barely remembered it.

Nick was dead. His body was at the morgue in Hillsborough County. Blythe took Tom there and stood by as he identified the remains. Tom didn't cry. He looked at

Nick, his face serene, his body covered in an evidence sheet, and felt nothing.

Back in his condo, the sun was getting low. There was a soft knock on the door and Tom answered, still dressed in his suit. He'd just been sitting on the couch, staring at the door to the garage.

Charlene was on his front stoop, her face wrenched with sorrow. Her husband stood behind her, hunched over with his illness. Tom let them in. Charlene had a grocery bag and put food into Tom's fridge. He stood in the kitchen, watching, not really seeing.

When Charlene had finished putting the groceries away, she turned to Tom. At last, without even knowing he was going to do it, he stepped into Charlene's embrace, and he cried.

CHAPTER THIRTY-EIGHT

TUESDAY

The alarm clock went off but Tom was already awake. He stared up at the ceiling fan, lost in thought.

He began his day with a pot of coffee, reluctantly forgoing his swim. He didn't want to run into any neighbors, and he was dodging the press. Alone in his condo, he fielded calls from eager reporters, telling them "no comment." Blythe and Turnbull both phoned. Even Coburn called. Coburn was surprisingly gentle and sympathetic. He apologized for the secrecy about Nick. But he assured Tom that Nick's death would have a silver lining — they had more evidence than ever against Mario Palumbo. "You know," Coburn finished, "you ever think about switching to County, there would be a spot for you in vice narcotics."

The County crime scene bureau had been and gone from his condo, but Tom's blood still stained the floor from McDermott dragging him through the shattered glass.

He was staring at it when there was a knock at the door. Tom figured it was Charlene again, but it was Detective Machado, and behind her was Katie Mills. Mills had taken over the autopsy on Sasha Clay.

Tom wasn't feeling very hospitable, but he showed the women into the living room.

"We wanted to tell you in person," Machado said. "We don't think Nick killed Sasha."

"We found her car, as you know," Katie Mills explained. "Sasha came down from Tampa on her own. In the car was a backpack with a suicide note inside. Her handwriting is all loops and swirls — who writes in cursive anymore? And the spelling . . . well, we got a handwriting expert and it took some time to decipher." Mills blinked at Tom, her eyes wet with emotion Tom hadn't expected. "The note mentions you, Agent Lange, and it mentions your brother. It says that she loved him."

Machado added, "We believe Sasha chose Naples because of what's in the note — that she felt close to you and Nick, even though she believed you couldn't ultimately help her. She went to the bridge near Tin City and committed suicide there because Nick's office was close, but she also makes a reference to the bridge as having some other significance. Do you know anything about that?"

It was the first thing to break through Tom's two-day malaise. He felt his blood flowing again as he straightened up in the chair. "Yeah, maybe. When I first met her, she told me about how she'd been homeless for a time as a kid. She said she'd lived under a bridge in Macon with her mother. Maybe it's something, maybe not. Maybe it's just the only bridge around high enough to do something like that."

The women exchanged looks. Tom knew they weren't obligated to come here, and that the information on Sasha's past, or theorizing about the bridge, was something they could have done without him. They were here to try to make him feel better, to tell him that Nick wasn't a killer.

"I wish he hadn't run," Tom said.

"Me too." Machado lowered her eyes.

There was a brief silence, then Tom asked, "What about Ward? Where's he, now?"

"In County jail, awaiting arraignment," Machado said. "He'll do time in federal prison." Her eyes found him again, and Tom saw a kindness there he appreciated. Machado was good people, no doubt. "I talked to Agent Blythe this morning. She wants to see you herself but she wanted to give you . . . space. For one thing, she wants to help us nail Josh McDermott for what he did. For another, she's also dealing with her own issues, pertaining to Ward. But, they're going to need you — Mandi hopes you're going to be able to work with Ward's prosecution. When you're ready."

Tom glanced around the condo. He'd been here alone since Charlene had left the night before. The thought of going back out there, dealing with reporters and court rooms and cops and people was unpleasant. Walking out that front door and back into the world, this time a world where Nick did not exist, that was worse.

Tom stood up. "Let's go," he said. "I just need to get changed."

The women rose as he walked out of the room.

"Help yourself to some coffee."

In his bedroom, he dressed at the bureau, looking at the picture of him and Nick as kids. Tom with that slightly pensive look, Nick's wide grin. Both of them bare-chested, standing with their arms around each other's shoulders.

When Tom returned downstairs, Machado and Mills were quietly talking in the kitchen, with mugs of coffee. They set down their drinks and smiled as he entered, fixing his tie. Machado glanced at the tie, then approached him. "May I?"

Tom let her redo the knot.

"I want to open a case on the dog track in Bonita Springs."

Machado stepped back and admired her work, and brushed some lint from Tom's shoulders. "That's a good idea."

Mills said goodbye outside and left in her own car. Tom and Machado got settled in her unmarked Ford Taurus. Tom glanced at the garage. The door was left open. The space was empty.

"You need to get your department-issued vehicle," Machado said.

"Yeah. I do."

THE END

TJB
3/23/16 – 10/28/16
Etown & Naples

Acknowledgments

I'd like to thank the following people for contributing to this book in all the best ways. Jenifer Bulkley, my sister and a former Sheriff's Deputy; Steve Buzzell, my stepfather and a criminal defense attorney; Geoff Pierce, my friend and writing ally; Kristy Wilson, my cousin and a New York state trooper; Dava, my supportive wife and voice of reason; James, my father, who is a retired probation officer living in Naples, Florida, where the story is set. Thank you.

Thank you to Jasper Joffe, and everyone at the amazing Joffe Books. And my gratitude to Emma Clements, a fantastic editor whose insight and precision sharpened the story.

Special thanks to Lee Clark Smith and her husband Sergeant Andrew Smith, aka "Smitty." Lee's keen eye and cop knowledge helped pull the book together in its late stages, and Smitty contributed his experience pertaining to police surveillance, drug crime, and Southwest Florida weather.

It is to their credit any technical accuracy in the book must be given — any faults in police or legal procedure are my own.

It has also been my intention, while remaining accurate in the depiction of police procedure, to exercise restraint when detailing certain police tactics — Smitty would not like it one bit if this book helped educate the bad guys about what the good guys are doing.

Thank you for reading this book. If you enjoyed it please leave feedback on Amazon, and if there is anything we missed or you have a question about then please get in touch. The author and publishing team appreciate your feedback and time reading this book.

Our email is office@joffebooks.com

www.joffebooks.com

ALSO BY T.J. BREARTON

HABIT
SURVIVORS
DAYBREAK

DARK KILLS
DARK WEB
GONE

HIGHWATER

DEAD GONE

75355796R00202

Made in the USA
Columbia, SC
16 August 2017